ACCIDENTAL REBEL

A MARRIAGE MISTAKE ROMANCE

NICOLE SNOW

ICE LIPS PRESS

Accidentally hitched to a dream. Now for the catch...

I didn't even say "I do."

One crank call and I'm insta-wife to a tattooed behemoth and mother to his kids.

He's paying my idiot boss a fortune for the perfect lie.

Because trouble found Miller Rush, and he found me.

A rock hard, overprotective rebel with a cause.

Father of the century.

Abs wound tighter than his attitude.

A broodylicious bull stomping around my house, barking orders.

Something's got to give, okay?

But it won't be me.

Not my courage, even when my nosy mother smells drama.

Not my heart set on helping two little angels and their perma-grump dad.

Definitely not my body screaming *Mayday* because his bedroom eyes are magnets.

Deep breath.

It's only a few weeks.

It's only a whole mess of freaky secrets.

It's only pretend and I'm *so not* letting Miller run off with my heart.

Riiight. Why didn't anyone warn me some knots can't be untied?

I: RING-A-LING (GWEN)

"Oh, for Heaven's sake!" I slap my desk with both hands so hard the round plastic holder full of pens and pencils nearly topples over.

This damn ringing is officially driving me *nuts*.

With writerly things still clinking together, I shove my chair back, letting out a loud huff. Remind me why I'm here again?

All the hours of unpaid overtime recovering data from a computer that must've been on Noah's Ark is punishment enough. I've put up with rudeness, last minute requests that add on hours to my day, every nuisance imaginable since working here, but this...

This constant freaking ringing? I think I'd rather spend all day spraying nests of angry hornets.

I've had it.

Standing, I stretch angrily and march across the room to yank open Manny's office door.

Every room of this oh-so-prestigious – *gag me* – law office is smaller than most broom closets. But that's life. It's also my tragic joke of a job.

I'm an 'ass-ociate' of Stork, Storkley, and Associates. A place where the Storkley part is fictitious and so are the associates.

Manny Stork, Esquire, is the only real lawyer here, and it's a stretch to say that. And, well, as the only other soul here who could be called an 'associate' in the vaguest sense, I haven't done anything but kept my nose shoved in an ancient computer for weeks doing data recovery.

Beggars can't be choosers, they say.

But I'm wondering if I'd be getting better job experience rattling a cup for loose change on the street. Too bad this was the only legal job available in Finley Grove, Minnesota, one more small town among the pines.

Unless I wanted to sell out waiting tables, playing overnight cashier at the gas station, or working a fast food drive through, the choice was clear.

This is the part where I wish I'd taken a better look at my choices. Because right the heck now?

I think anything would beat Stork, Storkley, and Associates.

Growth pains. I could blame it on them.

Apparently, I'm still 'growing into my feet.' A phrase Mother loves using to describe my almost comical mess of a life and six-foot-tall height.

So I'm not the most graceful person.

Waitressing? Been there, done that. It didn't work. My one and only paycheck went to cover all the dishes I'd broken.

And I think those little drive-thru gas pumps are even more claustrophobic than Manny's law offices. They can also be dangerous.

I may be tall with a head full of untamable red hair that at times could scare the pants off any would-be robber, but I'm a chicken at heart. So cashiering overnights at a convenience store wasn't up my alley either.

Then there's that pesky paralegal certificate on my resume. The thing I'd shelled out good money and years of my life for, telling myself law would be stable. Glamorous. Exciting.

Right. Let's just blame it on too many *Law and Order* reruns and cut our losses.

My losses. Anyway...

So here I am, following an obnoxious nonstop ringing in the stuffy office of a lawyer who has more side gigs than real clients on the books. That much I've figured out from the data I'm recovering.

Part of me wonders exactly what some of his *gigs* are all about. Admittedly, I'm intrigued, which is probably the only reason I haven't handed in my resignation yet.

The noise is coming from Manny's desk. Just a constant, steady basic bitch ringtone that only goes quiet for a few seconds before it goes off like an air raid siren again.

Sighing, I pull open the desk drawer. My brows knit together as I glare at the obnoxious phone that's been blaring for the last hour.

The rest of the metal drawer is empty. God.

No wonder this thing sounded like an elephant stampede echoing off the walls.

Odd. It's one of those disposable pay-as-you-go cell phones. Some off-brand I've never seen or heard of before. I frown.

This isn't like my illustrious boss. Manny has a sleek new Android phone that's larger than his palm and forever glued to it.

I lift out the phone just as it quits ringing again.

Honestly, I don't know if I'm happy or disappointed.

The stupid plastic device just shattered my last nerve. To

think I was looking *forward* to planting the tip of my heel in the screen, pressing down with a satisfying *crunch,* and putting an end to this insanity.

My finger taps the button on the front, turning it on.

"Seventeen missed calls?" I whisper out loud, reading the screen. "At least seventeen. More like seventeen hundred." I scroll down. "Twenty-two text messages? Again, at least."

All from Unknown. *Damn spammers.*

I flip the phone over, looking for the off button, when it buzzes in my hand again. My fingers shake so violently I feel like I'm holding on to a restless frog trying to leap away.

It's another text. Mr. or Mrs. Unknown again.

Confirmation needed on tomorrow's meeting ASAP. Answer me.

I shake my head, pursing my lips and staring at the message. I almost feel sorry for Unknown.

Whoever they are, they've put an awful lot of confidence in this firm. And if they're stupid enough to believe Manny Stork is as good a lawyer as he believes he is, that's their problem, not mine.

The message disappears, and I notice the time. "7:15? Christ. Maybe I'm the stupid one. There goes another *four hours* I'll never be paid for."

Saying it confirms how done I am with this day.

I've been here since seven this morning. I grit my teeth. As my boss, Mr. Asshat, Esquire himself, has said in the weeks since I've been here, 'working long hours doesn't always equal smart hours.'

He doesn't have the saying quite right, but the meaning's there. For me, I think it means one more day shot in the head.

But tomorrow's another day. There's always a teensy-tiny chance it might suck a little less than this one.

It might even be the day I'm done with this shady data

recovery crap so maybe, just maybe, I can actually start working on a real case like Manny promised. Something I can sink my teeth into and hopefully, enjoy. Not to mention make my education pay off.

Hopefully I'll remember what I supposedly learned. I graduated with a degree in marketing and went back for a paralegal certificate later, but have to admit, writing was always the one thing on my mind, which didn't make me the best student.

The phone buzzes again.

Another text.

Confirmation ASAP!

I stare at the words until they disappear, feeling a tug of anxiety. *Should I, or shouldn't I?*

Obviously, it's a total invasion of privacy to play with a mysterious stranger who wants to reach my boss *really* badly over the phone. But it's an invasion of a girl's sanity to have no fun ever at work.

What the hell? I am an associate, after all.

Manny keeps his schedule in his phone, but I'll be here all day tomorrow. And the next day, and the day after that, searching through old computer files that barely hint at anything. This could be one of his side gigs where I can get some answers.

I click on the text icon, and then type fast, before I lose my nerve.

Confirmed.

Then, practically shaking in my heels with a snicker, I jet for the door.

When I reach to click off the light, I realize the phone's still in my hand. I consider putting it back, but probably should scroll through the messages so I know what time this meeting is that I just confirmed.

Manny won't miss the phone.

He won't be back until nine a.m. tomorrow morning. I'll be here by seven. Besides, if he wanted or needed it so badly, he'd have taken it with him.

Since my wonderful boss has been so amazing to me, I'm glad I could return the favor.

* * *

AT MY DESK, I drop the phone into my purse, turn off the old dinosaur computer and the newer laptop, and then lock the office door. I lock up the outside door of the small brick building as well, and then climb in my Buick Regal.

Don't laugh. It's an old boat of a car, but I *need* the head room. In all honesty though, the old girl's showing her age.

A decade of savage Minnesota winters, driving on ice and salt covered roads, is always hard on cars. I'm going to miss this beast if and when I can ever afford a new one. She's never failed me.

The old US Mail slogan comes to mind: neither snow nor rain nor heat nor gloom...

She delivers. And I'm thankful I have one thing in my life I can count on.

Tonight's no different, and Old Pearl – although her pearl white paint has faded into a dull ecru color – and I are soon pulling into my driveway. Or Mother's driveway, to get technical.

Technically, she owns the townhouse I live in.

Technically, she owns the entire building and rents out the other three places, too.

Technically, she acts like she's doing me a huge favor, even though without me keeping an eye on things, she would've had to sell these spur-of-the-moment rental investments a long time ago.

Sigh.

I'm so *not* bitter.

Even if I do sometimes secretly dream of following in her footsteps. *A New York Times Best Selling Author.*

That's my mom, M.E. Court.

May Ericka Courtney to those of us who know her.

I've even figured out my pen name. Gwen Lynn. That sounds miles better than Gwendolyn Courtney, and much shorter, too. It'll look nicer than Mother's slanted, floral script on covers, too.

I want the huge, blocky style that's right at home with thriller novels. Books full of intrigue and mystery. Romances are Mother's signature genre and her claim to fame. Even though she and my father didn't exactly have a happily ever after.

I don't even know if they had a happy for now.

I barely remember him. They'd divorced long before he died.

Hitting the button to open the garage door, I wait impatiently for...nothing?

That's what happens, and it can only mean the batteries are dead. Stupid thing.

No warning. Just dead.

I scan the area with an ever-familiar eerie sensation tickling the back of my neck before shutting off my car. This could be one reason I've never finished a single one of the many books I've started working on.

Confession? I'm afraid of the dark. Of my own shadow. Of dang near everything. The cowardly lion skipping his way to Oz had more courage than I do. I get to the point in a story where the intrigue gets deep, and I creep myself out and let my imagination go wild and just...stop.

Like I'm doing now. I shake my head.

Convinced the coast is clear, I jump out of the car and make a mad dash for the front door like a flock of flying monkeys are after me. Someday, I'll get over this ridiculous fear of everything.

That's what I keep telling myself, and I hope someday, I'll be right.

Inside, with the door locked, I can breathe easy again.

In another life, I must've been chased through the night by a serial killer or something. It *had* to be another life because it sure hasn't happened in this one.

Still, I've always felt like I'm waiting for the other shoe to drop. Like I know something dark and sinister is going to happen.

Someday, it won't matter, I tell myself again. Probably whenever I'm finally rich enough to lock myself inside and finish writing a book. A damn good one that will have me hitting the charts right alongside Mom.

I kick off my shoes, leave them by the door, and walk across the plush new carpet. Mom had the place re-carpeted before I moved in, all beige because it doesn't show traffic like white does.

That's my mother, though, and I love her. Drama and all.

Before I reach the kitchen, my purse buzzes like an angry hornet found its way inside. It's not my phone. That's a guarantee.

The number of people who have my phone number is next to nil, and most of them are far too busy to light up my screen at eight o'clock at night.

Real trepidation crawls up my spine as I pull out the cheap phone and set my purse on the counter. I take a deep breath and hold it, glancing at the text displayed on the screen.

Will she be there?

Forget the trepidation. Now, it's a full-on shiver.

She? She *who*? A *she* hasn't entered Manny's office since I started there.

What have I confirmed? Manny's not married, and he doesn't have any daughters or sisters that I'm aware of.

Crud.

This must be one of his side gigs. Secretive, under-the-table projects that don't leave much of a trail. Probably for good legal reason.

But I just know they're how Manny keeps making money outside his skeletal client base. Far more than any lawyer makes writing up wills and settling small-time estate feuds.

I set the phone down and back away from it slowly.

The phone can't hurt me. It's ninety percent plastic. I have no good reason to be afraid of it. *So why are my hands shaking?*

Because deep down, I know this might be Manny's Pandora's Box, and I just opened it.

"Get a grip!"

My own voice makes me jump.

"Sheesh!" I head for the fridge and grab a bottle of water, downing half of it without coming up for air.

Better. At least I'm no longer shaking like a leaf.

Deep breath. I go through it in my head.

Manny is a snake, but he's more like a gardener than a rattler. It's not like he's in the business of *killing* people. Or shacking weirdo Unknowns up with shes for a price.

Eat something, I tell myself.

That'll help. I haven't eaten since noon, when I wolfed down the leftover pasta salad I'd taken to the office yesterday.

Listening to my small amount of common sense, I pull out more deli food, and tear open a container of fresh salad. It's some sort of spring greens mix with chicken and seeds and avocado and raspberry vinaigrette dressing. I put away the rest and plop down at the small breakfast bar to savor a few bites.

I don't get far before the phone buzzes again.

Oh, crap.

I don't glance at it, but that doesn't stop my mind from conjuring up a thousand different scenarios. The mind of a writer is never silent. It's always working on overtime, creating what-ifs and heroes and bad guys that'll grab you by the throat and scream *read me*.

It's worse for me, though.

Because I was *trained* from an early age to observe the simplest things with intense scrutiny ever since Mom realized I had an interest in her craft. One time, in her pre-millionaire days, she kept me occupied describing the nacho cheese machine at a gas station in such gory orange detail, I've never been able to eat the stuff since.

Add in the fact my mother told me I should write thrillers because it would cure my fear of the dark, and, well, I'm screwed.

That's all there is to it. I always imagine the worst, never the best.

Like whoever's texting right now just has to be a serial killer or a sicko looking to put some poor lady on an auction block to pay off Manny's debts.

Ugh.

It's exhausting, I know, but in my hamster wheel brain, it's too real.

The phone goes off again three times before I'm done with my salad. The food helps. I'm no longer thinking the absolute worst.

Well, serial killer is still in the back of my mind, but I'm also *pissed* at myself for grabbing the damn phone out of Manny's desk.

But I made my choice. It's my responsibility. So now what?

Grabbing the phone off the counter, I read the messages,

all asking if she'll be there. Before I lose my nerve, I stab back at the keys on the screen.

I'll have to confirm that. Hold on.

Smiling, satisfied I've bought some precious time, I set the phone down, rinse my dishes, and put them in the dishwasher. Then I go upstairs, change into a pair of yoga pants and t-shirt, and take my hair out of the tight bun that keeps it halfway manageable most days.

Another text comes in hot, making the phone jump against the counter as I'm heading back downstairs.

My eyes suddenly itch. I probably should just ignore it, but, of course, I can't. There're three new messages.

Confirm what?

What sort of shitshow is SS&A? I don't have time for this BS.

You guaranteed your end of this deal. Guaranteed. And I'm paying out the ass.

Whoa. At least I've managed to *confirm* there's something majorly hinky here.

And that's about the second the air in my lungs locks up.

I pace the small kitchen area frantically. *Oh, God.*

What have I started up? Whether Manny drives me nuts or not, this seems serious.

He hired me, gave me a chance, a job, when no one else would. If I screw this up, I'm screwed to the place you go where you don't have good screwing puns anymore.

Bad news is, I *need* this stupid job. Even if it comes with a slight risk of major, enigmatic weirdos barking demands through cheap phones.

I swore I'd never accept another dime from Mom after college. Even if she has enough dimes in her investment account to rebuild the Tower of Babel.

Mom doesn't owe me anything. I already owe her a lot.

She covered my tuition in full, not to mention she's letting me live here practically rent free.

But now I've just put my ticket to adulthood in freaking jeopardy.

Maybe *worse*.

Worse, meaning, I could be knocked off or arrested for being involved in...whatever this is.

Crap, crap, crap, crap. Also, crap.

I take a deep breath and hold it, contemplating my answer before I start to type carefully.

Stork, Storkley, and Associates has a sterling reputation.

Lame, but it's the best I can come up with right now.

Within seconds, a new reply buzzes in.

Fuck your reputation. Can you deliver what I need or not?

"I don't know what you need!" I shout at the screen, getting flustered all over again. I know if I could see my own reflection, my face would give my hair a run in the red department.

I'm mulling over how utterly frustrated I am, mostly with myself for thinking a little fun wouldn't come back to bite my rump, when it happens.

The phone rings again. And I almost pee my pants.

"Crap!" Why the hell did I text Mr. Unknown back? Now I have to answer it. Have to!

It keeps ringing. There's no voicemail set up. It would've already rolled over to it a long time ago if it were.

Taking a breath that scalds my lungs, I tap the answer button. "Stork, Storkley, and Associates," I say.

The long silence on the other end allows my lungs to empty. For a second, I'm relieved there's no one there. I start peeling the phone away from my ear, but then there's thunder.

A rough, gruff voice.

"You her?"

Her? Hell no!

"Are you her?" The voice grows louder. Angrier. Mr. Unknown sounds even more pissed off than his texts.

"Excuse me?" I mutter.

"You deaf? Asked if you're her?" He snarls again. "Lady, I don't have time for games. There's too much at stake. So I ask. You answer. *Are. You. Her?*"

I swallow a boulder in my throat. I'm not sure I'd ever know what to say.

But Unknown cuts in again before I can squeak anything.

"Look, I've been driving for eighteen hours already and still have to make it across North Dakota. I need to know everything's in place. We'll be there tomorrow."

It's not just fury in his voice. There's desperation, too, but that's not what makes me go stock-still.

Another voice in the background does.

A child's voice, saying they have to go. Anyone who's ever heard a kid desperate for the nearest bathroom knows the urgency I just heard.

"It's in place," I say. "Confirmed. I'll talk to Mr. Stork and make sure–"

The phone goes dead before I even finish.

Holy hell. Fingers quivering, I set it on the counter again like it's alive and might bite me.

What. Is. This?

I have no idea how long I've been pacing the floor, wondering if I should panic call Manny when the phone rings again.

I stare at it, my eyes ready to crawl right out of my head. Kidnapping crosses my mind. What if that's what this is? Some soulless creeper rounding up kids for God only knows what?

But then, I remember the child said Dad. *Dad, hurry up, I have to go!*

Unless their dad kidnapped the boy from his mama. That happens all the time in the news.

He could still be a serial killer, and a kidnapper to boot. Or maybe she's the big bad wolf, and he's just trying to get the kid to safety. Or maybe...

Ugh.

Maybe that's why Manny's side gigs are practically classified. Child custody cases. People will pay big bucks to keep their kids – especially from psycho exes.

Picking up the phone, I click on the answer icon, and whisper a "Hello?"

"Sorry," the gruff voice says. "It's been a rough trip. I just need to know everything's set. Finalized. It's too late to—"

"It's set," I say impulsively. "Everything."

"Your law office tomorrow morning?"

I close my eyes, suddenly sick to my stomach. "Yes."

"Nine a.m.?"

I squeeze my eyes shut harder. "Yup. Nine it is."

"Thanks. See you soon."

There's a bleeping sound. The line goes dead again. Cue my entire body turning to mush.

Then I'm just slinking down on the floor, wondering what I've done.

I always wanted to write thrillers. Not *be* in one.

II: HOLDING OUT (MILLER)

I've never been so goddamn tired or so spooled up.

It's been over thirty-five hours since the last time I've closed my eyes, and we've still got several hours on the road till we hit the Twin Cities.

At least Shane's feeling better. *Christ.*

It must've been those ratty nachos from that last gas station in the sticks upsetting his gut. That slimy fake cheese crap is enough to give anyone the shits.

It rattles me something fierce that I can't do more for him, like give him a few hours rest in a decent hotel bed, or a real meal. Maybe this wouldn't have happened in the first place.

But time isn't of the essence.

It's fucking essential.

If I don't keep flooring it halfway across the country, if we don't get to our safe house, if I stop for even an hour just to catch our breath, the vultures will come.

And these are the kind of buzzards that won't even wait for us to die before tearing us limb from limb.

That's why I keep going. Why I keep counting my blessings through this sick ordeal, even when my family's being hunted. Why I'll give everything to make sure this hunt doesn't become a kill.

I count my blessings where I can. Both my kids have been troopers through this mess, which is far from being over. I couldn't ask for a better rockstar son than Shane, or a better daughter than my little Lauren.

I look at my boy now, twisting back into boredom in his seat. He gives me that look like he wants to ask *are we there yet?* but knows better not to.

I smile. You could've knocked me over with a feather the day they'd been born. Twins.

Maybe they were born to be rock solid from the second they came into this world. Nothing started easy. They never met their mother, after all.

Willow died moments after Lauren was born, barely a little while after Shane arrived.

An aneurysm.

Undetectable. Unimaginable. Unfair.

Unforgettable.

Up till the last couple weeks, I thought that fucked up day would always be the hardest of my life.

I had no idea.

"Are we almost there, Dad?" Shane finally cracks, asking the question that's been gnawing at him from the back seat.

"Getting there, kiddo. How're you feeling?" I ask, glancing at him in the rear-view mirror.

He flashes me a grin and his big blue eyes grow wide. "Better. But after this...I don't think I'm ever gonna eat nachos again."

"I told you it smelled like a skunk," Lauren says with a yawn from the seat beside him, rubbing her eyes.

"It *tasted* funny too," Shane admits, scrunching up his chipmunk face at the memory. "Blech."

"Then why'd you eat it?" Lauren asks.

"I was hungry!" he says, slapping his knees.

"I offered you one of my bananas," she replies.

He shrugs. "You only had two."

Warmth flows through my veins. They really are good kids. Nice kids. Generous to each other and other people.

Some days, I wonder how they're turning out as decent as they are. It hasn't been easy. Raising them alone, all these years, running my ass off for the company that's put me in this bind.

Rage flares deep in my gut. It was all going so well, our old lives back in Seattle.

I'd climbed the proverbial career ladder, securing the life I knew they deserved, despite not having a mother. Money can't buy everything, but it can make life easier.

They had toys. Friends. Vacations. A damn nice roof over their heads. Whole weekends with me, where I'd take them camping to Rainier or the Olympic Mountains, or we'd all climb aboard Keith's sailboat with his family and sail around the Puget Sound.

Sure, it could be boring. Suburban. Safe.

There are worse things. Like the utter shitshow we're starring in now.

All because I saw something I shouldn't have and couldn't keep my yap shut.

Then all hell broke loose. I think it's *still* breaking loose, actually, considering we're not even to our safe house yet.

Yeah, I'm taking a big risk trusting this shifty fuck of a lawyer. Beggars can't be choosers when they've got a loaded gun pressed to their family's head, on the run with two kids.

Goddammit.

How had I let this happen?

I should've realized the sky was about to fall before I even looked pure evil square in the face. How good we had it should've been fair warning.

Life isn't that easy. Not forever. Not for me. Never has been.

If I'd caught onto what was going on behind the scenes at Mederva sooner, I could've extracted us, could've made it far, far away from them before sounding the alarm. Before it put our lives in danger.

Our lives. Shit.

I can deal with my own, but no one fucks with my kids. Once I get them to safety – us to safety, technically, because they need a father who keeps his own neck intact – I'll make sure every last bit of info that'll put an end to Mederva Therapeutics goes global and winds up in the hands of someone who can do something.

I knew things there didn't smell quite right for the past year or more, but convinced myself that my past was making mountains out of molehills. I wish I'd listened to my instincts from day zero.

My gut was never wrong in war zones, and it hadn't been here.

It was the coin blunting my faith in myself. Money.

I was being paid too well to work there, and that salary became the lifeblood of everything. Our nice house with a sweet view of Mount Rainier. Good schools where they excelled. Name-brand clothes. Awesome eats. Fun.

All the shit I'd craved when I was young but never got. I tried to give my kids the universe, and it might've delivered them to the mouth of hell.

"Hey, Dad, will we be able to eat at a real restaurant today?" Shane asks. "Get some real food?"

I nod. "Yeah, buddy. Just need to make it through our meeting first."

I've never lied to them. I had to tell them as much as I

could in this situation. Enough to make them accept the fact that I tore them away from their home and friends without any warning for good reason. Enough to make them understand I'm doing this to save our lives.

I hoped like hell it wouldn't come to this, but it had, practically overnight. Our options were next to nil. When you're hunted, you just *run.*

Fly like the wind, hoping you'll be smart enough and careful enough and lucky enough to sort the rest out later.

It's a small mercy the school year ended last week. At least I don't have to worry about the system looking for me and claiming truancy, or worse.

I remember that from my younger years, how they always caught up with us. I must've gone to eight different schools my sixth-grade year. That sucked royally.

"Daddy...um, is the meeting where we'll meet her?" Lauren asks.

My eyes snap to the rear-view mirror, glancing at her. She looks about as nervous asking it as I feel hearing that question. I force down the boulder in my throat.

Goddamn. How do I even *begin* to answer?

Lauren isn't stupid. She knows what's up and what the stakes are. We all know what *her* means, even though we haven't even met *her* yet.

"Right," I say, clearing my throat. "It's not much farther. A quick introduction and then we can finally settle in."

"Will there be a town?" Shane asks. "Not like Seattle, I know, but...bigger?"

We've been on back roads all the way from the Seattle city limits. Had to be.

I couldn't take the slightest chance of being seen on major highways, even though I bought this SUV right before leaving town. If all goes right, we'll be out of the country before the title change hits the DMV databases. The salesman thought I was a cheapskate because my main concern was how long the license plates were still good for, then looked at me in bewilderment when I paid all cash.

"A little bigger," I tell him. "Nothing like home, but I think there's an ice cream place. Probably a DQ or something."

The kids smile, threatening to shear my heart in two. It's torture knowing they're grateful for such small favors.

From what I can tell, Finley Grove, Minnesota, isn't much. Just another small town an hour or so north of the metro area clustered near two big sister cities. A bedroom community that's mostly made up of newer middle class housing developments where people do little more than sleep and mow their lawns on weekends.

For our needs, it's perfect. Quiet. Secluded. *Safe.*

Not that it matters. We won't be here long enough to smell the roses. The lawyer Keith set me up with, Manny Stork, promised we'd be in and out the door within a week or two. I'm buying efficiency and sweet time.

On paper, Stork's a man shady enough to do what I need, but clean enough so no one suspects he's in on anything.

In reality, he'd *better* follow through.

Because I'm about to pay this weasel out the ass, trusting he'll be our ticket to a new country and new lives. Our *only* way out of here.

I had my doubts last night when no one would answer my calls or respond to my texts. By about the fiftieth attempt, I could feel my eyes going bloodshot in the North Dakota darkness, wondering whether or not I'd have to turn off abruptly toward the Canadian border and take our chances.

A woman finally picked up, though. She confirmed everything. I'm trusting her and the man who's got her on payroll.

"You guys got any snacks left back there to hold you over till after the meeting?" I ask.

"Yup!" Lauren chirps. "I rationed them, Daddy, just like you said."

"No, she's wrong," Shane cuts in. "We ate up everything a couple hours ago. Right before we hit Minnesota."

"Nuh-uh. I just hid them so you wouldn't wolf it all down. We've got cheese sticks, an apple, and a bottle of water," Lauren says, digging in the bag beside her, holding up each item as proof.

"Aw, sis, no more *cheese!*" Shane groans.

"This is real cheese." Lauren taps the cheese stick on the leather seat. "Not that fake goo stuff you ate." She hands him an apple. "Here, eat this first. You'll be fine."

I pinch my lips together. She's like a mini-mother. Has been since she was old enough to walk.

Willow would be proud of her. Of both of our kids, really, for shining through in a time of stress.

For me, I think pride would be last on her list of stormy emotions. Hell, there isn't even a silver lining in this mess I've created, sending us across the country like we've got warrants for our arrest.

I wish it were that simple.

The police don't make people disappear into an unmarked grave. And no dirty cop has millions at his disposal making sure we're found.

Fuck.

Was Willow right all these years? That was the main reason we'd never married.

She couldn't trust me to keep my nose clean. That's how she'd described it. I'd promised her I'd changed my stripes since returning to the States after my last big stint in the Army, and I'd asked her to marry me for the third time. She'd agreed, and I'd been ready to put the ring I'd bought on her finger before she went into labor.

I never got the chance to see how we would've worked as

one big happy family. The laughs, the love, the fights, the anger, the disappointment most couples go through weren't meant to be.

"What's this place called?" Shane asks between bites of apple.

Eyes focused on the road, I point at a green sign.

"Finley Grove," I say. "Twenty-nine more miles."

"I wonder if they'll have a library?" Lauren muses, biting her lip.

"Library? How about an arcade? A big one with laser tag!" Shane thumps his small fist against his chest. "That's way more fun than a bunch of musty old books."

"Don't knock it unless you try it." Lauren sticks her tongue out, turning her face back into the paperback resting on her lap.

It's some new kids' book by Olivia Woods, who writes about brave little girls with magic powers to kick ass and mend broken hearts. I'm just glad Lauren isn't into the author's sister, Milah Holly, once the screaming, beating, musical heart of teen rebellion.

I don't interrupt their debate on libraries versus arcades, nor do I comment on the fact that we won't be in Finley Grove any longer than absolutely necessary. It shouldn't be more than a day or two before Keith calls and we get the go ahead to board a plane, but we won't be joining him in Ecuador.

All four of us are bound for Ireland: one man, two kids, and a wife.

This isn't the way I'd always wanted to take the kids overseas. I don't mind soaking in new cultures and old world charm, but hell.

This isn't a family fucking vacation.

As soon as we're settled in a little village off the map, I can talk to Keith half a world away on secure lines. Then the real work begins; how we'll unfuck our lives permanently and end this threat so we can come home.

It's still on my mind less than half an hour later when we roll into town. The law office isn't far.

The building looks nondescript, worn, tired. It's a one story made of faded brick, a block off the main road that cuts through Finley Grove. It's the kind of place you'd miss if you blinked after stopping at the four-way stop sign.

I'm careful not to make that mistake now.

Glancing at the time on the dash as I put the car in park in front of the building, I let out a huff of relief. Nine o'clock on the dot. Maybe that's a sign things will start going our way.

"This it?" Shane asks.

"We wouldn't have parked here if it wasn't," Lauren answers for me. "Can we come in, Daddy?"

I nod as I open my door. I've already told them what I expect. They know how serious this meeting is. There's no need for behavior reminders.

While they climb out, I collect a backpack out of the back hatch. It's stuffed to the brim with payment for services rendered.

The kids follow me to the glass door. I pull it open and we walk inside. A sign for the law firm hangs above a door halfway down the hall.

Stork, Storkley, and Associates.

What a bullshit name. I don't know how Keith even found this Manny guy when he's halfway across the country from Seattle, but I'm *counting* on this lawyer coming through. Handing me everything I need.

A wife.

Pretend wife.

One willing to lend us cover, then travel to get us the hell out of the country.

There are no other signs hanging over the other doors, which leaves me to believe the rest of the offices are empty.

Good. Discretion is the name of this supremely screwed up game right now.

The kids walk at my sides, and I give them each a quick scan. Remarkably, they look no worse for wear after a road trip that seemed like it'd last forever.

Their freckled faces are clean. Shane's dinosaur t-shirt doesn't have a single nacho stain, surprisingly. I don't need to inspect Lauren's pink unicorn shirt. It's as neat as the freshly combed, brown hair hanging around her face and down her back. Her pink shorts look fine and so do her sandals.

I tap Shane on the shoulder as we arrive at the door. "Pull up your shorts and tie your shoes."

Nothing new there. His lanky frame doesn't have any hips, so his pants are always falling down, and his shoes are forever untied. His hair is cropped short like mine. Otherwise, it'd be sticking out in every direction. No denying he's as much a boy as Lauren's a girl.

And I love them for it with all my heart and soul.

I wait till he's done tying his shoe before reaching for the doorknob. The door is mostly glass, but there's a vinyl blind hanging on the other side so I can't see through it. The blind bounces against the glass as I push the door open.

We're not alone.

A woman with golden-red hair sits behind a desk. Her big green eyes lock on me, but the rest of her seems frozen stiff. I wonder what the lawyer told her about me, about us.

Her deer-in-the-headlights look doesn't change, and she doesn't say anything. I wonder if she's like other chicks I've met half a lifetime ago. One of the quiet, hot ones who's also battier than a castle?

"Nine o'clock appointment," I say, stopping just short of waving my hand in front of her face.

"Oh, uh, of course!" she stutters, coming to life.

Wait. *That voice.*

I recognize it from the phone last night. My eyes shift up and zero in.

She stands then, and I'm surprised at her height. Closer to my six-foot-five frame than most women, even if I'm still taller.

Her loose-fitting, flowery dress enhances a figure that's in perfect, lush proportion to her height. Her hand moves up to her head, and the bun holding back her thick hair shifts, letting several corkscrews fall around her face.

Goddamn. If I had time to stop and drool, I just might forget our hellish predicament long enough to grow a hard-on like diamond for this ginger-red fox of a girl.

I've always been partial to redheads, and this one's pure gold from head to toe. But there's no time for lusting. No time to gawk and admire her many assets, much less hold up the show.

Giving my head a slight shake, I nod to a door on the other side of the room. "Is he in yet?"

"Who?" She shakes her head, waving one hand too far, which hits a plastic container of pencils and pens. Reaching for the container as the contents fly out of it, she says, "Oh, Mr. Stork, right. That's who you mean."

She spins around, scrambling to collect the pens and pencils before they roll off the desk. "Ugh, I *knew* that," she mutters under her breath.

Lauren darts forward, catching a couple pens before they hit the floor.

"Thank you!" the woman says, offering my little girl a timid smile as she takes the pens. "I really appreciate it."

Then her jade eyes flick to me with something like savage shame and annoyance. "He'll be here very shortly, I'm sure. Thanks for your patience...sir."

I fight back a grin at how slow she is to add it. Maybe it's the long drive, but there's something amusing about making her day more interesting.

Gingersnap.

That's a good name for her. Just like the cookies that pack a touch of sweetness and some serious bite behind their rusty glow.

Not only is her hair a similar golden-red, right now her face could teach cherries how to blush.

"You're welcome," Lauren says, stepping back. "I just wanted to help if you're busy."

"Oh, no. Not yet. Mr. Stork isn't here," she says, stuffing her things back into the container and setting it neatly on the desk. "But he should be any minute." She waves a hand to a small sitting area. "You're welcome to wait."

"Dad? Can I use the restroom?" Lauren looks at me.

"Of course," Gingersnap says. "It's straight across the hall. Can't miss it."

Lauren looks at me, waiting. So does Shane. They're probably wondering what fucking spell just came over me.

Slowly, I nod, shrugging off my stupor. As both kids reach the door, I say, "Leave that open, please."

They do, and I turn back to the woman. "Should be, or *will* be?"

She frowns, her brows knitting together underneath that brilliant head of hair.

"Stork. Should be here any minute, or *will* be here?" I ask, trying not to snarl. "Lady, I've come a long damn way, and I really don't have time to waste. Or any room for misunderstandings."

She purses her lips, wringing her hands together, then pulls them apart and sets the pencil holder on the other corner of her desk.

"Will be, will be." Under her breath, she adds, "God, I hope."

I lift a brow, letting her know I heard that.

Her smile comes out strained and wobbles. "Don't worry just yet. He's...he's usually here somewhere between nine and..."

I lift both brows, waiting for her to finish.

"Nine thirty!" She grimaces, glancing at the wall behind me. "Seriously. That's the latest I've ever seen him in. I'm sure of it."

I turn. The clock hanging there says it's ten after nine.

Fuck. I really didn't need to see that to know she's stretching the truth, trying to keep the peace.

"It's always before ten," she rattles on. "Can I get you a bottle of water or some coffee?"

There's a small fridge in the corner near the waiting area, and a coffee maker sitting on top of it.

My dry mouth throbs like my burning eyes at the thought of throwing more caffeine down my throat. Now, I'm getting worried.

"No, nothing. Our appointment was for nine," I say. "Your boss shouldn't make promises he can't keep."

"Oh, I understand, and I'm sure he'll be here in just—" A sound stops her.

I heard it too. The outside door.

I'm off, heading for the door, glancing down the hall impatiently. I hope it's that damn lawyer and not anyone tracking us. Christ, I'm so tired I think I left my gun in the glove box, and the others are even more locked away.

Then I see a tall, dark-haired man in his late thirties or so hurrying toward me. Hardly the profile of a lethal mercenary on clean-up duty.

"Mr. Rush?" he asks, forcing a smile. "Manny Stork, at your service! It's a genuine pleasure."

"Our meeting time was nine," I growl.

"I know. Traffic held me up. Unreal this morning."

I blink at him. This town only has one four-way stop on the GPS. "Traffic?"

"A train!" he says. "A really long one. I, uh...got caught taking a little delay after fueling myself up for the day."

Finally, the bastard gets to the truth. The tall cup hanging in his hand, filled with some syrupy sweet Franken-coffee I can smell steaming through the plastic lid.

Train, my ass. It's only my kids' lives at stake while he gets his morning fix.

I want to throw him against the wall, spilling that shit all over his pressed shirt, and ask him if he'll take this *seriously.*

But I'm too pissed, too desperate, to menace this clown who's still our only pathetic hope.

I evil-eye him instead, finally stepping aside as he rushes through the open door.

"Right this way, Mr. Rush. I read you loud and clear. No need to hold things up any longer." Glancing at the woman as he hurries to his office door, he says, "Hold all my calls, Ms. Courtney!"

"Got it." She nods and looks up at me. "I'll watch for your kids. They'll be just fine out here with me."

I stare back out the door, across the hall at the restroom doors, slowing. For a second, I hesitate, hating the idea of leaving them alone with *anyone.*

"Or I can send them straight to Mr. Stork's office, if you'd prefer?" She must sense it, the feral, protective spark lighting up my face.

"No," I snap. "Keep them out here. Please."

I'm asking for an honest favor. Don't need the kids seeing my reaction if Stork doesn't have everything he promised in place. There may be smoking craters left behind.

She nods, then looks toward Stork's open office door. I

cross the room, enter the office, and pull the door shut behind me.

"Sorry I'm late again," Stork says as he settles himself into the overstuffed leather chair behind his desk. "Please have a seat."

"Don't tell me that's her?" I ask.

A huge, heaping part of me hopes it's not.

Gingersnap is a looker from the way her hair falls around her face to the way those long legs move when she's nervous. I damn sure don't need a diversion like that in any way, shape, or form.

This shit makes me nervous enough. I'll be exposing my kids to a stranger, making them pretend she's their mother, something they've *never* had.

What kind of chick agrees to that, no matter how well it pays?

Hell, what kind of woman takes on any of this for money? She'll be taking a big risk.

Any sort of mistake, hiccup, or malfunction, and the same sick fucks who are after us will be on her.

Stork's eyes drift to my backpack and stop. "Did you bring the money?" he asks.

My fist tightens. I hold out the bag by the strap and let go, watching as it hits the floor.

He tries to peer over the desk worriedly, as if the bag will sprout legs and wander off like a tortoise.

Asshole.

It's not hard to see where his priorities are. His suit is expensive, tailored, and his obsession with the bag shows how much he likes his money. I know plenty of men like him, ones willing to do whatever it takes to get more of their favorite green fix.

My skin crawls just being here, standing in front of his beady little eyes.

I'm not sure what sort of connections Keith used to find this guy, but I remember there's no choice. Stork's obsession with a fatter bank account just might save our lives.

"Right there," I answer, stepping in front of it as he stands up. "You can count it later. Let's not put the cart before the horse."

He blinks and nods. "Oh, of course. Your arrival's earlier than expected, Mr. Rush."

"Things change," I growl. "We had to leave earlier than planned. I gave you plenty of notice."

"Yes, yes, I got the message..."

"And? You able to deliver or what?" It comes out like acid, words wishing they could burn a hole through this greedy pig.

It's not his life on the line. His future. His *kids.*

His gaze goes to the door. After a dull silence, he nods. "Absolutely. However, I still have a few last details to finish before you're on your way to the Emerald Isle. I hear it's a nice place this time of year, all soft breezes and beer to die for–"

He drifts off when he notices my death glare. "I don't give a fuck about Guinness. Two week turnaround. Ideally less. That's what you promised."

He forces the world's most awkward smile. "Right, right! It's been a long trip here, I get it. No worries, my friend. You're in great hands now. This won't take long. As you've probably noticed, Finley Grove isn't a big spot on the map. You'll be nice and cozy here until everything's set. No trouble will find you here."

For your sake, you'd better be right, I think to myself.

This dark hunger rises in my veins, an ache in my fists I've had ever since Keith and I barely blew Seattle with our lives.

I'm not happy with his answer, but I haven't been happy with much for weeks. "How long?"

His mouth goes crooked while he thinks. Or he tries to cook up the best answer to avoid upsetting me.

"Hmmm...no more than another day or two to get this going? It should be fast." He reaches over and turns on his computer. "It's just paperwork, really. Legalese making sure the I's are dotted and the T's are crossed."

"But the woman, that's set? And a place for us to stay?"

He pauses for a strained second, then glances at the bag on the floor again. "Sure, sure, but...not to sound crass, I'll need the money up front. That's not all profit. Some of this is just covering our travel fees."

He winks. I just pretend the insufferable cock didn't.

"*Half* the money," I bite off. "That was the deal. You'll get the rest when we, *my family* and I, board the plane. Not before."

"All right," he huffs after a long pause. I can't tell if he's nervous or just that greedy. "Half now and half then. That was the deal. Right-o, captain."

My fist tightens again. He flicks his tongue over his lips and nods again as a sly grin forms. "I'm sure you'll be very comfortable at Ms. Courtney's home. She lives a somewhat simple, secluded life, but unless I'm mistaken, that should fit your present needs like a glove?"

I force a nod. He rubs his hands together.

Goddamn. I can almost *see* the wheels turning inside his head like the cogs in a machine set to scheme-mode.

Keith better be right. I have to believe he knew what he was doing when he contracted this guy.

I know he made it out safely, at least. His other guy in Phoenix didn't let him down. Let's hope this one's just as reliable.

Clearing my throat, I sit up straighter. "So, when will I meet her? You never answered my question about that."

Stork holds up a finger and stands. "Very shortly, Mr. Rush. And about that...I'll be back in a jiffy! I just have to go speak with my receptionist and make sure all the arrangements are in place with no more delays." He rounds his desk and bolts for the door before I roar back. "I won't be long. Make yourself comfortable!"

Comfortable? He's got to be shitting me.

I haven't been *comfortable* in weeks. I wonder if I even forgot the meaning of the word over the past thirty-hour hell-drive here.

Sighing, I can't help but guess what rock Keith found this snake under.

III: IT'S ONLY A WEEK (GWEN)

*Y*ou know that ringing dizziness you get when someone says something so outrageous, so unbelievable, so upsetting?

Yeah. It's a minor miracle I'm even standing.

"You're *serious?*" I ask him, too stunned to say more.

I run through all the reasons why I might've heard wrong. Maybe I didn't get enough sleep last night, or that pasta salad did something funky to my head. Maybe that little game of phone tag with Mr. Snarlypants gave me a terrible case of second guessing. Maybe I never woke up this morning and I'm still freaking dreaming, waiting to fly up in a rush when I really *do* wake up past my alarm and try not to be too late for work.

Because what Manny told me – what he's *asking* me to do – is so unreal I have to be dreaming. *Right?*

He can't be serious about some strange man and his two kids moving into my house. Oh, but his lips are moving again, every bit the beak that makes him look like his Stork namesake.

"You have two bedrooms, don't you, Ms. Courtney?"

"Um, yeah." I shake my head as soon as I answer.

I can't believe I'm not screaming.

The number of bedrooms in the townhouse doesn't *matter*. Not for this.

I knew I was up the creek without a paddle the second Manny pulled me into the hall outside our office, obviously for privacy. The guy he's talking about – the super tall, very well-built beast who looks more like a jacked cop who hasn't shaved for a week versus the creepy serial killer kidnapper on the run I'd been imagining since hanging up the phone last night – is *still* in Manny's office.

But his kids are in the waiting room, perched on the secondhand furniture. They're busy flipping through the small stack of old magazines on the end table, financial journals that wouldn't interest most adults, much less children. I feel bad for them.

"I don't even know him," I hiss, my eyes bouncing to the closed door behind us like he'll hear through it. "Those might not even be his kids for all I know."

"They're his rugrats. He's all they've got in the world from what I understand, and the poor guy's in trouble." Manny follows my glance to the door. His voice softens strategically. "Poor things. They barely had time for it to sink in before big daddy hit the road. No time to even say goodbye to their friends."

I'm *so* not falling for this. He's not pushing my buttons. I don't know if Manny Stork could manipulate a potato into growing eyes.

Still, I feel for those kids, and it has nothing to do with his hilariously selfish persuasion.

Something akin to sympathy fills his face as he looks back at me. "You don't have to know someone in order to help them, Ms. Courtney."

"Help them—" I stop myself before the compassion that

started sprouting inside me last night gets any bigger. "No. Hell no," I add, trying harder to convince myself this is *not* something I want to be mixed up in.

Forget wanting to know more. Screw the big mystery. Curiosity killed the cat, and I have a feeling the truth here just might leave *me* roadkill.

"Ah, yes, I thought maybe you'd be reluctant. I'm not asking you to do this *pro bono* – Lord knows I did plenty of that crap when I was bright-eyed and bushy-tailed right out of law school. You'll get paid for it, Ms. Courtney!" He beams like the sun, lifting a brow, waiting for me to start jumping up and down. "Paid well," he adds.

I barely hold back a snort.

"By who?" I know it's not my boss who'll be signing the check.

He's a true believer in *starting salary*. One that barely reaches above minimum wage for wearing a whole hat rack as his secretary, receptionist, data recovery specialist, sometimes paralegal, and part-time office maid.

"Don't look so shocked. I'll write you a check right now if you want me to put the money where my—"

I shake my head, holding up a hand to stop him. "No. Forget it."

"Fine then, cash!" he says a little more sharply. "You'll be paid in cash. Nothing less for your services rendered, just as soon as you agree. No tricks, no games, no fuss. An incredibly generous offer, Ms. Courtney. How's that sound?"

I huff out a breath. "It sounds like I'm still saying *no*. I won't do it."

His face darkens. He opens his mouth, but I head him off.

"Don't you *dare* think about terminating me on the spot. Employer or not, you can't make me take work this far outside my job description. It's one thing to ask me to slave over your stupid computer with your 'gigs' when I've barely so much as swapped out a hard drive. Forcing me to open my home to strangers is against every employment law on the books. A *major* violation of privacy."

For a second, he looks mortified, then angry, then bemused.

That makes two of us, I guess. Mom would be proud of me for showing some backbone. I think I'm even a little proud of myself.

"Whoa," he whispers. "Whoa, Ms. Courtney, now hang on a minute. I'm not asking you to–"

"To *what?*" I snap. "Seems like you've asked for plenty more than I was hired for ever since I started here. Hey, what's one more little task?"

He freezes. We both know what *task* means. That's what Manny calls it, as if he's doing me this huge favor asking me to run around like a hen on fire. Diverse 'tasks,' all for the 'experience.'

"Ms. Courtney...Gwendolyn..."

I cringe as he says my name, something he rarely does. All part of the mock prestige at this fake law firm, I guess.

"I'd never force you to do anything you don't want to do, or that would breach your personal sense of ethics," he says. "I simply *assumed* you wouldn't mind helping this guy out. He's on the up and up, you know. A hero of sorts. A whistle-blower. He just needs a safe place to stay with his munchkins until it's time for him to jet and reveal his sources. Somewhere he won't have to worry about shooting himself in the back of the head five times."

My jaw drops a little. Both at the morbid fake suicide analogy and because it tells me this is as deadly serious as I feared.

Curiosity bites harder. So does the way my heart aches for those poor kids.

What does Manny *mean?* Really? That someone would

actually kill their father over whatever 'sources' he has? That someone would murder all of them?

A chill sweeps up my spine. It's a balmy day in an office with craptacular A/C, and I'm suddenly shivering like it's winter.

I think about the two adorable kids on the other side of the door. Twins. Fraternal. Ten years old.

I had to try hard to get even that much out of them.

"Whistleblower for what?"

"Well, I'm not privy to all the dirty details," Manny says. "That's not really my role."

"Exactly what *is* your role in this?" I cock my head, crossing my arms.

Even though we're the only two people in the hall, and every office space in this building except ours is empty – available for rent – he lowers his voice. "I'm not at liberty to say. It's part of the contract."

"Your contract with who?" My eyes narrow. If there was ever a time I wanted to yank on his stupid tie, royal purple with mock-royal heraldry...

"Sorry, Ms. Courtney. Can't say. And you've already made it abundantly clear you aren't interested, so..."

He turns his back but barely gets a step away from me before I yell out.

"Wait!" The wheels in my head spin like garden whirligigs. "Who do you mean? The government? Is this, like...part of some elaborate witness protection plan?"

He shrugs slightly, offering me a wry smile. "I truly can't say. It's classified."

A rare tingle of excitement fills me. "I'm right, aren't I?"

Adrenaline surges through my blood. It's making more and more sense. So maybe his gigs aren't all weird, under-the-table deals with creepers.

Working with the Feds *would* explain why there's so much

encrypted data on his old computer. Heck, it might even explain how he manages to keep the lights on and the fans running at this joke of a firm, which probably hasn't ever turned a profit.

"It'll be short term," Manny says. "Him and the kids staying at your house, I mean, if you're willing to reconsider..."

"*How* short term, Manny?"

He reaches up, stroking his pointy chin. "Oh, shouldn't be more than a week. Maybe two at most. Let's say...ten days?"

Oh, God.

I'm caving. Little by little. Piece by piece. Even though I *know* I shouldn't be.

I'm simply too intrigued with this man, a real life thriller hero who just walked through the door. My palms are going sticky, my mind racing with possibilities.

This could be it. The lucky break that gives my muse something meaty to chew on, a chance at real research, real experience for my book.

The best of the bestsellers don't just materialize from nothing. They happen when writers get butt in chair, words on paper, and bleed *experience.*

"...and you'll be paid in cash," Manny says, bringing my attention back to him. "A considerable sum, as I said earlier."

I frown. "Considerable?"

"Three year's salary, tax free, Ms. Courtney. We'll round up a few thousand because I'm nice like that."

What the what? I reach up and rub my ears, wondering if they're hallucinating again.

"A *hundred* grand?" I'm flabbergasted. Ready to go falling through the floor.

Manny nods. "If you're willing to do more, I'll see if we can get that doubled. This client has ample resources."

"Doubled?" I squeak, too stunned to even be embarrassed.

"You heard me, young lady." He nods, chuckling to himself. "Play your cards right, and you won't even need another degree to make some big lawyer bucks."

Holy Toledo. Screw the degree. Screw *law.*

If he isn't just playing, filling my ears with a fairy tale, I could quit working here on that type of money. I could lock myself away and write my novel. I could give it my very best for a couple years before I'd have to worry about anything. "Manny...are you serious? Tell me this isn't some kind of weird joke."

"Scout's honor. It's all real." He glances at the door again. "But there are a few stipulations."

Oh, of course.

Of course, it's too flipping good to be true.

"You have to pretend you've known Mr. Rush and the kids for several years." He shrugs, a funny look on his face, his eyes shifting around. "Almost like...they're family or something. Long lost relatives, if that makes sense."

I eyeball him warily. *That's it?*

I was expecting to lose a limb or something.

This whole thing still sounds too easy, too basic, too good to be true. "Where's the catch?"

Manny grins. "That's it. A little theatrics, if anyone comes sniffing around. But I think the chances of that are very unlikely, and if all goes according to plan, Mr. Rush will be gone before he even leaves a caveman-sized dent on your sofa."

A week. Maybe two. That's hardly a big deal, and my social life is blander than porridge.

No one in the neighborhood would even notice a man and a couple kids staying over, keeping a low profile. So I guess pretending I've known them for years has no bearing on my decision whatsoever.

"I'll tell you what," Manny says, raising a finger. "I'll even give you the rest of the day off, paid, so you can show them where they'll be living and get them all settled in. We want Mr. Rush and his family to be comfortable. They've got a stressful time ahead."

"A day off *with pay?*" I can't stop shaking my head.

This case must be extremely important to him. That thought makes me pause. I look him square in the face. "When I called you this morning, you sounded almost surprised that your appointment with him was today. But if you've been waiting for this so long, shouldn't you have known?"

"Guilty as charged. I was surprised, Ms. Courtney," he says, sounding strangely honest. "My contact originally said it would be next week he'd be coming by. But circumstances changed, him and the kids had to leave earlier than planned for their own safety. That's why I'm kind of in a bind, asking you to help. The lady I'd originally asked to put him up can't do it on this short of notice. I didn't have time to get ahold of anybody else who usually assists me with these sorts of cases."

Intrigued, I ask, "How many of these witness cases are you involved in?"

"Now, a gentleman can't reveal everything. Particularly in *this* line of work. I've already said far more than I should have, I hope you're satisfied with the answers. Wouldn't want to breach my contracts or my ethics letting more slip."

I almost laugh in his face. Up until now, he's never had an ethical bone in his body.

But what if I'm wrong?

What if the shoestring, penny-pinching lawyer-by-day persona he wears is just an act to shore up his real work?

Again, he seems weirdly sincere, and uncharacteristically honest.

Witness protection? Holy crap.

This is spectacular stuff.

Stuff I could really use for books, without ever revealing the true cases of course. For once, Manny's potential goldmine might have a few nuggets for me.

"Okay, fine," I tell him, and have to take a deep breath before adding, "I'll do it."

For a moment, I wonder if my boss is going to hug me, and I take a step back. Because that would officially be more than I could handle. Plus, I have a personal space bubble I rarely let anybody pop.

He doesn't hug me but does smile from ear to ear while patting my shoulder with his manicured hand. "Great decision, Ms. Courtney! I knew you'd come around. Thank you, thank you." Stepping toward the door, he adds, "Now for the easier part. I'll just need a few minutes to get everything in order with Mr. Rush."

"Is that what I'm supposed to call him? Mr. Rush?"

"That's the name, Miller Rush. The kids are Shane and Lauren." He gives me an affectionate nod and then opens the door and holds it for me to enter.

I walk back in from the hall. While Manny sails past me, heading for his office, my nerves do the jitterbug as I see the children still in the waiting area. Big Daddy's standing next to them.

Miller Rush.

Forget jitterbug. I think there's an entire stampede in my belly.

He's taller than me by several inches – a rarity to begin with for guys – but it's so much more than that. He's *hot*.

Like fashion magazine underwear model picture-perfect hot. Like eyes so ladykiller, Congress should pass a law against them. Like the kind of man who'd never give me a magnetic stare.

His black polo shirt clings so tight I get a good idea what

he'd look like without a shirt, and his black jeans...holy hell. My imagination spins into overdrive. And not just because of this whole crazy witness protection thing I somehow signed up for.

"Mr. Rush?" Manny says from his doorway. "All ready for you."

The man doesn't say anything to the kids, Manny, or me as he storms past my desk into Manny's office. The door shuts and I finally heave out the air that was locked in my lungs.

One week. Seven days. Maybe a few more.

I can do this for more money than I've ever had in my life. It's not like it's any huge burden on my privacy or barely-there social life either.

The townhouse has two bedrooms, and the guest room has bunk beds. They came built-in from the original owner. The couch in the living room is also oversized and comfortable.

I slept on it last winter when I tore the tendons in my ankle while skiing and couldn't manage the stairs real easily for a couple of weeks.

I can sleep there again if they want both rooms. It's just a week or two. No big deal.

"Excuse me?"

I snap out of my thoughts and smile at the little girl staring up at me. "Hey, what's up?"

"Um, I was just wondering...does this town have a library?"

I can't help but smile. A girl after my own bookish heart, which I probably got from Mother.

Crud. Mother.

I forgot about her. She'll have more questions than I do about this situation if she even gets a whiff I've thrown my door open to total strangers.

But for this chance? It's a risk I'll have to take. I'll just have to brace myself to cross that bridge if and when we get there. "Oh, yes, there's a nice big library off Main. Biggest in the county, it serves people from several towns over. It's not too far from the grocery store." I walk to the waiting area with her. "It's not like a big city or campus library, but they do circulate books with larger places, so they have a good selection. Do you like to read?"

A smile lights up her cherub face. "Every day!"

"She's a bit of a nerd. Always has her nose stuffed in a book," her brother says. "She read three whole paperbacks on our drive here. Big ones." He rolls his bright-blue eyes.

"Not *that* big," she says, nudging him with an elbow.

"Three books? How long was your trip?" I ask.

"We left home yesterday morning," Shane answers. "Dad said it takes like twenty-five to thirty hours to get here from Seattle. Sounds 'bout right."

Holy crap. That kind of drive would turn me into a puddle of sleepy mush.

Not wanting them to think I'm being too nosy, I keep talking books. "You read three whole books in one day? Wow, that's impressive at your age. Any age, really. I read somewhere most adults are lucky if they read *one* book a year."

Lauren nods shyly. "They weren't super long, and I have a book light so I could read after dark. Daddy said we should wait before using the tablet so...I read the old school way."

I nod, turning to Shane. "How about you? Read anything good on your trip?"

He shakes his head. "Nah, I kept Dad company. Think he liked having somebody awake most of the time to talk to on the road. It gets lonely driving that many hours," he tells me proudly.

Lauren gives him a formidable look. "And you ate nachos that made us have to stop at bathrooms every thirty miles."

I quiver. "Gas station nachos? The kind where the cheese sauce just festers in one of those metal urns? My condolences."

"Yup!" Lauren laughs. "It smelled *awful*. I told him to be careful but...he was starving."

Shane nods and grimaces. "All right, all right. Lesson learned. No more orange goop ever."

I fight back a laugh. They're both so adorable. "Smart choice. That stuff makes me quiver just thinking about it," I say, cringing all over again. "I opened the lid once."

"It was really gross inside, wasn't it?" Lauren asks, wrinkling her nose.

"Pretty much. Gross might be an understatement."

"I knew it!" Looking at her brother, she says, "Told you."

Shane puts his hands up defensively, trying not to grin.

She glances up at me again, her little eyes twinkling. "I told him those things are never washed. They're all unsanitary."

"The one I opened up hadn't ever seen a wipe down, that's for sure," I tell her.

"Why would you ever open one?" Shane asks, standing to stretch.

"It was...a project of sorts. A challenge, I guess you'd call it. I had to describe the cheese machine in painful detail," I answer, hating how it sounds as ridiculous as it actually was.

His face wrinkles with a frown. "What kind of project is that?"

"Something to do." I shrug. "I liked to do a lot of writing growing up."

I decide to leave it at that. It sounds better than explaining how Mother was always doing research for her books, locked up in her writer's cave, and because I was usually with her, I was given assignments, things to research and describe in vivid detail to keep me busy.

"Sounds like you need an iPad, Miss," Shane says dryly.

A giggle bubbles up my throat as Lauren nudges him with her elbow again, shaking her head.

"What kind of books do you like?" I ask her.

"All of them," her brother mutters. "Real boring stuff."

"Says you! I like history, fantasy, mysteries..." She shoots him another daunting look before rattling off a number of children's series.

Some older ones that I'd read when I was young, and some newer ones I've barely heard of but haven't bought because they're kids' books. Mother would shake her head if she knew I was interested in reading them.

I sit down on the extra chair and ask her about the ones I've read. I remember the characters like I'd just read the books yesterday instead of years ago. That's something I'd agree on with momsy, the endless power of a good read to stick in your head many years later.

I'm supposed to be the adult here. I could go on, tell the kids some sage wisdom about how books open doors, and Lauren should never stop reading, and Shane should read more, but...

We're still talking about a series that was turned into a Netflix show recently when Manny's office door swings open.

"Ms. Courtney?" Manny calls. "Allow me to formally introduce you to Miller Rush."

I stand up abruptly, trying to steel my knees, nodding at the man as he steps closer.

He may be tall. He may be hot. He may be gruff.

But if I'm going to do this, I *can't* let him scare me anymore.

"Miller, please meet Gwendolyn Courtney. Your partner

in crime for however long you'll be staying here in little old Finley Grove."

For a second, Miller turns, giving him a vicious look.

Manny holds up his hand. "Sorry. Poor choice of words maybe. By partner in crime, I certainly didn't mean–"

"Enough," he growls before turning back to me.

Oh, crap. There's that racing heart again. Except now it feels more like a turbo powered lawnmower screaming against my ribs.

He's standing still, the dirty look fading off his face, waiting.

I can do this. I swear, just a quick nod and a handshake and we'll be like old friends.

Yeah, I'm delusional.

My hands start shaking the instant I move closer, and he holds out a hand.

Curling my right hand into a tight ball to quell the trembling, I force myself to hold out my fingers.

"Thanks for agreeing to help us, Ms. Courtney," he says. "Means a lot to me and my family."

Whatever else I expected, it's not this.

Sincerity in his tone, in his eyes. They're the same bright sky-blue as Shane's.

I push my hand out farther. "Happy to help!" I say.

He says nothing else. Just takes hold of my hand firmly.

Oh, God.

Then it happens. The brush fire heat of his palm touching mine sends a bolt of pure electricity racing up my arm. I pull my hand away. Unable to think of anything to say, I nod, and then look at Manny.

"Everything's all set," my boss says, oblivious to the weird energy exchange powerful enough to short-circuit me. "I think Miller here has been awake for over a whole day, and he's ready to get some rest. So don't let me hold you guys up a minute longer. See you around, Ms. Courtney."

I nod at Manny. He's probably not wrong.

Miller's eyes do look dog-tired, and there's a five o'clock shadow covering his jaw. Tongue-tied again, I nod, then walk to my desk where I shut down my desktop and pull my purse out of the bottom desk drawer.

Manny says goodbye again and just like that we're walking out the door.

Once we're outside, I point at Pearl. "That's my ride. You can follow me to my place, it's not far."

"Got a restaurant or drive-thru on the way?" Miller gestures at the kids climbing in the back seat of his Equinox. "They're hungry as hell. It's been too long since we had a real meal."

Oh. Right. They're probably starving.

"There's a hamburger joint along the way," I tell him. "This small local place that serves up breakfast and sandwiches and other diner fare. I hear they do the job."

I can't speak from experience. I've never eaten there.

Shrugging because I don't know much about the taco place on the far side of town, either, I let him think it over. Finley Grove sprawls out across several miles, all thanks to the newer housing developments, but the town doesn't have much of a business base. "The only major sit-down restaurant nearby is about another five miles away. I'm not sure if they open before lunch, though. I know for certain the other restaurant at the golf course doesn't open until four."

That's the only one I've patronized, with Mother, more Friday nights than I want to count. There's a bar there where I do drinks with friends the rare times they come into town.

"The drive-thru will do," he says.

I hope he's right. Because I kind of feel like I'm being stared down by a huge, hungry giant.

"Follow me. We'll be there in no time," I say.

Pearl fires right up, and I back out of my parking space, onto the road. Miller does the same, staying close as I lead him a block or two up to the highway.

We stop briefly at the four-way stop sign before crossing the road. Glancing in my rear-view mirror when he follows me through the intersection, my lips sag into a frown.

Something's off.

I think it's that vehicle.

The baby-blue Equinox just doesn't fit him. He seems more like the sort of man who'd drive a hulking four-by-four pickup. Black and tall and snorty like a dragon, so high the kids would need his help to scramble up in it.

But what do I know? I've known this guy for all of an hour.

Taking the next corner, we pull into the hamburger joint. I don't know if he wants to go inside or not, so I park on the side of the lot. He drives past me, straight into the drive-thru lane.

I wait patiently until after he's ordered and pulled forward before I flip a U-turn so they can follow me after they get their food. My place isn't far. Only a mile from here.

And I can feel my nerves revving up with every second ticking by.

"No backing out now," I whisper. "It's a week or two. Big money. You can do this."

I wrinkle my nose, just knowing those words are going to be my personal prayer for however long this lasts.

* * *

THE ROW of four-plex townhouses backs up neatly against the golf course. There are two other sets of units just like mine, and then four separate, but attached homes farther down on Seventh Avenue. About where the road comes to an abrupt end, right next to the eighteenth hole of the golf course.

If I were the superstitious type, I might start to wonder if that number means something.

During those last few minutes while I wait for his Equinox to round the building, I take a few deep breaths, reminding myself I'm doing the right thing. Helping them. Helping myself to the serious moolah Manny promised.

And it's for a good cause...isn't it? Knowing it's a witness protection program is comforting.

Only innocent people can use that program, especially if it's sanctioned by some alphabet soup agency like the FBI. Right?

I hope so.

I'm still debating it, and my own judgment, when Miller's Equinox appears in my mirror. Drawing in another breath for the road, I hold it and shift Pearl into drive.

Within a matter of minutes, we're rumbling up my driveway. I push the garage door remote, now hosting a new battery, and pull in close to the far wall, leaving plenty of room for his vehicle next to mine.

The two car garages are another reason Mother bought this place, and then the other three rental properties, years ago. She claims a garage is a must in wintry Minnesota.

She's not wrong, but right now, I'm even more thankful for the garage, plus the large door that slowly closes. It almost feels like I need to keep Miller and the kids hidden.

Like they're a secret, a treasure I have to protect. It seems like the stakes are high with the amount of money I'm supposed to get from all this. But every time, I come back to the glaring, chilling fact that for them, it's worse. It could mean their *lives.*

"Lauren, you can carry the food while Shane and I grab our luggage," Miller says as he shuts his car door.

I walk around my car and see Lauren looking down at her hands. One's full of books, the other's holding a heavy looking backpack.

Smiling at her, I say, "No worries. I'll get the food."

"Thanks, Ms. Courtney!" Shaking her head, she whispers, "*Men.*"

I want to bust out laughing at the sour expression on her face, but just wink at her instead. "This way," I say, once I collect two bags of food and a tray of drinks out of the front seat.

I lead her through the living room, not worrying about my shoes, and then into the kitchen, where I set down the food. Miller and Shane have their hands full with the suitcases. "There's a bedroom just up those stairs, and another one right around the corner. Can't miss them."

Shane looks around, frowning. "Why does your house look so big on the outside, but so small on the inside?"

"Because it's a townhome," I say.

His frown deepens. "What's that mean? It's only half a house?"

"Sort of," I answer. "There are actually four houses here, all connected to each other."

"Weird," he whispers. "I remember Dad talking about living in something like that growing up and–"

"Shane." There's a commanding edge in Miller's voice. "Luggage."

The boy blinks, nods, and starts up the stairs with a suitcase in each hand and a backpack on his back.

Miller follows him, and I smile at Lauren. "You can put your stuff on the sofa or carry it upstairs. I'll get plates and set the table."

"Oh, no, I'll help," she says, setting her backpack on the

sofa and books on the coffee table. "I like your house. It's bright and pretty. Nice flowers on the wall."

I follow to where she's looking, no heart to tell her the floral arrangement is a total fake.

"Thank you." I hand her three plates. "You can put these on the table while I fetch you guys some silverware and napkins."

"Aren't you going to eat with us? Dad bought you a chicken sandwich and a soda." She looks at me expectantly. "I wasn't sure...we just thought you might like chicken over a burger."

"That's very kind of you." I grab another fork from the drawer and then a plate out of the cupboard. "Thank you."

I'm not that hungry, not with my stomach turning itself into knots, but how can I refuse? I'm not that rude.

I think.

Honestly, now that they're here, I'm feeling way out of sorts. Like I'm a stranger in my own home. Almost as out of my element as these unexpected guests I'd agreed to on a whim.

Well, and a heartfelt six-figure payout, but I'm not sure an extra zero behind that would make this less weird.

Lauren and I are working on getting the food plated and the four sodas on the table when Miller and Shane come back downstairs.

"This place isn't so bad! Your backyard is huge," Shane says, jumping off the bottom step. "Those kinds of places back home cost a *fortune,* don't they, Dad?"

"Right, son." Miller shrugs, taking in the scene.

"It's not all *my* backyard." I point out the sliding glass door behind the table. "That pond is the water trap for a golf course. It starts back there, right behind my little patio."

Shane speedwalks around the table. "Golf? Cool! I love golfing."

"It's time to sit down and eat, bud," Miller says, pulling out a chair at the table for him.

Empathy fills me. He's looking more like death warmed over by the minute. It's strange to see a man with his size and looks so utterly drained, like he's just had the life sucked out of him.

The kids don't seem affected, but I imagine they slept while he drove. "Once you're done eating, we can walk down to the course," I tell Shane. "There are always golf balls around the water trap people leave behind."

Shane's eyes light up. "There are? Can I keep them?"

I shrug. "If you want. Or you can turn them into the club-house. They'll probably pay you for them."

"They will?" He grins. "Sweet. I wanted a way to make some money this summer."

"They use them for the driving range, mostly. Always need a good supply."

Shane looks at his father. "Can we go look for some?"

"I'll take them," I say before Miller has a chance to answer. "While you take a nap."

"You won't mind?" he asks, looking relieved.

I shake my head. "Not at all! It's nice outside, and I have the afternoon off thanks to you. It'd be a shame to waste such a beautiful day."

For a moment, he hesitates, something dark turning behind his eyes.

"Thanks," he says. "I appreciate it. Just remember, kids, you stay with Ms. Courtney. Anybody comes around asking about you, about us, you–"

"Dad, I know. We run and find you. You've told us a hundred times." Shane nods, gobbling up his burger. "We've been cooped up *forever*. Can't wait to walk around."

The rest of the meal gets eaten without much conversation. Once we're done, the kids help me clear off the table while Miller thanks me again, tells the kids to behave, and goes upstairs.

"Hey, Shane," I say, pointing at a drawer. "There's a bag in there you can use to save the golf balls you find."

"Awesome!" He opens the drawer and pulls out a bag, then runs for the patio door. "Let's go. I'm ready."

Frowning slightly as he pulls open the door, he says, "Oh, but one more thing...should we call you mom? Or is that too freaky?"

Ice instantly grips my spine, freezing me in my tracks. *Mom?*

"No, silly," Lauren tells him. "She's just our pretend mom, remember? Dad's pretend wife."

Wife?

I feel sick.

IV: FINE PRINT (MILLER)

*E*ven in my dreams, I can still see her smile.

It's subtle, sly, intense. A faint crescent smile like the Mona Lisa, if da Vinci's model had been a cold-blooded demon.

My eyes want to bore through this witch. I wish I had superpowers so my gaze could set her the fuck on fire. After what I'd found, after what I *knew* she'd orchestrated, if anybody ever deserved their own special VIP seat in hell, it's Jackie Wren.

But in my fitful dreams, every time her cruel lips open, she always asks the same question.

"How much, Miller?"

I don't have time to answer.

There's just the fierce sound of Keith screaming, bones breaking, and the deafening *thud* of my own pulse.

* * *

"Shit!" I bolt up in a cold sweat, wiping my brow.

Almost the same nightmare as the other few times I've slept since everything fell apart. I wonder if I'll ever have a normal night of shut-eye again.

Disoriented from sleeping so hard, it takes a second to remember where I am.

Finley Grove. Minnesota. Gwen's place. Safe.

For now.

I'm scrunched in a twin-sized bottom bunk bed so short my knees are practically touching my shoulders. I roll over onto my back and shove my feet out over the foot board. Sweet relief rolls up my legs, into my back.

I needed that, both the stretch and the sleep.

I'd been so dog-tired, I barely remember my head hitting the pillow. Even with the nightmare ending, I feel better.

Reaching beneath my head, I rub my neck, working out the knots. It takes a lot of pressure to relieve the tension.

The plywood above me is painted bone white, almost glowing in the darkness, just like the rest of the wood used to make these bunks. They're sturdy, friendlier than the slabs I had in my Army days, and if they were longer, they wouldn't be half bad.

The mattress is soft, yet firm enough for support. The kids will sleep just fine in here, but considering the height issue, I'll have to find an alternative. I could never crash here for eight hours straight.

There's a king-sized bed in the room across the hall, but that's Gwen's. That redheaded fox who, for some unholy reason, agreed to this madness.

Also, the woman I barely even know, who's currently watching my kids so I could rest for a few hours.

Pulling my legs back on the bed, I roll to my side to sit up, careful so I don't bash my head.

Stretching my arms in front of me, I pop both shoulders,

then twist my neck till it pops too. Nothing like shifting bones to make a man feel more awake, more alive.

Movement across the hall catches my attention.

I can't see anything, but there's something, or someone, in there, breaking the stream of sun shining through the window. Gwen, I think, stopping in her room to fetch something before I hear her long, sexy legs carrying her away again.

I look down with a growl, staring at my badly behaved hard-on.

Not something I need while I'm a guest here.

Not something I need any day while I'm trying to get through this without behaving like a complete fucking Neanderthal.

I shove off the bed and cross the room. More white everywhere. The walls, the wood work, the bunk beds, the doors, and even the carpet is that same ivory tone. The curtains are pale green. Same for the bedding and the framed modern art hanging on the walls in more snow-white frames.

The room's a pretty good size, just like the bathroom at the end of the hall.

I move down the hallway and step into the threshold of the other bedroom. It's much larger, clearly the master suite, but also painted cloud white. The curtains and bedding in this room are bronze, closer to the color of Gingersnap's hair – who's in there pacing back and forth in front of the sitting area near the French doors that lead out to a small balcony.

I must not have heard her come up again.

She senses me and turns, doing a double take like she's not sure if I'm really standing there or not. There goes my dick again, springing to life, hounding me to do the impossible – make a move on this peach tree of a woman I want to shake something furious.

"You're awake." She cringes slightly, her green eyes fluttering. "Did I wake you? I didn't mean to."

"No. I needed to get up anyway." I run a hand through my hair. "What time is it?"

She gestures toward the bed, where a digital alarm clock sits on one of the bedside tables. "Almost five."

"Damn. I slept longer than I thought," I admit. "Where're the kids?"

"Downstairs. Lauren found my little library and Shane's busy mastering my smart TV." She points at me. "Um, actually, Miller...we need to talk."

My gut tightens. "What'd Shane do?"

Her tone says it all. He's a good kid, but high-strung, a little hyperactive. To someone not used to kids, he can be a handful.

"Oh, Shane didn't do anything."

Hesitant, I ask, "Lauren?"

That'd be a new one. I can't remember the last time little Lauren ever did anything out of sorts, but you never know what this kind of stress can do to a ten-year-old.

Gwen shakes her head. "Not anything she did either. We had a nice time wandering around the golf course. They found about ten bucks worth of balls they turned in." She nods her head. "They split it equally."

I can't help but shake my head. "Then what's wrong?"

For a second, she glances around, before moving across the room. Stopping at the French doors, she twists the knob. "Out here, please, so they can't hear us."

I cross the room and follow her onto the small balcony that hosts two white rocking chairs and a small table. White again. I've never seen so much damn white in my life. "You do know paint comes in a variety of colors, yeah?"

She frowns, looks at the chairs, then grins slightly. "Not

my style, honestly. My mother owns this townhouse. She let an interior designer do everything."

I close the balcony door. "Where does she live?"

"The other side of town."

Shit. Extended family. That's not a good thing when you're trying to keep a low profile.

More people finding out we're here, asking questions, means more room for leaks to the wrong people.

"And that brings me to what we need to talk about." She shifts in place, hands hugging the rail, staring off into the distance before she suddenly looks at me. "Miller...why do your kids think I'm their mom? Your pretend wife?"

Fuck me.

Whatever else I expected, it wasn't that. The fact that she's even asking throttles my pulse, makes me wonder if that bastard lawyer wasn't as honest as he insisted about all the details being set.

Calmly, I walk over and lean one hip against the balcony rail, cocking my head. "Because that's what I'm paying you for, right?" Nodding toward the door, I add, "Your money's inside, if that's the concern. Every last dollar stashed away in my bag. You want me to get it now?"

Her eyes widen. "You mean you're carrying around like a hundred thousand dollars in that bag?"

"A hundred thousand?" I try not to snort. The muscles in my neck slowly tighten. I'm paying her boss *a hell of a lot more* than that.

She nods but holds up a finger. "Manny said he'd be the one to pay me."

"How much is he paying you to do this?"

Grimacing, she says, "He said he'd negotiate a bigger cut. Something like two hundred thousand?"

"For you?"

She nods so fast I think her head might pop off.

It'd be adorable, watching her all flustered, cheeks going redder than her hair, if I wasn't so baffled.

I shift around to fully face her, resting my elbows on the railing behind me. "I'm paying him five times that total. If you're not even getting half, he's screwing you."

And if he's screwing her over, what's he doing to me? I wonder, biting back a snarl.

She grabs hold of the back of one of the rocking chairs. "Wait, what? A million dollars? A million freaking dollars for a place to stay for a week? Holy...what kind of witness protection thingamajig is this?"

"Witness protection? Is that what Stork told you?"

Now, it's starting to make a sick kind of sense.

Now, I'm getting royally pissed.

Nodding, she walks around the chair and sits down like her long, sleek legs can't hold her up anymore. "Yeah. He said you're a whistleblower and you needed a safe place for the next week or two."

Fucking. Shady. Lawyer.

Of course he did.

Cautious, because I'm ninety-nine percent sure she's still my only hope, I nod slightly. "He's right about one thing. I *am* a whistleblower, so to speak, and this is a little like witness protection, but the fee's not just for a place to stay. It's all under the table. No official agencies involved."

I think about adding *they can't be trusted, not when I'm running from a multinational octopus like Mederva with a third of Congress tucked in its pocket,* but don't. I'm worried I'll scare her, blow everything if she refuses to cooperate.

"Then what?" she asks, "And what do you mean 'so to speak?' Are you some kind of criminal? Is someone blowing the whistle on *you,* Miller?"

My skin bristles at the irony of her even asking something so fucked up. But if the lawyer left her in the dark, it's not her fault.

My brain turns over. Maybe words aren't the best approach here. I could do better showing her what's next, convince her she's already in too deep to back out, or if she does...it might be the end of us. "Hang on. I'll be right back."

She sits up straighter, her brows raised. "Where are you going?"

"Something you need to see." I leave the balcony and fetch my bag out of the guest room. The whole way, I'm mentally cursing Manny Stork for bullshitting her – or at least conveniently omitting what she's truly signed up for.

Returning to the balcony, I sit down in the other chair, open my duffel bag, and pull out the manila envelope Manny gave me.

There's nothing in here she can't see, so I hand her the entire package.

"Go ahead. Look inside," I growl, trying not to scare her.

Frowning, she takes it and opens it up. Glancing at me, she starts pulling things out.

Passports, driver's licenses, Social Security cards, birth certificates, and a marriage certificate. Several of them have her name on it with my last name attached.

Ms. Courtney won't exist by the end of the day as far as government databases are concerned.

She's Mrs. Gwendolyn Rush, and has been for several years.

"What the *hell?*" She shuffles through them a second time, her jaw hanging open wider with every document. "No way. These are forgeries. Fakes. Miller..."

She's not wrong. They're fakes, but damn good ones. Six-figure fakes formally endorsed by insiders being paid hefty bribes. I hope to God the rest comes through.

"Those are all part of this deal," I tell her. "Same gig that'll give you half a million dollars, if you don't let him short you. Manny gets the other half."

"Half a million—" She shakes her head, then rubs her temples, like she's trying to massage the words into her brain to make sense of them.

"Gwen, look. I didn't plan it this way. He was supposed to be honest, upfront, make sure you were on board with everything before–"

I don't get a chance to finish. She bolts up out of her chair, pain rippling across her sweet face.

"Before *what?* What's going on here? We're married or…or you're going to tell me that's all just a fake too?" Standing up, she backs away from me. "No. No, Miller. I never agreed to anything like this." Tossing the envelope onto her chair, she adds, "This is ludicrous. Not to mention illegal. I bet I could go to prison alone for the fake passport and Social Security number that's not actually mine. *God.*"

She's right. This has to be elaborate, creating fake lives right down to the last detail, everything changing except our names so there's more confusion in the databases.

Just enough to buy time to get the hell out of the States without anyone noticing.

Now, I wonder if there's even a chance that'll happen.

There's not a whole lot I can say, except the truth. "It's not like I'm having a grand old time either, lady. It's the *only* way I can protect my children. After the shit I witnessed…"

I hold off, stop just short of letting the full horror tear its way out of me.

I'm angry, afraid, more desperate than I'd like to admit.

But I also know scaring her more won't do us a lick of good.

Gwen stares at me, her green eyes somehow sharper than the flames licking at her cheeks.

Then her expression softens, and she grabs the envelope off the chair. "Forget it. I'm calling Manny right now."

She throws open the door and enters the bedroom. I follow, closing the balcony door, and then the bedroom door after I step into the hall.

I have no goddamn clue what her idiot boss is going to say, but he'd better not back out.

We'd barely left Seattle in the nick of time and don't have a backup plan. I doubt we could slip across the Canadian border without arrangements on the other side, and Canada's just as vulnerable as the rest of the States for a Mederva kill team to come crashing through our door some night.

Then there's no saving us. Just the final heavy *thunk* of a bullet going through my skull before the demons do the same to Shane and Lauren.

Fuck.

I force my lungs to work, greedily sucking in a breath so I can think.

I have a little time. Absolute worst case, I can throw together a Plan B, as much as I hate it. Hard to believe it could be worse than hating *all* of this.

Up till now, I've never needed anyone's help with something like this. I've never been so helpless. Even in the war, it was a matter of hunkering down in the rocks outside Kandahar, waiting for the air support to show up and wipe out the insurgent assholes pinning me and my boys down in an ambush.

This is worse by a long shot.

There's no unit. No friends, not with Keith half a world away. No cavalry in the sky.

Just me, two kids, a shady-ass lawyer, and this wildcat redhead I hope to high hell will show us a shred of mercy.

"Hey, Dad," Shane says as I step off the stairs into the living room.

"Did you have a good nap?" Lauren asks. She's curled up in a big cream-colored chair with a book.

Shane is stretched out on a matching colored sofa, remote in hand. "Gwen has the Discovery Channel."

"Cool," I say to him before nodding at Lauren, "Yeah, I did. I hear you found golf balls and made a little coin."

"Sure did!" Shane answers. "Got ten bucks for them. We split it."

"Sounds fair," I say. "You guys getting hungry?"

I know I am. That paper-thin burger I scarfed down hours ago is long gone.

"Is Gwen still upstairs?" Lauren asks.

"Yeah, she's on the phone." I try to ignore the outcome of that call as I walk into the kitchen to check the cupboards, wondering if a trip to the store will be in order.

It takes a lot more to feed four people than one, and Stork hardly gave her any notice we were coming.

Hopefully, I'll find enough here to throw together something for supper.

Yes, I know the dangers of going grocery shopping while hungry. With hungry kids, too, it could be disastrous.

Gwen might be calling her boss to tear his ear off over this deal, but I'm moving forward, assuming we've got safe harbor. At least for tonight.

The cupboards and fridge are as neat and organized as the rest of the house. Almost as sparse, too.

There's a bag of rice, little glass bottles of seasonings, a bag of frozen shrimp in the freezer plus some garlic bread. A quick scan shows several different salad kits in the fridge.

My wheels turn, trying to figure out what I can throw together. Seeing a coconut water tucked in the back of the fridge does it. Reminds me of Oahu, where I spent some time doing training exercises back in the Army.

"Garlic scampi and rice sound good?" I ask the kids, even

though there really isn't another choice if they say no. I'm sure they won't. They both like scampi, especially baked with rice and plenty of garlic. An old North Shore favorite a couple guys who were from Hawaii taught me how to cook.

"Yum," Lauren says, tilting her little face back happily.

"Sure," Shane chimes in. "I'm starving!"

"You're always starving," Lauren says, gently ribbing him for being every bit the growing boy.

I leave them to ramble on about their appetites while I find bowls and bakeware, then a colander for the shrimp. They're fresh, so deveining them should go fast after they defrost.

"Daddy, can I help?" Lauren asks, having left her book in the living room, already washing her hands in the sink.

I smile.

"You can mix up the salads." I check the water I've put on the stove for the rice, seeing it's coming up on a rolling boil.

She digs around in the fridge. "Hmm, looks like...two bags of Caesar? We all like that, and Gwen must too since it's in her fridge."

"Right," I agree, breaking the tails off my now defrosted shrimp in the sink. "You see anything more fun than golf balls back there today?"

She grins and tells me about the wildlife while we assemble the meal. A red fox, several frogs, and a garter snake all came out while they searched the grounds for golf balls. She mentions how nice the clubhouse was, along with the man who paid them for recycling the balls.

By the time Gingersnap comes downstairs, I've got the rice and shrimp ready. Every last shrimp is slathered in crushed garlic and seasoned butter, simmering away in the oven, and Lauren has the salad in a bowl, ready to add the dressing once the scampi's done.

Not bad for improvising.

Still, I clear my throat, side-eyeing Gwen. "Didn't mean to raid your kitchen. The kids were hungry, and my stomach started growling like a bear. Figured the least we could do tonight is make us all some dinner. My thanks for putting us up."

She stands at the edge of the kitchen and gives me a subtle nod. "No problem. Thanks."

Shit. I wonder what that really means in the lexicon of a woman who must be hair-on-fire freaked after checking in with her pants-on-fire boss.

I still wouldn't mind introducing my fist to Stork's face. But I can't knock out the clown who might be our only ticket to freedom.

"Dad's making shrimp scampi," Shane tells Gwen. "It's really awesome."

She smiles at Shane. I study her closely, deciding it looks real. I *hope* it's real.

"Smells delish," she admits, stepping fully into the kitchen.

The muscles in my neck tighten. I can't tell by her expression if her phone call with Stork went the way she wanted or not.

Her smile could just be show for Shane, just to keep the peace, or to hide how tangled up she is inside. Is she trying to figure out how to kick us out gracefully without upsetting the kids?

"I made some Caesar salad." Lauren glances up at me. "Should I set the table now, Daddy?"

I keep my eyes trained on Gingersnap. "Sure."

She doesn't meet my gaze, just steps around me and opens a cupboard.

"If it's even half as good as it smells in here, you guys did a great job with dinner," she says while lifting down a stack of plates.

She doesn't *sound* pissed, anyway. I relax a notch.

Still looking for clues about how the call went, I take the plates from her hands. "I hope you like garlic. These shrimp are one with it now and forever."

Opening the next cupboard door, she replies, "Who *doesn't* like garlic?"

"Vampires, duh," Shane says from the living room.

Leave it to my son to give the best answer.

Gingersnap laughs, and showing her teeth makes her eyes light up. My heart slams something fierce for all the wrong reasons.

This is no time to celebrate. Much less imagine how she'd look sprawled across this counter, that mane of fire-red hair wrapped in my fist, giving me those *teeth* as I piston between her legs like the world's about to end.

Goddamn.

I instantly turn away from her, forcing my mind back to earth, carrying the plates around the center island to the table in front of the patio doors.

Whatever else I think, wherever else my half-fried thoughts go, I can't do this.

Can't let this get any more complicated, and fixating on how damnably attractive she is could bring me down like Humpty Dumpty.

I take my sweet time setting out the plates and step out of the way when her and Lauren arrive carrying glasses, silverware, and napkins. They're talking about the book Lauren borrowed, and I hold my tongue, keeping my lewd thoughts and worries over tomorrow to myself.

Still can't seem to control my eyes.

They won't stop scanning her. Every contour, every

curve, calls to me like a siren. From her bare toes to the top curls of her golden-red hair.

It dawns on me then. Something more awkward than any of this.

She must have a boyfriend.

Anyone with her looks couldn't possibly be alone. *Shit.*

That's reason number ninety-nine this won't work, isn't it?

No man with any balls would put up with something like this, a stranger moving in on his chick, no matter how well it pays. If she's taken, I'll have to find someone else.

I got the sense from Stork that he didn't have anyone else lined up. Almost like Gingersnap was a spur of the moment pick.

I noticed it before but didn't want to believe it then. I'd been too tired, frayed, nearly dead, and just wanted a couple hours of shut-eye so I could think straight again.

Now that I've had it, things are clearer, even if they're also as muddy as quicksand.

Son of a bitch.

I really need this to go off without a hitch. Need to know *now* if there'll be complications in her life that make this thing doomed from the start.

The timer I'd set on the stove goes off. I walk around the table, past the island where Gwen and Lauren are busy juicing lemons.

"Is it done?" Shane asks hopefully. "A grizzly's got nothing on my stomach right now."

"Just time to put in the bread," I answer, sliding the pan into the oven. "But go shut off the TV and wash up, Shane. It'll be ready in about eight minutes."

"I'll put the dressing on the salad as soon as Gwen and I finish the lemonade," Lauren tells me.

Unable to wait any longer, I nod at Lauren as I step up

beside Gwen and lean a hand on the granite countertop. "How'd it go?"

She freezes, her eyes flashing to me. I wonder if she's shocked I'm asking her out in the open like this. Hell, maybe part of me is just as surprised, but I don't have any choice.

I need to know what's coming.

Gwen pours the lemon juice out of the bowl into a pitcher. "Just fine, Miller."

Just fine? I frown.

Her poker face still doesn't give a hint.

"Did he even answer?" I whisper.

She lifts a brow. Up this close, I notice there's a short line of delicate freckles along the curve of her high cheekbones. A teasing finish on a face that'd look too good all over my body.

"He answered, all right." She dumps a cup of sugar into the pitcher and then hands it to Lauren. "Fill it up three quarters of the way full, please. I'll get the ice."

I'm frantic now. Whatever game she's playing, I'm not in the mood. I stop just short of grabbing her wrist, before she can pull away.

"What'd he say?" I ask quietly after Lauren carries the pitcher to the sink. "Are we still on, woman, or what?"

"You're welcome to stay here for a week. It's okay." She doesn't even blink. Just rattles it off like it's the fucking weather report, then spins around and pads over to the fridge.

What the hell does that mean, 'okay?' We're on?

Or Stork's looking for someone else to fill her shoes before I rip his head off?

I can't be in limbo like this. I need a wife right now.

I turn, ready to tell her that, but just then the front door opens, and I've got another worry.

"Yoo-hoooo, Gwendolyn!" a female voice sings her name, a soft beam of sun clashing with my mood.

I'm not the only one who's surprised. Gwen whips around, her eyes as big as saucers.

Fuck, what *now?*

She closes her eyes and her chest heaves reluctantly, drawing in a deep breath.

"Hello, Mother. What brings you by?" she asks, handing me the ice bin in her hurry around the island to escape into the living room.

"Oh, Dylan's in town, and we're meeting at the clubhouse. Lord knows I've made that man enough money to buy a second home, so the least he can do is buy me dinner at the most expensive place in—*Oh.*" She sidesteps around Gingersnap, eyes wide. "You have...company, darling? My, my."

My, my, my ass.

It's a miracle I'm not completely sneering as this lady gawks at me like a new, exotic beast in the zoo.

She looks like she's roughly fifty. Draped in what appears to be layers of white cashmere material, the woman has hair that's several shades darker than Gwen's, almost a dark burgundy. She's shorter, too, by more than half a foot, but her eyes and cheeks are as close as a mother's could be to her daughter's.

All in all, she's attractive, for her age. Fit and well-kept and totally unwelcome here.

Realizing I'm still standing like a fool, I have no choice but to smile and nod, considering the fact that her eyes haven't left me once. "And who might this lovely specimen be, Gwendolyn?"

Gwen turns, looking at me over her shoulder, mouthing an apology. "My company, Mother. This is Miller, and his daughter Lauren, and this—" She waves as Shane walks out of the bathroom. "Is his son, Shane."

"How lovely!" Her mother clucks, glancing at Gwen, light flashing in her eyes like tinsel. "I'm May, Gwendolyn's mother."

"Nice to meet you," I lie, moving a hand to Lauren's shoulder as she steps up beside me. I slide the ice bin over to her.

It's not fun gabbing while our lives are on the line.

Not while I have no idea what Dumbass, Esquire, told Ms. Make Believe.

Not while I'm drawing every breath under the gun, literally and figuratively.

"Hi!" Lauren's eternally cordial little voice rings out while she's scooping up ice for the pitcher, snapping me out of my trance.

"Hey, ma'am," Shane echoes. "Nice to meet ya."

"Twins?" May's eyebrows leap up as she glances slowly between Lauren and Shane.

"Sure are," Gwen tells her. "Now you said you're meeting Dylan at the clubhouse? Probably smart not to keep him waiting, so if you just want to–"

"Oh, wine and my next contract can wait, dear." May waves her hand like an empress dismissing a subject. Then, with her eyes on me again, she smiles with the whitest teeth I've ever seen. "You, I don't recognize, Miller. Where'd you blow in from?"

"Out West, Mother. Miller and the kids are just staying with me for a few days," Gwen says, cutting in before I have a new dilemma on my hands.

May's eyes damn near roll right out of her head. "Staying here? With *you?* Really now?"

Her face is practically twitching with questions trying to get out. Luckily, the buzzer goes off on the stove, so I'm not sure if Gwen ever gives her a real answer or not. I head straight for the oven.

"Lauren's quite the avid reader, Mother," Gingersnap says, smiling sweetly, trying to change the subject.

May tilts her face sourly but has a syrupy smile for my daughter. "Not my stuff, I hope?"

I pull the scampi and the bread out and set the pans on the stove before turning to see Lauren nodding. "Um, yeah. What stuff?"

"No, surely not, you're far too young. And somehow I think Big Daddy here wouldn't like you sneaking anything too terribly grown up." May nods at me, mischief in her eyes.

"Wait, you write books?" Lauren asks, suddenly far more interested.

May flips one end of her white scarf over her shoulder as she walks closer to the island. "Sometimes I think the books write me. But yes, doll, I'm constantly spinning yarns with damsels in distress on white sand beaches and the men-to-die-for who steal the show." She winks.

"You're an author? Like a real life published author? What's your name?" The excitement in Lauren's voice goes to eleven.

"M.E. Court," May says.

The name means nothing to me, but it does to Lauren. She squeals so loud it bounces back off the ceiling.

"Dad, Daddy! You know those books Heather reads? The ones she said I couldn't borrow, but some of them have been turned into movies that I watched with her and...the Arcadia Island Cove movies, I mean? This is her! She wrote them!"

"Correct," May says cheerfully. Still looking at me, she smiles. "Don't worry, daddy dearest. The movies are quite toned down from the scenes in my books to fit the studio's demands."

Fuck me upside down.

So, it's not just a nosy mother across town I have to

worry about on top of everything else. But a *famous* one who must've sold millions of books to wind up on the big screen.

Let's cut the crap. I'm going to slaughter Manny Stork before it's over. And I think I'm willing to go to prison to make his lying, incompetent carcass pay big time.

"Oh, my gosh, I can't believe this!" Lauren's still gushing. No surprise. "Heather would fall right over for a chance to meet you!"

May just smiles like a cat sunning itself. No doubt whatsoever she's heard it a billion times.

Doesn't stop Lauren from pressing both hands to her chest. "Me too! This is amazing. *Amazing!*"

"Whoever this Heather is, tell her she's welcome to email my site for a signed copy of her favorite book on the house."

Lauren bites her bottom lip and glances at me before saying, "She was our babysitter before we moved. And wow. *Wow.* She'll be ecstatic!"

"What time are you meeting Dylan, Mother?" Gwen cuts in, her tone pointed.

May darts a frown back that asks why she's trying so very hard to ruin her fun. "Oh, don't worry about him. He'll be there when I get there."

"Well, as you can see, I'm afraid we can't join you tonight. We're about to sit down to eat ourselves. Dinner for *four.*" Gwen folds her arms.

Sweet hell, this woman.

She's feisty and beautiful and riled. And it's not lost on me that for now, she's trying to help.

"Shame, your dinner smells scrumptious. Reminds me of the food trucks I adored on Oahu." She looks away from me to Gwen. "Curious. Garlic shrimp isn't your style, Gwendolyn. Have you finally been taking cooking classes?"

"Nope. Miller made dinner tonight."

May storms over then, grabs Gwen's arm, and pulls her

close without even lowering her voice. "Oh, dear Lord, where did you *find* this incredible man? All three of them, really? I want *details,* dearie. Might even make a good sketch for a book."

Scrunching up her face, Gwen shakes her head, tearing herself away. Her ma pouts while she rubs her head like she's suddenly got a crippling migraine.

Feeling her pain, I say, "We met through a mutual friend. Not Hawaiian, but I did learn to cook this stuff over there in the Army."

"I knew it! Well, Miller, it'd be rude to say hello and goodbye without offering you a night off dinner duty, wouldn't it?"

My eyes shift over to Gwen. The look in her eyes says that headache she's nursing isn't just a phantom pain.

Fuck.

I say nothing, just stare at her, waiting for the next thing out of her mouth to hit me like a brick to the face.

Gwen just shakes her head faster and grabs at May's arm, tugging her firmly toward the door. "Mother! The kids are starving and so am I. I'll call you tomorrow. Tell Dylan I said hello."

May walks haltingly beside her, mainly because she doesn't have a choice, but her neck twists and she cranes her head, still glancing over her shoulder dead at me. "You'll come to my place for dinner later in the week, and bring those little darlings with you."

There it is.

Bad turning into worse. But I don't have the heart to go ballistic when I'm still too busy walking a tight rope.

I remain stock-still. This is Gwen's call, not mine, and it's her mother to deal with.

She nudges her mother around the small entryway corner, so I can't hear what comes next.

Whatever she says must keep the peace. Because May Courtney hardly seems like the kind of woman to back down without raising hell if she doesn't get her way.

A moment later, May pokes her very smug face around the corner one more time. "Ta-ta, everybody. It was a pleasure meeting you all. See you *soon*."

V: MORE TO CHEW ON (GWEN)

*M*other steps outside, *finally,* and then I shut the door and lean against it.

I use the same weight I would if I was worried a black bear might barge in. At least the bear would have more manners.

Oh, my God! What in blue blazes do I do?

Not just with her and this stupid dinner invitation, but *any* of this?

Predictably, Manny was no help at all, besides laying on his guilt trip as thick as molasses. He apologized up and down for leaving out the *little details,* but the fact remains. He doesn't have anyone else who can help this family.

Family. That's the part that's hitting so hard.

A single dude – even one as handsome as Mr. Stormy, Inked, and Mysterious – I could jettison on his butt without much guilt. But with these poor kids, supposedly in grave danger...

What *am* I thinking? A single man wouldn't need a pretend wife, a make-believe mother of his children, in order to fool Federal TSA databases to exit the country.

Ugh.

I didn't fully understand that part until Manny explained it. He says they scan for names, behavioral profiles, criminal backgrounds, or holds of any kind. The system won't flag a near duplicate entry for a man with kids who have fairly common names. There must be at least a dozen Miller Rushes out there with kids named Shane and Lauren.

And if this Mederva place put some kind of illegal hold on him, it'll miss it the second our fake passports come up as one big, married, happy family who've always lived in Minnesota. The Rush family they're looking for is from Washington, sans the non-existent wife.

That's just one of the many fun details Manny left out this morning. He apologized for forgetting that part, too.

Asshat. I'm not stupid. He left it out on purpose to get me to agree to this after he waved his dirty money in my face.

I'm expected to fly to Ireland with them.

Ireland!

A place I've always dreamed of visiting one day, but totally not like this. My father was from Cork, a small-time musician who swept Mother off her feet when they were both too young to know what they were doing.

Maybe that's why Mother refused to ever travel there. She won't like the idea of me going, either. Much less with a man who could raise the temperature in Hades itself, and no end date.

Actually, can she even *know* where I'm going? Where we're going?

Crap, what's wrong with me? I can't possibly go to Ireland with them and make my mom's hair stand on end. Knowing her, she'd probably have one of her Hollywood people reach out to Scotland Yard or the Irish equivalent to hunt me down.

Why did I think I could ever do this?

"You okay, Gwen?"

I snap open my eyes at Miller's question. My fake husband leans against the short wall that separates the entryway from the living room. And to be perfectly honest, he looks like he just stepped out of one of my mother's books.

Awesome.

Just what I need right now. A brutal reminder of how huge and hot he is, and how he's probably as sick of this stuff as I am.

His dark hair is cut short, still rumpled from his nap. His black shirt hugs his broad chest like a second skin. So do the black jeans, and even in his socks, you could just eat him up. Whipped cream optional.

The worst part is, it's a normal, almost boring look. *How can that be sexy?*

Hell if I know, but it is. Something hums in my veins I've never felt before, this heated rush that has far too much to do with *Mr. Rush* and not the adrenaline attack of the past twenty-four hours.

"Gwen?"

I try to nod. My name rolls off his tongue like warm caramel drips down the side of a scoop of vanilla ice cream.

His bright-blue eyes no longer look so tired, so worn out. Now they have a shine to them.

There's more, too. He's concerned. Rightfully so.

This guy and his twins are on the lam. That's got to bother him deeply. Heck, I'm not even him, this isn't my mess, and it's not any easier for me.

If only that were true. Because I went and made it my mess when I let Manny talk me into helping Miller Rush twice.

I push off the door, hating how flustered I must look. "I'm fine. Let's just eat."

"Hoped you'd say that. It's ready."

He doesn't have to remind me. My entire house has never smelled this good in my life. It pales even compared to the time I tried to cook a whole turkey dinner for Mother and her happy little M.E. Court team. She wound up rushing to my rescue. Turns out my cooking skills are far more impressive in my head.

Maybe I'm dreaming this. An overly handsome, wildly sexy stranger in my house has just cooked up a fabulous meal from my meagerly supplied cupboards. That's more than a dream.

It's a flipping fairy tale.

Who needs a glass slipper? Not this girl.

He's very good at making me forget the price for all this.

I step away from the door. "I'm excited to try this stuff. The smell alone makes me want to camp out in this kitchen for the next week."

He cracks a grin that would melt Minnesota in January. "The kids and I don't mind earning our keep." He turns and walks beside me into the living room. "But I'll need to go shopping for next time."

"Ya think?" A laugh bubbles out. "Old Mother Hubbard has nothing on me. With all the hours Manny makes me put in, I'm lucky if I have enough energy to crawl to the fridge and pull out something instant."

We arrive at the round table, where the kids are patiently sitting, wearing somewhat weary smiles. They've been watching carefully since their dad said 'next time,' almost like they can sense the tension.

Guilt pinches my stomach at the thought they're worried I'll kick them out.

"Sorry for keeping you guys." I sit down. "But hey, now you've met my mother."

Another twinge of guilt rolls through me for using her as a lame excuse.

"Your mom's so cool, Gwen!" Lauren gushes. "I can't believe I met a real life author. A bestselling romance author with movies, even." She glances at her father. "I just wish I could tell Heather."

Miller pulls up the chair next to me, then piles rice and shrimp from the pan onto Shane's plate. "You'll see Heather again, baby girl. Don't you worry."

She'd mentioned Heather earlier.

I have a weird feeling she's more than just a babysitter. Especially due to the way Miller's hand tightens on the serving spoon. His knuckles go white.

"And Max and Josie?" Shane asks, then lowers his voice weirdly. "And...and Keith, Dad?"

"Yep. Give it a little time." Miller reaches over and picks up Lauren's plate. "You'll see them all again before you know it."

The white-knuckling doesn't stop. *Hmm...*

"Heather was our babysitter," Lauren tells me, taking a bite of her food. "Her husband, Keith, is Dad's best friend, and their kids were our friends. We've known them since we were born because Dad and Keith were in the Army together, and I guess they—"

"Lauren," Miller says sternly. "Grab some salad and pass it on. Please," he adds, almost an afterthought.

Her face turns cherry red. I get a sense that she's said more than she should have. But why?

The silence that follows as Miller lifts my plate, spoons shrimp and rice on it, and then sets it back down in front of me only confirms my fears.

This isn't family fun time. Or a simple meet-and-greet over really good food.

It's not just a matter of secrets, this whole situation. More like terrible secrets, dangerous ones, cards held close to his chest because they could do God only knows.

I pick up my glass, already full of lemonade, and take a nervous sip. "Lauren, sweetie, this lemonade turned out perfect. Tangy and sweet. Great job."

"Thanks, Gwen," she says. "I filled the glasses while you were saying bye to your mom."

"Thanks for that, too." I set my glass down and take the bowl of salad Miller hands me. "Everything looks delicious."

"It's even better if you eat it," Shane jokes. He's talking, grinning, and chewing at the same time.

I smile back at him. It's a small relief he's still just a little boy, even in the middle of this insanity.

"How about you pass the bread to the rest of us, son?" Miller suggests.

After the bread makes the rounds, I take a bite of scampi and just...die.

Heaven has nothing on this stuff. Flavor cascades along my tongue, salt and butter and garlic and shrimp so succulent I can't believe they were ever on ice.

Holy Hannah.

I want to just close my eyes and savor it forever. But I think I enjoy not looking like a total weirdo in front of them.

Instead, I stare at Miller, and after I swallow, I ask, "How in the world did you manage to make something this divine in *my* kitchen? It's seriously restaurant grade."

There's that grin again. The ladykiller flash of teeth and subtle dimples in scruff that make my insides somersault.

"Secret recipe," he growls with a wink. "Nah, I learned it in Hawaii while I was stationed at Fort Shafter. This stuff is pretty popular there. You'd be surprised how many people will spend hours in line and pay out the nose for a good garlic shrimp plate."

"That's nothing! Dad can cook all sorts of things," Shane says. "He's like a celebrity chef without the accent. Hardcore."

"Manners, son. Don't talk with your mouth full," Miller tells him, casting a glare.

I raise an eyebrow. "I see he's got a little of the temperament, too."

Everybody laughs. These kids really are cuties.

It's not hard to see Miller in both of them, mainly their eyes. For kids, they're very well behaved. He's done a great job as a single dad from what I can see.

Understanding Shane's plight, I ask him, "Always hard to chew and talk at the same time with food this good, huh?" When he nods, I add, "You're so lucky, having a dad who knows how to cook like this. I bet I'd have grown up spoiled."

"Does your dad know how to cook?" Lauren asks, a careful look on her face.

"Well...I have no idea if he knew how or not," I answer. "I don't remember him, exactly. He died a long time ago." There's no reason to go into the sordid details, mainly because I'm not privy to most of them.

Mother kept that part of her life buried. She'd tell me whatever I wanted to know when I'd ask, but it was almost like hitting her up about some obscure ancestor rather than my own father. So I rarely did.

"That must've made your mom sad," she says sincerely.

"Maybe." Honestly, I don't know for sure.

They never had any plans to reconcile.

I'd guess Mother was sadder than anything that my father hadn't lived long enough for her to show off how much money her hobby eventually brought in. She made several snide comments over the years about trying to support Dad's music at the expense of her own art.

Her big success came long after he died and his indie album was long forgotten. Her net worth really skyrocketed the past ten years, from great money to movie star type dough. I still can't believe it sometimes.

Growing up, we'd eked by on whatever part-time jobs she could find that would still let her spend most of her time hunched over her computer, researching facts and tearing up words.

She never doubted her work. She always knew she'd hit it big someday if she just put in the time. She'd been right, and when she struck gold, it snowballed into a fortune.

I'm not jealous, even if I'm still waiting for my ship to come in. I'm ecstatic and proud of her. Especially when I saw firsthand how she worked her tail off for what she has now.

I also know what she sacrificed, what we *both* sacrificed in the early days, which makes me look at Miller across the table. They're sacrificing even more than we ever did just for basic human comfort. Safety.

It's so different from what we experienced, but in a sense, I can relate.

The rest of the meal passes in relative silence.

I can't help but blame myself for that and feel rotten about it.

So after everybody's finished, I say, "Thanks for the best meal I've ever eaten here. How about I clean up and throw together some malts for dessert? I've got strawberries and chocolate syrup, I think."

Lauren and Shane both smile, nodding eagerly.

"Strawberry sounds yummy," she says.

"I'm down for chocolate anytime!" Shane slaps a hand on the table, which gets him a hilarious side-eye from his dad.

"They're both my personal kryptonite." No joke. I'd be ten pounds lighter if I didn't keep the freezer stocked with fresh berries and ice cream. It's always time for a grocery run when I'm getting low. "How about you, Miller?"

"Strawberry works. No need to put yourself out on our account."

I open my mouth to tell him it's nothing, but before I can, Shane bolts up, rounding the table, his plate in his hands.

"We'll help you clean up so you can work on the malts, Gwen!"

This kid is too adorable. He's just not quite big enough to take all the heavy ceramic plates to the sink in one go.

Since I don't want his crazy enthusiasm risking broken dishes, I stand and gather a few. "You've got yourself a deal, mister."

Miller stands, too, but I take his plate before he can head for the sink. "Not you. You already did your fair share, chef."

He glances at the kids, who are both carrying things into the kitchen at lightning speed. Nodding, he says, "Thanks. I'm gonna take a shower while you're doing dishes and playing malt shop."

"Perfect." I gather up his silverware, casting a glance at his muscular back as he stands and stretches.

Dear Lord.

You don't even need to see his face sometimes to know exactly how butter under a heat ray feels.

"Towels are in the closet in the upstairs bathroom," I call out. Gesturing toward the bath off the living room, I add, "The one down here's only a half bath."

"Thanks, Gwen. Won't be long."

I *purposefully* don't watch him leave. I really, really don't need the images my mind tries conjuring up.

Miller in the shower. My shower. Naked. Wet. Slick.

Ginormous muscles flexing and popping and turning over like some huge, feral thing straining in its pen.

Big hands, big shoulders, big *everything.*

All just no good, very bad news for every red-blooded woman in sight.

Potentially lethal for a girl like me. I've spent more date nights with dirty books and battery powered stand-ins for insufferable jerks on Tinder.

"Sink, not the dishwasher, Shane!" Lauren hollers. "We've got to rinse the buttery stuff off first."

"Why? It's a dishwasher," her brother says. "It's a waste of water and makes no sense if you have to hand wash before you throw 'em in it."

"The dishwasher sanitizes them. It can't always cut all the grease. Doesn't it, Gwen?" Lauren turns to me.

Not wanting to start an argument, I say, "Good question. I think dishwashers have a kind of mini hot water heater so they use hotter water than washing them by hand. That's usually enough to work out the grease and the germs unless we've really made a big old mess. But it certainly wouldn't hurt to let the pans soak for a few minutes."

They look at me for a moment and then nod, seemingly appeased.

Just like when they were looking for golf balls, they team up and soak the pans, then get the dishwasher loaded in practically no time before zooming to my side to help with the malts.

"I hope I didn't bug you asking about your dad. We don't remember our mom, either," Lauren says somewhat out of the blue.

I stop with my hand on the ice cream scoop, looking at her carefully. "Oh, no, honey. You've got nothing to apologize for. It was a long time ago. I didn't know him, so it's not like there's bad memories to bring back." Or any memories at all, really.

"Same for us. Mom died when we were born," Lauren says, pulling out chocolate powder.

I'd wondered where their mother was, if she knew they were on the run. That answers it.

Dropping several metal scoops full of ice cream into the blender, I mull over how to respond.

My experience being around children lately is almost nil. And unlike me, they're still at an impressionable age where not having another parent could hurt.

"I'm sorry, guys," I say. Lame, I know. "I'm glad you've got a cool dad. It can't replace anyone, but I consider myself pretty lucky every day I know there's somebody on this planet who loves me. Even if Mother *is* incredibly good at riling me up. It's always just been us, and we care about each other. That's always been enough."

I focus on the malts, trying not to ramble. My face heats, wondering if I've said the wrong thing.

"Us too! Dad swears he's never getting married again." Shane's cheeks turn cherry red. "I mean...not for real married. He always says it's us against the world and we don't need a fourth wheel."

Interesting. I'm dying to know if Papa Bear has ever been on a date sometime this century, but of course I'm not brave enough to ask.

"Looking good, guys. One chocolate coming up and strawberries on the way. You two certainly are good helpers." I pass Shane the frozen berries to drop into the bigger batch of strawberry malt. "And your dad's cooking? Oh my God. I wish I could hire him full time."

Yep, I'm still being lame.

I know it, but I'm completely out of my element in this entire situation.

I'm also not exaggerating anything about those shrimp.

"We like playing around in the kitchen." Lauren picks up the milk container. "How much should I pour in?"

I stand over her shoulder and guide her, telling her when to stop pouring, and then wait for Shane to do the powdered malt. He puts the lid on the blender last before I tell Lauren to hit the ON button.

A minute later, we've got ourselves some Instagram-worthy malts in tall glasses with bubblegum pink straws, and the kitchen is even back in order when Miller reappears.

His dark hair is still wet, a little wilder than before. He's wearing blue jeans and a white t-shirt that are just as form-fitting as the black jeans and polo shirt. "Those look good."

Crud. If I hoped he'd magically be a tad less sexy after showering to save me from more shameful gawking...nope. Not my lucky day.

Forget the malts. He's what looks good here. A tall, strapping sip of raw masculinity I really need to stop ogling. "How about we drink them on the patio?" I say. "Lovely evening out there."

"Let's do it!" Lauren picks up two glasses, carrying them outside ahead of us.

Shane grabs the other two malts and follows his sister.

"Gotta love it when they take the initiative," Miller says, waving for me to walk ahead of him toward the door.

As soon as we sit down on the patio furniture, the kids point to the pond and start talking about how they found a ton of golf balls near it. There were even a few geese earlier, stragglers from Ontario who hadn't moved farther south for the summer.

They monopolize the conversation, chattering on and on about their dreams of making fifty bucks off lost golf balls before they have to leave.

I'm okay with it because at least it's a safe subject.

My mind goes off on its own, focused on Miller again, while the rest of me tries hard *not to.* Like I ever had a chance. The same questions keep coming, fast and furious.

What type of trouble is he in, and how did he get there? Why?

Will it ever be over?

He seems like such an average guy with a good mind and knock-you-down looks, raising his kids, apparently successfully. Ever since the day they were born.

Raising kids alone is hard and expensive. I know that much from growing up with Mother.

But where did he get the insane amount of money in that bag upstairs? Or is he just bluffing? Messing with me and Manny? I wouldn't even blame him for teaching my boss, Greedy McGreederson, a well-deserved lesson.

I haven't seen this money, though. He could be lying. And if he is, what else would he lie about?

"Is that okay, Gwen?"

I look over from Miller to the children, who stare at me excitedly. Uncertain, I shrug, looking at Miller. "Sorry, is what okay?"

He nods toward the kids. "They want to go hunting for golf balls again."

I shrug again and smile. "Oh, yeah! Fine with me."

"Will there be more golfers coming past? How busy does this place get?" he asks, his eyes narrowing, scanning the open course.

I shake my head. "Usually not real crazy until summer. This is also the eighteenth hole. Most evening golfers only play nine holes, and they're all on the other side of the course. It's a pretty huge place."

"Okay," Miller tells the kids. "Just stay where I can see you. And be back well before it's dark."

Shane and Lauren take off running for the course. Miller takes the final swallow from his malt and then sets the glass on the table. "That hit the spot. Could've used a shot of something. You're not half bad at making drinks, Gingersnap."

I almost choke on my own drink.

Gingersnap? He's got to be kidding.

When you grow up with hair like mine, the nicknames never end. But he just might've found a new one. And I can't decide if I'm feeling that awkward, in-denial, over-the-top crush again, or if I just want to slug him.

"Look at 'em out there, running their little legs off. They've got a lot of energy to burn after being cooped up in the car for a day."

I set my half-full glass on the table. "They're nice kids, Miller. They've been lovely all day."

"My own pride and joy," he says, keeping his eyes on them as they race around the pond. "Just wish I didn't have to drag them through all this shit."

My lips twist. Seizing the opening I ask, "What is all of this exactly?"

He doesn't take his eyes off the kids, his bright-blue eyes burning through the evening dusk like they want to compete with the stars barely beginning to materialize.

He doesn't answer, which makes me tense.

I know he heard me, and I'm about to scrounge up the courage to suggest it's only fair he lets me know more. But then he turns and looks my way, that sharp blue flame in his eyes aimed at me.

"You really want to know? Swear you can keep it secret."

*Holy...*my heart starts pounding so hard I can't speak. Balling my hands into little fists, I nod as vigorously as I can. "Of course. Mum's the word. I just...I want to know, Miller. What did I sign up for?"

Slowly, he sighs, turning away from me again, back toward the creeping night. "The company I worked for was buying and selling some very illegal...merchandise. Let's just fucking call it that. I found out what they were doing and decided to put a stop to it. My friend, Keith, he was on board to help but...we both had to flee. Shit got complicated. Had to save our own skins, and our families, before we could do anything." He looks at the children again, who are searching the ground near the pond, laughing as Shane plucks another ball they'd missed earlier from the leaves. "I can't go to the police or some Federal agency over this. Not when this company has its hands everywhere."

"Oh," I murmur weakly.

Something tight constricts my throat. I'm choked on this awful cocktail of sadness and fear.

Then he turns, and I see the brutal look on his face. It hits home, all of it there, scrawled in his mask of raw hatred, torture, *rage.*

"They threatened my kids. I goddamned had to get them away. But I won't let sleeping dogs lie. The second I know we're safe, and I can talk to Keith, we're leaking this shit and making it public. We're going to make them burn for what they did, Gwen. That's why I need your help."

God.

Despite the warmth of the evening air, I'm flash frozen.

Being the chicken I am, I'm not even sure I want to know more about exactly what type of merchandise he means. So I just change the subject. "Your job must've paid well for you to have so much cash on hand."

He looks at me with a single brow lifted. "It did, but not this well. I knew even before the threats started that we'd have to leave, so I cashed out my investments, my retirement, and sold our place to a flipper. All cash. Fully furnished. Didn't take too much of a loss in this market in a good Seattle neighborhood. Nothing like the kind of loss I'd take spending another second in Ballard..."

His tone covers me in goosebumps. I cross my arms, trying to rub warmth back into them.

"You don't need to worry, babe. Not yet. I didn't leave a

trail of any kind the whole way here," he says. "You're safe. I know how to throw a bloodhound or two off my trail."

"Not yet?" I ask, clearly reading the undertone in his voice. When he doesn't answer, I ask, "What type of job did you have there?"

"I worked security. Spent years in the military before that. I'm no stranger to this bull, even if I bit off more than I could chew this time."

That doesn't make me any more comfortable. I'm not sure he was trying to make me be, either, but I do appreciate his honesty.

Well, kinda-sorta honesty. I wouldn't call it a cold shoulder or a ringing confession. He's certainly not an open book, but for a man fleeing for his life who I've only known for a day, it's a start.

He leans back in his chair. "So, your ma, are we going to her house for dinner later this week? I looked her up and thought it over. Not gonna lie, her status worried me at first, feared it could blow our cover."

"Oh, jeez. I didn't even think of that. It's weird when your mom's a celebrity and it just seems normal." I sigh, rubbing my face. "Manny really screwed you, didn't he?"

He nods, but his face ignites in the darkness, exploding in that brilliant smile I've seen a few times before with the kids adding so much life to his granite features. "Sure did. But we could do a whole hell of a lot worse than you and your hospitality, Gwen. Might've even wound up in a place with no golf balls to keep the kids busy."

I feel guilty as hell for laughing. But I can't help it. Between the nerves and the weirdness and this hot, intense beast-man staring me down, I just...

I lose it. I have to cover my mouth to avoid giggling like a crazy woman.

"So, Mother," I say, once I've regained control. "You're really okay with it? She can be overwhelming. Fair warning."

"If I can't handle your ma for a few hours, then we're in deeper trouble than I thought," he says, reaching for my hand, giving it a quick squeeze.

There it is again.

The same sultry, electric spark I felt this morning in Manny's office, shaking his hand for the first time.

I pull my hand away so quick his eyes twinkle and he tilts his head. But I have to keep control of something. I have to *try.*

Even if it'll be nothing but wishful thinking by this time on Friday.

There's never any control at Mother's house. And I freaking cringe to imagine what sorts of nosy, inappropriate, awkward-turtle things she'll drop on us.

Poor Miller. Hard to believe the bad guys after them might be the least of it.

This beautiful man has no earthly clue what he's gotten himself into.

VI: LIKE A HAWK (MILLER)

*A*t the sound of a door opening upstairs, I close out of the program, yank out the USB jump drive, and shut my laptop.

On second thought...

I lift the lid, click on the browser button, and bring up a major news site. I want it to look like I'm just catching up on current events. All the usual crap that's fit to print.

Disasters. Scandals. Human tragedy in its sad fullness, peppered with a few happy special interest stories on local art and new movies.

It's still too close to home, but Gwen and the kids won't be any the wiser. My eyes scan the screen as I scroll down. Politicians fighting to save their own asses. Malicious criminals who seemed like *such nice people* only yesterday.

What the fuck else is new?

If I wanted to type Jackie Wren into the search bar now, I know what I'd find.

Endless stories praising her charity. Rave interviews worshiping her brilliance in cutting edge medical technology. A polished, carefully curated Instagram feed where she looks fit to rule the world.

None of them reflect what a demon she truly is.

When it comes to powerful people and black markets, it's the blind leading the blind. No one ever knows till it all comes crashing down with one little slip someday – or till somebody stops turning a blind eye.

My hand clenches, forming a fist I'd love to throw through the screen. The blind eyes I've dealt with still piss me off, and so does how high up this shit at Mederva Therapeutics goes. I don't even know if Jackie is the top of the pyramid, but I do know she's a cog that'll break the whole machine if she's removed.

If I can just get to safety long enough to–

"You *can* sleep in the bed tonight, you know."

I glance up at a soft, feminine voice and need to hold my breath.

Gingersnap rings more true all the time for this woman.

She's hotter than she's got any right to be like this.

Her hair, a wild mass of copper-shaded curls. The bright pink t-shirt and black shorts hugging her ass are all wrinkled from being slept in. And her luminous green eyes are still sleepy enough to make me want to throw her over my shoulder and haul her back to bed.

But not to sleep.

Fuck no.

Red looks exactly like the face in my dreams that woke me up hours ago. Not a nightmare, for once, but it left me no less restless. I had to jump on my computer to get my mind off her.

Scanning my dirt on Mederva to see if there's a better way to thwart them was the only thing strong enough to do that. Until now...

"I knew the couch would be too small for you," she says,

stepping off the stairs. "Let me take it if you want to go back to bed. I'm a little shorter. It's easier for me to sleep there."

I finally find my voice. Have to in order to quit staring like I've been struck by lightning.

"No, the sofa was fine. I'm just an early riser."

The couch wasn't uncomfortable. In fact, before my dream bit me awake, I'd slept better than I had for a good, long while back at home in my own bed.

Her smirk says she doesn't believe me, but she won't argue. Not verbally. I try not to grin.

I've discovered that about her fast. She doesn't always say what she's thinking, holds her cards close to her shy, dangerously teasing chest, but the woman's always thinking.

Gathering info, hashing it, trying to fill in the gaps and string together the dots. Whether that's the parts of my crap she still hasn't sorted, or it's watching the kids to see if they're up for dessert. I recognize it because I do the same thing.

"Guess that makes two of us. Coffee?" she asks, trotting across the kitchen, tempting me with another downright *torturous* view of an ass I could bite.

"Please. Nothing fancy. Just brew up whatever you've got."

Eyes on your screen, dammit, I tell myself, pretending to make it look like this random story I've clicked up is far more interesting than her.

It's an article about some escaped convict and a dead mayor in a little town called Heart's Edge. A nowhere place in Montana I think we passed by on our way to Minnesota.

Small comfort knowing I'm far from the only poor bastard in big trouble, marooned in a small town.

Still, I'd be fooling myself if I said anything on this screen was more interesting than Gwen and her peach-shaped ass, no matter how many pages I scour. Yet, that's what I do for the next few minutes. Glue my eyes to the screen.

Try like hell to find something that'll hold my attention and keep my cock at bay.

An ad for a novel draws my eyes for a second. She said she writes, didn't she? Or is that just her ma?

Her mother was pretty well-off and talked like a big shot. So what's Red doing working for a ratty-ass small-town lawyer who does an even rattier job handling clients like me?

I'm still processing that when a cup of steaming joe lands next to my computer on the coffee table.

"It's black. Kinda thought you might like it that way, but I do have French Vanilla creamer. Plus milk and sugar."

I pick up the cup and take a nice pull off it. "Black's fine. Thanks."

She smiles knowingly – maybe even a little proud of herself, which doesn't help the situation below my belt line.

Then she sits down in the chair flanking the big couch and takes a drink out of the big red mug she's holding with both hands like it's the best thing ever. There's a book on it, I realize, open to curly printed strokes on white that say, *Kick ass. Take names. Write.*

Going off her love of malts, I say, "Bet you like a splash of coffee with your cream."

The smile that appears behind her cup makes her eyes shine, two emerald pools flickering in the light. "That obvious, huh? Shame. I hoped I'd be a bigger mystery."

I stare at her for a moment. A dozen things run through my head like a snorting freight train, and they're all innuendo.

Thankfully, she takes another sip of coffee and then tilts her head toward the coffee table. "Oh, uh, house rule. There's no smoking here. Just so you know."

I don't know what she means till I follow her eyes.

Shit.

The jump drive looks like a lighter, one of the more expensive ones I could find with this kind of detail. I snatch it up and tuck it in my pocket. "Don't smoke. You and your ma won't have anything to worry about if you're planning to rent this place out again someday."

"Oh, but...so you just carry a lighter around for fun?"

I hesitate. There's no way to tell her what it really is without bringing down questions like an avalanche.

"Right. Never know when it'll come in handy." I pick up my watch and clip it on my wrist and then shove my billfold in my back pocket. "Actually, this one's a bit of a memento. My Uncle passed it down. Keep it around for luck, I guess."

Fuck, I'm just digging myself deeper, even if she just gives me a dull nod.

I don't have an uncle.

I make a mental note to buy an actual lighter that looks like this. With my luck, she'll ask me to use it at some point to prove it works. This thing doesn't. It's just a jump drive without a flame.

She takes another long drink off her cup and then stands. "Okay, well, I'm going to hit the grocery store before the kids get up. We'll need more food to keep all four of us fed."

I shut down my computer. "I'll go."

"You? Is that even...safe?"

"Yeah. Not like anybody here knows me, aside from Manny Numbnuts and your ma." My jab at her boss gets a giggle out of her as I stand. "Anything specific you need?"

"Nope, think I'm good. Whatever you guys want to eat." She stands, too, ticking off her own list mentally. "Wait, though. You don't even know where the grocery store is."

I point to my watch. It's one of the newer smart ones that's paired with my phone. "GPS, babe. Besides, I know what the kids like and what they won't touch to save their lives." I walk to the door that leads to the garage and slip on my shoes. "I won't be long."

* * *

ONCE I'M on the road, I pull out my cell and dial Keith's burner number. It goes straight to voicemail, just like it had all day yesterday.

What the hell? His new line shouldn't be compromised already, and if it is...

No. I'm not letting the ugly possibilities rattle my brain.

Setting down the phone, I grip the steering wheel tight with both hands. To say I'm concerned is an understatement.

I've known Keith for almost twenty years. A giant with thick red hair and a pointy beard, he'd fit right in if it were him heading to Europe instead of me.

We'd met in the Army, served together, trusted each other with our lives. Small world finding out we were both from Bremerton, and we'd both enlisted as soldiers because the Navy was too close to home.

We stayed together after our service ended and wound up working for the same security company. He was there when the twins were born, when Willow died. He kept me from the grief, from the bottle that did in my old man when life went off the rails.

His wife was there too, Heather, this slip of blonde sunshine any man would be lucky to call his. They're the whole reason I was able to keep my head above water.

When Keith heard Mederva Therapeutics was hiring, a top-notch medical company, he convinced me to go there with him. It was a good gig. The money, the benefits, the people.

Just not *all* of them.

For years, we thought we'd hit the jackpot. Lived the

good life with plenty of extra cash to go around.

Until that fateful night when Keith stayed late and noticed some very fucking unusual activity at the other warehouse. We'd both recognized something was out of sync for months.

Had been since the new CEO stepped in, Jackie Wren, the queen of phony bitches. But neither of us expected what we found a few days later, following up on the shipping logs.

Illicit goods. My stomach clenches at the memory of what I'd seen.

Darkness incarnate.

Sick.

Evil.

No one should *ever* be involved in shit like that, but it all made sense how, once we started stringing pieces together. Why Jackie created so many 'new' positions, including in the security division, and why Keith and I were limited to overseeing the shipping of only one division, the original.

The newer one, the *expansion*, was all black market, with a line of *investors* that floored us both.

Those investors are also the reason we can't simply go to the Feds. Fucking politicians.

Lives don't mean shit to them unless it helps their re-election. If it doesn't, they'll do anything to line their pockets, including bending rules that cost your soul.

* * *

I'M STILL in a mood when I start paying attention to where I'm at.

The GPS tells me I've arrived, and I turn into the grocery store parking lot. I try Keith's number again before heading inside, and again after the groceries are loaded and I'm driving back to Gwen's place.

Every call still goes straight to voicemail.

Fuck.

This doesn't make sense.

I know he made it to Ecuador. Not even his busted up bones would've prevented him from getting his family to safety.

The original plan was for Heather to take their kids and mine with her, while Keith and I blew the whistle on Mederva. That was before a couple of Jackie's henchmen caught us off-guard.

The garage door opens as I'm driving up the street, pulling my mind off Keith. Every sense I have has spent the last few weeks on red alert.

I slow down and scan the area before turning into the driveway. Shane stands in the garage, waving, a plucky grin on his face.

"Where's the rodeo, cowboy?" I roll down the window to hear him as he runs up.

"Gwen told me to watch for you so I could open the door," he says. "She has another garage door opener for you to take next time."

He pulls open the backseat door before I've even shut the vehicle off. "What'd you get, Dad? I'm *starving.*"

Ah, there's our rodeo. Food is damn near as important as oxygen for a boy his age.

I reach back and ruffle his hair. "Yeah, yeah, figured you would be, son. Let's get this stuff inside so you can eat."

He grabs bags with both hands. "Yes, sir!"

In the kitchen, I fry up pancakes, eggs, and sausage, my go-to big breakfast for the family. Try to keep my eyes off Gingersnap the entire time. Not very successfully.

Her hair is still damp from the shower she took while I was gone.

When they're wet, those copper curls hang past the

middle of her back, and a pale-green sun dress reveals the flawless skin of her neck, arms, and shoulders. It almost gives me a stroke to see her shapely calves, her feet, her little toes painted pink.

If I ever got those legs wrapped around me, I think I'd chain us both to the bed.

"Gwen says she doesn't have to go to work today, Daddy," Lauren tells me once we're all seated at the table. "Her boss gave her the day off."

I glance at Gwen. "Manny the Idiot did you a solid?"

She nods. "That was part of the deal. With pay, of course. I'm learning how to look after myself."

I hold my breath. It's not all great news. Part of me looked forward to having privacy, so I could focus on other things, like the crucial data stored on my fake lighter.

That barely happens. Her and the kids go hunting for golf balls again and visit a park next door, but even then, I can't concentrate. Not while I'm watching out the window, checking to make sure some asshole hasn't snatched them off into the ether.

Making sure whatever's silencing Keith doesn't do the same to *us*.

Later, I finally join them and walk over to the clubhouse. It looks like a nice, posh place for a beer and snacks. This time, Shane and Lauren end up with eight dollars each. I buy everybody this big order of brisket beef nachos to share plus drinks.

Gwen smiles at me over her glass of wine, thoroughly pleased. Maybe she's just glad her second day on the job – being my *wife* – goes down easier than she expected. For me, it's a little harder, and I need a second beer after watching her pull that cabernet into her heart-shaped lips.

I take another stab at the data again that evening, doing some research online, and sneak off to dial Keith's number several times while Gingersnap has the kids outside. She'd found an old set of golf clubs in the garage that keeps Shane busy. Lauren's nose is buried in another book she'd picked out of the dozens sitting on the shelves framing the big TV that hangs in the living room.

An hour later, I content myself with the latest progress and try not to think about Keith's mysterious absence. It's bizarre how downright *natural* this feels, setting the table while we bake a big pile of enchiladas I picked up from the deli. Decided to keep it simpler tonight.

That's a lot like how it goes down the next three days.

It rains a lot, and I try not to think of home. It might be the first time in my life heavy rainfall actually brings down the mood, the dull, somber landscape outside reflecting the hopelessness of what I feel like I'm wrangling with.

The kids stay inside, content with sleeping in, books, and video games. I take Lauren to the library on Wednesday, where she loads up on a new stack of books using Gwen's card, and grab them milkshakes and burgers again for lunch.

Gingersnap goes to work and puts in seven or eight hours each day for Manny Dickface – who's making me increasingly nervous since he hasn't said a peep about our Ireland itinerary as the week grows shorter.

It's a small relief, having her away for a few hours. I try to conform to her schedule for focusing on my own work.

Because I know come evening, my life becomes a terrible distraction every time she's in the same room.

That amber hair. That smile. That laugh. That pair of legs and palm-sized tits and luscious, round ass.

Every last bit of Gwen Courtney slays me in a different way. It puts this whole charade in real danger because nothing good happens if I start sharing a bed with my fake wife.

Fuck.

So much for simple. I knew it never would be, but at least I have an idea where to start with rescuing my kids and then driving a stake into Mederva's cold heart.

But with Gingersnap? I'm at square one.

And if I'm not careful, it'll turn into ground zero, an explosion triggered by my own stupid lust.

* * *

FRIDAY COMES and the rain lifts.

Small miracle I've survived four nights here without stress-jacking my dick raw to this woman, who won't stop parading her body around in the mornings. To be fair, it's not her fault ordinary sleepwear puts fire in my blood every time I look at her.

She's home by noon, happy to take the kids out for a walk, where they round up a few more golf balls to sell.

"Don't forget, we have to be at Mother's by five," Gwen says as they're walking inside. "The kids decided Lauren would clean up first, then Shane."

I smile, knowing exactly what *decided* means. Shane's all boy, just like I was at his age. Convincing him to take a shower on schedule is like pulling teeth sometimes.

"Sounds good," I say, giving Shane a look that says *bath time, Mister.*

His smiling nod makes me wonder if my look was even necessary. I'm grateful they seem relaxed here, at least. After several days, we're settled in.

It could be a hundred times worse, considering our situation.

"Daddy, Gwen wants to braid my hair," Lauren says as she heads upstairs. They'd talked about it last night.

Gingersnap follows her. "I'll show you the shampoo you'll

want to use. Think you'll love this stuff, it smells just like a flower garden."

My nostrils twitch. If it's the same thing she used this morning, it smells damn good, all right.

I've been getting faint whiffs of Gingersnap all week. I close my eyes, then pry them open and try to focus on my laptop again.

Shane plops down on the sofa next to me. "I like Gwen, Dad. She's handy. Don't you?"

Leave it to my son to find a loaded question and blow my head off.

I hesitate, and not just due to my own obvious attraction. Truth is, I can't have him or Lauren getting too attached. We're not supposed to be here much longer.

I want them to be comfortable, yeah, but this is temporary. In a few weeks, Minnesota should be a distant memory and an entire ocean away.

"She seems nice," I agree. "Can't complain about a chick who's a great host."

"She rocks!" He scoots back deeper into the sofa, scratching his ear. "She's pretty smart, too. She knows where to find golf balls and always points us to the best spots." He lets out a big sigh. "A guy could get *rich* living out here, you know, finding all these balls."

"You think?" I ask, smiling to myself at his simple logic. I wish life were so easy.

"Yeah!" Nodding, he adds, "I've already made thirteen bucks, Dad. Not even counting earlier this week. Lauren made that much too. So that's over thirty dollars." He snaps his fingers. "Just like *that*."

I snap mine, too. "Just like that? Really now?"

"Heck yeah."

He's clearly proud of himself. I shut my computer and lean back next to him, stretching out my legs. "So what're you planning to do with all your money, Richie Rich? Build a pool and dive into it?"

He shoots me a glare so sour I grin. A thoughtful expression forms on his face. "Ya know, I've been thinking about that and..."

Oh, he's been thinking, all right. I wait to hear what he has to say.

"You see, Dad, I think I could make even more money. If I just had a bike, or even one of those golf carts they have at the club, I could find a whole lot more balls. Bet they're hidden all over this place. New ones probably get lost all the time over by the beginner holes people play. It'd be faster too because I'd be riding, not walking."

I nod. It's pretty ambitious for our short time here, but what's the harm in letting him dream?

"Got a goal in mind, or are you just gunning for the Fortune 500?"

His eyes grow brighter, so much like mine it hurts. "Hundreds is my guess, and it wouldn't take long. Not long at all."

Not wanting to disappoint him, I nod. "You might be onto something, bud."

"I *know* I am, Dad." He shakes his head and frowns. "There's just one problem..."

I lift a brow, but before I can say anything, his name rings out upstairs. Lauren, calling for him loudly.

"You're up, big guy!" Red adds.

Shane leaps off the sofa. "Gotta go, Dad. You can take your shower after me."

"Okay," I say, even though I didn't know they'd *decided* I had to take one too.

A short time later, after Lauren and Gwen come downstairs with their hair done and both wearing dresses, I figure I better change too. Fair is fair.

Shane wanders out of the bathroom, so I shower, and by the time I come downstairs, everyone's waiting.

"We late?" I ask as they spring off the sofa.

"Nope," Gingersnap answers. "They're just excited. They really want to see my mother's place and talk to her and," her voice drops to a whisper, "that's a good thing. Any distraction for Mother, I mean. We'll take my car."

I can count on one hand the number of times someone else has driven while my kids and I are in the same vehicle, but I nod. Whatever.

It's a chance to get a better look around this town. Not being able to get a hold of Keith is starting to worry me more and more. He still hasn't picked up or called back for days.

Radio silence isn't like him.

Not something he'd do without a damn good reason.

I just hope it's him making the choice and not somebody else. There's no room for error.

Hopefully we haven't overlooked something crucial.

THE DRIVE to her ma's place isn't far, and I'm in as much awe as the kids when we pull into the big circle driveway.

"Whoa, it's like...it's like a mansion!" Lauren nearly starts hyperventilating from the back seat. "I knew she made it big!"

"Sure is," Shane agrees. "I bet this lady's got security guards, guard dogs, maybe even guard lions!"

I try not to roll my eyes at his vivid imagination. Then again, is he really so far off?

May Courtney could own a few lions. She must have eight figures to her name, easy. There's no way we're looking at a house that costs less than ten million.

It's an estate. A huge white brick house with yawning

double doors, all wood, more like a castle than a sleepy old farmhouse expanded to forty thousand square feet or more.

The manicured lawn and flowerbeds say she must have a good staff to take care of it, practically on a daily basis. There's not even a flower petal out of place, and the huge white urns beside the front door are full of them. Real ones. Fragrant already, even though some are still coming up to bloom.

The huge front door opens as we arrive on the stoop.

"Hello, hello!" Gwen's mother says. "I'm so excited to have you all join me for dinner this evening. Come on in."

I get a glimpse behind her and grab one of Shane's shoulders with one hand and Lauren's with the other.

They both glance up at me with apprehension. I don't have to rein in their behavior often, but don't want to in this place at all. Hell, I'm worried we might break something just stepping inside this place.

By the time I'm done paying Gwen and her boss for their help, we'll probably be damn near broke, so I don't need some sort of expensive doodad or exotic rug hand-sewn in Antarctica ruined tonight.

"Behave," I whisper quietly, but with warning.

"Oh, of course they'll behave themselves like darlings!"

I look up. May must have ears like a wolf for her age. Smiling at the kids, she continues, "You can call me May, or May-May. No Ms. Courtney and *definitely* none of that Ms. Court nonsense I only save for interviews."

"*Mother.*" Gingersnap snaps. Her eyes say she'd love nothing better than to follow that up with a *behave* comment of her own.

"What?" May smiles innocently, holding out her hands to Shane and Lauren. "Come on in. I've set out some games you might like. Let me show you around."

As she guides the children across a huge tiled foyer, I

glance at Gwen and can't help but ask, "Why the hell are you working for Manny Stork?"

Without missing a beat, or a single step while following her mother, she smiles. "Because none of this is mine. It's Mother's, and I'm no mooch."

Respectable. I get that, but it still doesn't make sense to me.

May's loaded, yet her daughter's car is older than my twins. The two of them don't appear to be estranged at all, which only makes it weirder.

We enter a large living room. May and the kids are at the far end, where a large wooden table, an elaborately carved antique, has game boxes stacked on it from one end to the other.

"Wow, that's...*way* more than a few games," Shane says, rubbing his eyes in disbelief. "Holy crap. It's like the game store at the mall. I've never seen this many in my life."

"I wasn't sure what you liked, so I bought one of each," May says, giving a little shrug. "I bought us a few other things, too. There's a couple remote control cars and jewelry making kits. Oh, and some markers and paints. Go ahead, dig in, it's all for you."

Both Shane and Lauren look at me. So does Gwen.

I'm so stunned I can't even speak.

She shrugs and whispers to me. "Mother loves playing the hostess with the mostess. She's always like this. Just let it happen."

I give the kids a quick nod, then give Gwen a slower one. I did well while working at Mederva Therapeutics, real well with one of the highest security specialist salaries in the city, but *nothing* like this.

I'm not a multimillionaire. One wall has a line of framed movie posters, and beneath each one there's a framed book cover, blown up so huge you could read her name a mile away. No joke.

M.E. Court.

Here, at home, her name sounds more like true royalty than some author spinning modern day pulp fiction.

"Miller, I took you as a beer man." May pops the top off a black long-necked bottle of beer and passes it over. "I wasn't wrong, was I?"

"Nope," I reply, taking the bottle gratefully. A drink will keep my head from spinning, especially a rich porter like this with higher alcohol content. "Thanks."

She sets the opener down on the table and picks up a bottle of wine.

"My instincts rarely disappoint." May pours two glasses of wine and hands one to Gwen. "Darling?"

"Thank you, Mother."

Once again, she's dressed in a flowery outfit, this one several shades of pink. May waves a hand to a long white sofa with matching chairs flanking it. "Come, let's sit down. Dinner won't be ready for half an hour or so. Chef's just wrapping up the final touches."

I follow her over, Gwen at my side, my eyes drinking in how bright she's blushing.

"I also guessed you're a steak man, Miller," May says. "Ribeyes. Nothing fancier than Argentina imports. Grilled, of course, with sautéed mushrooms and onions and plenty of sides."

Goddamn, she's nailed me.

Did she make all this money writing books or reading minds?

"Sounds delicious," I say, trying to get over how weird this all is.

I wait till she sits on the sofa and Gwen takes the seat next to her before I move into one of the chairs.

What am I even doing here? I need to keep a low profile.

This gaudy, outrageous millionaire dinner party shit is anything but.

Getting mixed up with a famous author and her daughter? Definitely not the way to do it.

Everyone in Finley Grove must know who they are. Hell, maybe half the state.

My stomach churns. Even the beer I slug down doesn't do much for the anxious fire raging in my gut.

This isn't going to work.

I should pack up the kids tonight and go. Head for Canada. We can find another guy smarter than Manny up there to get us to Ireland. There's still enough money.

I know that's just my worries talking, though.

I need to get a hold of Keith. Make a change in plans.

My gaze goes to Lauren and Shane, my number one concern since the day they were born. Before then, actually, ever since Willow told me she was pregnant.

That's the moment they became my responsibility, my life, the other pieces of my soul. I've never let anything come before them. The fact that their lives are at risk thanks to someone else's filth and greed infuriates me.

Far more than it should while I'm in this posh chair, guzzling beer fit for a king, eyeballing Gingersnap and her ma rambling on about books I've never heard of.

Christ.

The hair on the nape of my neck stands up, and I see the reason. May.

She's staring at me expectantly. Taking another swig off my beer, I take a moment to search my mind, see if I unconsciously heard whatever she said.

If I did, it's not registering. That's almost as concerning as her reading me like nothing when it comes to beer and steak.

She's intuitive. Able to find her answers without even asking for them.

Another excellent reason to make a change of plans *fast*.

"Sorry," I say, lowering my beer. "I didn't hear. I was watching the kids." That's true enough.

I was looking their way, where they're totally engrossed in the games she'd set out. Making all of this harder.

I hate depriving them of anything. I want them to have a good childhood, good lives, and they will, after this hell is over and we no longer have to worry about hitmen showing up to murder us or worse. But it's harder, denying them the simple things, even though my main solitary focus is keeping them safe.

"Ah, yes, I'm thrilled those little dumplings sure are enjoying themselves," May says with a self-assured smile. "I asked what you do for a living. My telepathic abilities do have limits, Miller." She winks.

"Security," I answer. One word, point-blank.

Gwen looks worried, apologetic. Not her problem.

May nods. "Quite the norm for former military, especially men who served in special forces."

My spine stiffens. *What the fuck?*

How can she possibly know I was more than a regular?

Gwen shifts awkwardly. "Sorry. Um, Mother's years of research has made reading people a hobby of hers..."

"Hobby? I'm close to an expert, dear," May says. "Look, I know an amazing man who works for the FBI and a fabulous P.I. with military experience too. They've both given me several very helpful tips over the years for my books. Personality clues, key actions, identifying strengths and weaknesses, mannerisms and deviations. It's fascinating." May takes a long sip of her wine. Almost celebratory. "I've never hoarded my knowledge. Always shared what I know with Gwen for her to use in her writing."

Gingersnap's face twists, tenses, like a secret just slipped out as I look at her. "So you're a writer too?"

She pinches her lips together, giving a single shake of her head, mouthing *no. No.*

"Oh, yes, she is!" May answers. "She just hasn't honed her chops yet. She will though, soon." Glancing at her daughter, she carries on. "Dylan asked me when you'll have something ready for him to read and shop around."

"Mother!" Gwen shakes her head. "That's not your place. Or Dylan's. I'll find my own agent someday, thank you very much."

Grinning, May shrugs. "Darling, he's the one who brought it up. Not me. He remembers that half-written book you turned in last year. It seems you're the only one who felt it wasn't worth finishing."

"Can we not?" Gwen's voice shifts, a sharpness in her tone.

Then a tinkling, musical chime sounds from another room. A sorely needed distraction if there ever was one.

"There's our dinner!" May stands, finishing her wine and sauntering across the room.

I rise at the same time Red does, and tell Lauren and Shane to put everything away.

"They can just leave it and play again after we eat," May tells me.

"They can put it away now," I say. "We'll be leaving after we eat."

May lifts a brow and glances at Gwen.

With a smile that's more like a grimace, she nods. It's no secret I'm offering her an escape.

I can't say May looks terribly miffed, or shocked, but the wheels are definitely turning in her head. This whole mother-daughter drama is more than I need right now, too.

I'll have to call Stork, tell him to find me a different plan. I can't afford for this to fail because a world-famous romance author decides to get up in my damn business.

"Right this way," May says politely as the kids arrive. She sets a hand on each of their shoulders. "Let me tell you two the ground rules."

They glance up, wide-eyed, and she grins. "Anything you don't like here, you don't have to eat."

The relief oozes out of them. And me, but I can't let mine show the way they do.

"You scared me there for a minute," Shane admits.

May laughs loudly. "Oh, my dear boy, you didn't wait for the other rule. If there isn't *anything* you like, the chef will make you something different."

My son isn't the only one who does a double take. This is too much.

"Really?" Shane wonders, his huge eyes going to me.

"No." Looking at May, I add, "They'll eat what's put in front of them. No worry."

"Miller, Miller..." May guides the children forward, keeping eye contact with me. "Trust me, I can believe that's the rule at your house, but this is mine. And it applies to you and my lovely daughter just as much, too. Don't like it, don't eat it. Special requests are always granted. I pay my personal chef beyond his wildest dreams for a reason."

Is that *reason* to show the fuck off?

I wonder as I watch her touch Lauren's shoulder and point at one of the massive paintings on the wall. My daughter smiles like the little lady she is, fully enchanted by this Beauty and the Beast magic castle bullshit.

Gwen lays a hand on my arm. Her warm palm relaxes me, sends its heat all the way to the base of my spine, where I struggle not to let it go lower.

"Mother's chef is wonderful," she says, leaning closer. "She's not embellishing that part."

"Not the chef I'm worried about, babe."

Gwen sighs. "Me, either. We'll leave as soon as we're done eating, okay?"

Her eyes search mine.

Big and green and pleading.

For some reason, she wants this to work. Get through dinner without another hitch. *Fine.*

We follow May and the kids out of the room, and as we walk down a long hallway with more framed pictures of book covers, I ask, "So are you really an author too? Is law just a side-hustle?"

"More like side-show," she whispers, shaking her head. "But no. I'm not anything like Mother."

"Why?" We move together. There are also framed pictures of May herself on the walls, next to some people I do recognize. Movie stars. Producers. Singers. Household names. "Looks like your ma has all the connections you'd ever need to catch up to her."

"That's the problem," Gwen says as we turn a corner into a large, formal dining room that May and the kids have already entered.

The table is set, complete with place cards. While gesturing to our assigned seats, May says, "My daughter doesn't need connections, Miller. She needs confidence. She's a very talented wordsmith, and someday, she'll write a bestseller to outshine even *mwah*. She just needs to stop being so afraid of her own shadow."

This woman must have a bionic ear. "Afraid of what?" My question goes to May, but I'm staring at Gwen as I pull out her chair for her to sit.

"Her own dear heart," May answers with a theatrical swoop of her hand to her chest.

I hold her chair and after she sits, move to mine, unsure what her mother means.

"Gwen and I struggled for years, you see," May tells us. "Financially. Just like most artists, it's feast or famine for authors, too. My writing career didn't flourish until nearly ten years ago. The ebook revolution changed the industry as much as TVs did for cinema. Before that, I'd had enough rejection letters from the big publishing houses. I could've heated our apartment all winter burning them, but then, after I started making a name for myself through a small digital imprint, all the big boys came a calling. They wanted my books, and lucky me, they were willing to pay handsomely. It's worked out marvelously for all of us."

Has it? I wonder as I look over, studying Gwen, whose face is somewhere between *not again* and *shoot me.*

"I want to be an author when I grow up, too!" Lauren's little blue eyes dance up and down.

"Then an authoress, you'll be," May says with a smile, plucking a chilled shrimp the size of a small drumstick out of the fluted bowl sitting on her plate. My stomach growls loudly. There's no denying the appetizers look good. "All you have to do is put your mind to it and never, ever quit for anyone or anything, young lady." She dips her shrimp in cocktail sauce. "Try one, everybody, before I eat them all. They're delicious."

We all have fluted bowls on our plates that look like they came from Versailles.

If she was worried Lauren or Shane wouldn't like them, she's wrong.

I've been making their meals since they were born. Because I'm not a fan of mac and cheese or peanut butter sandwiches all the time, they aren't either. My cooking and the Seattle creative scene have given them a sixth sense for good food.

The children wolf down the shrimp – we all do – while May talks about how Gwen once won a writing contest.

She'd been in sixth grade, and because her poem made it to the newspaper, technically, Gwen became a published author before May had.

Lauren is all ears, and Shane follows along too.

May's stories don't stop there during the break in courses. She tells them about research trips her and Gwen would take on long weekends.

It's interesting how when they went anywhere, they studied their surroundings in screaming detail: trees, birds, buildings, houses, people, words, animals, crafting whole journals about everything under the sun.

That's dedication. I'm not much for art, but I do admire grit.

When she mentions Gwen describing a nacho machine so thoroughly that she still nearly gags whenever she sees one, Shane has *plenty* to say about that. I stop him before he ruins the meal summarizing our long ride here.

I also don't want him giving more details for the elder Courtney to sink her teeth in.

He can spin a story well, too, even if he's no writer. May and Gwen are damn near wiping the tears of laughter out of their eyes with linen napkins before I finally chuckle.

It's nice to laugh again.

I'd started to forget what it felt like.

The meal arrives in five full courses. Sunchoke and whitefish soup follows the shrimp, then salads, steaks grilled to noble perfection alongside spicy caramelized brussels sprouts and creamy twice baked potatoes piled high with all the fixings.

The entire meal could leave a five-star restaurant in the dust. Dessert isn't half bad either.

Some kind of fancy molten lava brownies with vanilla ice cream. Didn't think I had room after devouring a steak as big as my head, but I think my sundae disappears faster than the kids' while Gwen looks on with her green eyes twinkling like stars.

At least the whole evening isn't a total loss.

Everybody at this table thoroughly enjoys every morsel. The conversation May keeps steering about her life isn't half bad either.

She even brings the kids back into it. Whenever there's a lull, and they're quiet, she asks Shane or Lauren a question, or shares another Gwen story that leaves her cheeks painted red.

No denying it. All in all, the enjoyment on Shane and Lauren's faces send guilt rolling around my overstuffed gut.

They've never had anything like this. A form of extended family, almost.

If Willow ever had any relatives, I never knew about them. Her parents died when she was young, and her grandma shortly after we'd met.

My ma died while I'd been in boot camp. A heart attack, I'd been told.

Probably brought on by smoking like a chimney, going through four packs a day sometimes. A bad habit she picked up after my old man left her, drinking himself into an early grave.

My folks died too young, barely in their late fifties.

Not a great inheritance for the kids.

Willow and I both came from gnarled family trees that'd been torn out at the roots. Plenty of broken dreams, a hearty dose of self-abuse, and *misery loves company* ought to be etched on the family coat of arms – if they handed them out to people like us.

Maybe that's why I'm even more determined to make sure me and the kids aren't the latest Rush tragedies. I'll be damned if my boy or girl shuffle off their mortal coil early.

Hell, with the mess we're in, not having extended family is a good thing.

No one can use it to chase us down.

At that thought, I lay down my napkin, but before I can say anything, Gwen speaks up.

"Dinner was delicious as always, Mother," she says. "Thank you. Now, Miller has some work to catch up on, I think, so we'll just–"

"You're very welcome." May pats her lips with her napkin and then sets it aside, cutting her off. "Chef's skills never fail, but it was the company that makes it truly enjoyable." She points at the children while standing, one by one. "You two, you're with me. I'd like you to pick out whatever you want to take home. The rest goes to charity. I know Gwen doesn't have much for you to play with at her house."

Shit.

I should protest, but I can read people, too. May is doggedly determined to make sure the kids won't leave here without a few of the things she's purchased. So, instead, I hold up two fingers for Shane and Lauren to know the limit. Two games each.

They each pick out a couple, then say thank you and goodbye. We're on the walkway, almost to the car, when Shane leans close to Lauren.

"Ya know, I wish Dad really *was* married to Gwen. Not just pretend, because then May would be our grandma," he says.

Lauren answers with a muffled laugh, nodding her head.

The hair on the back of my neck stands on end.

Not because what they said is so outlandish, but because I know who's listening.

Watching us like a hungry, all-too-curious hawk.

May stands on the front steps, her bionic ear probably at full power because she immediately calls my name. "Miller?"

"Keep walking," Gwen hisses, tugging at my arm. "We're almost there."

I should. But I don't. May is already behind me, running at a good clip when I turn, breaking Gwen's urgent arm-pulling.

Her mother's expression is beyond somber as she stretches onto her toes and leans closer, so only I can hear her. "Careful. I'm a *very* resourceful woman, Miller. Hurt my daughter, and you'll find out what kind of hell money buys."

Like I don't already have a good idea.

My eyes narrow and I look at her, sizing her up.

"Keep your change, May. I won't be around long enough to hurt a single hair on her head, and I wouldn't dream of it," I say, then turn around and quick-step to the car.

May gives a parting wave, shifting back into the sweet old author lady who'd never threaten a bee, and blows kisses to the children before yelling after us, "I'll call tomorrow, darling!"

"Thanks again, Mother," Gwen huffs out as she shuts the driver's door and starts the engine.

Her gaze settles on me as she puts the old car in drive. Obviously wondering what her mother said.

I'm too tired to care, much less kindle more drama, so I glance into the back seat. "All buckled?"

"Yep," both Shane and Lauren answer.

A moment later, I realize I shouldn't have asked. It's like I just gave them permission to relive the last couple of hours that were nothing short of magic to them. They gush about the games and food and fairy-tale estate all the way to the townhouse, and then race inside ahead of us to play with their new toys.

Goddammit. This isn't getting any easier.

"Sorry for all that, again. Thanks for being a good sport.

Mother can be a little overbearing," Gwen says as we climb out of the car. "And by a little, of course I mean brutally."

I shut my door and walk around the front of the car. "This isn't going to work."

"Huh? What isn't?" Her eyes light up.

"Us staying here, Gwen." I start for the door. "Manny's going to have to find someone else. A backup."

"There *is* no backup. He's clueless. Do you think we'd have even met if he really had somebody better lined up and wasn't just flying by the seat of his pants?" she asks. "I guarantee you, we wouldn't. Look, I know this isn't easy, I know you're in a lot of trouble but...I'm your only option. And I want to help."

I spin around. "You're no option at all. Not when your ma will be sniffing around every move we make, and probably flipping her shit to Jupiter and back when she finds out we've left the country!"

It comes out harsher than I intend. But fuck, I've reached my limit.

I hate not being in control, having to rely on help like a beggar.

Can't even remember the last time I had all the say. Total control of my life, my fate, my kids' futures.

She shakes her head, disbelief turning to anger. "You're being ridiculous, Miller. She won't do anything crazy if she just understands what's up."

"Good one, babe. She already threatened to tear me a new one if you decide to kiss this frog, looking for your prince," I growl, too pissed off to mince more words. "What do you think she'll do if she knows the stakes? If the assholes coming after me catch *you* in the middle?"

I don't want to scare her.

I regret it the second it's out of my mouth. She just looks sad. Worried. Frustrated.

"Jesus, I can't believe she...you know what, fine. Go ahead and call Manny if you don't believe me. Then you can hear it from the horse's mouth, and we can talk about how we're going to figure this out."

I just about lose it.

"Manny, that fucking idiot? He was supposed to find me a safe house. A woman who could pass as my wife to get us out of here. You're plenty nice, but shit, with your liabilities, that sure as hell isn't you. What don't you understand, Gwen? Your ma's a famous author. I'm guessing Stork knew that, too, and he still screwed me over."

"My mother has *nothing* to do with this. I'm the one trying to help you, Miller, not her."

I scoff at that.

How is it possible for any girl to be this gorgeous, this innocent, this persistent?

"Like hell, she doesn't." There's no way May Courtney will ever let Gwen leave the country with us, that's as sure as the sun coming up in the morning.

And it's the last hitch I need. Being dragged into some tabloid drama with the internationally bestselling author – whose daughter leaves the States with a man she just met.

I know the media. The paparazzi would be all over that shit like piranhas on a rack of ribs. I can't even risk a flap on Instagram about it, knowing Jackie's people watch *everything*.

"The kids and I are leaving. Whether Stork can find someone else or not, it's time for Plan B."

"Plan B?" she hisses, crossing her arms, glaring. "And where, pray tell, might that be?"

"You're the last person I'd tell. Not when it might make it back to mama."

Her fiery stare sharpens into hellfire. "You know what, Miller? For raising such sweet kids, you're a big effing dick."

VII: TIME TO FLY (GWEN)

I haven't been this mad at someone in years, but *whoa, mama.*

I'm pissed at him. We're talking dagger eyes and the rocket's red glare in my blood.

Turns out, Miller Rush is kind of an asshole.

And I guess I am too for getting involved in something so stupid, so reckless, so ridiculous. And that goes double for Manny, who roped me into this, and...*ohhhh, I'm furious.*

I can't blame Mother, but I'm mad at her, too, for butting in where she doesn't belong. It doesn't help the fact that while sitting at her table, I saw exactly what she's always wanted.

It was there on her face, in the glow in her eyes, in the almost too smug twinge of her lips.

She's always claimed she wanted to be an author more than anything in the world. Make a name for herself, a fortune, and she's done all that in spades.

But tonight, I found the last thing fame and riches haven't given her. Or me, with my desert of a dating life.

A family.

She was in her glory with Shane and Lauren. Showering them with gifts she could never give me when I was that young. Even now, when she can afford to, and often insists, I won't let her because I'm an adult and need to stand on my own two feet.

Heck, I'm several years older than she was when she had me. By the time she was my age, she was working two jobs and still being wonder-mom.

Despite working all day and staying up half the night writing, she never missed a PTA meeting, or parent-teacher conference, or field trip, or concert, or play, or *anything.*

She gave me everything I truly needed, and it wasn't material.

I never knew how badly she wanted to keep on giving those things until I saw her tonight. Her interest in the kids wasn't just faked for politeness.

She was glued to every word they had to say, and she adored telling them about me. Even when some of her tales were embarrassing, I couldn't stop her, because she's worked her butt off for me since the day I was born.

What a flipping mess this entire thing is.

That's what infuriates me most.

How I've let *two* asshat men screw things up so bad, so fast.

I should've fought harder, absolutely refused this kind of crazy, taken my boss to court if he insisted. Then I wouldn't be where I am right now.

Right at the edge, where I'd relish telling Manny and Miller and maybe any man whose name starts with M to buzz off out of my life.

But at the same time, I stuck around, didn't I?

I fell for the magic trick, the illusion, the *lie.*

I'll never admit it, but Mother and I are too alike. What

we had for a couple hours at her place tonight is exactly what I've always wanted.

A family.

A badass husband.

A couple kids running around, complete with adorable little issues and triumphs worth all the agonies and laughs and feels.

Something greater than just me and Mother. People we can share our past escapades and memories with, our hopes and dreams, and our futures.

Miller might be a huge swinging dick, but his kids aren't.

They're pure sunshine. They've already touched my heart in ways I'm afraid to admit. But I let my guard down. And for that, there's no one to blame but Toby.

Back up.

It's not quite the same, Toby was a dog, this sweet little beagle, but at the same time...that's what I'm remembering, comparing these feelings to.

He'd shown up at the little house we'd rented south of the Twin Cities years ago, barging inside like he owned the place one fine evening when Mother left the back door open. Because he had.

Or rather, the people who owned him, had.

They'd built a new house across town and rented out their old one. Somehow, Toby had gotten out of his new place and ran all the way to his old home.

He spent a week with us before his people thought to check with us.

God, I'd loved that pooch. So had Mother.

So had his owners, who he'd gone back to live with again.

Now, Miller's going to take Shane and Lauren away just like Toby's owners took him. And even if I kinda-sorta-wanna march right up and let my hand fly across his face for the verbal lashing he gave me, you want to know the worst part?

I hate, hate, *hate* that he's going to take his big, snarly face away from me, too.

The same rough, beardy face I've imagined kissing far more times than I even want to count since the second he showed up.

A little while ago, Miller stormed past me into the house. I haven't gone after him because I'm worried he's about to make the kids pack. So I drag myself inside later, bracing for more misery.

"Gwen, there you are! Want to help me make a necklace?" Lauren asks, perched on a stool.

She has the jewelry making kit spread out on the kitchen island, one of the two things she picked at Mother's place. The girl's got good taste.

"Sounds like a plan, Lauren," I tell her.

I peer around the corner, toward an odd buzzing noise. Gripping his new controller, Shane's busy making the remote control car speed around the coffee table in quick laps.

Movement draws my eyes to the sliding glass door, where Miller paces the small deck, phone pressed to his ear. I look at him, subtly glaring, but he doesn't meet my eyes.

Go ahead, Mister. Feed your ego.

Manny will tell him exactly what I just did.

Shrugging, I walk over to the island. "So what kind of necklace are we making?"

"I haven't decided yet. There's a ton of styles here." Lauren points to the supplies laid out neatly on the table. "But there's plenty of chains and beads and little copper pieces, so...we could make matching ones if you'd like?"

"Not a bad thought," I say, pulling out a stool to sit down.

"I always liked copper and beads. Something simple and rustic."

"Me, too!" she chirps. "We could even make one for May. Then we'd all match."

Something hot and totally annoying stings my eyes as I nod. "I bet she'd like that, Lauren. She'd like it a lot."

Just then, a hulking grizzly bear comes inside as we're laying out a bead design, but only long enough to grab his laptop off the coffee table. Miller takes it back outside without so much as a glance at me, closing the door behind him.

God.

Where did this caveman learn to push my buttons so well?

The kids don't say anything about that. They don't notice, so I pretend I don't either. Until Shane asks if he can take his car outside.

"I don't care," I answer, "but maybe ask your dad? The noise might bother him while he's working."

"Got it!" Shane says, scrambling up. "But he won't mind."

Strangely, I know that's true.

I may be pissed at him, and think he's a major league ass, but there's no denying Miller his status as superdad. I've never seen him be anything but kind and caring and fair to these kids.

Even the warning looks he gives them that he thinks are stern are full of love. For their own good.

So much goodwill, it makes my insides tremble.

They're lucky to have each other.

The thought of something awful happening to them because of this stupid mess or an even dumber fight makes me feel sick. And yeah, okay, slightly less like I want to spit in Miller's handsome face.

"So your mom must be really proud of that poem you wrote," Lauren says, smiling at me.

Mother pointed out the framed newspaper hanging in her dining room like it was a herald sent from above.

"I guess. It isn't much, really. Just a sappy little thing I wrote about a summer day. Crickets, frogs, lightning bugs, sunshine, and stars. I was eleven." I don't dare mention that she has two other copies hanging upstairs, one in her bedroom and one in the hall. "It's not exactly Shakespeare or even Dr. Seuss."

"Are you still writing? Something besides poems?"

"Oh, yes," I answer, trying not to shudder at the dozens of half-completed manuscripts on my computer and the boxes of spiral notebooks under my bed. "Someday I might even finish a book."

"Finish?" Lauren asks. "You mean you haven't..."

She looks down, too shy and polite to finish what we already know: I suck at this authoring thing because I have a hard time turning in my homework.

"It's okay to laugh, Lauren. I know how crazy it is. I just get about halfway through, going great guns with my characters and plot, but then...I want to start the next book. I see a shiny new plot bunny I have to chase all the way to Wonderland."

Her little face scrunches as she frowns. "Is it...?"

I shrug. "Different reasons, I guess. Or maybe I just have the attention span of a squirrel."

"No, I mean, is it writer's block?"

I smile at that. She's sweet for giving me some way to save face.

"Perhaps."

Her face lights up then. I can practically see the invisible light bulb over her head switch on. "That's no prob! Maybe we should write a book together. That way when you get stuck, I can write, and when I get writer's block, you take over."

A writing buddy isn't the worst thing in the world. I never thought I'd consider pairing up with a ten-year-old. No matter how smart she is, I don't think she'd be at home with my kind of thriller books, but...what if I let her be my pint-sized muse?

What if she gives me new ideas? Fresh inspiration?

"Now there's a thought," I say, resting my hand on my chin.

"We could start on it later tonight after we finish our necklaces." She's gushing now.

Poor little thing.

Only a matter of time until she finds out what it's like having me as a freaking author-buddy.

Threading more beads onto my chain, I ask the inevitable. "So what would our story be about?"

"Hmmm..." She's quiet, thinking while putting more beads on her chain. "Hey, I know. How 'bout two kids who find buried treasure while looking for golf balls?"

"Fun idea. And realistic, too," I say with a wink.

But actually, my mind goes to a man and woman who are forced to live together due to bad guys chasing them down. A grumpy, handsome man with knockout blue eyes and savage ink crisscrossing his skin, who falls in love with Ms. Impossible against the odds.

Too real? Or too ridiculous like my kiddie poem?

"A huge treasure...and then there's like a bad antique dealer who used to be a pirate who tries to steal it but...but they outsmart him and build themselves a mansion to live in with everyone. Their mom and dad and grandma!" Lauren sets down her necklace, smiling like she's just cracked the secrets of the universe. "That would be a really good story with a happy ending, wouldn't it? That's important. People love happy endings."

"They sure do," I agree.

The thin real life details she's basing her tale on don't have a chance of ending the way she wants. There won't be happy endings for me and Miller, and the only treasure I've got coming is one I'm not sure I want anymore.

But there can happier times for her and Shane.

I hope with all my heart they'll find it, wherever they wind up.

Someday, once her father gets them out of this jam, they deserve nothing but the best. Tonight, at least I'm here to make sure she has a happy-for-now. Despite her beast-daddy being a butt and a half.

We finish our necklaces and put them on, comparing how they look.

Not half bad for an amateur effort.

I won't be tearing up the runway any time soon – do jewelry shows even *have* modeling runways? – but it's better than one of those ugly summer camp projects I had to do a few times as a kid.

After putting the rest of the kit back in its plastic case for safekeeping, we find ourselves a gift bag for the third necklace she's made for Mother. I'll hang on to it until I see her again.

The closet also has several spiral notebooks, so we take two out and carry them back to the kitchen, where we sit down and start brainstorming her wild treasure hunter tale.

"Is it okay to use real names in a story?" she asks, biting her little lip.

"Well, it's yours, so you can use any names you want to. No famous people, but common names are fair game. That's part of the fun of writing. Creating the characters. You give them looks and names and plenty of attitude. Any way you want to slice it, honey."

"Wow, I never thought of it like that." She nibbles on the end of her pencil. "Sooo...I could have a girl with pink hair? Who only wears white clothes? And, oh, has a cat, too. A big fat tabby with black and orange stripes!"

"Only limit here is your imagination." It's sage advice I wish I could follow.

Her eyes nearly sparkle. "And the cat's name is Tiger, and hers could be Sally. I've always liked that name."

"Genius," I say, giving her shoulder an encouraging pat.

She starts writing furiously, scratching the paper so hard I can hear it. "This is gonna be so fun!"

Ah, another wish. Finding her kind of carefree satisfaction writing again.

When you're an adult with a bestselling mother, it's different. Books are minefields of second-guessing, agonizing revisions, ego-bashing feedback, and that's just the beginning.

I've never even made it to the real arena, where you're at the mercy of agents and publishers and big fricking bookstores, then the professional reviewers and the readers who will either think it's the best thing ever or will want to light your little book-baby on fire.

My chin slips off my hand, and I sit up, blinking. I'm thankful Lauren's still busily scribbling away so no one saw it.

Okay. *Focus.*

Just like Mother used to do for me when I was younger, I etch out an outline for her, complete with directions on how to create a beginning, middle, and ending to her story that should flow naturally.

I *hope* that's what it does, considering I've never finished a book.

The entire time I'm writing, a completely different story forms in my head.

The one with the man and woman forced to live together, and how they fall in love. A slow burn hate bleeding into love like a spring thaw.

I've never tried to write a true love story. I didn't want to follow in Mother's romancey footsteps.

But for some reason, this time, a weird rush of magic fills me like never before.

While Lauren pencils away at her story, I start outlining one of my own and quickly become engrossed.

Miller finally comes inside and tells the kids it's bedtime. I'm surprised at the time we've lost. Over two hours have gone by, and now it's well past nine o'clock.

I close my notebook and tell the kids goodnight. But then, as soon as Miller follows them upstairs, I open the notebook back up to write down one more thought about the hero, and another, and then describe the flag and eagle tattoo on his upper left arm.

So maybe it *is* a lot like Miller's, but that doesn't mean anything.

Honest.

Neither does the fact that the hero has short dark hair and sky-blue eyes and this irresistible scruff that would feel like the finest burn ever on a woman's soft skin.

Sigh.

At least my hero's name is Graham Rivard, right? That's nowhere even *close* to Miller Rush.

Other details? There might be an artistic resemblance. But only that.

Too bad the sixth-sense tinge inside me says he's right behind me. I close the notebook and spin around.

"Working on the next great American novel?" he asks, one brow lifted.

I don't say anything. My pout look tells him it's none of his business.

He nods and leans a hip against the side of the center island top. "Sorry about earlier, in the garage. I wasn't myself. Didn't mean to put your head on a pike over my shit, Gwen."

I wasn't expecting an apology. But I can figure out why I'm getting one.

"Oh? You called Manny, didn't you? And he told you there's no one else except little old me. So you're stuck here, just like I said."

His grin is half smirk as he nods again. "Yeah, babe, that's pretty much what he recommended." He pushes off the counter with one hand. "But I'm not stuck with you. Or I should say you aren't stuck with us. We're leaving in the morning, bright and early."

My heart leaps up in my chest. "Leaving? Going where?"

"Can't say."

"Can't or won't?"

He hesitates, then shrugs. "Both, maybe. I'm still working on our route. Still, the less you know, the –"

"Don't say it. You don't even know if it's for the better, Miller."

I know how ridiculous it sounds. I shouldn't care so much.

In fact, I should be ecstatic to be done with all this, out of whatever danger zone he might be putting me in every day he hangs around, but...

But I'm so not done.

Him leaving like this, practically storming out, just leaves me living the very definition of *unfinished business.*

"Listen, I'll pay you for letting us crash here. I know it wasn't easy."

"It's not about money," I throw back, hurt and disgusted

at the same time. The worst part is, I can't even say more without digging myself a deeper shame pit.

Through his eyes, I'm sure he sees a silly, overly emotional girl. Not an adult. Not someone who ever should've been his fake wife and his lifeline to begin with.

Well, he's flipping right.

He lets out a half chuckle. "I almost believe you, Gingersnap."

I look up, anger burning in my eyes at that stupid nick-name. "Almost?"

He nods.

This isn't helping anything. I pick up my notebook and stand. "I was right about one thing – you really are a ginor-mous dick." Heading for the stairs, I add, "Enjoy your last night on the couch."

* * *

MORNING TAKES FOREVER TO COME.

At the same time, it comes well before I want it to.

Before I'm ready for it, even though I hardly sleep a wink.

I dress quickly, clip up my hair, and brush my teeth before heading downstairs, where the smell of coffee brewing fills the air. It's almost haunting, this thick roasted scent in the air, like leaves in a crisp bonfire blazing away to ash.

The way he's erasing our little...I don't even know what to call it.

Arrangement? Ships in the night? Pretend marriage?

Miller's in the kitchen, pouring a cup. My mind flashes between reality and fantasy, and for a second, I freeze.

This image, a man wearing jeans and a t-shirt, barefoot, pouring coffee could be straight out of the romance thriller novel I started last night. Of course, in it, he'd turn around smiling, and hand the heroine a steaming mug of coffee that's perfectly fixed to her liking.

Back in reality, I'm expecting him to scowl, or look up anxiously, just hoping to keep the peace so he can leave.

But sometimes, reality blurs.

Miller turns, sees me, grins oddly big, and reaches around. He lifts a cup off the counter and holds it toward me. "Half a cup of creamer. Just how you like."

Damn!

My insides nearly melt for absolutely no reason at all.

Or for every reason I shouldn't be feeling.

"Thanks," I whisper, taking the cup and stepping back as he carries his into the living room.

"The kids know we're leaving this morning. I told them last night," he says, "but I said I'd let 'em sleep in. It'll be a long-ass day on the road again."

My heart clenches. I'd hoped, prayed, that he'd come to his senses during the night.

Probably as foolish as believing I could finish a novel. Toby the dog bolts through my mind, and I pinch my lips together, forcing it to go away.

Forget the dog. This is *worse.*

I'm a grown woman. Shane and Lauren don't belong to me any more than Toby did.

Neither does Miller.

And it's totally my fault if I've let them crawl under my skin, heading for emotional nooks and crannies I should know to guard against all the painful, disappointing crap life loves to hand out like Halloween candy.

Turning, I watch him in the living room. The blankets and sheets he'd used are all folded neatly and stacked on the end of the sofa. His computer, suitcase, and duffel bag are gone. Everything.

"Any luck on that route? Figuring it out, I mean?" I ask, staring glumly into my cup.

"Ontario, probably. Then maybe all the way to New Brunswick. The closer we can get to a transatlantic flight by land in a place without too many people, the better." He looks at me sharply, his gaze softening. "You've done your part. No use worrying about us. I had to leave something for Manny Fuckface, and I'll be sure you get your cut."

No. A sense of near panic hits.

"You don't have to leave!" I'd spent a good portion of the night wishing I hadn't been so quick to fume. I'm usually not and can't say why I was last night, even if he kinda deserved it, but I won't be this morning.

Cool, common sense is what I need. "I said I'd help you, Miller. That hasn't changed. I'll go to Ireland or wherever else. I'll make sure Mother doesn't get in the middle of it. Just leave that to me."

He sets his coffee cup on the coffee table with a *clink.* "Babe, your help isn't the issue."

Sighing, I walk into the living room and sit down on the chair. "Then what is? What's changed?"

Shaking his head, he says, "I can't risk being compromised."

"Compromised? By me? By Mother?"

A brief smile flashes on his lips before it turns deadly serious.

"By anyone, Gwen. The kids and I need to get the hell out of this country. Safely. Soon. The devils I worked with have big bucks at their disposal. They could hire whole strike teams to find us. Can't take any chances on someone discovering where we are before then and tipping off the wolves."

I nod, my chest tightening. Even if I already knew, hearing it doesn't help. "I'm not going to tell anyone. I barely know anyone around here to begin with."

"But everyone must know your ma? She's famous."

I look up, puzzled. Then it dawns on me why he'd think that. "Right. She is, but she's also a very private person. That's why she picked Finley Grove. Most people don't recognize her, and the few that do..."

The way he's shaking his head has my words fading.

I'm not convincing anyone, least of all him.

I'm not even sure why I'm trying, stringing this along.

"Still too close for comfort," he growls softly. "Sorry, I just can't take the chance. You're a celebrity's daughter, and that alone makes you newsworthy. Your connection to her. Someone could easily tip off the gossip rags about a man living here with you, about the kids, and our cover would be blown to kingdom come."

Sigh.

I can't deny what he's saying. Because in a different sense, if I ever *do* finish a novel, it's the same reason I won't use Mother's contacts. I don't want someone buying my work simply because I'm M.E. Court's illustrious daughter, and surely the apple doesn't fall far from the tree.

"You get that, don't you?" he asks. "I can tell by the look on your face."

"I understand your concern," I admit, "but I have my own, too. Mainly about Shane and Lauren. They're comfortable here."

"Right now, comfort isn't what they need."

As if on cue, a *thud* sounds upstairs. We both glance up.

Miller stands up and steps around the coffee table. A heaviness pools in my stomach like molten lead.

Hopping to my feet, I twist for a better look up the staircase. "Just wait. I'll talk to Mother and—"

"No," he says. "Gwen, I'm damn sorry, but this is how it's got to be. The kids know we're leaving. They're throwing their shit together. Let's not make it harder."

I've never felt so powerless before, so torn.

I really don't like how it's just getting worse every ten seconds.

He lays a hand on my arm, rough and calloused. It's as thick and comforting as the rest of him.

I so don't want to stare into those hypnotic blue eyes of his. I so don't want to get burned. Maybe I just wanted to dream. That never hurt anybody, right?

"Thanks for everything, Gingersnap. You made my kids very happy the past few days during the worst time we've ever had. I'll always appreciate that. Never, ever gonna forget it."

He's. Killing. Me.

I have to close my eyes, hating how torrid my emotions hit, how bad I am at fighting back the sting of tears.

The burn gets worse as he moves closer, his warm lips briefly touching my cheek. It's so quick, it's gone when I open my eyes.

And so is he.

Unshed tears blur my vision as I watch him disappear, climbing the stairs.

I hear the murmur of voices then and just know he's right, that this will be hard enough on the kids already. So I move into the kitchen, using a paper towel to dry my eyes and dig the ingredients for breakfast out of the fridge.

I'm not much of a cook, but this morning, that'll change.

It's the least I can do to give them one more nice sendoff.

* * *

Nice sendoff?

Yeah, right.

Half an hour later, Miller's busy yanking the battery out of the smoke alarm while Shane holds open the back door, coughing. All so I can carry the pan, burnt beyond any future use, outside.

Miller put out the fire with baking soda before he got a chair to silence the smoke alarm.

When the kids first came down, they'd been somber, sad, carrying their luggage slowly to the garage like it weighed ten tons. Now, even though our eyes are burning from the smoke, we're all laughing at my disaster – with relief. And still sputtering a bit as we suck in fresh air while standing on the back deck.

"That was so cool!" Shane laughs. "I never saw bacon catch on fire before."

"Well, I've never seen Daddy leap over an island before," Lauren's face scrunches up like an elf. "He looked like a superhero!"

"Nah, Ninja Turtle!" Shane says, jumping off the deck.

"Then what was Gwen?" Lauren takes a big leap too, following her brother.

"Awesomesauce, that's all I know," Shane tells her. "Shame it's stinking up her place."

I was hardly awesomesauce – his words – but I guess I had swept Lauren off her feet and hauled her out of the kitchen when the flames began roaring.

"You sure you didn't get burned?" Miller asks me.

"Positive," I answer. "I just wanted the bacon to cook faster, so I really cranked up the heat."

"Bacon's not something you can hurry, Gingersnap," he says, grabbing both of my hands and flipping them over, searching for burns.

I spread my fingers wide, letting him look, before I say, "See? Everything's still in one piece."

He nods, face deadpan, and then pats his chest. "Good. I'm still not sure about the heart attack here."

My own heart nearly stops, until I comprehend he's

teasing. I give him my best teasing grin back, although I haven't used it often. "I took a CPR class once. Lucky you. I know what to do in a medical emergency...fire, not so much."

He laughs. "Like you know how to cook bacon?"

"I was improvising, okay? Can't help it if my usual breakfasts just involve yogurt and berries."

The glimmer in his eyes swells as he steps closer. "Improvising?"

My heart stops again, but this time only because it needs a second to shift gears. Right into flights-of-fancy mode.

Heat flushes through my system and I can barely breathe. Trying to hold it together, I nod.

"So would you improvise with CPR, too?"

Probably, because I've never actually used it, just took the classes years ago.

He leans in closer. "Like the mouth to mouth part?"

Holy hell.

His gaze shifts from my eyes to my lips and back again, this hungry glint that nearly causes another fire emergency here.

The idea of his lips touching mine? Unreal. Unbelievable. Unforgivable.

My mouth goes completely dry, though. My knees tremble, threatening to give out.

Yet, I can't peel my eyes off him. Off his face, his smile, his mouth. Off every *what-if* thudding in my pulse.

He smiles again. "Fuck. You're making me wish I *was* having a heart attack, Gwen."

I fight the urge to lean forward. It's only a matter of inches, and my lips will touch his, but I can't do it.

I can't.

But the next thing I know, I'm being pulled through the open patio door, into the house so quickly, I stumble to keep up with him. He wheels me around the island and into the kitchen before stopping.

"I shouldn't do this," he whispers.

We're face to face, mere inches apart, and all I can think about are those furious lips of his on mine.

"Screw it," he whispers. "You'll forgive me later."

I think ten things happen at once.

His lips touch mine.

His tongue twists, mine curls, and then all ten of my fingers and ten little toes scrunch up in pure, unadulterated bliss. *Oh. My. God.*

I taste him. Hints of coffee and mint toothpaste and, more importantly, Miller Rush.

It's delicious, raw, masculine, and heavenly.

It's so intense I forget to breathe, just oozing into him, his ragged stubble grazing my skin as he pulls me closer.

My knees nearly go out again. But this time it's the heat – *oh, hell, the heat!* – this raging, aching sweetness pooling between my thighs, sending lightning to my core every time his tongue chases mine and–

The kiss stops just as abruptly as it started. Those big blue eyes of his are narrow now, focused and on fire.

He reels me in closer, his big arms holding me tight. My chin rests perfectly on his shoulder.

That's never happened before with the few guys I've dated. I'm so tall, dancing with men is awkward, let alone hugging. Their heads are usually below mine, not close to being level, and never above.

It feels so good, so right, so natural I swear on everything I could just pitch a tent and camp out forever on Mount Miller Rush.

I'm bracing for him to kiss me again, wanting to give back as good as I get, when a familiar, annoying, and *totally* out of place voice sounds.

I jerk up in his arms, his fingers going tighter. We both listen.

No freaking way. It can't be?

"Gwendolyn!" Mother says again, calling so loud there's no mistaking it.

Crud.

We fly apart like someone just lit a firecracker between us. He spins toward the stove and I march to the living room, where Mother must've conveniently let herself in, now rounding the divider wall.

"What on earth?" She waves a hand in front of her face, her nose wrinkling. "It smells like burnt bacon in here." Giving me a look that includes a thoroughly *mom* head shake, she asks, "You weren't trying to cook it, were you?"

I huff out a heavy sigh. "No, Mother, I was trying to burn the place down so you could never rent it out again. Surprise!"

I don't even care about the embarrassment. I'm steamed that her ambush just ruined one of the hottest, most spontaneous moments of my life.

She cocks her head, her greying hair bobbing, and stares for a moment.

Something deep inside tells me she knows. There's no hiding anything from her freaky sixth sense. Bringing a boy home to do anything wasn't even possible in my teens for good reason.

She knows. Just *knows* that Miller and I were on the verge of making out only seconds ago, and now we're hosed.

"So glad Miller was here to save you," she says firmly, leaning to look around me to where he's wiping down the stove, "and this lovely townhouse."

I swallow the bitter lump in my throat. I can't even manage an annoyed nod.

"It wasn't that bad, May," he calls from the kitchen. "Just a little bacon grease. Got it under control and we're working on the cleanup."

Mother saunters to the table, where she can inspect the big pan with its full pound of charred bacon still wafting smoke outside on the glass table. "A *little* bacon grease? I've seen prettier mishaps on the Fourth of July."

The kids see her and come running inside. *Just great.*

The truth that it was more than a little bacon grease will definitely be out now, so I look toward the kitchen, but my feet don't want to move. If they do, I'll be close to Miller again.

Too close to the perfect man who's in the middle of trying to pack up, hit the road, and leave me forever.

As the kids start spouting stories about superheroes and Gwen the Firefighter, I decide Miller just might be the safer bet after all, and I force my feet to walk.

He has most of the baking soda wiped up. The grin he beams my way helps me regain a tiny bit of pride. Not to mention self-control.

We clean the kitchen while Mother shows the kids the brand-new gifts she'd brought this morning while she was "just out shopping."

A new set of young adult books for Lauren and a video game for Shane.

We busy ourselves making breakfast all over again, trying to ignore the latest drama. This time, it's Chef Miller cooking and me following his lead, whatever I can help with.

There's no more bacon, thank God, but Miller manages to whip up a platter full of French toast and a big pan of scrambled eggs. I slice up some strawberries and set a container of whipped cream, plus some syrup for the French toast, square on the table.

"Will you stay and eat with us, May?" Lauren asks my mother.

I hold my breath, glancing at Miller. It's a miracle neither of the kids have mentioned leaving yet.

"I wouldn't dare miss it, you sweet little thing," Mother says, walking over to shower more affection on the girl with kisses to the head.

He just shrugs.

I suppose it doesn't matter.

They'll be leaving right after breakfast, won't they?

My heart sinks clear to my toes again and stays there. I'll never know whatever strange, beautiful thing was about to happen before Mother barged in like a dragon breathing shame instead of fire. And maybe that's a good thing.

Someday, I'll get over it, I tell myself. *Someday.*

"Come get it while it's hot." Miller carries the platter of French toast to the table.

We all find a chair and sit down to eat. The food is incredible, the kids keep Mother occupied, but there's a heaviness growing in the room.

It's so intense by the end, I can barely swallow, and what I do manage to get down, curdles.

Even Mother seems unusually quiet, listening to the kids, and that only adds to my discomfort. Nothing gets past her. Never has.

So it surprises me when, as soon as she's done eating, she stands. "That was delicious, Miller, but I'm afraid I have to run. Call with my publicist. I just came by to look in on Gwendolyn. Let's meet again soon, as long as you're in town, hmm?"

Miller nods without saying a word.

Both Lauren and Shane turn more somber. The sadness in their eyes at Mother's words, at what she doesn't know, is enough to stab me right in the heart.

"I'll see you all later," she tells them cheerfully. Her gaze bypasses me, and she turns to Miller. "Say, Miller, would you be so kind as to walk me to my car?"

Uh-oh.

Whatever's coming, I knew it. I open my mouth to protest, to lie, but he just places a hand on my arm and squeezes.

"Gladly, May," he whispers, never taking his eyes off me.

I feel sick.

He stands, and as they head out together, my shoulders slump. I can't follow, not with Shane and Lauren watching me. Fresh hope shines in their eyes, as if Mother can wave a magic wand and change Miller's mind into staying here.

She can't. Nobody can. I know that, and I'm trying like mad to accept it.

It's difficult, but I try to catch the cheerful bug from Mother as we clean the kitchen together. Once that's done, since Miller still hasn't returned, and because I know the inevitable is coming, I give the kids each a couple grocery bags and say they'd better fill them with snacks.

It's only fair. Miller paid for it all after another recent grocery run to stock up, and I won't even eat half of it, so they might as well take it with them. I know I won't have a real appetite for some time.

He returns just as the kids are finishing up, and seeing the kitchen clean, he nods. "Come on, guys. Time for us to go," he says quietly.

The children don't even protest. They're too well behaved.

Lauren throws herself at me first, then Shane. I've never wanted to keep hugging anyone this bad.

Miller doesn't make a move, and I don't expect one. He's a smarter person.

I'm dragging my feet as I follow them into the garage and

hit the open button while they're climbing inside the Equinox.

"Thanks again. For everything, beautiful," he says, lingering with his hand on the driver's door for a second before he climbs inside.

I don't trust my voice to work, so I just nod.

My eyes are burning up and my heart's blazing down. This feels like it did all those years ago, when Toby's real owners drove away with him, but amped up on steroids guaranteed to cause one thing. *Heartbreak galore.*

Go ahead and laugh. Mock. Chastise.

Yes, it's foolish that I've gotten so close to all of them so quickly.

Yes, it's stupid that I kissed a man I've only known a week, who I'll probably never hear from again for many reasons.

Yes, it's reckless that I wish he'd stay, knowing the kind of risk it brings down on everyone.

But no amount of foolish or stupid or reckless changes what I feel. No shame changes what's ahead.

The instant he rolls down that driveway and disappears from view, there's nothing left for me but to swallow my agony and just *deal.*

Deal with it.

Miller starts the car and puts it in reverse. Shane and Lauren roll down their windows, giving me a final sad wave as the car backs away.

I wave back, even though I can hardly stand to watch. I've reached my limit for torture, so I turn around and walk to the door to the house.

I'll just wait. Close the garage door once they've backed out. Like the final curtain scene of a play.

Over. Done. The end.

The end of something that'll stay with me like the taste of poison for a long, long time.

That's the worst part. They'll be gone, half a world away, but never out of mind.

None of them.

When I think enough time has lapsed for them to be out of the driveway and too far down the street for me to see, I suck in a deep breath and turn.

Huh?

The car's still there. In the driveway. Not moving an inch.

I walk closer and see Miller's on the phone.

The look on his face turns my walk into a *run.*

VIII: HEART OF THE MATTER
(MILLER)

I've never heard this desperation in Keith's voice.

A goddamn *breach,* he calls it. No, it's so much worse than that.

They know where he's at. They've found him. And his safe harbor just became a minefield.

He's taken his family deep into the Ecuadorian forests, trying to shake the half a dozen or more lethal killers he's seen from the Mederva strike team swarming in. He hasn't slept in days. He's just been moving, recruiting help, diverting, hiding.

Eyes and ears are everywhere. He's paying out the wazoo for bodyguards, locals who'll get a princely sum if they manage to survive this. Lucky for Keith, he has more cash than I do to try to salvage a very fucking unlucky situation.

Even now, he's talking so fast I can't even catch it all.

"Miller, just listen! Don't...anywhere, goddammit. They'll...right after...and the kids. Stay put."

Worst part is, his phone keeps cutting in and out.

"Keith!" I snarl hoarsely, cupping my hand against my

cheek. I try to conceal it from the kids, how thoroughly fucking freaked I am, but I know it's no use.

They're as worried as me. Silent as the grave in the back seat. And yeah, I know, making grave analogies at all is bad juju.

"Keith? You there?"

"Yeah, yeah! This...stupid thing. Listen. Keep your ass where it's on...turf. Nothing's safe anymore. No roads. No hotels. No...airports. No one knows where you're...not unless you blow...cover. It's all been...compromised."

Shit.

It's not a total shock based on everything else he's said, but to hear that word? *Compromised.*

It's like a death sentence.

"Keith? Talk to me." Every word feels like ice shaking up my throat.

"We're safe for now. We just have to...moving. I'll call you again in—" he cuts out again.

"Call when? Keith?" I say when the line goes completely silent. "Keith!"

I have an ugly feeling he's not coming back. Then I look at my phone and see the call's been disconnected.

"Dad?" Shane starts in first, braver than Lauren. "Dad, are you—"

"Daddy, what's wrong?"

I can't think. I'm paralyzed. I ignore the questions coming from the back seat while slouching my head back against the headrest, waiting to see if he'll call back.

It's no use. The line's dead.

Fuck.

My insides are shaking, burning, adrenaline coursing through my system like venom.

This whole situation just went from bad to worse to *compromised.*

An almost military euphemism for *fucking fucked.*

I nearly jump right out of my skin when a pair of soft fingertips tap gingerly at my car window.

Gwen.

She doesn't say anything, but her eyes are full of questions. She's seen enough through the windows to know something's up.

Sighing, I drop the car into drive, roll down the window, and tell her, "Shut the garage door after I pull in."

She nods, running back into the garage, and I drive forward.

"Daddy, are we staying?" Lauren asks, her voice shaking. "Do we get to see Gwen longer?"

"Yeah, are we, Dad?" I've never heard Shane try so hard to sound tough, unfazed by this, but I know deep down he's more freaked than I am.

I have to head it off. I can't control what's happening to Keith, but I can damn sure let my kids know we're not in any imminent danger.

Not yet, a sick voice growls from the back of my mind. *Be careful.*

"Yeah, guys. Change of plans. We'll be here just a little while longer." That's all I can manage as I shift into park.

Their unsure, but undeniable smiles cause my guts to feel like I just chugged broken glass.

It isn't fair, dammit. I can't put Gwen in this kind of danger. But I can't risk ignoring Keith's warning either.

"It's okay. I'll carry in the bags, Dad." Shane says, opening his door, looking at me anxiously in the rear-view mirror.

"Later. Leave 'em in the car for now," I say. "You two go inside. Get some fresh air on the patio. I need to talk to Gwen."

Lauren lingers a little longer, her sweet little eyes staring at me through the glass. Quietly, secretly asking if it'll be okay.

Eyes locked, I nod.

I don't know how, not anymore, but I'm not letting this sickening terror infect my children.

Somehow, someway, I'll save them.

I'll be the father, the man, the hero they deserve.

"Go on now," I mouth to her, and she scampers inside.

* * *

I'M NOT sure what's worse: facing the kids or *her*.

Gwen stands beside the Equinox, staring at me with concern glistening in her huge, green eyes.

I wait till long after the kids are in the house and I've closed the door before climbing out of the small SUV. "We need to hang here for a few more hours. Sorry."

"A few hours?" She blinks and shrugs, her tall frame doing this seductive bounce I need right now like a hole in the head. "Take your time. Whatever you need, Miller."

I nod as the conversation I'd had with her mother circles around in my head. "I hate jerking you around. Something came up. I just...fuck, I need to figure out what to do."

Those heart-shaped lips curl into a worried line. "You know, maybe if I knew more, I could help. Two heads are better than one."

"Maybe." I shake my head. "But you already know too damn much, babe. Not gonna put you through more."

"I barely know anything, really."

"Which is still too much."

"Miller—"

No. Not now. Not ever.

I hold up a hand to stop her. More words can't help.

Then her little hand reaches for me and I grab her wrist.

It's hell keeping her away from my own body when I'd love nothing more than to slam her into the nearest wall, bury my lips on hers, fist that wild red mane, and *move* on her like the fucking wind.

But she seems to understand.

She pulls away, and I use the hand holding hers a second ago to scratch at my tingling scalp. None of this makes sense.

If Jackie's people found Keith in Ecuador, a foreign country he'd run to after doing everything he could to throw them off, then we missed something critical. All the plans of mice and men just crumbled. We'd been frantic, in a rush to save our own asses and our families, but we knew what we were doing.

We covered every base.

We thought we did.

But if they're hot on his tail on another continent, then it means one thing: we're sitting ducks here in Minnesota. Fuck.

I lurch around and slap a hand on the roof of the car so hard it zings through my bones. Caveman shit, I know, but this is too fucking *much.*

Gwen tries her luck again, laying a hand on my shoulder. This time, I can't fight her off.

"Miller...I'm going to head inside and see if they need anything. You're safe for now, I bet. We'll figure this out, whatever it takes. I'm here."

Sweet girl, no. I think to myself, grinding my teeth, but I can't find the words. *Don't talk that shit to me, or you might never talk yourself out of this.*

"Take some time and come inside when you're ready, okay? Miller?" She says my name so sweetly it takes everything in me to fight back the urge to sink my teeth into her lip.

I want to feel her so bad and I can't.

"Got it," I whisper, reaching up to stroke her fingers with mine. "I'll be in soon. Thanks for everything...again."

My insides are cold with dread, yet smoldering. Absolutely livid. And at the same time, Gingersnap's quiet, patient kindness fills me with a warmth I haven't felt in years. A peace that only comes from knowing someone cares enough, gets enough, to give space when needed, and the assurance that they'll be there, taking care of things, when you need them.

I know because it's something I've rarely experienced. Know how precious it is.

She pats my shoulder one more time, then leaves.

I slump forward as soon as the door to the house closes, leaving me alone.

I'm so fucking sick of living this hell. Of needing help. Of thinking I've found it, only to realize it was wrong with Manny, or not good enough to outsmart the monsters on the prowl.

It's hard enough. I've never needed help before. Not even when the twins were born.

I hardly slept for months then, looking after two newborns on my own, but they were mine, and I took care of them by myself.

That's what a father does. He comes to the rescue again, and again, and again. Forever.

What pisses me off is that I can't do it alone anymore. This isn't as simple as having Heather babysit while I was working. It couldn't be more different. I need help keeping them safe, make sure they *live* through this.

Goddamn. That hellish responsibility nearly guts me.

I turn slowly, staring at the garage wall without really looking at anything.

May, and what she said before I tried to leave, swirls in my mind. She's whip-sharp. Knows there's something going on with me, some kind of trouble, and swore she'd find out what.

She will, too, sooner or later. I feel it.

What then? Endanger Gwen's mother, too?

If she sticks her proud beak where it doesn't belong, even her high-profile status won't protect her. Mederva has many, many ways of making a bestselling author look like she expired from perfectly natural causes.

What the fuck do I do?

I rack my brain furiously, but can't come up with a single other soul I can contact. There's no one. And if there were, I wouldn't want to drag them into this either.

The desperation I'd heard in Keith's voice fills my mind. If they'd found him in Ecuador, they'll find us here, or in Ireland. The rot inside Mederva won't stop till all loose ends are severed. That queen of bitches, Jackie Wren, sure as hell won't.

I close my eyes, trying not to puke. Wishing, hoping, praying something comes to me.

I've never had time to slow down long enough to take a step back and *think* this through. Not since trouble found Keith and me.

Maybe that's the biggest problem.

* * *

Weeks Ago

"STAY LOW," I tell Keith as another cargo van backs into the loading dock.

We both know the authorization badges on our chest don't cover this lot. We'd killed two security cameras in order to sneak in, and we hope to hell to get back out and turn them on before anyone notices.

Keith won't shut up about what he accidentally saw in those coolers.

Right now he's a human grenade. His huge jaw is set, his gingery-red hair practically standing on end and ready to burst into flames.

He's convinced, but I'm not.

It's impossible. Nonsensical. Incomprehensible.

"Miller, that's them," he whispers. "Same kind of package I saw...just like what those fucks are hauling in."

The coolers may resemble a mad scientist's version of high-end camping coolers, but they're medical grade, and they cost an arm and a leg. Designed to withstand anything thrown at them, known for keeping ice solid and contents preserved for days if not weeks.

These are smaller ones, whole rows of them. Each can't hold much more than fifty to eighty pounds.

I keep count as a dozen get unloaded by the driver and a security guard. A thick envelope is exchanged then, and the driver, carrying it, climbs back in the van while the guard closes the overhead door and then follows the van to the locked gate.

Once the guard steps back inside the guard shack, punching in the code to open the gate again, it's time.

Waving a hand over my head, I signal for Keith to follow me. I'd scrounged up a set of building plans from the time when they'd added this section, and know another way in.

That is, if the blueprints weren't revised.

We keep low, out of the way of the cameras we couldn't hack. These are night vision, so there's no tell-tale sign of flashes when there's movement detected.

I hope like hell we pass, but I have a plan in place for that too, if we don't.

I've broken into the main security control program and will delete any footage taken retroactively, hopefully before anyone else has a chance to see it.

Between the warehouse and the back wall of the office building, I find the ladder. We both shoot up it to the roof, then slip down inside the warehouse.

It's pitch-black. We use our flashlights sparingly, cautiously approaching the area where the coolers are stacked neatly, waiting for the next leg of their journey.

Each one is labeled with orange biohazard stickers. CAUTION. EXPERIMENTAL TREATMENT DEVICES.

"My ass," Keith growls as he unhooks the rubber latches with one hand, pushing his wavy hair out of his eyes with the other. "Look."

I've never known him to lie, to be so wrong, but hope he is this time.

My heart jackhammers as I hold my breath, waiting for the lid to fully open.

It does with a pop, and I shine my flashlight into the cooler.

Then my stomach erupts. Pure wretched violence. Revulsion.

Fuck!

I can't puke here. I have to swallow, choke back my own bile.

"See? It's fucking sick," Keith snarls, gagging. "I looked this up on medical sites. Too small for adults. Not even from a fucking–"

"Shut it!" My voice is inhuman, almost thunder.

He looks at me sharply and closes the lid, pinching the locks back in place. We do the same thing with three more chests before I've seen more than I can stomach in this lifetime.

Every muscle I own twitches with rage.

Thoroughly nauseated, I finally ask him, "What the hell are these bastards doing here?"

"We're going to find out," Keith says, shaking his head. "And put a stop to it."

* * *

Present

"Miller?"

I turn, watching Gwen step into the garage and close the door behind her. Can't blame her for wondering. I've been out here too long, lost in my own head.

I shake my head, dispelling the last of the gut-wrenching flashback, and swallow more bile churned up at the memory.

"The kids?" I ask. "They sorted or what?"

"They're fine. Just resting and playing quietly with the new stuff Mother gave them." She frowns, moving closer, this tall, redheaded angel too good to be in the same room with the evil in my skull. "So, this is weird. Mother just called and said she wants to talk to you. I told her you were busy. But she wants you to call her, I guess. Right away."

Shit.

May really knows how to go straight for the balls.

"What's going on, Miller? I mean, really? Is this about her asking you to come out to the car right before you..." She stops. Swallows. Looks right through me with that wanting jade stare.

Somebody up there in heaven really loathes my ass. Or is it someone down below?

I don't want to answer, but there's no choice. Not anymore.

For her sake, I need to tell her more.

Shaking my head, I look her dead in the eye and speak. "Keith, my friend the kids mentioned, worked at the same place I did. In security, just a little higher up than me. Well, some grade A bastards much higher up than him had their hands in bad shit, Gwen. Illegal shit. Found out we'd seen more than we ever should and...long story short, we fled. He took off with his wife, his kids, just like me. I found out less than an hour ago he was ambushed in his new country. Nearly fucking killed. Him and his family got out of the worst alive, but—" My throat feels raw. I need a second.

"Are they okay?" she asks softly, her eyes searching mine.

I nod. "For now."

She goes a shade paler. "But you and Shane and Lauren? And...and me?"

"The airports aren't safe, babe. We can't fly to Ireland as planned anymore." I hold up a hand, hoping she'll believe me. "You aren't in danger. I swear, I believe with every bone in my body we're okay for now. The wrong eyes at the airports gave Keith away. No one followed us. Nobody knows where we went."

"But they will," she whispers, pressing a small, curled fist to her chest. "Eventually, they'll find you, Miller. Even here."

I shake my head, then nod. "Not gonna let that happen."

"What do these people want? What kind of information, what evidence do you *have?*" She chews her lip, still in agony. "Whatever it is, can't you just get rid of it?"

I'll never ditch what we saw. "It's too rotten. There's more to it than that. What I'm holding on to, along with Keith, might be the only evidence anybody ever has to stop this."

"Did you call the police? The FBI?"

If only it was that simple.

I smile bitterly. "The cops wouldn't know what to do, not with this shit. A cleanup crew sent by the company would be down their asses hushing it up before they ever got it into the right hands. As for the Feds, they...fuck. Let's just say they can't be trusted. Not when they depend on other people giving orders and signing their checks."

Her eyes get bigger. "I don't understand."

"You probably won't," I growl. "We couldn't just tell the authorities. Never an option. We needed to gather the means, the proof, rock-solid intel on the people behind this, so when it's exposed, those savages get more than a slap on the wrist. They get put away for good, and the shit going on ends."

"But *what* was going on?"

That part, I can't tell her. I won't. I've done enough damage, and I don't need to scar her for life on top of it.

Confusion fills her face, souring her sweetness. I search for a way to make her get it without blabbing more than I should. "The people behind it are above the law, Gwen. That's the important part."

"No one's above the law." She shakes her head fiercely. I think it's more for herself than me.

"Wish that were true, Gingersnap," I whisper. "If the world still worked that way, we'd all have ourselves a Merry Christmas."

She closes her eyes, thinking. Then opens them. "So what does Mother want to talk to you about? Will you at least tell me that?"

"Your ma's a smart cookie. Whoever baked her did a damn fine job. She knows there's something bothering me and it's not right when you never mentioned us before, me and the kids just showing up, staying here."

The seriousness on Gwen's face deepens tenfold. "That's my Mother. She's a sleuth. Loves her unsolved mysteries and research, I think, and obviously she's good at it. If there's anything to uncover, she'll find it. Won't stop until she does."

She presses a hand to her forehead. "I'll go call her now. Let me handle this."

I grasp her wrist as she tries to pull away. "No. I'll talk to her. You don't need to get more involved in this than you already are. And you damn sure don't need to cover my ass."

Truth is, I *can't* let her get more involved.

I refuse to let that happen.

Never should've kissed her earlier, either, which only poured gas on flames of confusion. Sure, I'd fought the desire, but not hard enough.

How can I blame May for digging into my history? I'm probably the biggest wrecking ball to ever bust into her daughter's life.

"What's her number?" I growl.

She shrugs. "I don't even know it by heart, but it's in my phone. I'll go get it."

I follow her inside, just wanting to get this shit over.

There's no getting around May anymore. Not with this unexpected extra stay in Minnesota.

I'll just have to figure out a way to throw her off course. Throw her a few bones so she doesn't keep chasing the red meat.

Once we're inside and Gwen dredges up the number, I call her and discover just how damnably persuasive May Courtney can be. Before hanging up, I've agreed we'll all be at her house for a barbecue by noon – barely a few hours from now.

Whatever happened to that 'call' with her publicist? I snort inwardly, knowing I could learn a thing or two from that woman about cover stories.

She's not shy about dropping hints either. Even now, I can't keep my mind off her curious little promise that I'll be *mighty glad* if I come and *real sorry* if I don't.

I'm sure she's not talking about the Tennessee style rub

on the ribs.

The kids are ecstatic to go, of course. Gwen and I, not so much.

A few hours go by like nothing, Gwen keeping busy tidying up the house while I brood in the living room. My laptop holds no answers, nothing new, and I close it as Gingersnap saunters in later.

The apprehension on her face mirrors mine. As Lauren and Shane rush upstairs to get whatever they think they'll need, I ask her, "Be real with me. How trustworthy is your ma to keep secrets?"

Shaking her head, she steps forward. "It's nothing you should worry over." Laying a hand on my arm, she squeezes and adds, "She's relentless when it comes to the truth. I watched her stick her nose in an active money laundering case with a billionaire once just to get ideas for her big romantic re-telling of Bonnie and Clyde. Word is, she helped crack the case, and the guy was in handcuffs before she even sent the manuscript off to her editor."

Shit. Just my luck.

My stomach clenches. I brush a wayward hunk of copper hair from the side of her face. "Just wish you weren't involved in this."

"I've told you a hundred times, it's fine."

Except it isn't.

Gwen looks at me, all wine-red hair and ivory skin and those eyes that light up like a lioness. She leans softly into my arm, teasing parts I can't even acknowledge right now.

My regret deepens. "We thought we had it all figured out. Figured a couple, a man and woman with two kids and mismatched family details in a database, wouldn't draw any attention at the airport when it came time for us to jet. I chose Ireland because no one runs away there."

And because Keith and I knew the farther away from each

other we kept ourselves, the better. That way if the unthinkable happens to one of us, the intel on Mederva, the proof, won't be lost forever.

A grin flashes across her face. "You're right about that, I guess. I can't say for sure, but it seems like everyone escapes to Canada or Mexico or some island. Hardly romantic places for a secret agent man in exile."

"Nah." I shake my head. "I'll have to come up with another place."

"Were the tickets already bought?"

"No. That was Manny's job. He'd planned to buy us tickets with something off. It was supposed to look like a last-minute change in family vacation plans. Arrive at the airport, talk to the ticket agent to make corrections, and fly the hell away."

"Okay, fine. So we'll find another place to fly away to."

I stare at her, needles pricking my skin.

She's not dense; she just doesn't *get it.*

There's no longer a *we* in this. Not one that includes her.

As if reading my mind, she nods. Then, as a thud sounds on the stairs – probably Shane trying to bound up them too fast – she leans forward and kisses my cheek. "We'll talk about it later. Sounds like it's time to go."

Spinning around, she walks to the bottom of the steps. "Ready, guys?"

The kids shout back that they are.

"We'll take my car again," she tells them.

"Here we come, Old Pearl!" Shane yells, running for the garage.

I've never had an innocent peck on the cheek affect me so much. My skin flares hot, sending a current through my entire system. I don't even know what the fuck to do with this, considering everything else going on, but my cock knows exactly what it'd like to do.

It's pure hell trying to keep my eyes off Gingersnap's lush, round ass as she bends over a chair to fetch her keys and purse.

"Ready?" she asks me. "Or were you looking for something else? Did I forget–"

Does this girl hear *herself?*

Clearly, she's oblivious to the darkness entering my brain while my eyes were glued to her ass five seconds ago. Somehow, that makes this urge to do the unthinkable even worse.

"No. Let's go." I pull my shit together and nod, then walk to the garage. "I'll drive this time, if you don't mind."

"Okay," she agrees.

Good thing too because right now, I need control.

Shane and Lauren chatter away with Gwen the entire drive, and May steps out of the huge front door as soon as we're through her gate, pulling up the long, rounding driveway.

"Hello, hello!" she shouts as the kids bound out of the car. "Are you little bees all ready for a barbecue and dip in the pool? It's a little cool today, but that's why God made heating pumps for us Minnesotans."

The kids run toward her as she walks down the curved steps to meet them.

"A pool?" Shane yells, laughing. "You have a pool here too?"

"I do. And my own indoor spa, but I can tell you're not the type who'd enjoy being basted in scented oil. Maybe when you're older, with the right gal." May turns, winking at me. "Didn't I mention the amenities here?"

"No way!" Lauren answers before she turns around and looks at me. "But...we didn't bring any swimsuits."

She's right, and there's nothing I can do about that.

"Let me handle it," May says. "I entertain guests often and always have a few spares hanging around for boys and girls of all ages." She gives each of the kids a quick hug before looking at Gwen. "Darling, show them to the changing house, will you? Miller and I need a little privacy, then we'll meet you at the pool."

"*Mother*," Gwen says sternly, her eyes flashing neon green. "Don't pressure him, whatever you're thinking."

"Oh, it won't be me doing the convincing, dearie."

I walk up and grasp Gwen's wrist. There's no need to shake my head or mouth more words. She knows what I'm trying to tell her.

I emphasize it by looking at Shane and Lauren. She glances toward them, and then back at me.

I've got this, babe.

Still, there's a struggle on her face. She's torn between pleasing the kids and just having a normal time here and, in her mind, protecting me from God only knows what with Mama Bear.

But I'm not the one who needs protection.

"Go," I whisper.

She shoots a parting glare at her mother before her lips form a sugary smile for the kids. "Right this way to the pool! You'll love it. One of the things that makes this place bearable for the half a year it's not a frozen tundra."

"I'm gonna dive and do laps!" Shane shouts. "Is there a diving board, Gwen? A water slide?"

"Are there really bathing suits?" Lauren wants to know.

Whatever Gwen answers is covered up by May, waiting not-so-patiently.

"This way, Miller." She whirls around and walks up the steps.

She's once again dressed in flowing layers today, this time pale greens. I follow as she enters the house and crosses the massive foyer.

We're heading for a huge room. She opens the left door of

a set of massive, curtained French doors and motions me in so she can close the door behind us.

I step inside and try not to bristle at the sight of a man standing there.

I don't know him, never seen him, but his mere presence tells me May found something on me, all right. Now she's acting on it.

"Miller Rush," she says as the door clicks shut behind me. "I'd like you to meet my friend, John Thomas Riggs."

He's short, but husky, with dark-black hair turning grey and wearing a western cut shirt, half unbuttoned to show off furry curls on his chest as well as several triple gold chains hanging around his neck. Looks older than me by a couple decades, but he's still fit as a whistle. His muscles still large and well-used.

"J.T., this is Miller Rush," May says. "Our new client."

Client? What the fuck?

He nods at me.

I remain stock-still, numb.

Nothing puts me at ease.

Neither does whatever arrangement May's trying to spring on me.

Hell, he could be one of Jackie's goons for all I know. An infiltrator protecting what her and Mederva are dealing in. But he doesn't look like one of the sleek, younger, hardass men Wren would find with most dirty mercenary agencies. They're all products of recent wars, not middle aged like this guy.

My mind goes to the kids, and I glance sharply at May.

I don't know her well, but she's not stupid. She wouldn't put my children or her daughter in danger. Eyeing her, I ask, "He's your guy?"

"Yes, sir." She moves to a white sofa flanked by two chairs

and plops down. "A very old and dear friend. Let's all have a seat, shall we?"

This is her office, I realize. Bookshelves fill an entire wall, and the others are covered with framed photos of more giant book covers and movie posters. It's a shrine to M.E. Court everywhere, except the wall that's covered with the huge rock fireplace centered between two huge floor-to-ceiling windows.

J.T. moves to a chair, and I step over to the other one, sitting across from him. It feels like some weird version of the Oval Office, sitting with the president.

"Miller," May says, clearing her throat. "Did you know that way back in the day, law enforcement couldn't arrest anyone on the Sabbath, but bounty hunters could?"

My spine tingles. I cock my head, nodding at J.T. "You're a bounty hunter?"

He gives a single, short nod.

"I believe the politically correct phrase nowadays is 'fugitive apprehensive specialist,'" May says. "Among other things, J.T. also owns one of the oldest P.I. firms in the state. He's an ex-Marine. Marine Corps, special forces, wasn't it, J.T.?"

"Yes, ma'am," J.T. answers with another single nod. "Vietnam. Sixty-eight and sixty-nine. FORECON up till the day they sent me home with a metal plate in my head."

Holy fuck. Force Reconnaissance. One of the toughest units in the war, embedded deep behind enemy lines. Their missions were so legendary we studied them even in my unit.

So much respect washes over me, I momentarily forget the danger this man could pose.

Men of his generation who fought that war, engaged in the battles they did, are bigger living badasses than most anyone today could ever dream of. Hell, FORECON guys could munch on Navy SEALs and Army Rangers for breakfast back in his day. They tangled with the best of the best

North Vietnamese units, commanded and equipped by their Soviet and Chinese advisors.

You know what? Screw caution.

I lean over and give his hand a fierce shake. "Pleasure to meet you. Thank you, J.T."

He knows what I mean, what I'm saying, and nods again.

"Same to you," he says, his eyes glowing a little brighter. "Different wars, but same mission."

"Yeah." My service was nothing compared to his hell, in my eyes, yet I nod in acknowledgment. Each time he's spoken, I've caught a bit more of his accent. It's not Minnesotan.

"What brought you up here?" I ask.

He grins, showing off several silver teeth. "A little gal from Minnesota caught my eye years ago, and I followed her home from Missouri. Good thing, too, 'cause she was plump full of babies and those babies have given us sixteen grand-kids so far."

Math alone tells me he must be close to seventy, if not a few years older. I'd have never guessed that. Not by looking at him.

May clears her throat, and we look at her. "I asked J.T. to join us today, Miller, because I needed a few answers after meeting you for the first time. He came through with those answers, just as I knew he would." She smiles at J.T. and gives him a respectful nod of her own. "Now, in the past, I've only picked his brain for my books. Being able to hire him for something more serious was a bit thrilling."

They're both looking at me now like I'm the main course at the dinner table.

Shit.

"Thrilling?" I echo her, wondering just how fucking cooked my goose is.

IX: THE DEEP END (GWEN)

I'm trying my best to be impressed by Lauren and Shane's swimming abilities, but I can't help but keep one eye on the house.

Mother *would* have to stick her nose in this. God forbid I have anything to do with a man without her having her own freaking private police report written.

The sad part is, it's not out of place here. If she finds the trouble Miller's in...there's no telling what she'll do. And that's the part that makes me wish I had somebody besides M.E. Court to call mom.

Actually, it's more than that. She won't stop even after she has an exact count of how many hairs are on his chin. Whenever she figures out he's in this witness protection thing, especially if it's his own design, it's over.

Everything involving Miller Rush is right up her dark, sleuthing alley. Fodder for future books to last a lifetime.

I cringe, knowing she probably started outlining it after meeting Miller for the first time.

There's no arguing the obvious. He's one hundred percent pure hero material.

Throw in his secretive background, two adorable kids, and some sinister mystery, and she's died and gone to writerly heaven. I guess that makes *two* of us, but my interest in this beast is hardly just professional.

Crap, by this time next year, everything that's happened since I met him, and more, could be a made-for-TV movie. Or making its way to the big screen. Her Hollywood connections are some of the very best.

I die a little inside. Just thinking of her going after more fortune and fame off this man's mystery, not to mention swiping my muse out from under me, all while she's *trashing* my love life?

None of her business.

No, I don't even care if the love life part feels like a huge, honking mistake. It's mine to make. Every bit of this, and besides being concerned for my well-being, she shouldn't be up in this at all.

It's bad enough when she's the main reason I've never had a real boyfriend.

The only guy I ever introduced to her before Miller freaked out and ran, scared he'd end up in one of her books. I worried too, based on her reaction to him, that she'd kill him off by chapter ten. Or maybe even in real life.

Ugh. There's a reason *that* didn't work out.

"Gwen, Gwen! Watch me do a somersault!" Shane shouts from where he's bouncing on the diving board.

"I'm watching, dude," I say, waving at him.

Part of me flinches as he springs off the board, wondering if he'll hit the end of it.

But he doesn't, and I clap my hands raw, even though his flip was more of a half twist than a somersault, and the splash that blasts water droplets in all directions says he hit belly first.

167

"Are you all right?" I ask once his head pops out of the water.

His smile tells me that's an affirmative. "Did you *see* that?"

"I saw, big guy. Nice ninja moves, maybe you could be a SEAL someday."

He grins. "That'd be cool. I'm gonna do it again."

"Wait!" I lift my feet out of the water and stand. "I'll meet you at the diving board." I walk around the pool as he swims to the edge so he can climb out. "Just want to make sure you're getting enough height to make a full somersault. You aren't standing close enough to the edge of the diving board."

He shakes the water out of his spiky hair and wipes his face with one hand. "Huh? What do you mean?"

I step onto the diving board. "Here, let me show you. I used to do this all the time in high school. See how my toes are right on the edge of the board?"

I wiggle them for effect. He nods.

Yes, it's been awhile, but this is like riding a bike. You never forget.

I count each time my toes touch the board, using each practice bounce to propel me higher into the air. Then, on the count of three, I spring up high and tuck myself into a ball, making a full circle in the air.

This is the part that's not as easy as it was at fifteen. I'm taller and older now.

But I stretch, hands pointing downward, and slice through the water flawlessly.

Their shouts are muffled by the water, alongside the clapping, but once my head emerges, I hear both Shane and Lauren clearly.

"Awesome, Gwen!" he shouts. "Why didn't you say you were part mermaid?"

"I've never seen anyone dive like that except on TV,"

Lauren chimes in from where she's floating on a blow-up chair in the shallow end. "You looked so graceful!"

"Do it again," Shane says, pumping his hands. "I wanna see everything."

Small victories, right? It's nice to be admired for something.

Smiling, I swim to the edge of the pool. "You try it first, Shane. You have to hug the edge of the board with your toes and shoot as high into the air as possible. I'm right here."

"Okay." He jumps up on the board, finding his footing a little more carefully. "Watch and see how I'm doing?"

"I'm watching." I point two fingers at my eyes, then at him.

Aaaand he flies.

Definitely an improvement this time, but he still does a belly flop.

"You're getting it," I say. "A few more tries and you'll have it down pat."

"Can you show me again?" he asks. "I'll pay more attention this time, honest."

"I want to see it, too," Lauren calls, sitting up in her float-chair and watching closer. "Please, Gwen."

"Sure." I use the ladder to climb out of the pool. "Just watch how I tuck into the somersault as soon as I leave the board. It's all fluid, one motion, like you're becoming the ball."

"Do two?" he begs. "Just two more!"

How can I say no?

"All right." I step onto the board and walk to the end. "Eyes on me. Ready?"

"Yeah!" Shane yips.

"Me too!" Lauren adds.

I give myself three harder bounces this time, giving more momentum to spring higher into the air, then tuck tighter and roll twice before straightening out to glide seamlessly into the water.

Their flurry of muffled shouts and clapping echoes again, but as my head emerges, I realize it's more than just Shane and Lauren congratulating me.

My cheeks ignite like an instant sunburn when I see Mother standing there, but she's not the reason I'm blushing.

It's him. Miller, right there at the edge of the pool with his eyes pinned on me.

"See? The girl's a natural. She's the real reason I had this pool put in," Mother tells him. "From the time she could walk, she loved to swim. Even won several awards on her high school team. If I didn't know any better, I'd swear she's part dolphin."

"I thought you said you didn't grow up in this house?" Miller says, his blue eyes aimed down at me. They catch the sun and shine just as bright, but I wonder...is it just the light or does he *like* what he sees?

My hands move self-consciously over my chest, wishing I could hide. But there's nowhere to run here.

So I swim to the edge of the pool instead, trying to pretend I'm not half naked in front of a man so tall and muscular and gorgeous it hurts. "Right. I didn't. It was public pools before. Mother bought this house a few years ago and made some additions."

"Because I *knew* it'd get you over here to use the pool." She glances at Miller. "Swimming is the one thing where her height is an advantage."

"Don't forget reaching the cupboards above the fridge," I say. That's the other thing she always points out.

Miller smiles, never taking his eyes off me. "Always a plus."

Goosebumps everywhere.

"Over there." Mother points toward the small changing

room attached to the house, but it looks like it's not because of the lattice and hanging plants. "You'll find some freshly laundered swimming trunks if you'd like to join in the fun."

"Yeah, Dad, come on in!" Shane shouts.

"Hurry up," Lauren squeaks. "So I can swim, too."

"You can swim now," I say, studying her timid expression. "Do you want some help with the diving board?"

She shakes her head vigorously. "No, I–"

"She's afraid," Shane says quietly. "Dad always lets her ride on his back. That's what we always did back home when he'd take us swimming."

"She doesn't know how to swim?" I ask him.

"She knows. We both took lessons, but she's still nervous."

I've heard of that before, but it's so foreign to me because water might be the one thing I've never been afraid of. I truly can't comprehend the revulsion. But that doesn't mean I don't try.

Swimming over to her, I duck down under the string line of small, glittery buoys that separates the deep end from the shallows. "I'll swim with you, Lauren."

She shakes her head, biting her lip. "No, thank you, I'll just...I want to wait for Daddy."

Fair.

Still, I want to help, so I ask her, "What scares you the most about the water?"

Her face scrunches up, and she shrugs. "I don't really know. It just scares me. Not being able to touch the floor, floating around...that's why I like the shallow end, where I can still touch something when I stand up."

"Then let's swim right here," I say with a smile. "We'll stay on the shallow side so you've got nothing to worry about. You can still practice your moves there. I'll be right beside you."

She glances around nervously. "You won't leave me?"

"No way! We'll swim from side to side, right here, where you can touch the floor anytime." I nod at the changing house. "I can even get you a life jacket, if you'd like?"

Something akin to fear flashes in her eyes. She grabs the sides of the floating chair tighter. "No, thanks. I don't want a life jacket."

"No worries. I've got you, all the time, I promise."

Mother sits down in one of the long lounge chairs nearby. "Gwen was a lifeguard for years, Lauren. Almost every summer. You're in very capable hands."

Nibbling on her bottom lip, Lauren looks at me. "You were?"

I nod and smile. Not wanting her to be forced into doing anything she doesn't want to, I add, "But you don't have to swim with us. You can stay right there enjoying the chair if you want."

"No, I want to swim, it just...it scares me."

"I'll be right here, honey," I whisper. "The whole time. Just me and you and Shane. And your Dad, if he decides to–" I look up and notice Miller's disappeared.

After another hesitant moment, she nods. "Well...okay."

I hold the chair as she slides off it.

Once she's standing, I push the chair over near the steps leading in and out of the pool. "Let's start slow by floating, getting used to the motion. The water can make your body as light as a beach ball if you'll let it."

She stares at me for a moment. Then her little head nods slowly.

"That's it! You just have to relax. You can float around as easily as that chair you were sitting on."

"Really?"

"I'll show you. Here, let me hold you up a little. Just lay back like you're on a bed, nice and flat. Lay your head on one of my hands and I'll put the other one under your legs so you know you won't sink. I won't let you, honey. Cross my heart."

She struggles to relax, but finally, with enough coaxing, her body goes limp in my arms. The water instantly supports her weight.

"See? Once you give in, the water helps you stay on top."

"Kinda nice." She nods slightly, a little confidence entering her eyes. "I remember this part from swimming lessons."

"Good." I start slow-walking through the pool with her, real gradually. "Just imagine yourself floating like the chair does, that's exactly what you're doing. You're just flesh instead of nice foamy, squishy stuff. I'm right here beside you." I keep talking softly to her, reminding her to relax, as I walk from one side of the shallow end to the other.

When I think she's ready for more, I ask, "What else do you remember from your lessons?"

"Hmm...I'm not sure." She blinks nervously.

"Let's try something then, okay? I'll help you roll over on your stomach. You'll just hold your breath and put your face in the water, but you'll keep floating just like you are now."

"But you'll still hold on to me, Gwen?"

"Wouldn't dream of letting go."

Satisfied, she rolls over and soon floats up on her stomach.

"Go ahead. Turn your face sideways and take a big breath of air," I say.

She gives me a sweet smile and does it perfectly.

"There, just keep doing that. Turn, breathe, turn." I pause, watching her. "Again. Turn, breathe, turn."

Once she's got a rhythm going, I loosen my hold ever-so-slightly. "Now, start kicking your feet. That's it. Good girl."

I guide her, turning around across the pool again before encouraging her to start paddling. That's when I notice

Miller, wearing a pair of red, white, and blue swim trunks, stepping into the pool.

Oh, wow.

I'm suddenly not sure who's more jittery – Lauren or me?

Very different reasons, obviously.

My toes curl against the bottom of the pool. He's all huge, rippled chest, bearish muscle covered with dark curls and several tattoos. Then I see how well those muscles move without a shirt, biceps and triceps and some man-ceps I'm pretty sure are new to me.

You remember the slow, sexy runs that would happen on *Baywatch?* Yeah, I thought it was cheesy too, but this...

Holy hell.

Smiling, he holds up a hand, waving. I stop walking beside Lauren and let her swim to him on her own. She kicks away, adding her own hand paddles, totally focused on her goal.

"Great job, baby," he says as her hands reach the sidewall.

She drops her feet into the water and spins upright again.

A twinge of guilt pinches my stomach. I'd promised not to leave her side. Too bad I'd gotten horribly distracted by big daddy and his chiseled abs. A manly washboard if there ever was one, made for *far* wickeder things than pressing clothes.

Frowning slightly, Lauren asks, "Hey, I swam over here all by myself?"

I nod, breaking into a grin. "Sorry, honey, I had an itch."

Feigning scratching my neck, I hope no one notices what kind of itch I really mean.

"Sure did, Lauren," Miller tells her. "We watched you do it all by yourself. Knew you could, me and Gwen both."

"Wow," Lauren whispers, this time more excited. "I did it! I really swam all by myself."

"You did amazing," I say, moving a little closer to them.

"Can I maybe try again?" Lauren asks.

"Anytime." Miller lays a reassuring hand on her shoulder. "Swim to Gwen, then back to me. You'll have it down in no time."

Lauren pushes off the floor, back into the position I taught her. I see her trying to count.

She does it perfectly, and again a few more times.

When she stops and drops her feet to the bottom of the pool next to her father, those little eyes are shining brighter than her wet skin glistening in the sunlight.

Shane starts clapping first, but the rest of us aren't far behind.

"I did it, Daddy. I can swim again!" She leaps up, splashing her hands in the water.

He pulls her in, wrapping her in a hug and lifting her out of the water.

Somewhere on the scale of ugly cry to adorable father-daughter moment, I know where this is.

Heat stings my eyes, watching how happy they both are.

I glance at Mother, finally, who's removed her sunglasses and looks on with a face that says she's touched. Even Shane is quiet, respectful, smiling at his dad and sister.

Miller lowers Lauren back to her feet. "Try it again. As many times as you want, Lauren."

"Okay!"

She glides onto her stomach without a shred of fear and swims to me, then flips around and swims back to Miller.

Shane swims over and stops in the water next to her. "Let me swim next to you, Lauren. We can do laps, and once you've got that down, races!"

I move out of the way, heading for the center of the pool so they have more room.

Soon, they're swimming back and forth between the walls of the shallow end.

Miller paddles over to me.

"Thanks for helping. She's been scared for a few years now. Didn't know if she'd ever get over it."

"Why?"

"I wasn't there, but one time, Heather took the kids to a pool. Guess Lauren was still in there when Shane and Heather's kids ran to change their clothes. While she was swimming to the edge, trying to catch up, a bigger kid jumped in and landed right on her. She went all the way to the bottom of the pool. He felt bad and pulled her out right away, but she's been afraid to even try it since."

"Poor thing!" I say, hands sliding down my cheeks. "God. That's plenty to scare anyone."

He nods. "I saw everything. The way you did that, had her float first, relax, and stayed by her side, was exactly what she needed." He reaches over and takes my hand, his grip strong and grateful. "Thanks. I mean it, Gwen."

The heat of his palm against mine, and the way he squeezes my hand, sends a rush flaring up my arm. The way he's looking at me so intensely makes my knees go weak.

Good thing we're in the pool. Where, supposedly, I should have plenty supporting my weight.

But I shift my feet nervously, and, suddenly, lose my footing.

I'd been standing next to the buoys, where the steep slope to the deep end starts. There's no saving me from going under, so I suck in air, hold it, and sink beneath the water.

I swim to the far end of the pool before resurfacing. Miller pops up next to me there.

Not wanting him to think I was trying to escape him *that* obviously, I say, "Sorry. Lost my footing back there."

He gives his head a shake exactly like Shane did earlier, spewing water droplets. "Funny how that happens."

There's that smile, Mr. Irresistible incarnate, making me wonder if I'll melt right into the pool.

We're both holding on to the edge, shoulder to shoulder, my fingers gripping it so tight my nails ache. I can't even begin to describe this sensation winding through my body, or the desire curling through my nerves like a lit fuse.

I can't stop staring at his lips, firm and full and smug, hooked on imagining him kissing me again. It's been a long time since I had a boyfriend. An even longer time since I've had sex.

But now? With him? I think I'd give up my right leg and still do it with a freaking cane.

"Dad, catch!" Shane shouts from nowhere.

Miller flips around just in time to catch the beach ball right before it would've smacked me in the head.

I try not to laugh too hard. Or wonder if it's what I need to stop thinking stuff I really, *really* shouldn't.

Miller tosses the ball in the air with a low growl and gives it a good punch like a volleyball, serving it right back to the other end of the pool.

"Sorry," he says, turning to me again.

"No harm, no foul." I dive into the water and surface near the buoys, waiting for the kids to send the ball my way.

Maybe it'll help distract me from this outrageous need to do the horizontal mambo with Miller right here in the pool.

Wish granted – well, one of them.

Soon, there's a game of beach ball volleyball happening between the four of us. It's fun, but the most rewarding part is watching Lauren chase after the ball through the water with comfort and ease. She's even laughing.

This time, my heart does a somersault.

The game ends when Mother calls us for lunch.

Barbecue, right. I'd totally forgotten.

She hands us towels as we climb out and says there's no

reason to get dressed because we'll eat outside, at the table past the far end of the pool.

That's when I remember what I'm wearing and blush. A skimpy pink two-piece, and now I don't even have the water to help me obscure anything in front of Miller.

I wait so I'm the last one out, and as I take the towel she holds out to me, I ask her, "What happened to the rest of my swimsuits?"

She feigns confusion. "Aren't they in the changing room?"

"Nope. This is the only one that was there." I wrap the towel around me, snug beneath my arms, and tuck in an edge to keep it that way. Playing in the water helped, but my insides are still on fire, thinking about sex.

Hot sex. Wet sex. Sweaty sex. Angry sex. Bitey sex.

Sex, sex, sex with Miller Rush and every dirty, seething inch of him.

Mother shrugs. "Maybe they're in the laundry. I had Gemma make sure everything was refreshed this morning, and she never misses anything. Hmm, what if your new *friend* hid them? Can't blame a man for tilting the odds in his favor, can we now?"

"Tilting–*Motherrrr.*" I doubt that very much. "This isn't a romance novel," I hiss.

For all I know, *she's* responsible for my amazing disappearing swimsuits.

"Never said it was, dear." She lets out a low whistle. "But you know, he certainly is hero-worthy. The *bad* kind. If only I was a decade younger..."

She holds up her hand in a tiger claw, making a cringe-worthy *rawr.*

"Gross. You're even not going there while I'm around!"

"I like this new side to you, Gwendolyn. Very territorial. It's refreshing." She grins and then speedwalks to catch up with Lauren and Shane, gushing over how well they swam before I can whine some more.

Much as I'd love to, I can't interrupt this.

Miller slows down and waits for me to catch up next to him. "Lauren hasn't spent that much time in the water in years. You worked a miracle with her."

"I'm glad I was able to help her."

"You've helped more than her today, I think," he says.

There's that look again. Blue-eyed burn and mystery and gratitude. And there goes my desire again.

I draw in a breath, trying for control, and focus on something else.

That's easy enough once I pick up on what he means. Mother. "So what did she want to *chat* about?"

"Tell you later. After lunch."

Goosebumps rise, peppering my arms. His entire expression changes as soon as it's out of my mouth. His eyes have dulled.

"Miller! What did she say? What's she up to? I'm dying here." A thousand crazy scenarios race through my mind.

One of them even includes her having a magic elixir to make herself a decade younger.

Damn. I really don't need the image that conjures up in my mind.

I already have enough illegal, very wrong brain-fodder with me and him locked together, alone in this pool, free to do whatever we–

"You were right," he says quietly, breaking my trance. "Your ma could outsmart Holmes and Watson. But later, babe. Promise."

My lungs tighten. *What does he mean?*

X: GET A ROOM (MILLER)

*T*he ribs are so tender, the meat falls off the bone and melts in my mouth.

The sauce is perfect too, sweet, yet spicy, a lot like Gwen herself. I'm trying to focus on all the nuances with the smorgasbord of dry rub and saucy meat she's got laid out. Hard to make it happen when I've got something a hundred times more appetizing laid out in front of me.

That little pink bikini she's wearing leaves nothing to the imagination. Nothing except how bad I want to take her in every position I can till my hip damn near snaps.

Walking out of the changing room, seeing her guide Lauren around the pool, took my breath away for a different reason. Yeah, I could get off on her eyes, her globe tits, her ass, her fiery hair, but this attraction isn't all raw, animal, and physical as much as I wish it was.

Gwen hits me somewhere I don't even want to go. In a matter of minutes she coaxed my little girl back into swimming.

It took me a long time to even get her back into the shallows again, and months more than that to convince her to hold on to me while I swam.

This woman has a way with the kids that's foreign to me.

Their faces light up every time she looks at them, smiles at them, teaches them something new.

I know that feeling. There's something about her, a glow that simply makes everything brighter and better. Inside and out.

She's genuine. Nothing fake about her.

All in all, she's one of those people that are too easy to like and too dangerous to love.

More reason to keep my guard up. Swimming lessons and swimsuits I'd love to tear right off her can't change facts. There's too damn much at stake.

Her mother knows it, no thanks to her P.I. buddy. May fully knows what her daughter's involved in now. She even admitted to hiring J.T. to dig up intel on me.

But there was another reason she brought him on board today for a bigger role – the help I'm lacking, saving my sorry ass and the kids.

Accepting that is hard to swallow. But I have to and hope like hell J.T. is as good as him and May say. Neither of them said much about Manny Stork, except that he's the best person in the state when it comes to fake IDs.

With Keith unreachable, J.T. seems like my only option. So for now, I've swallowed my pride, hoping like hell I haven't made yet another mistake.

He and May swear I haven't, but I'll need proof before believing anything.

I didn't reveal all my cards.

Just enough to warm up J.T.'s hound-dog senses. They were piqued, all right, and he said he'd be back in a few hours. I'll know then if I've made a mistake or not and will go from there.

My heart clenches as I look around the table.

At the kids laughing, eating, enjoying life.

Shit, I really can't afford more mistakes. Or more surprises like what Keith got himself into.

For their sake, I wish I'd never gotten involved in this, but when Keith told me what was in those coolers, and I saw it for myself...there was no other choice.

I couldn't turn a blind eye to Mederva's dirty laundry.

Sure, I'd seen plenty in Afghanistan. Gruesome, horrible things, but what I saw that night was an order of fucked up beyond any battlefield.

Pure nightmare fuel that has no place in this world.

My throat locks at the memories. I grab my glass of water, hoping it'll settle my stomach so I can try to enjoy this delicious food.

"More ribs, Miller?" May asks, already reaching across the table.

Swallowing hard, I shake my head. "No, thanks, they were great, but I'll burst if I overstuff on this grub."

No lie. The food was immaculate with perfectly cooked spices and sweetness and more sides than I could count, but my appetite's obliterated.

I wonder if I'll ever be able to get through a good meal again without being haunted.

"You really have a chef and maids, May?" Shane asks. "Do they live here with you? Like in the movies?"

"Yes, they do, my boy," May tells them. "They have their own private quarters, plenty of space and privacy to keep them cozy. A happy employee is a good one."

"Wow! You must be so rich," he replies.

"Shane." I give my son a warning look.

May smiles at him, and then shifts her gaze to me. "The boy's hardly wrong, Miller. I only hire the best, and I'm incredibly proud of it."

I know she's not just talking about housekeepers and her talented chef. She's straight up referring to J.T. The guy has a resume that doesn't quit.

After his time in Marine FORECON, he became a bodyguard for some of the most famous people in the States during the seventies, and then he'd studied martial arts in five different countries. He had proof of everything he said, except for the claim that his father died while driving a bootlegging truck for Al Capone.

He couldn't prove his reason for enlisting in the Marine Corps either. Supposedly he'd been caught stealing semis for a local mob boss in St. Louis when he was young, and a judge gave him a choice: join the service and shape up, or go to jail.

He didn't need proof for me to believe it. A large number of men were given that choice in those years, and most chose the military route for the better.

"I wanna be rich like an author when I grow up," Shane muses, blotting a smudge of barbecue off his chin. "This house, the lawn, the pool...May, you've got *everything.*"

She smiles her trademark grin at him, basking in the praise. But there's something else.

Almost like a hint of sadness? Regret?

"Hey, um, if there's still time...can we go swimming again?" Lauren asks shyly.

"Of course you can, dear." May says. "You can paddle around to your heart's content all afternoon."

Both Shane and Lauren look at me, and I nod.

Truly, May's house might be the safest place for them right now. And it could be a backup if my cover ever gets blown like Keith's.

She has a top-notch security system. Despite being a famous author, the location here is probably a well-kept secret known by very few. Celebs aren't idiots. They love their fans, but adore their privacy, and learn how to maintain a healthy balance.

That's how I've heard May describe it.

People and personals. A balanced diet, she says.

I want to remind her there's not a security strategy in existence that can't be breached, but if it ever happens to her, I know I'm the most likely reason.

Same for Gwen. If her daughter gets hurt, I'm the asshole, even if I'm a victim of fate.

My mind traces the inevitable what-ifs.

If only we'd taken a different route right from the start. Then neither Keith and I, nor our families, would be in the situation we are now.

We had to know more, though. That's why we tracked those coolers as they were packed in crates and shipped out to Galentron, another local bio-research company with a bad rap over their shady business deals. Like Mederva, they're flush with illicit ties to major politicians.

Not only local yokels and state legislators, but national ones.

Keith and I realized fast that calling the FBI, the CIA, even the local police, was out of the question. When things are this corrupt, turning Mederva in would end with us looking like the ones caught with our hands in the cookie jar.

That's why we both knew we had to leave before we could leak anything.

"You know, I'm in the mood for a good sit in the sun with an afternoon Mai Tai. I'll keep an eye out while the kids swim," May says with a yawn. "Gwen, show Miller where the hot tub is. The two of you can have a soak and let your food digest. Lord knows it does wonders for my acid levels."

The wide-eyed glare Gingersnap shoots at her mother makes me pinch back a grin.

Maybe May's a bit more accommodating than I think. I

also love how it makes Gwen squirm, knowing what her ma might be up to.

I nod. "Sounds good. Thanks for giving us a chance to relax."

I'm not going to bite, no matter how appealing the bait is, but I have nothing else to do while waiting for J.T. to return. Seeing Red's perfect body wearing nothing but that bikini for a little longer could be dangerous, but I've been in real danger for weeks now.

Red tucks her towel tighter beneath her arms as she stands. I rise and follow her around the large screened-in porch that the maid used while serving us.

* * *

IT'S A GORGEOUS PROPERTY.

On the other side, there's a large pergola with white curtains that hang all the way to the ground. We walk to the far side, where the curtains are pulled back, exposing the hot tub housed inside.

A bottle of beer and glass of wine are already sitting on the sides of the tub.

Okay. So this matchmaker shit might be a little twisted. But I'm not complaining, and neither is my raging hard-on if it gets me alone with this woman.

"Your ma really takes this hostess gig to the moon, doesn't she?" I ask, dropping my towel and sliding into the tub before she can see how hard I am.

"Among other things." Gwen sighs, rolling her eyes.

I lower myself into the swirling hot water and let out an exaggerated groan. It feels damn good, but more than that, I'm waiting for her to drop that towel.

I haven't been this attracted to a chick in eons.

Even though I know I won't act on it, not fully, I'm

enjoying the anticipation, the desire, the sense that anything could happen. It's also the distraction we need from worrying about Mederva and hitmen and whether or not we'll eventually crack under the stress of all this bull.

Slowly, she leans against the edge and drags one hand through the warm water.

"Aren't you getting in?" I ask.

"Dunno."

I cock my head. "Why not? Water's fine."

"Because I know what Mother's playing at. It's so embarrassing. I'm just surprised she went from doing everything she could to shoo boys away when I was younger, to playing matchmaker like this is some warped *Bachelor* episode."

I laugh. "Babe, I get it."

She frowns, studying me. "Then...why are you just going along with it? Isn't it kinda humiliating?"

"Because, despite what everyone thinks, we're adults. Fully capable of making our own decisions. Long as we've got our wits, you'd better believe I'm going to take a few minutes to enjoy the quiet, the drink, the hot tub, and hopefully, your company."

Her frown deepens, but she tilts her head.

I take a long pull off my beer. Another nice, cold Belgian brew. "How 'bout a story?"

"Story?" she blinks. "You mean–"

"Nah. Not more cloak and dagger shit. I'm talking about something lighter. So you can hear about the man I was before I got mixed up in bad vibes."

Slowly, she nods, coming closer and leaning on the edge of the tub.

"When I was in Afghanistan, twelve or so years ago, a decoy went out and got hit on a supply run. There was an abandoned truck full of contraband. Something that'd gotten caught in an ambush and had to be left behind a few weeks before. Smokes, snacks, socks." I shake my head, remembering how *priceless* new socks were to guys spending their days in remote arid deserts with assholes shooting at them.

"So, the enemy was smart, used the old truck as bait. Anyone going near it would get ambushed. We all knew that. They had trip lines and some shitty Russian mines they'd salvaged circling that truck, with snipers taking shifts in the hills. It was a deathtrap, but we plotted anyway, hoping to get to it. Every idea we came up with had its pitfalls, but our hankering for a smoke, a piece of beef jerky, clean socks was so strong, we couldn't let it go."

She climbs up on the edge of the tub a few feet away, engrossed now. "So what'd you do?"

I take another swallow of beer and set the bottle down. "Plotted some more at first."

Leaning closer, fully interested, the tucked edge of her towel slips. "And?"

"Keith and I stayed up half the night, coming up with a strategy that wouldn't fail."

She doesn't notice how the towel crumples, pooling around her waist.

Her firm, full breasts fill the triangles of material completely. Even her nipples are hardly covered.

I get a hint of darker skin that circles the little nubs pushing against the pink fabric.

Goddamn.

The idea of licking her tits, flicking my tongue against each nipple one at a time, makes my cock diamond. Bet she gets wetter than the pool with a man taking it nice and slow, gradually igniting her.

Can't say the same for myself.

I'd damn near explode to see my dick in her mouth, coming my brains out at that delicate red hair haloing every inch of me. I'm not small.

For a second, I have a flash of it, and wonder how far she'd get down my shaft before she–

"Well, what was the plan?" she asks, giving me a playful little shove.

"I'm getting there," I growl.

Hardly sure if I'm talking about the story.

I shift in place, giving my dick a tad more breathing room in my trunks. I'm playing with fire, yeah, but so what? It feels too good to stop.

Being a single dad hasn't given me much time for women, and the shit going on the last few months has completely overridden everything else.

Glancing up as I throb, the sun shines down between the wooden slats overhead, helping me remember my place. "When the sun comes up over there, it's so bright against the sand and rock, you see things that aren't there."

"Mirages?"

I nod. "And insight. Almost like visions."

Her mouth forms an O. She's equal parts enthralled and enthralling. I spread my legs.

If she looks into the water, she's sure to see the tent in my trunks.

A devilish part of me likes that idea. Reaching over, I pick up the glass of wine and hold it out to her, knowing she'll have to slip into the water to get it.

"So was that the magic bullet then? Insight?"

I'm shaking my head. "Yeah, but it wasn't just the landscape. It was thirst. When you're rationing your water and instant coffee, you start to get real thirsty for anything better. Some of the guys swore up and down there'd be a few bottles of Jack in the truck, too."

Pushing the towel away, it falls over the edge and onto the ground. I hold out the glass and she takes it.

Fuck.

The skimpy bikini bottom gives me a glimpse of her pussy's outline before she lowers herself into the water, sitting less than a foot away.

She takes a sip of wine before repeating, "Desperate times and desperate measures. Am I right?"

My hands physically ache to touch her, to stop these games and grab her, pull her close, feel the silkiness of her skin. So much for *control.*

It takes me a little while to get past that and remember what we'd been discussing.

"Insight," I say, inching closer to her, "is half desire and the rest inspiration. That's when you finally notice things you may not otherwise. Keith and I figured we'd be able to see where the sand hid the landmines, and we did. Demolition was one of our specialties, so we created a few small remote-controlled devices. Then that evening, while the sun was setting, we did it."

"What?" She's almost breathless. It comes out too much like a moan.

Ah, hell.

Her face is inches from mine, so caught up in the story I'm telling, she leans closer still.

I lower one hand beneath the water and plant it on the tub seat where the edge of it brushes against her thigh. "We made ourselves a diversion. Blew up our latrine."

"Oh, no." She starts laughing. "No way. Was it even near the truck?"

"No, and that was the point. One of our guys was hauling around a fifteen-pound bag of jellybeans sent by his sister. Guess she worked for a candymaker or something, almost a miracle they didn't melt in the Afghan heat, but they were bright with all the colors of the rainbow. Thousands of 'em. So we used the entire bag, filled up the latrine that evening and let it rip." I spread my fingers wide across her thigh. Another inch and one finger could slip beneath her bottom.

Gwen giggles.

"The latrine was on the other side of our base camp. It was almost dark by then, so while everyone was busy, especially the snipers, watching and probably laughing at the jellybeans flying in the air, Keith and I used our remote-controlled devices to set off enough mines for us to make it to the truck. The insurgents never knew what hit 'em. We came back heroes with cartons of cigarettes, bags of snacks, and a full box of socks before anyone knew it had happened."

"Miller!" She gently slaps my arm. "That's the moral of the story? You risked your *life* for cigarettes, snacks, and socks?"

"I've risked my life for better things, too." I lean closer. "And will again."

"Miller...I don't...is this a risk you really want to take?"

My lips brush hers. "Damn right, Gwendolyn, if it means having another taste of you."

Adrenaline hits my veins in a rush as I take her mouth, pressing my lips hard against hers. Her plush, pink mouth parts with my tongue, and I slide it in, pushing my fingers into her bikini bottom.

She twists, moaning, and loops her arms around me, spreading her long, fuck-worthy legs.

It's like heaven just opened its gates. She whimpers into my mouth as my hand finds her pussy folds.

My thumb rakes her clit, just brief enough to make her stiffen. Then I slide two fingers up in her, loving how tight and hot and wet she is for me.

Snarling, I pull out of the kiss, my ears burning as she whispers.

"We...we shouldn't do this."

"Bullshit." I twirl my finger inside her, finding her sweetness, making her body jerk against mine. "Tell me again. I'll stop if you want, but I think I know better."

She answers, running the tip of her tongue across my bottom lip. "I don't want to stop, but this isn't exactly private."

"There's a curtain, Gwen. The kids won't get out of that pool till they have to. And if anybody comes knocking, we'll see them coming."

I rub harder, loving how she bucks against my hand. Her pussy drenches my fingers. Even in this water, she's fucking soaked, and I can't stop thinking what it'd be like if I replaced my hand with something else.

She lowers a hand, runs it over my chest, and then down into the water right as I find her clit. "Okay, I just–oh! God, right *there.*"

"Fuck." A groan snags in the back of my throat when she gives it back, her little hand brushing the tent of my cock in my trunks.

Spreading her legs wider, she whispers, "I haven't done this in forever."

I shrug. "Good. You're wet enough to break both our dry spells."

She sucks her lip, doing terrible, terrible things to me.

Her eager hand slips inside my trunks and folds around my cock. I almost lose my rocks right there and shame myself forever.

Shit, it feels so good. Normally, it's easy holding my own with a woman, even redheads.

But none of them were this tall, this beautiful, this ready to be held down and mounted good and proper. I push her against the edge of the tub, moving between her legs, smothering her lips.

My teeth find her bottom lip and I suck. I bite. I show her

how much of a madman I can be, courtesy of one damnably fine Minnesota girl.

She kisses me harder, whimpering again, getting into it. Her pussy shifts against my cock.

Is it even dry humping if it's in the water?

Whatever it is, I want my trunks and her bottoms *gone* like yesterday.

"We shouldn't do it here. Not all the way but...there are other things." Her hand glides up and down my cock.

"You'd better tell me what you're thinking, Gingersnap. Clue me in."

She flushes hellfire red. "Oh, I mean..."

"Say it, babe. You want me to bring you off with my hands harder than you've ever been in your life? You want me to bury my face in your cunt? You want me to fuck your mouth, and you want to swallow every drop of come scalding my balls?"

Her eyelids flutter. She's speechless, breathless, but I haven't even got her really going yet.

Sliding another finger inside her, I frig her pussy faster, substituting what I'll do to her with my dick later. "Tell me, Gwen. Might just stop if you don't."

"I...I...." She lightly pinches the head of my dick, then looks at me with those wide, shimmering green eyes. "I like the way you think, Miller. And I think I want us both to come."

Just like that, I'm fucking gone.

Hearing this woman say it – *come* – is closer to a verbal command than I'd like to admit.

So I press down against the nub of her clit with my thumb.

I go to town.

I light her the hell up before I squirt off in her hand.

"Miller!" she gasps, arching into my hand, throwing her head back. "Oh, right there. *There.*"

Sex marks the spot.

I dip my head and shove her pink top aside, taking one tit in my mouth, sucking like my life depends on it.

She works my shaft faster, harder, pumping it with such rhythm I could come right now, but won't. I'm going to milk this as long as possible. I won't give it up till she does first.

Latching on to her other tit, I suck harder, loving how her pussy clenches my fingers and her hand pumps my cock, building a vicious O inside both of us like nothing else.

I feel the fire at the base of my spine, blazing hotter every time her hand glides up my balls to the swollen tip of my dick.

"Holy hell," she gasps, her hips working against my hand, adding her own friction to mine. "Miller, Miller! I'm going to–"

"Come for me, babe. That's what I want you to do," I growl, right before attacking her mouth with mine. My tongue plunges in, finds hers, and owns it.

She's close, breath drawn in, legs shaking. I can tell she's about to burst, but that doesn't stop her from working her sin on me.

The way she's jacking me off never slows, never misses, even when she arches against my hand and her whimper turns shrill, frantic.

I sense the second she's about to tear loose, and keep my mouth locked on hers, muffling her moan as her pussy convulses, turning to slick heat against my fingers.

I keep pressure on her clit, swirling my fingers inside her as her body stiffens.

My muscles harden, too.

It's coming on like lightning.

I hold it back, focusing on hers a little longer, working feverishly till her legs tremble and I know she's coming down off her O. Then, I give in, let myself erupt with a loud snarl.

So fucking good, I get fully lost in the pleasure.

It burns and gnaws and ruptures loose, fully encompassing me as she continues stroking till I'm fully spent. Till every last bit of my cock goes numb in her hand.

We both slink backward, up against the wall of the tub.

"Holy shit, that was intense," she whispers.

"Yeah."

No fooling.

And now I can't help but wonder what the hell I was thinking to let this happen.

XI: THE COST OF LEMONADE
(GWEN)

*W*ell, crap. What did I just do?

Had the best orgasmic high of my life for one thing. But the distant, contemplative look scrawled on Miller's face makes me worry it's a new low.

I leap to my feet, grab the railing, and race out of the hot tub. As I snatch my towel, shifting my swimsuit back into place, I mumble, "I'm going to check on Shane and Lauren. Be right back!"

I'm actually running away, but I can't tell him that.

Did I really just have sex in my mother's hot tub? Not full-blown sex-sex, obviously, but a form of sex.

Good sex. Great sex. Memorable sex. Sexy sex.

Sex with a loud, confusing, deliriously gorgeous beast-man I barely even know.

I nearly run around the screened-in porch, and as I approach the pool, I toss aside my towel and then dive in the water.

I swim the entire length of the pool, under the buoys, all the way to the shallow end.

Shane and Lauren are there. As soon as I surface, they ask

me to watch as they dive for the weighted rings they throw to the bottom of the pool.

I'm glad for the diversion, honestly. It's a whole lot easier to digest than that man and...whatever *that* was. After they collect them all, I offer to toss the rings again. Mother must've wandered off for a bit to take one of her evening walks shortly after I showed up.

Lauren stays in the shallows, but her comfort with the water has grown. Shane wants the rings tossed into the deeper side, so I find a spot near the buoys where I can toss rings for both of them, and I try to forget what just happened in the hot tub.

Like that's even possible.

I'll never forget *that*.

Ever.

I can't believe I'm standing here, in Mother's pool, tossing diving rings for Miller's kids, after what just happened with Miller himself. This can't be real. It's more like an M.E. Court novel, the part where Mother's characters do something terribly reckless but inevitable, right before the sky comes crashing down on their heads.

More to look forward to, I guess. The sex was certainly right out of a romance. *Freaking unbelievable.*

I came so hard I literally saw stars. It's never been like this.

I've had sex before with three different guys. Mother never held back teaching me about the birds and bees and the importance of a healthy sex life. It's the relationship part she had a bigger problem with, and that's what I've always lacked.

Like everything else, it scares me.

"Gwen, Amelia has some treats for the kids," Mother says, returning to the poolside.

Amelia, her maid, sets a platter on a nearby table. Various

desserts, including homemade coconut ice cream bars dipped in chocolate and coated with more coconut shavings, candied mango, and a pitcher of lemonade with carafes of milk and mineral water next to it.

"Come on, you two," I tell Shane and Lauren. "Snack time."

Shane instantly starts swimming to the side of the pool. "*More* food? I love this place! Are you the luckiest lady on earth or what, Gwen?"

I smile. It's hard not to seriously consider the answer to his question after the past hour.

But then, depending on the aftermath, my luck could change rapidly.

Lauren hands me a diving ring.

"I love it here, too. It's just nice all the time. No stupid worries." She smiles, but there's a hint of knowing sadness in her eyes. "I wish we could stay here forever."

My throat thickens. They will leave. Probably very soon.

I've known it from the beginning, but it hits harder now.

For her sake, I put on my best fake smile. "Well, right now, let's not worry about that and have some good stuff. Swimming always makes me feel starved."

Miller finally shows up shortly after we sit down on the loungers by Mother.

Much like I'd done, he dives in the deep end off the board, swimming the entire length of the pool in a slow, refreshing lap.

"Care for some dessert, Miller?" Mother asks as he emerges.

My heart jumps in my throat as he stands, and my mind goes back to the hot tub.

Heat braises my cheeks as his blue-eyed gaze meets mine, only growing as he grins.

Of all the things I'm afraid of, this should be king.

Miller freaking Rush and the squirmy, conflicted, impossible way he makes me feel. He was *made* to flash danger until my entire system short-circuits.

"Looks tasty," he says.

I grab a towel off the pile on the chair next to me and wrap it tight, desperate to hide how my body reacts to him all over again. Even at this distance.

His look sharpens as he waves at the changing house. "Think I'll get dressed first."

"Does that mean we have to quit swimming too?" Shane yells from the pool, his mouth full of ice cream.

"No, son," Miller tells him as he walks by. "Keep having fun till we leave."

Shane lets out a happy yelp and takes another huge exaggerated bite off his ice cream bar for effect.

Gotta love that kid.

"You know, I've been thinking about having a gazebo with gables and gold trim built out there," Mother says, pointing to a blank expanse of her backyard, covered with perfectly manicured green grass that eventually flows into a grove of oak trees. "White and gold, with a tiled floor to die for."

"Sounds pretty!" Lauren chirps.

"Oh, it will be," Mother replies. "That's the one thing this place has always lacked. Something more formal for outdoor parties and big events like weddings. It'd be perfect for that. I think I'll have Miller build it."

I tear my gaze off the changing house and look at her like she's lost her mind. "Miller isn't a carpenter, Mother."

"No, no, Daddy could build it!" Lauren throws back. "He built our house in Seattle almost by himself. Another guy helped run the wires, I think, but the walls, the roof, the sweet little finishes...that was all him."

Mother gives me a knowing grin, far too proud of her uncanny instincts.

I shake my head, shifting my gaze back to the changing house, waiting for Miller to emerge and hoping I'll have an excuse by then to make my escape.

Because that's what I need to do with this. *Run.*

Get as far away from him as I can so I can process.

Ah, but there it is.

That familiar, overwhelming fear I'm used to, rising up inside me as I stand.

"Where're you going, dear?" Mother asks, looking up from the book perched in her lap.

"Bathroom break," I say and head toward the house, even though there's a bathroom in the changing house. Once inside, I take a second to catch my breath and regain control over my own body.

I'm on total overload right now. This is just too much. I'm used to calm and cool with no surprises. Dull and safe.

Not a hulking, wound-up beast who can make every nerve sing soprano one second, and then flay me open with his razor-sharp blue eyes the next.

I head down the hallway and use the bathroom, taking my sweet time. When I finally muster up the nerve to go back out to the pool, Shane and Lauren are the only two there, flopped down in the chairs under a couple big umbrellas.

Shane sees me and jumps off the lounger as I walk across the warm cement.

"Dad said we couldn't go back in the water until you came back, and only if you're staying out here with us."

I scan the area, making sure I hadn't missed Miller or Mother. "Where did they go?"

"Inside. Been gone for a while now. Guess they had a lot to talk about." Shane bounces from foot to foot, casting an antsy glance at the pool. "But you're staying here, right? We can go back in the pool, can't we?"

I shouldn't feel so disappointed by Miller's absence.

But I do.

I'm also worried about what he and Mother have going on that they have to 'talk' again. I never did get an answer about the oh-so-secret discussions happening under my nose ever since we showed up here.

"No worries, I'm staying," I say. "Go ahead and get in the water."

"You'll swim with us, won't you, Gwen?" Lauren asks sweetly.

I agree, hoping it'll be a good distraction, and join them in the pool. We stay there until Miller finally returns.

I study him closely, but there's just...nothing. An impassable mask. The stone-cold look on his face doesn't give me any hint what he discussed with Mother, other than the fact that he's clearly not happy about something. *Uh-oh.*

"Guys, time to go," he tells the children. "Dry yourselves off and start getting ready, please."

Disappointment shows on their faces, but they don't argue or beg for more time in the water. I follow them into the changing house, making sure they shower off the chlorine before getting dressed, and then do the same myself.

Mother hugs us all goodbye before we head for the car. I cast a worried glance back at her, wishing *someone* would cough up the truth about what's really going on.

Miller climbs behind the wheel of my car, waiting not-so-patiently. I get in the passenger seat while the kids get settled in the back.

At least someone walks away happy. They chat about the fun they had on the whole ride home, while I watch the broody thunderhead on Miller's brow deepen with virtually every passing second.

God, what happened?

What did Mother do this time?

Once we're home, the kids, with their limitless energy, head outside to play by the golf course. Miller collects his laptop and takes it out on the deck, obviously hoping for privacy.

My mind swirls like a jet engine as I try to buckle down and focus on a few mundane household chores. Not so easy.

Everything that happened today feels more like a novel than real life. After I'm through vacuuming, I pull out my own laptop and transfer everything I'd written in my notebook into a new document.

I find a better distraction here. In no time, I'm buried deep in the story again.

The thing about writing both mystery and romance is, once you've got it down, the words can't fly off your fingertips fast enough. Intrigue comes easy because there's plenty to work with lately.

I use everything I know about Miller and let my imagination fill in the blanks.

Shane interrupts me a little while later when he asks if I have any lemons.

"I think there's enough on the counter for a pitcher," I say, closing my laptop cover.

"Just one pitcher?" he asks. "I wanna make it like May's lady did. That stuff was delicious!"

I laugh as I walk to the fridge to fetch him a gallon of water. "How thirsty are you, Shane?"

He grins and shrugs. "Nah, it's just...you'll see."

I hold up the bag that contains three big lemons. "There. Perfect for one nice, cool pitcher of lemonade. You know how to use the ice maker, right?"

"Yup. It takes three to make a whole pitcher, yeah?"

"You got it." I set the lemons on the counter. "I think the

secret to the good stuff is throwing the sugar in some water over a low boil so it fully dissolves. Should be something we can handle without any fires." I smile at him.

"And how many glasses is that?"

I cock my head, staring at him.

What gives with this sudden new interest he's developed in lemonade mechanics?

Then again, isn't this the way most ten-year-old boys are? All over the place after they've found something new and fun? *Thanks, Mother,* I think to myself.

"Let's see...I think that's plenty for the four of us. Unless you're really thirsty, you can have my glass. Just give me a sec to get the sugar out and we'll get started."

"Oh, no, that's okay," he says, shaking his head. "Never mind."

I pause. "You don't want any lemonade now?"

"Nope. Guess I just changed my mind. Sorry."

I open the fridge door again. "Well, okay. There's always bottled water in the fridge if you need something else."

"I'm not thirsty."

I glance at the clock and am a bit surprised at how late it's getting. Somehow, we've already been putzing around for hours. "Getting hungry?"

He shrugs again. "I can wait. We had a ton of food at May's and Dad's still busy on his computer."

Miller must've been out on the patio for a couple hours now. Lauren sits next to him on a lawn chair, quietly reading. I'm pretty sure Shane's remembering how I almost caught the place on fire this morning with my attempt at breakfast.

Was that really just this morning? So much has happened since then.

Giving my head a clearing shake, I ask, "Do you like pizza?"

"Who doesn't?"

"I'll order some for supper. What kind do you all like?"

"Pepperoni, and it's Lauren's favorite, too. Dad likes everything on his. Plenty of meat and veggies."

"Okay, two pizzas coming right up. One pepperoni and one supreme with some extras." I pick my phone up off the counter. "The pizza shop is just up the road, next to the convenience store, so it won't take long for them to get here."

"How long?" he asks.

Finding the place with a Google search, I say, "Half an hour, probably. We'll have piping hot pizza here in no time, or it'll be free. They still do that in this town." I show him my phone. "It says so right here. One of the perks of small town livin'."

He nods, but his gaze goes to the lemons again. "Oh, uh, I forgot to ask...how much are lemons, anyway?"

"The price varies by season, I think," I say, hitting the call icon. I point to the tag on the bag. "Those were six for four dollars. Cheap for organic in these parts."

The pizza place finally answers, and while I rattle off our order, Shane runs upstairs. He comes back down and walks out the patio door while I'm giving my card number to the pizza shop employee who'd taken my order.

After the call, I make a fresh pitcher of lemonade, which he obviously wanted but was playing coy with for some weird reason, and set it in the fridge to cool before our pizzas arrive.

Then I set plates, silverware, napkins, and glasses on the counter in case Miller wants to eat on the deck. I can't help but wonder if he's really that into whatever he's doing on his computer.

Serious business, maybe?

Or is he just trying to ignore me thanks to what happened this afternoon?

He probably regrets it.

For all I know, he hasn't given up on looking for someone else to help. Another fake wife.

There shouldn't be a pang of jealousy. But of course there is.

This morning he said they just needed to stay here for a few more hours.

Then Mother called. For him.

He said we'd talk about what they'd discussed later. My stomach bunches up wondering what the big secret is.

Maybe she found another place for them to go? Somewhere safer than here.

I couldn't even guess all the well-connected people she knows to save my life. By helping Miller, she probably thinks she's helping me like she's always done, taking the stress and the weight and worry off my shoulders.

Whenever I've been afraid to try something before, she's always been there with a solution.

Why would this time be any different? Only thing I can't figure out is why she decided to play matchmaker if the plan is to hand Miller a get-out-of-Gwen's-life free card.

I should be glad about it. Him and his tight-lipped scary business leaving. The kids moving on to happier times.

But I'm not any happier than I was this morning.

I snatch my phone off the counter, but the doorbell rings before I pull up my call log.

Miller shoots in through the patio door like some gladiator. "Expecting someone?"

"Yep." I drop my phone on the counter. "The pizza guy. I'll be sure to check his credentials," I tell him, sass in my tone.

Miller frowns at me.

I point to the clock as I walk to the door. "It's after eight. The kids must be hungry."

He storms past me and beats me to the front door, pulling

aside the curtain over the window at the side of the door to peek outside.

The aura surrounding him is so intense the hair on my arms stands up.

Apparently, joking about this doesn't take the edge off.

God. He really believes we could be ambushed here by someone uninvited, someone dangerous...and I keep running my mouth like it's nothing.

I actually feel a little bad.

"I-it's just the pizza man," I say, trying to downplay it, half-questioning whether that's true. I'm afraid of my own shadow and sure as hell don't need him making it worse.

Miller nods after looking out the window, satisfied, then steps back around the partition wall. "Pizza's here."

Huffing out a breath, which does little to calm my nerves, I open the door. After adding a tip, I sign the receipt and then take the two warm boxes from the gangly kid holding them. I try to be as pleasant as possible, hoping the delivery boy doesn't drown in the tension filling the air.

I shoulder the door shut and nearly jump out of my own skin when I spin around and see Miller standing there. Again, I slowly exhale, trying to soothe the anxiety.

His hands come out. "I'll take those."

Irritated by both myself and him, I step around him. "No. I have them just fine."

In the kitchen, Lauren stands near the table looking at us. I'm instantly annoyed by the look of apprehension on her face.

Awesome. He's making her nervous too with his big, silent, secretive guard dog act.

With a bright smile, I say, "I ordered pepperoni, honey! I hear that's your favorite."

She turns slowly, toward the patio door.

"Go tell your brother it's time to eat," Miller tells her. "I'll grab a knife to slice up any messy pieces."

Biting her bottom lip, she spins around, then shoots out the patio door.

Ugh.

The last thing I want to do is argue, but I saw how Lauren bolted. Miller sure is talented at pissing me off.

"Did you see that?" I drop the pizza boxes onto the counter. "She's afraid. You, acting like Charles Manson was ringing the doorbell, and then snapping at your daughter."

He runs a hand through his hair, flashing me a look. "I didn't snap at Lauren, babe."

"Yes, you did! And don't you *babe* me. Your tone was just like it is now. *Nasty.*" I flip open the boxes. "Didn't you see the look on her face? She was already nervous, the way we've been tiptoeing around here ever since we got home. Now, she's scared."

"Scared? Of me?" He shakes his head. "No. My kids have never been afraid of me, and never will be."

"Says who?" I pull a spatula out of the drawer and slam it shut.

"Their old man, Gwen. And I don't need you or anyone else trying to stick their fucking nose where it doesn't belong."

I toss the spatula on the counter, where it rolls to a stop. "Correction: you're the one who stuck *my* nose in this whole flipping mess by hiring me. Remember?"

"Like yesterday. Doesn't give you the right to say anything about my kids, no matter how damn gorgeous you are and how much you care about 'em."

Already on my way to the patio door to check on them, I say, "Miller. It's my house. I won't let anyone be scared or upset or just wound up while staying here." I step out the door. "No matter who they are. Not even *you.*"

Deep breath. I zoom away before he can throw more crap at me.

Weird.

Outside, I don't see Lauren or Shane, so I walk off the patio into the grass, scanning the area. My heart skips a beat when I don't see them anywhere.

Oh, no.

Oh, Jesus, no, no, no, no.

I don't even remember my legs moving. Suddenly I'm just running at full speed, rushing to the short wrought iron fence that butts up to the side of the house and separates the backyard from the road.

It's a tiny relief when I see Lauren's small silhouette on the other side of it, walking toward the road.

"Lauren, baby!" I shout, almost out of breath by the time I've reached the gate. "Wait up!"

As I open the gate, I hear Miller coming, hurdle-jumping the fence. "Where are you going? Where's Shane?"

We both stop at Lauren's side. That's when I know something terrible happened.

Tears roll down her plush little cheeks, red like the middle of a dartboard.

"Honey, what's wrong?" I ask, kneeling down next to her, clenching her shoulders.

"Where's your brother?" Miller demands. But he isn't angry anymore, his voice is too tight.

She shakes her head. "I don't know, Daddy. I don't..."

I can hardly stand to look at him. I've never seen anyone go completely pale, his face twisting like someone just stabbed him between the shoulder blades.

Miller looks up, scanning the horizon, his eyes hollow.

He sucks a deep breath and turns his faded eyes to me.

"When was the last time you saw him?" he asks.

Now, I feel the knife, too. It's a struggle to even speak, to hear him over the rushing sound of my pulse drumming in my ears.

I shake my head. "Half an hour ago, maybe. Around the time I ordered pizza. He was asking about lemonade, so...so I made him some and ordered pizza for supper. He went upstairs and then ran back outside. I thought he was with you but..."

He scans the area, then kneels down in front of Lauren. "Listen, baby girl. Do you know where he is? Any idea at all?"

She shakes her head, another sob tearing free from her lungs. "No, no, Daddy. I just don't...I can't..."

Miller clenches his jaw so hard I see his temples bulge. He tears his gaze away from her.

Trying to figure out where Shane could've gone, I ask Lauren, "Did he go hunting for more golf balls? Go to the clubhouse to sell them, maybe?"

She shakes her head furiously.

"Lauren," Miller says. "You have to tell me what you know. Exactly what you remember."

It's clear he's trying to hold in a temper, a fear, a fury the entire world should fear.

If anyone took Shane, they're dead.

No question.

"H-he said he had a plan for us," she answers, more tears falling from her eyes. "One that would make it so...so we wouldn't have to leave here. That's what he told me, Daddy."

Miller turns his head slowly so she won't see the curse he mouths. *Fuck.*

It's like his inner agony takes over his face, this silent poison oozing out of him. I close my eyes, blinking back tears.

"Wh-hat kind of plan?" I stammer, still desperate to help, wrapping an arm around her trembling shoulders.

"For making money. He said if we made enough, we

could just give it to the bad guys so they'd stop chasing us," Lauren says, her sad eyes huge in the moonlight. "So then we wouldn't have to leave. We could just stay here with you and Daddy and May."

"Bad guys? Oh, honey, no. Don't ever worry about them. We've got you."

Do we? My stomach spasms as I fold her into a hug, glaring at Miller.

His expression looks like pure anger and shock had a bastard lovechild.

I hate how I can't think of anything better to comfort her. But my very presence seems to help.

I want to say children don't have to be told. Some things they can figure out on their own. And as mad as I am, I'm also scared for Shane, for Lauren, for Miller, for myself.

Whatever this is, it's horrifying to see a grown man with a heart of steel scared for his son's life.

I can tell that's what's going on behind his thousand-yard stare, and frankly, it scares the crap out of me.

Until now, I hadn't thought something like this would happen. A sudden threat, a kidnapping.

There's no question Miller loves his kids. For him to have involved them in something, in this, it has to be bad. *Really freaking bad.*

"We have to find Shane," he growls finally, turning. "Have to go *now.*"

He gets a head start, then we run to the front door behind him, into the house, and then into the garage. I usher a sobbing Lauren into the back seat while Miller climbs in Pearl's driver's side and starts the car. He doesn't ask permission, and I don't care.

He just shifts into reverse the instant the garage door opens, but he doesn't back out. For a second, his eyes are glued to the rear-view mirror, brow furrowed.

I'm afraid to even look. I can't hear what he's saying as he looks at me, my heart beating so fast I swear I'm about to pass right out.

But he moves like lightning, slams the car into park, and throws open the door.

Miller surges out of the car and runs.

XII: TRUTH OR DARE (MILLER)

The emotions tearing through me as I see Shane running up the street with plastic bags swinging in each hand are so conflicted, I have no fucking clue which one to act on.

I've never been so thankful to see my son in my life. At the same time, I've never been so pissed at his behavior. And I've never been as scared shitless as I was thirty seconds ago.

Thinking I'd never see him again nearly brought me crashing to my knees.

Nearly fucking *broke me.*

I race out of the garage and meet Shane in the road. My first reaction is to grab him, hug him, press him to my chest so hard I might not ever let go.

But eventually, I do. Thanking every god and power in this universe he's safe, he's alive, and I've got a second chance to keep him in one piece.

Then I set my boy back on the ground and tell myself to stay calm. To listen. "Where have you been?"

He bites down on his bottom lip. He knows he's done wrong before he even sees the look in my eyes.

"Shane." Still fighting to contain everything bleeding out of me, I say, "Don't lie to me, son."

"I just...I wanted to buy some lemons," he says quietly, scraping his shoe on the ground. "I'm sorry, Dad."

I grind my back teeth together. "Lemons?"

He nods slowly. "Yeah. At that gas station mini-mart place up the street."

My eyes go to the bright-yellow citrus swinging in his hand. He's got a whole big bunch of them, probably twenty or thirty bucks worth of lemons in two bags.

"Why?"

A soft hand falls on my shoulder.

Gwen kneels down beside me and gives Shane a quick hug before saying, "The pizza's getting cold, guys. We'd better go inside and talk."

Pizza? Who the fuck cares if it's cold?

I could've lost my son over a goddamn lemon run.

My mind snaps then. It's not about pizza, I realize.

It's about where we are.

She's too smart. From what J.T. said, our location might be compromised. Gwen figured out why I was so on edge even before Shane vanished.

I just move. Pick up my son, lemons and all, and though I haven't carried him in ages, bring him into the garage.

Gingersnap hits the button to close the garage door, and then we all walk into the house. Lauren is there, waiting in the kitchen, face in her hands, crying.

I've never regretted this shit with Mederva more than I do now.

Seeing my kids like this guts me.

I set Shane down and keep an arm around him, pulling my daughter into a hug.

These two are life.

If anything ever happens to them, if anything gets them

due to me, I'll – my throat constricts. I close my eyes against the painful, broken glass sting in my eyes.

"Miller...why don't we all sit down while the pizza warms up?" Gwen whispers.

I release the kids.

Again, she's right.

It's time to act normal. Not scar them more with my relief.

She takes the bags from Shane. "Oof, they're heavy! This is a *ton* of lemons."

Shane nods.

Laying a hand on each of their backs, I guide them to the table.

"How much did you spend on these?" Gwen asks, hauling the huge bags to the counter.

"Thirty-one bucks plus tax," Shane says meekly, plopping down in his usual chair.

"From the money you both made finding golf balls?" Gwen puts her hands on her hips, adorably confused.

Shane nods first. Lauren joins him, bowing her head shyly when Gwen looks at her.

Then it's my turn. I get her green eyes, conflicted and staring, wondering if I have any clue what this means.

I'm as lost as her. Sitting next to Shane, I finally ask, "Why so many lemons? What in the world were you planning to do?"

"Make lemonade and sell it to the golfers," Shane says, his voice small, unsure. "If I sold them drinks for a buck or two a glass, that way I'd be making plenty. And if they bought it and told their friends I had the best lemonade ever...maybe it'd all spread by word of mouth. Maybe I'd make so much we wouldn't have to worry anymore."

He certainly put thought into this. That makes part of me

proud. It also makes me worry what the hell got in his head to make him do it in the first place.

"Son, if you're worried about our cash running out, we're good. I told you before we left home, I've got plenty. Enough to start over."

"What makes you think golfers would buy lemonade?" Gwen asks him.

Shane looks up at her, then at me. "Well...I saw this girl in a golf cart sell them cans of pop, so I figured they must get thirsty out there playing golf. Especially with hotter weather coming and all."

I want to tell him most of those golfers were probably buying beer, not pop, but instead ask him, "What's got you so interested in making money? I told you, we're okay financially."

He cringes slightly and looks at Lauren.

She shrugs, then nods, her eyes saying *tell them.*

I've seen them do that often, communicate without speaking, especially when they were little.

Shane dips his head, staring at the table. "Max told us before we left...he said bad guys hurt Keith, and that's why they were leaving town. When we left, we figured they were after us, too."

Shit.

I should've known they knew more than I ever let on. They're growing up too fast and they've got damn good instincts.

From the time we left, they'd been angels, agreeable to almost everything. It truly went beyond good behavior. Now I see why.

Even when I told them we were meeting a woman who was going to pretend to be their mother so we could fly overseas, they never questioned it. Just went with the flow.

"Dad, everybody *knows* the only thing bad guys ever really

want is money. So we just figured if we could make a bunch of it, we could pay them off, and they'd leave us alone. Then we could stay here. With Gwen."

Children's minds certainly aren't simple.

They're complex. Too complicated for their own parents sometimes.

"That's not a bad plan for making money," Gwen says softly, "except for one very important thing." She kneels down between Lauren and Shane. "Leaving, without telling anyone where you're going, should never be part of any plan. You scared us, guys."

"I...I'm sorry. I thought I'd be back before anybody noticed, before the pizza arrived." He lets out a frustrated sigh. "I would've been, too, but it took me several trips to carry all the lemons to the counter. I couldn't find a basket."

"Tell you what, Shane." I fold my arms, trying to soften my gaze. "I'll let you decide like usual what you think should happen."

"I know, Dad. I know."

Since early on, whenever they've done something bad, I let them decide their punishment. It helps instill responsibility, fairness, self-reflection.

"You think about it while we eat pizza." Gwen might think that's a cop-out on my part, but it's not. I consider not glancing at her, but I can't help it.

She merely smiles her caring, sexy-as-hell grin, then saunters into the kitchen.

A sense of normalcy finally returns as we eat pizza and drink lemonade. Then, without being asked, the children clear the table and load the dishwasher. Slowly, but surely trying to make up for what happened.

"We're going to bed now, Dad," Shane tells me. "Can we talk more about this in the morning?"

I nod, holding open my arms. They each give me a hug

goodnight. The love I have for these two fills me so completely, I feel it in my bones.

Nothing in this world will ever snuff out that flame, no matter how bad it gets.

For them, for Gwen, for myself, I'll be their man, their protector, and their rock.

* * *

MY EYES never leave them as they walk over to the counter, giving Gwen a hug for good measure, before they head upstairs. The bags of lemons are still sitting there.

"Can't believe a damn gas station had so many lemons on hand," I growl, shaking my head.

"Cocktails, Miller. It's a little mart connected to a liquor store," Gwen says. "My guess is, lemons and limes are probably close to the only fruit they stock."

I nod. "You're probably right." Then, because I owe it to her, I say, "Thanks for keeping your wits while mine went to shit. You were real calm, Gingersnap, and we needed it."

She lets out an exaggerated laugh. "Calm? Is that how you saw me? Because, um, calm was the last thing on my mind. I thought they'd been *taken*."

I hate how brutal that word sounds coming out of her mouth.

"Could've fooled me," I whisper. "We got lucky."

She picks up the lemons and carries a few to the fridge. "Yeah. I was faking it, keeping it together for their sake. And yours. But I guess I get it now...why you were creeping around the house, ready to tackle the pizza guy if he was someone else. It's like being hunted."

She isn't wrong. And until all this ends, until I make it go away, there's only so much I can do.

It's bad enough the kids are freaked over the assholes

tracking us. This is the first time I've heard Gingersnap truly scared, and that makes this primal roar build in my blood like rolling thunder.

I need a distraction.

For some inexplicable reason, I want to ask her if she was faking it in the hot tub back at her ma's today. Even if I already know the answer.

Nobody comes that sweet for me without meaning it. I never had a woman go off with so many fireworks, pussy hot and slick as cream, whimpering against my tongue when we both came fire.

With everything else so fucked up in my life lately, that little moment counted.

Hell, I don't even know how to explain it.

Not just sex. Not just pleasure.

Something raw, something real, something totally her.

It was like I had a real partner. Someone I could interface with on a different level than I can with the kids or anybody like Keith.

I haven't had a woman to make me feel shitty over or feel shit *for* in over a decade.

Haven't ever had one who makes me this crazy, wishing I could unravel her even now.

"Were you faking, too?" She opens the cupboard door above the fridge and pulls out a bottle of vodka and a drink shaker. "I saw the worry, but you were focused. In control."

"I was damn scared," I admit. No sense in hiding it. "Thought my worst nightmare came true. I don't even want the kids to sleep alone tonight, but fuck."

"Rightfully so." She squeezes the juice from two lemons into the shaker, dumps in a good amount of vodka, then water, sugar, and a handful of ice.

After shaking the metal container, she pours the mixture into two martini glasses.

"Here you go." She hands one to me. "We both need this."

The drink isn't just refreshing, she's dead right about needing it.

A swallow of booze could do wonders to take the edge off my still burning nerves. Neither of us speak till we've downed our drinks, given over to biting lemon and numbing vodka.

Gwen shakes up another batch after refilling our glasses, looks at me, and says, "Let's go outside. We need to talk."

No denying that.

So I walk to the patio door and hold it open for her to step out first.

She sits down on a chair. "This is Minnesota, in the summer, Miller. That means we've got about half an hour at best before the mosquitoes drive us back inside. So start talking fast." She takes a long sip off her martini.

"Where the fuck do I even begin?" I growl, taking half my drink in one swallow.

"How about who's after you? What do they want? We'll get to Mother after that."

I don't want to tell her. Not because she doesn't deserve to know, she's earned the truth several times over.

Honestly, it's because I've never had to describe what I saw in those coolers back at the Mederva shipping center. I never wanted to touch it again unless it was in front of a judge or someone we could trust a hundred percent to make things right.

Right on cue, a little vampire bastard lands on my arm. I smack the mosquito into the stone age before it draws a drop of blood.

"See? Thing about this place is, that pond next to the golf course. It gets to be a breeding ground for them into summer, Miller, and when dusk hits...they're out in force.

That little nibble you just had will be nothing compared to the swarm in twenty minutes or so. Let's hear it."

Sighing, I set down my drink, staring into the night. "You remember before, right after we met, when I said the place we worked for was dealing with some real bad merchandise? That's what Keith and I discovered. That's why shit hit the fan. They want to shut us up."

"Details, Miller. What *merchandise?*"

I turn around, my lip curled, shaking my head. "Believe me, babe, you don't want the details. Not if you want to keep from puking up your drink."

"Probably not, but it's kinda important so...don't mince words. Just tell me, Miller. *Please.*"

My eyes go to the dusky sky again, the night creeping in. There's this blanket of darkness that suddenly feels downright suffocating.

Taking a deep breath, my balls crawl upward as I try to find the words. "It was body parts."

"Body parts? What kind of parts do you mean?"

"Human, Gwen."

"Well, yeah, I figured that much. That's terrible, but...what were they? You mean organs? Hearts. Lungs. Kidneys? The kind you'd store for transplants?"

"Transplants. Research. You fucking name it." My throat swells shut with rage before I form a fist, regaining control. "Every part there is."

"Every part? That's not even possible, I think. I'm no doctor but–"

"It fucking is. They were selling parts of *children,* Gwen. I saw toddlers dismembered with my own eyes, and not ones who'd died from natural causes."

Gwen slaps a hand over her mouth and doubles over the second I turn.

Keith confirmed the worst from the records.

Somehow, they'd murdered these kids and put them on ice, then flown them in for every sick fucking prick who wanted to get their hands on the remains.

The real vampires out here aren't the damn mosquitoes.

They're the demons among us who bend the knee to the almighty dollar, sacrificing these poor kids to the highest bidder. Whatever shark-infested bio-research firm wants to pay good money and turn a blind eye to where they source their specimens.

Even now, it gets me madder than a warhead.

I have to dig my fists into my sides, physically fighting the urge to pick up my chair and hurl it into the night.

A second later, I'm at her side, grabbing her arm, knowing full well the horror, the revulsion erupting inside her.

The flashes of what I saw are still in my mind, and I hope that by talking about it, I can keep them from overwhelming me. "I saw them myself. Little coffins stuffed with ice. Some kids whole, and some in pieces."

"Oh, my God, Miller. *Oh my God!*"

I want to rip her up into my arms. But I know if I move her too fast, she truly might get sick.

"They're being sent all over the map. Some for private buyers here at home, willing to do anything to get organs for their own kids. Mostly, though, they're being sold to a company helping supply research facilities with specimens for experimental treatments. Drugs. Any old thing involving young, healthy tissue."

"God!" she whispers again, pressing a hand to her forehead. "I...I heard something about that in the news a while ago. The black market organ trade, but Jesus, *kids?*"

"It's true," I growl. "And it gets worse."

"Worse? How?"

There's no simple way to summarize all the shit we

found, and why we couldn't go straight to the Feds. So I run a hand through my hair, trying to break it down.

"Ultimately," I say, trying to find a way to explain a cluster of a situation. "A lot of these places get government grants. They're Frankenstein public-private entities, with plenty of bigshots who lost their moral compasses a long time ago leeching the benefits. Whenever a new drug gets perfected and sold, the kickbacks to the insiders tally in the billions. Lucrative as hell for anyone in the know – especially the ones helping fund it."

She frowns, but I see the wheels turning in her head. "You're saying...it's the government behind it?"

I nod. "Parts of it, at least. Specific senators and Congress-shits and insiders with fancy titles behind their names. Assholes who help it along, reap the rewards, and then hush it up."

"But haven't there been crackdowns? Investigations? I swear I saw a documentary about this once and–"

"Babe, no. There're too many soulless players getting rich. There's never been a widescale, national sweep of the organ trade, and plenty of loose oversights at these facilities. Anybody who'd want to stop this shit in its tracks doesn't even know it's going down."

Her eyes go wide, and I hate it. Absolutely loathe her look as the full horror sets in.

She rubs her arms with both hands crossed, chilled to the bone, like it's thirty degrees out here instead of seventy.

"This has to be totally illegal. I don't get why no one slips up, how these...shipments even get anywhere without people noticing."

It guts me, but I nod. "Mederva Therapeutics is enormous. They supply millions of legitimate medical devices every year. These shipments are mixed into everything else, the normal distribution pipeline, hidden inside the company budgets. Keith and I sifted through the data and traced their suppliers to foreign sources, mostly. But nothing ever gets done to stop it if that info can't make it to the right people."

"That's why you need to get it out of the country, then?"

I nod. "Yeah. This is bigger than just Mederva, probably crosses national lines. Once I'm in a different country, somewhere safe, we can do a controlled burn. Get what we know out there some way it'll find the right journalists, and the right folks inside the Federal agencies who still aren't corrupted."

The plan sounds ridiculous even to me. Impossible. The severity of this thing hits me all over again.

I don't know if we can even pull it off.

Still, we have to try.

"Holy hell," she whispers, rubbing her eyes. "It's so wrong. On so many levels."

"Yeah."

"I knew it was bad, worse than I ever imagined when I saw your face after Shane went missing. Whatever you brought here, whatever you were running from, had to be true evil."

"Now you know. Hope you also see why I couldn't just walk away, why I'm paying a terrible fucking price."

Her gaze ignites with compassion as she looks at me. "You invested everything you have trying to stop this. That's—"

"Heroic? I'm no hero, Gwen. Don't even say it. Not unless I can end this while keeping my family safe." I pause, looking at her as she shakes her head. "And you."

She's quiet for a long while before asking, "Does Mother know about this? All of it?" She swallows. "The body parts?"

I shake my head. "She's good, and so's the guy she hired to look into me. Knows plenty from her snooping, but she hasn't filled in the deepest details. No one knows what I just told you except for me and Keith, and of course the bastards at Mederva running the show."

"The people after you...wanting to make sure you don't leak their secrets."

Again, I have to swallow hard while I nod. *Damn.*

She doesn't have a clue how many are involved. Far too many now.

It started out with just Keith and I, and it should've stayed that way.

Now it's our families, her, May and her people...

"So what's the plan?" Gwen asks. "You said the airports aren't safe."

"They aren't. Not anymore." I fully believe Keith's warning.

What I'm having a harder time with is J.T. The guy is good, don't get me wrong – within hours he'd uncovered more than enough to convince me he knows his stuff – however, I'm not sold on his suggestions.

The kids staying with May, for one. I have a feeling she's behind that more than anyone else. Well-intentioned, maybe, but after tonight, I don't trust anyone with their lives.

Being separated from them is too dangerous. I need to know where they're at all the time to keep them safe.

"So do you know if you've been followed?" she asks. "If someone really could come here and just take Shane and Lauren or..."

Me. That's what she wants to say. And the slightest possibility anyone could makes me see blood.

Fuck. I'm not sure of anything anymore.

I've reached a place I've never been and never expected to be.

I'd spent the evening online before Shane gave us a scare, researching anyone who may have any connections to this, and anyone who could be safe to contact. J.T. gave me tips on beefing up my encryption on this machine so even the toughest hackers can't break through and find us.

"Well, the mosquitoes will be getting reinforcements any minute," she says. "And I still have a lot of questions so..."

I swat at another needling sting on my arm. "Let's go in."

"You're probably done with questions for the night, huh?"

I finish my drink with a final gulp, refreshed by the melting ice.

"You know, Miller, sometimes it takes more courage to accept help than to refuse it."

"Believe me, I'm accepting, babe, and it's the last thing I want. Already tried with you and your boss, and now I've got May and her guy."

"Fake papers and a place to stay isn't what I'm talking about," she says. "I mean, solving this. Really fixing it. Getting what you need out to the world."

I wish it was still as simple as I hoped, an escape plan with a decoy wife. That idea, or the idea of her, rattles my thoughts. "Why don't you have a boyfriend?"

She blinks at me, confused. Then picks up her drink while standing and steps toward the door.

"Where you going?"

"Inside."

"Because I asked you a question instead?"

She opens the door. "Because it's getting dark out here and I don't fancy getting eaten alive."

I want to follow her, but I also want several other things that shouldn't be an option.

Like a repeat of this afternoon, another bad idea, so I linger where I'm at.

But not for long. It's like the mosquitoes know she gave me fair warning, and now they're descending in attack groups, ready to make a believer out of me for doubting her.

Red isn't in the kitchen or living room when I head in.

Locking the slider, I do a quick check of the front door, knowing it'll already be locked.

She keeps this place secure. Day and night. That hasn't just happened since our arrival. I'd say it's been a habit for this woman for years.

There's movement upstairs. Not needing the image of her prepping for bed, I turn on the TV and click to the news, but soon I'm bored. It's more disturbing fuckery I can't do anything about, considering my own predicament. Then there's weather and talk about baseball season going into full swing.

I set the remote on the table, noticing the spiral notebook there. It's the same one I'd caught her scribbling in the other day, with Lauren right beside her, writing in another notebook.

The noise upstairs has quieted, so I consider flipping it open. It's supposedly a story she's writing.

Lauren told me about it, and the one she's writing with the evil antique dealer and pink-haired girl with a little tiger cat.

Still, I respect her privacy, so I don't pick it up and surf more channels instead.

This is the real nightmare. *Waiting.*

Action, I can handle, but waiting around for disaster fucking sucks.

That's when the mind goes stir crazy, concocting all kinds of twisted scenarios.

I can't let that happen, and...yeah, hell, I'm staring at the notebook again.

Shit.

Yes, it's private. Yes, I'm a snake for snooping. But it's either this or be bored right out of my skull.

I move, picking up her notebook. Whatever's inside has to be better than what's on TV. I start to read her neat, curly handwriting one slow line at a time.

It's more than an hour later, almost midnight, when I hear a car door in the driveway. Setting the notebook down, I walk to the window next to the door and peer out.

It's J.T., right on schedule.

I open the door just in time to see another guy in a dark SUV backing it out onto the road.

"Everything's set, and I'm here for pickup duty," he says, stepping inside. "Where's your phone?"

I pull it out of my pocket. It's a disposable phone I'd purchased before leaving Seattle.

He hands me a new one. "Type in any numbers you need now. Anything critical. This one's untraceable. That old one might not be."

I quickly plug in Keith's number, and then J.T.'s. As far as I'm concerned, those are the only two I'll need.

Keeping his voice low to not wake anyone, he continues. "Send a text to your friend, so he has the new number, but do it discreetly. Use a phrase or a name that nobody but him will recognize. That phone's registered in New York. That's where it'll ping from for anyone tracking your friend's phone."

I use an old phrase from our Army days and send it to Keith. **Jellybeans.**

Both of us took every security precaution possible when we started this investigation, but Keith's last call proved it obviously hadn't been enough. That's why I'm trusting J.T. He's been in this business for years and gotten deeper into it than we ever were.

"Your car's in the garage?"

I nod, leading the way.

"Mederva's still handling this on their own," J.T. says as we enter the garage. "They haven't outsourced tracking you down to any outsiders. Too dangerous, I guess. The big boss you're so worried about doesn't want to be grilled by the board of directors, if too much ever comes to light."

"How do you know?"

He lets out a low chuckle. "I've got my sources, and they're good." Opening the driver's door of my Equinox, he adds, "Tomorrow, we're gonna send them on a wild goose chase. Should take them all the way to Mexico. Open the door. I'll be in touch tomorrow."

I open the garage door and close it again as soon as he backs out. Accepting help is out of the ordinary for me, and taking it from a seventy-year-old man is damn near unbelievable, but I'm out of options.

There are footsteps on the stairs as I close the door to the house. I'm hoping it's Shane or Lauren, but know it's not likely.

"Heard the garage door open," Gwen says, stepping off the stairs.

Fuck.

She's wearing a skimpy tank top and pair of shorts that leave her legs bare from her firm thighs down to her little toes. My hand quivers, remembering caressing her skin, and more.

The rest of me remembers, too. An instant hard-on forms.

Eyeing me critically, she skirts around me and walks to the door leading to the garage. She opens the door and flips on the light. "Where's your car? Who took it?"

Going for a nonchalant look, I shrug, walking into the living room. "Friend of your ma's. He's making a diversion."

"What friend? That guy you mentioned?" she asks, following me. "Miller, what's going on with Mother?"

I can't tell her that part, not till I know the next step. J.T. isn't finished setting everything up.

I nod toward the notebook on the coffee table. "You're

following in her footsteps. Couldn't resist taking a peek. What I read was good."

That does exactly what I want it to do, sidetracks her.

"You read it?"

I nod, unsure whether she's shocked or royally pissed.

It's not like I'm a critic. I've never read one of her ma's books, but I've read enough thrillers to know good writing, and that notebook is full of it.

The style wasn't the only thing that held my attention. Couldn't help noticing the obvious. "Every word, babe. Seems like a lot of similarities between your novel and our situation, too. And the characters. Hope I get my cut of the royalties when it's a hit."

"Yeah, right!" She plants both hands on her hips, glaring, but clearly trying not to smile. "Creative similarities. That's all they are."

"Now you're making sense." I give her a long, slow appraisal, which heats my blood ten degrees. "Because it's not like there's an *attraction* back here in real life."

She lifts her chin, batting her eyes a couple times. "No, certainly not."

I nod thoughtfully, taking a step closer to her.

Goddamn, she smells good, all fresh and clean and subtly sweet. I'm playing with fire and I know it. "Glad you agree. What happened in your ma's hot tub proves it."

Her mouth falls open like she's shocked I'd dare mention it.

"Because if there was an attraction, we wouldn't be standing around bullshitting each other." I step closer still, running a single finger up the length of her bare arm. "We'd be busy with a replay, Gwen."

She tries to hide it – tries so hard it's hilarious – but I saw *that* flash in her jade eyes before she closed them. *Pure desire.*

"Not going to happen," she whispers, catching her breath.

I let my finger trail back down her arm. Stopping near her elbow, I reach over and brush the nipple pebbled beneath her tank top. "Yeah, never."

Her eyes snap open. "Miller, I'm serious."

I've been at the brink of no return since she walked out of that hot tub this afternoon. I cup her chin with one hand. "I am too, Gingersnap. Never been more serious thinking how bad I'd like to lay you down real proper and fuck so hard we forget all our woes. Never had my fingers, my tongue, every inch of me this seriously riled in my life. Never wanted to kiss anyone so bad I pull the breath from your lungs, and make you give it back, give it good, or else you'll find out I mean *serious fucking business* for half-assing it when I make you come real sweet for me."

I wonder who's saying these words. This must be how I know I've lost my mind.

There's no space between us a second later. The air stalls in my chest at the way her body melts into mine, the way her lips race over mine, the way her tongue chases after mine so franticly I want to devour her.

We stumble up against the wall and I push her against it. *Hard.*

Kissing, tasting, feeling, fucking with our tongues.

My hands shift under her shirt, cupping and teasing her tits while my throbbing cock presses firmly against her soft belly.

She's got that little scrap of meat I like, the kind a man imagines knocking up real animal-like. The supermodels with their hard edges never did shit for me. Give me a woman with soft skin and belly and ass and tits any damn day of the week, and I'll make her *scream* like the happiest woman on earth.

"Gingersnap," I growl. "*Now.*"

I'm not screwing around. The heat in my balls that's been

driving me nuts all day since I shot off in her hands almost kills me at the thought of not having her.

She drops her hands from around my neck with a sultry little sigh.

Then with a sexy grin, she takes my hand and takes a step toward the stairs. "We have to be quiet," she whispers. "The kids..."

My heart thuds in my chest. "I'll keep you quiet," I whisper, fire in my blood when I imagine fucking her with a hand pressed tight to those pink lips.

Still holding my hand, she starts up the steps.

It's a manic dash to her bedroom. Once we're inside with the door locked, the passion that's been tangled up rips out of me. So does hers.

If I'm an inferno, she's dynamite.

Gingersnap kisses me back intoxicated on lust, on want, on all the filthy, forbidden things I'm promising right now. My dick rubs against her thigh through my jeans, horny as hell, my mouth pressed to hers so tight I suck her breathless.

We bang up against the wall once when I grab her ass, and she tears her mouth off mine. "*Shhhhh.*"

Right, the kids.

Fuck.

My son and daughter can sleep through a hurricane most nights, but they've surprised me before and could wake up if we blow it. Snarling, I take a step back, trying to tame this storm in my body, regain some basic human composure.

Gwen grins and points at the bed. I back up till my shins touch the frame.

Smiling, she gives a look that could kill a man. Raw confidence.

That's new. The energy dancing in my eyes is enough to tell her what it does to me.

She crosses her arms and grabs the hem of her tank top. I

watch with keen interest, dick jerking something fierce, as she tugs it off over her head. Have to swallow a jagged groan when I see those glorious, pink nipples I've been waiting for finally appear, perked and so ready for my fuckery.

They're flush with heat, almost as copper-red as her hair. This perfect complement to the rest of her skin, dangerous perfection made flesh.

My hands ache to touch her.

I wonder if she's in heat as bad as every bit of me goes into rut.

Walking closer, she pushes down her shorts, revealing a pair of tight pink panties that's too much like the bikini bottom she had in the pool.

I'll be damned if I'm waiting around again.

My hand flies out, grabbing her waistband and ziplining it down her long legs. She lets out a little gasp.

"Off, babe," I growl, enjoying the little kick she gives them at the ankle.

Then I'm just lost as her legs open, and I see glistening pink crowned by copper curls.

My cock wants to murder me. I'm pretty sure it'll find a way to strangle me in my sleep if I don't fuck this girl, and that single-minded purpose is muted by one nasty realization.

The hesitation must show on my face. Gwen frowns.

"Don't like what you see?" she asks quietly.

"Hell no." I grab both her hands and squeeze. "I love every bit of it. Think I want to spend the rest of the night spelling my damn name inside you with everything these hands and this mouth can give, babe. But there's something else I'd like to do and...fuck, you're gonna hate me." Shaking my head, I growl a confession. "I don't have any protection."

Her face wrinkles, a sly grin forming as she unbuttons my jeans. "Let *me* worry about that, Miller. And this too."

For a tall woman, her hands are so small. Another growl sticks in my throat as she rests her right hand between my legs, pinching me through my jeans, rubbing up and down my shaft.

I grab her hand then, push it down on my cock, mashing my forehead to hers, loving how her breathing matches mine. So raspy. So ready. So drunk on needing me.

"Babe..."

"Don't worry," she whispers again. "You just think about what you want to do to me."

My cock pulses, and she bares her teeth. My free hand shoots out, finds its way between her legs, two fingers up inside her. She's so soaked for me I want to take her then and there, condom be damned.

She closes her thighs around my hand as I thumb her clit, struggling to keep control, unzipping my jeans, rubbing me in all the right ways and some very wrong but so fucking good ways, too.

"Gwen, seriously, I–goddammit, we *need* a rubber."

I'm settled. Won't be able to stop till I'm deep inside her cunt, her long legs pinned around me, her teeth sinking into my hand while I come so hard in her pink silk she can feel it. I know that for *certain.*

"Take off your pants," she whispers against my mouth. "Miller, seriously."

I *love* the urgency in her voice.

I'm standing stock-still, fighting the do's and don'ts warring in my brain, but I know which side already won.

"Pants, Mister. While I get us a condom," she whimpers again, running her tongue along my bottom lip. "Or two."

"Bring the whole pack," I bite off.

Fine, so I'm overly excited.

Pulling back and pushing down my jeans, I ask, "You better not be playing, woman. You've got condoms?"

She walks into the bathroom. "A whole box. Unopened. They were in my Christmas stocking last year."

I kick aside my jeans and pull off my shirt. "Let me guess, your mother?"

She steps out of the bathroom, holding a black and violet box.

"Who else? Good thing too..." Her gaze drops to my hard-on. "Quite the shaft you have there, Mr. Rush."

"Shaft?" A sense of pride fills me at the gleam in her eyes, but it's a funny choice of words.

"Romance terminology. They go a little further in the dirty books."

"Then let's make our story filthy and call this a cock, babe." I chuckle, loving how she laughs in echo. "I've never read a romance book, but thanks to you, and the way you've gotten under my skin, I've been walking around with this all day. If anything, what we did in the hot tub just made it *worse*."

She giggles, opening the box as she walks over to me.

I take the condoms out of her hand and toss them on the bed. "Not yet. Soon."

"Soon?"

I dip my head, kissing down her throat and taking one nipple. "Fuck yeah. Gonna savor this nice and slow."

"Okay," she says, arching into me when my teeth pull her soft bud in for a tongue-lashing. "Ohhh-kay. Take your time. I don't mind one bit."

Neither do I, and we both feast on each other.

Exploring, tasting, fondling, tonguing, fingering, pumping.

Mostly, just gasping. Especially her after I kiss my way down her soft belly, bring my mouth up through her inner thighs, and push my face into her delectable cunt.

Even with just my tongue, I know she's fucking tight.

Her pussy tastes as good as her scent, the same faint traces I've been smelling on my hands for hours. I dive into her lush, wet heat and push my beard into her, making her ride it right through her first O.

I know it's coming when her legs start shaking. They're draped over my shoulders, trembling like mad, her little whines coming shriller and louder. Luckily, she knows she's getting too loud and bites the back of her hand.

That's my signal to bring her home.

My tongue smothers her clit. I eat her the fuck up, stroke by vicious stroke, and yeah, you'd better believe I do spell my name at least ten times. It's as insane as it is serious. I want to mark her that bad.

Because after tonight, after I've had her like this, I want her to think *Miller Rush* every damn time she touches herself.

She's coming so hard her eyes roll as her inner walls clench around me. I lash her with my tongue, quickening my strokes, faster and harder and wilder every time her body jerks.

Sweetness seeps from her pink slit long after I'm done, resting my head on her thigh, dick hammering so hard it drowns out everything except the soft sensation of her fingers tracing my jawline.

"Miller?" Gwen grabs the box of condoms on the bed beside us. "We need one now. I can't wait any longer."

Smart words. I've never been so willing in my life. I untangle myself from her legs and crash down on my back as she rips open a package.

"Here." I hold out my hand.

She shakes her head. "Let me do it. I want to feel you."

Thrilled at the idea, I thrust my hips upward, giving her a show. Can't even remember the last time my cock looked this huge, this swollen, this hungry.

She purses her lips together, smothering a laugh.

"What's so damn funny?" I growl.

"You're just...wow, you're pretty big, aren't you?" she asks, rolling the condom on my dick. "Not that it really matters, but – *wow.*"

Once, I read about this thing they called the *Wow* signal, supposedly a massive radio burst some scientists thought might've come from aliens. Right now, I think she's forever put that shit to shame.

Because hearing Gwendolyn Courtney describe my cock in one punchy, torrid word forever overrides anything else I'll ever think when I think *wow.*

"You tell me how it measures up, Gingersnap."

"Well, sure. Not that I've seen that many guys, but...of the few that I have, plus the ones online...let's just say you've got them beat by a long shot."

"Yeah? How do you really feel about that?" I ask, wondering if she's growing hesitant, if she thinks I'm too big for her. Wouldn't be the first time.

"Honestly? *Excited.*" The condom slides down my cock into place and she quickly moves to straddle me. "Show me it's not all hype."

I try not to grin like a fool. Because if there's one challenge I've never been so game for, it's making Gwen respect every impressive inch of my 'shaft.'

I'm off to a good start when I push in, push up, sinking deep. I grab her ass and shove her down, filling her pussy to the hilt, then push her face into my shoulder to stifle the sex whine spilling out of her.

"Careful, babe. Bite down if you need to. Also, two can play at this game. You want to see what this dick can do? Then you're gonna work that sweet ass and ride me for all you're worth."

Her heat clenches around me.

I smile because I know it won't take long to push her over the edge again.

She barely keeps up with me at first. I'm only a couple minutes in before she rears up, and I fist her long red locks, pulling so her face rests against the crook of my shoulder while I bring her over the edge.

"Miller, I'm–"

"Comin'? Fuck yeah, you are. Make it hurt for me, beautiful."

And she does.

Her pussy convulses around every inch of me, nearly bringing her off then and there, throwing this energy into her hips. I go right through her first O on my cock, moving faster, aiming the fierce burn of my pubic bone at her clit every time I thrust up, up, and away.

She's so hot, so tight, my eyes roll back as my lids close. "Good, Gingersnap. So fucking good."

She lets out a sigh as she recovers from the frenzy, regaining a little more control, then fully takes my length inside her slick depths. "You're not half bad yourself," she whispers.

Another challenge? Growling, I attack her mouth, binding her in another kiss while my hips go to work.

I clench her ass and pump harder, deeper, throwing myself into it and not caring if I lose.

I can't fucking wait any longer. I just want to bring her off.

She arches her back and joins in, sensing what's happening, fully enjoying the ride.

Her tits sway in our rhythm, perfectly positioned for me to suck, one at a time while I drive myself on.

It's like a dream how she holds nothing back. Giving me her pussy, her tongue, her body, her breath.

I wish we could go forever, but my release is too close, burning through me like a lit torch.

Hers isn't far behind. The instant I hear her gasp, watch her head toss back, and feel her straining, it's over.

I thrust up inside her, pull her hips downward, and every muscle in my body goes rock hard as I feel her pussy clench, engulfing me. We both twitch like we're wired on this sex, going over the edge simultaneously.

First her, this soft mess seizing up, her pussy wringing my cock so tight I wonder if the condom might break.

Mine hits a second later. My spine lights up and I feel the molten ropes hurling out of me, into her, coming so hard I can't even breathe for more than a minute.

I'm damn near suspended in time, enraptured like this. Having something like a vision that's all rolling curves, legs to infinity, ribbons of red hair, forest-green eyes, and the sweetest little moan sent down from Heaven's very own music hall of fame.

Consider me a total loss.

Whatever we just experienced was more than just sex.

XIII: CLOSING IN (GWEN)

*T*he sun is barely up, yet I'm wide awake and feel like I could run a marathon.

Maybe Mother was right. A healthy sex life seems pretty freaking rejuvenating right about now.

I'm even thankful for the box of condoms she'd stuffed in my Christmas stocking last winter. At the time, she was encouraging me to go after one of the waiters at the golf course with all the subtly of a golf club to the face.

I didn't, of course, and thank God. Turns out Mr. Flirty the Waiter had his wife make a public scene a month later over another woman he'd tricked into a romance.

The wait was so worth it.

Miller hands down blows away any lover I've ever had.

I let the memories of last night fill me as my eyes flutter shut. Then they pop back open.

The memories are there, and they're supremely wonderful, but I'm too full of energy to just lie here.

It's early, but Shane or Lauren could wake up anytime. I'm sure they'll be hungry after yesterday's excitement.

That's probably the reason Miller quietly slipped out of

bed and padded away a short time ago. I can't blame him for wanting to avoid any awkward questions from the kids about *Daddy and Gwen sharing the same room.*

They're old enough to take a good guess what that means. And their best guess might be completely wrong.

I still don't know what we're doing, what this means, if it's possible it's going anywhere good. But after last night, I'm not sure I care.

Sighing, I jump out of the bed, make it up, then grab some clothes and have a quick shower.

Miller's sitting on the sofa when I step off the staircase. He looks up and grins at me, his eyes glowing like sky-blue diamonds.

"Mornin'. Sleep well?"

I raise an eyebrow. "Um, yeah. Better than a long time." Obviously, I'm not talking about the sleep. "Now I'm in the mood for coffee. I'll get some on."

"Already done," he tells me. "Should be finished brewing now. I started it when I heard the shower running."

"Thank you."

He stands up. The feral, almost proud look on his face is close to what I'm thinking.

Danger, Gwendolyn Courtney.

DANGER.

We both want a kiss but can't take the risk. There's no doubt a quick, subtle good-morning smooch would turn into far more, probably ending with me bent over the counter, and that can't happen right now.

"I'm gonna take a shower before the kids get up," he growls, walking past me.

Then he stops, turns around, and marches into the kitchen where I've retreated to avoid the urge to feel those lips of his again. Apparently, it isn't up to me.

Miller takes my mouth, my tongue, my everything. We

kiss long and slow and so, so *good*, loving how his hand tangles gently through my thick hair at first, but then turns into a proper pull.

God, this man.

He really could be the end of me.

We've got inertia. It's insanely hard to make this stop. Slowly, I push against his chest, breaking off the kiss and staring up at him.

His eyes have never been sexier or more beautiful. "No morning kiss?" he growls.

"I think that was worth *ten*, Miller. As much as I'd love to, I don't think either of us like the idea of the kids walking in on us naked over coffee so...better shower. We'll work something out, later."

His hand saunters down my back and gives my butt a delicious squeeze. Then he's gone.

Close call. A few more seconds, and I'm pretty sure I would've been tangling up his shirt instead of pushing him back, begging for more kisses.

I couldn't even tell you how many rounds we went last night. At least half a dozen. My legs still have this sweet soreness today, thighs burning like I spent last night riding a horse and not something a thousand times more addicting.

I try to dampen my lust with caffeine, adding my usual cup of creamer, and close my eyes again.

Okay, so this whole thing has been beyond surreal since the day he showed up. But this morning, I'm actually enthralled with the dreamlike state I'm experiencing.

A soft murmur floats downstairs, and an instant later, Shane appears in shorts and a t-shirt with a robot on it that says, *Keep Calm and Automate.*

"Good morning, big guy," I say. "You hungry?"

"Hi." He plops down in a chair. "I dunno. Dad's taking a shower, then I guess we'll discuss my punishment."

Oh, crud. I'd forgotten all about that.

He sighs heavily. "We don't have any bacon, do we?"

I *wish* I'd forgotten about my little bacon fire too, but I'm not so lucky.

Wow, what didn't happen yesterday?

I look toward my purse on the table near the garage entrance. "No, we're out. But if you want, I'll go grab us some."

"You will?" He looks up like bacon means the world to him right now.

Poor little guy.

"Yup." I set down my coffee cup after another swig, deciding that's enough to get me going. "Tell your dad I'll be back in a jiffy."

I'm gone. I do a double take seeing Miller's Equinox gone, and then remember why.

The empty spot in the garage reminds me it's not all roses and sexy sunshine. Things got serious last night in more ways than one, and as I back out, I wonder if Miller took me like he did on purpose? Redirected my attention elsewhere, maybe, so I wouldn't worry too much over his predicament, Mother's weird involvement, this 'guy' she has helping him.

Ugh.

It's not like we hadn't thoroughly enjoyed ourselves, though. And honestly? It's not like we didn't sorely need the relief, either.

Living in constant fear and uncertainty does strange things to the brain. Now I know why my anthropology professor always said human nature came down to three things: *feeding, fighting, fucking.*

I think our behavior ran the full spectrum yesterday. In order.

Surprising, because even sex used to scare me.

I've never truly let loose before while having sex until last night. That's also why I haven't had it very often.

It always made me nervous, thinking someone else had control over my body.

But last night, that didn't happen. Miller had control without even asking. Surrendering to this man just felt natural, trustworthy, like I could happily fall over the ledge with him, and he'd catch me every time. I never once felt truly frightened.

That's new.

Having sex leave me with the attention span of a drunken gnat is new too.

That's why I drive right past the convenience store. *Oops!*

I decide to keep going a couple more miles rather than turn around. The bigger grocery store is bound to have better bacon, and it's not that much farther. If it takes the edge off whatever Shane's processing from yesterday, it'll be worth it.

I have to drive past the road to Manny's office to get to the store. I haven't stopped into work for well over a week, demanding my paid time off to deal with everything. I'm assuming Miller hasn't made an effort to claw back the money, despite the change in plans, or else my boss would be up my butt about the paid time off and everything else.

As I pass by the office, though, I do a double take.

Manny's car? That couldn't be his car pulling up to park outside the office. He never works on Sundays.

Weird.

Too curious, I turn on the next road and circle back around the block. Pulling up to the stop sign on the side street, I look harder and confirm it *is* Manny's car. A second vehicle pulls up just as Manny climbs out of his Tesla, probably the only person in Finley Grove who owns one.

The other vehicle is a sleek black beast of a Suburban.

I glance in my mirror, making sure I'm not blocking any traffic, and then turn. It looks like a group of sharp dressed people in full business attire, probably there for a meeting. At least three men in suits and a woman. Her hair is jet-black and tied up in a bun. She follows Manny to the door with the men flanking them with near-military precision, then he unlocks it and leads them inside.

Even weirder.

Maybe there's a good reason he's in this Sunday. *Another one of his side gigs?*

I shudder, knowing now all too well what one of those odd jobs involves. Who knows?

It feels like eons ago rather than weeks since I got involved.

Miller, Shane, and Lauren have made the days shorter. All the while filling them with more fun and excitement and energy than I've had in years. *Flipping years.*

No longer terribly concerned about Manny and his freaky business, I cross the street and head to the grocery store.

Used to buying for one, I pick up a basket. Then, on second thought, I put it back and grab a cart.

It's nearly full by the time I head to a checkout lane, loaded up on fun little extras. Every aisle had something I think the kids or Miller will like.

While loading everything in my car, I think of the big box of frozen hamburgers I bought and how I'll try to grill them to ease back into cooking. You can't screw up hamburgers and light them on fire, can you?

Oh, well, at least Miller will be there if I do try to burn the place down again. That alone makes me feel safe, ready to dip a toe outside my comfort zone.

I'd more than done it yesterday. I'd taken a giant lust-fueled leap of faith.

It's amazing how good, how liberating that feels.

Maybe I'm not just a huge *cluck-cluck* chicken after all.

What if I've just never had someone ready to catch me if I fall?

Someone besides Mother, of course. That could be the root of my issues. I was so used to her always being there, pushing her unwanted help. And I was so determined to live my own life, forge my own path, I started to worry so much about screwing it up that I'd invent my own monsters in the dark.

Actually, though, the darkness itself gets a pass. I'll always be afraid of it.

I put away the cart and climb in my car, utterly amazed at how different the world looks today. Even my selfish dick of a boss seems like less of a villain.

Like it or not, I owe all this to Manny. If he hadn't forced me to help Miller with his stupid misdirections, I'd have never found out so much about myself.

Thinking of him, I decide to drive past the office again on my way home, just to see if he's still there.

His car is still in the parking lot, but the other one isn't. His visitors, whoever they were, seem to be long gone.

My stomach knots. I can't shake the creepy, crawly sensation that something's wrong.

I also have no clue what's happening with my job when all is said and done. Miller seems to want me to keep my cut of the unbelievable cash he carries around. But even if I let him force it on me – which I swear to God I won't – do I still *have* a job? After all this?

Sighing, I want to just get this over with, or at least touch base with Manny to see where things stand.

So I turn off toward the office complex, park, and climb out.

The front door is still unlocked, and I can tell the door to the law office is open.

Eerie silence echoes in my ears as I walk down the hall.

My nerves are sharp as swords, as usual. But this time, I ignore the fear tap dancing up my spine. I really need to get over being scared of everything.

"Manny?" I call, stepping through the open door.

The office is just as quiet as the rest of the building. Like the lights are on, but nobody's home. Not even my creepy lawyer boss with his weirdo off-the-books clients.

"Manny?" I say again, this time a little louder.

Finally, there's a sound. This muffled noise from his office makes my stomach jolt.

I listen closely and get rewarded with a dull *thud.* Then I swear I hear my name, almost slurred.

My heartbeat quickens, unsure what I'll find. Do I even dare?

Today, I do, especially since I've already made it this far. Slowly, I walk to his office, which is halfway open, and grab the doorframe for courage.

I close my eyes and quickly count to three, then push the door open.

"Holy crap!" My eyes can't seem to land on anything once they're open, staring at the scene.

The place is trashed. His desk is swept clean, mugs and files and paperwork strewn on the floor, thick law books yanked from the decorative shelves behind him and dropped across the room. Or were they *thrown?* There are even several dents in the wall.

But no sign of Manny Stork himself.

Then I hear it. "Gwen? *Helllllp.*"

It's so faint, more like a rasp than a voice, I'm not positive it's even there at first. So I step closer, enough to see the feet on the floor behind Manny's desk.

Every instinct I own screams *run.*

But I can't just abandon him so I inch forward, clapping a hand over my mouth once he comes into full view.

It's Manny, all right. Huddled in a broken ball on the floor, his long legs splayed at a weird angle. Thick blood streams down a gash in his head, covering his face.

"Help," he whimpers again.

"Oh my God!" I rush to his side. "Manny, Manny! What happened here?"

"Gwen. S-sorry." He lifts the hand that was pressed to his stomach. "They...they beat me. I didn't want to tell them...*ohhh.*"

He's holding his phone, pinching his teeth together. It's smeared with blood. Still, he holds it out to me.

"Nine-one-one. I...I can't..." His eyelids flutter shut, and I wonder if he's passed out. Then they open again, and barely whispering, he says, "Leave. Run. While...while you can. They know, Gwen. About you and Rush. I'm so...damn sorry."

For the next ten seconds I'm just frozen, this terrible ringing sound lodged in my ears.

No, deeper than that, embedded in my brain, which struggles to grasp what he just said.

The full nightmare hits me *why* this happened, why my boss is a crumpled mess on the floor begging for mercy and straining to even breathe.

Jesus Christ, they found him.

The same people after Miller.

Shaking, I reach for my purse, for my phone, but it's still in the car.

I'm not sure if it's my head or my heart spinning faster. I feel like I just might pass out and join him on the floor.

But however scared I am, however confused, I can't.

Can't and won't.

Manny groans again, using what looks like the last of his strength to give the phone a good shake.

I grab it from his hand, and dial 9-11, while jumping to my feet. As soon as dispatch answers, I rattle off the address and say a man's been hurt bad. *Beaten.*

Manny gurgles again as the call ends. "Leave, G-Gwen. Go. Leave before they–"

I drop his phone on the floor a second before dispatch even hangs up, saying they'll be there shortly. "Manny, no. I have to make sure you get help."

And I also have to make sure this strange, newfound courage isn't the end of me. I can't leave a man who might be dying here like this. But I can't do this alone.

I kneel down again, find his hand, and squeeze with all my might as he grumbles.

Whatever Manny Stork is – modern day Scrooge, white-collar criminal, selfish prick, bad luck charm – right now he's a human being suffering mightily from his own bad karma. Even though I'm worried sick his agony might be contagious, might become mine, I can't walk away and leave him here alone until I know he's in custody, being treated, safe.

"Give me thirty seconds. I'm going to run to my car and get my phone so I can call for help." I wait for him to nod weakly before bolting.

I've never run so fast in my life, flying through the office and back across the parking lot.

Shaking from head to toe, I have to hit the unlock button several times before I can get my car door open. Inside, my phone is ringing, the screen lit up and vibrating.

I fumble around, sliding into the driver's seat so I can answer the call.

For a split second, I consider jamming my key in the ignition and flooring it away.

But I'm not Ms. *Cluck-cluck* today. I can't leave Manny like this. A surge of adrenaline rips through me.

"Hello?" I almost yell it, swiping the answer icon without

even looking at the number.

"Gwendolyn Marsha Courtney, get your butt to my place *now!*"

There's that terror again. I've never heard Mother so frantic in my life. You *know* it's serious when your mom uses your middle name.

"Mother!" I shout. "Where's Miller?! It's Manny, my boss, he's—"

"Miller's already here with the kids! He tried to call you ten times and said you wouldn't answer." Mother says. "Get over here now."

My teeth dig into my lip so hard I taste blood, metallic and acrid.

Briefly, I wonder if the shrill noise in my ears is panic setting in. Nope, it's real.

Sirens. Probably the ambulance and police escort the emergency dispatch told me were on the way.

"Gwen? Gwendolyn?" Mother sounds scared. Something I'm not sure she's ever been.

Holy hell, this is bad.

"Sorry. I'm coming. I'll drive right over."

Once I see the flashing lights in my mirror pulling into the lot, I drop the phone and hit the gas. I don't think I've ever pushed Old Pearl so fast.

More sirens shriek across town so close I can hear them, but that doesn't stop me from speeding, running stop signs, needing to get to Miller and Mother and the kids ASAP.

It feels like an eternity with the same noxious sweat beading on my brow. The same awful questions leaping up from their depths in my mind and poisoning me.

What if the people who did this to Manny are far from done?

What if we're not safe, even at Mother's?

* * *

HE'S THERE, standing in the driveway. And it's hard to fight the urge to just throw the car into park, leap out, and hurl myself into Miller's arms.

I also see Mother and a man I don't recognize in a bombardier jacket, grey hair, and a little scruff on his chin.

Oh God, he might be one of them, I decide, nearly hyperventilating.

I slam on the gas and aim Old Pearl directly at him. My car roars, unsure she wants anything to do with the taste of blood. Frankly, neither do I, but–

But nothing. Miller leaps in front of the stranger and spreads his arms, waving.

"Crap!" I slam on the brakes and wrench the wheel, barely missing Miller, right before Pearl plows into a large concrete planter with a worrying *crunch!*

Just awesome. I'm still trying not to scream, untangling my seat belt, when Miller rips open my door.

"He's after you!" I shout, crawling out, grabbing his collar. "They hurt Manny!"

"Babe, no. Come the hell here," Miller growls, pulling me out of the car, into his arms. "You almost just flattened the man helping us."

I fall down against him, relieved, thankful, but still so scared I even *feel* pale.

I'm not sure what happens next.

I can hear, see, move, but it's like I'm just a guest in someone else's body. A heavy fog takes over, blurs my vision, surrounds me, and chews up time and people and plans.

There's something about the older guy, Mother's guy, telling us we have to go. They've already got a place picked out a couple hours from here, apparently, somewhere to keep us all safe.

I hope to God they're right.

* * *

IT'S NOT UNTIL LATER, when we're in a new black pickup, traveling north with Miller driving, me in the passenger seat, with Shane and Lauren in the back, that the brain fog starts lifting.

"How're you doing?" Miller asks, looking over at me.

I pull my gaze off the kids in the mirror, who are both wearing headphones. They're blissfully encased in their own worlds and I don't blame them one bit. Shane plays a game on his little Nintendo, and Lauren follows along while an audiobook narrates a story on her tablet. A hint of seeing Mother hand the devices to the children, and of Miller telling them to put on their headphones before we pulled out of her driveway, flashes in my mind.

"What the hell happened?" I ask. "Where are we going, and who was that man?"

"The guy you almost made into a pancake?"

"Yes!"

"I take it you've never met J.T.?" Miller keeps his attention on the road. "He's a friend of your ma's. Former military, investigative experience, and pretty damn good at what he does."

J.T.?

"No, never met him," I say, though the name rings a bell, someone I remember her interviewing a few times for research. "But if he's just a friend, why's he involved?"

"Your ma hired him to help me." Miller's tone drops an octave.

The tick in his cheek tells me more. "You aren't happy about that?"

"Can't say I was real keen on it at first. I am now. Came around to the idea fast after Keith called, after plans changed, and now, hearing about your boss..." His jaw tightens, suddenly more chiseled than ever. He glances in the rear-view mirror at the children before focusing on the road again. "If it wasn't for J.T. and your ma, frankly, we might not be here right now."

I blink at him a few times. Trying not to make myself sick off all the grim possibilities he's hinting.

"What happened this morning? How'd you know about Manny before I did? I wasn't even gone that long, probably half an hour at the store..."

"J.T. was on patrol. Has been since he set up his guys with the Equinox last night, but maybe we were too late. He was watching your office, Stork's office, I mean. One of many things he's supposed to pay attention to. As soon as he saw who dropped by this morning, and IDed them positively, he called me, told me to be packed in five minutes for a ride to May's place."

That woman I saw? "Is she the one you're so worried about? The woman who met Manny, I mean. Tall, slender, black hair?"

"That's her," he growls, glancing at me. "You saw Jackie?"

"Yeah. I saw Manny pull into the office on my way to the store. Couldn't believe he was working on a Sunday, so I drove around the block and watched him and a dark-haired woman walk into the office. I just thought it was another client, not...not someone who'd beat him up. Not *this.*"

Miller's eyes are glued to the road.

"God, what if Manny didn't make it?" I ask, trembling at the thought. "The cops and EMTs were pulling up when Mother called, but I don't know how bad he was hurt. I stayed until they got there. I just couldn't leave him."

"J.T. will let us know. That was mighty brave of you, Gingersnap, hanging around for that worm. He owes you his life if he's still got one."

My stomach sinks. "I should've stayed longer. Maybe I

could've told the police something so they'd catch this Jackie person."

He reaches over and lays a hand on my knee. "No, you shouldn't have. It's J.T.'s job to worry about that. You did exactly what you needed to do. We had to leave. All of us."

My head hurts with more questions.

Picking and choosing the ones to focus on, I ask, "So did that J.T. pick you and the kids up?"

"May did," he tells me. "Soon as she heard from him, she was on her way."

"My *mother* picked you up? Um, just how involved is she in this?"

"Too deep now," he answers, shaking his head. "She also packed a suitcase for you. That lady thinks of everything."

Yeah, except for the way I scared her half to death when she couldn't get a hold of me.

Any other day, that would frighten me. Today, it doesn't matter.

"J.T. stayed at the office as long as he could, waited for Jackie to leave, then tailed her." He glances at me. "To your place. Her goons must've beat it out of Manny."

I slap a hand to my chest, feeling my heart leap into my throat. "You were already gone, weren't you?"

"Yeah, safe and sound at your ma's. Calling you, but you weren't answering."

"I was dealing with Manny." There's this nervous rush of relief and fear. A feeling like we just dodged a bullet, except there's no way to guess how many more are coming.

He gives a slight nod. "They won't find anything at your place, I made sure nothing was left behind."

"Did J.T. call the cops on them for breaking and entering?"

"They didn't hang around long enough to try. Almost like

they knew the place was deserted. Or knew they'd been compromised."

"Well, they beat up Manny bad. He has to tell the police. A sworn statement. That's evidence."

He shakes his head. "Only if someone can find her, babe. Can't put that witch away for shit till she's got no broomstick left to fly away on."

"I saw Manny, too. Once they get her, I'll tell them everything. Don't you worry."

He shoots a sorrowful look my way. "Not that easy. Even if they brought her into custody, she's got an army of law sharks and insiders lined up to help. We can't even have her arrested unless we're *sure* we can keep her locked up. Not till we find some way to release the intel on Mederva."

Frustration and anger scorch my veins. "Who is this Jackie, anyway?"

"She took over as CEO for Mederva Therapeutics a couple years ago," he tells me, then goes quiet.

It's not hard to figure out the rest.

"Is that when all the other stuff you told me about last night started?"

"Yeah. She must've been brainstorming it for years, had all the right pieces in place like lightning. Only area she slipped up was distribution, shipping, where Keith and I knew something wasn't right."

Another flash of Manny, of his trashed office, his beaten body, enters my mind, sending an ice-cold shiver down my back.

I swallow the burning bile in my throat before whispering, "She's pure evil. We really are in deep doo-doo, aren't we?"

Miller looks at me intently then, bristling. "No. Leave it to me. I'm going to get us the hell out of this. She'll pay a hundred times for making you suffer."

XIV: PROMISES MADE (MILLER)

I walk the perimeter of the cabin for the fourth or fifth time tonight.

It looks secure, and we're as deep in the woods as a cabin can be. These forests up here are enough to rival the thousand-year-old rainforests and overgrowth I'm used to back west.

It took us damn near four hours to get here, and it still doesn't feel like it's far enough.

Nowhere's truly far enough from a lioness on the prowl.

She'll find us, sooner or later. Find me. Just like she almost did this morning.

It's worse than I thought since she's come here personally. I always figured she'd send her minions. The risk of keeping the cleanup completely *hush-hush* inside the company must've been enough to pull her out of her ivory tower.

Not that it'd be the first time I've seen her personal thirst for violence.

Or maybe she just wants to settle score with me.

I had no choice. We barely survived our first brush with her and escaped with our lives.

Now, after beating the truth out of Manny, it's only a matter of time till Jackie the Ripper connects the dots between Gwen and May and this little cabin.

I have to be ready to fight. To protect Gwen and the kids and this place with a few savage surprises of my own.

Fuck.

Cold sweat beads on my brow. My insides clench, my heart wavers, like there's this huge fist hammering me from the inside out. I worried I'd already lost it all this morning.

I'd been so fucking scared when Gwen didn't answer her phone. Then when I pulled open her car door, after she'd come flying up in my arms, shaking uncontrollably.

It's not hard to see what this shit is, a slow acid drip ruining her life, and I hate every bit of it.

Seeing her safe rivaled even what I felt when I saw Shane running up the driveway carrying his precious lemons.

Relieved. Thankful. And so pissed off I want to personally impale Wren's head on a pike.

Small silver lining, her grocery run left us with a full food supply. We loaded it up from her car into the new truck J.T. loaned me, meaning we won't have to leave the cabin for several days.

I'd packed everything I could grab at her place, but knew we'd need more.

May saw to everything else with J.T.

The nondescript Chevy, for one thing, a great choice since it's just about the most common pickup on the roads in America. Gas for the generator. The cabin itself. It's a rustic place with a few rooms perched on a huge, secluded section of Rainy Lake. Ontario is less than half an hour away if things *really* go to hell.

However long we're here, the cabin isn't half bad. It's fully off the grid, and with the generator, it has all the conveniences of home. Only one road in and out, too.

Its A-framed shape and green tin roof blend into nature.

Probably renders it invisible from the sky with the tall pines and hardwood trees everywhere.

The kids were excited, treating this like one more stop on our forced vacation to the Upper Midwest. They instantly claimed the open loft with two twin beds as their space. The lower level has an open living and kitchen area, then a bedroom with a queen bed and bathroom attached.

The cinder block basement holds the water tanks and generator. I've already carried it up the steps leading from the basement and set it up in the sound-reducing shelter attached to the back.

There's also a wooden garage shed on the property. Big enough to park the truck in and to store various lake equipment, kayaks, a canoe, life jackets, fishing gear.

All the things I truly can't imagine May ever using.

Gingersnap, however, might be right at home. She's a natural water baby. Her abilities in the pool proved it.

If we get a second to enjoy ourselves, I want to check out the lake. Also wouldn't mind seeing her in that bikini again. Or even bare-assed and mine.

She's proved her many talents in that department and many more.

Right now, she's inside, putting away the fuckton of groceries she bought. Almost like she knows we'll need them organized. I'm sure it helps make the kids feel like this is a vacation rental rather than a hideout.

I'm thankful for that.

For all she's done, really, and I shudder to think where I'd be if I hadn't met her and May.

Still hate the fact I've put them all in danger trying to expose Mederva's human sacrifices.

But accepting their help has gotten easier. They're giving

people, every last one of them, and every day everyone's alive and in one piece makes me more grateful.

Now I just have to make sure I don't take advantage of that.

Once this is over, with Jackie and her crew behind bars, we'll be gone.

Not Ireland. Not necessarily home to Seattle. But somewhere safe, somewhere we can call home, where the kids can have normal lives.

Normal.

What the hell is that anymore?

I wonder when my phone vibrates sharply in my pocket. I yank it out and read the text message. It's from J.T.'s burner.

Manny Stork will survive. Just gave his statement to the cops.

Goddamn, that's good news. Hard to believe I'd ever wanted to wring his neck.

Another wave of gratefulness and guilt mingles, washing over me like a tsunami. Manny the Idiot may have deserved to pay the toll for his greed, but not like this. Not because of me.

This shit *has* to stop.

Another text message comes through then.

Eagle in place. He'll text as needed.

A picture comes in attached to it. A man in his thirties or so. Built. Blond hair. Blue eyes.

J.T. Riggs doesn't leave any open ends, that's for damn sure. Eagle's the lookout he said he'd send to guard the cabin, a local guy, someone to help keep an eye on things since J.T. himself can't be here constantly and sooner or later, I have to sleep.

Confirmed, I type back and hit send, then walk back to the cabin.

"Dad," Shane says as I step inside. "Did you know that May owns this entire lake?"

"Oh, no, even she's not that rich!" Gwen corrects him while folding up a paper bag. "She owns the only private property on this stretch for many miles. Everything else around here is state-owned, wildlife reserves and parks under special protection.

"You come up here a lot?" I ask her.

She shakes her head, that red bun on her head bouncing. "A few times last summer. Mother just bought it the winter before. We'd rented it a few times years ago. Thought it'd be another great investment, plus somewhere she could go to story jam with all her author friends." Her grin widens, those perfect teeth doing terrible things to me. "That's what she said, anyway, but I know the real reason. She wrote a story last year where the couple lives off the grid and needed to research firsthand exactly what that meant."

I nod, fully believing it. This place isn't roughing it by any stretch, but it's a nice taste of the North woods and a lifestyle with a nod to Paul Bunyan legends.

Gwen puts the bag in a drawer and closes it. "If Mother ever starts writing sci-fi, I'm leaving the country."

Can't help chuckling at that.

Remembering the story of hers I read, I say, "Your ma packed your computer and notebook."

"I saw!" She gives me a coy look. "You didn't tell her about it, did you?"

"Your story?" I shake my head. "There wasn't time. We had to get in and get out."

"I did." Lauren stows the broom she'd been using in a tiny closet next to the back door. "When we were at her house, yesterday, swimming. I told her about mine, too."

Gwen manages a smile. "Well, I bet she was happy to hear about yours."

Lauren nods excitedly. "She promised she'd have her editor and agent look it over when I'm done! It might make a good kids' book."

"Hey, wait a minute," Shane says from where he's standing in the middle of the living room area. "There's no TV?"

"No, bud, not here," I say. "You'll survive."

"Can I go check out the lake? There's a dock." Shane hops from foot to foot, realizing he'd better get his entertainment in during the daylight with nothing to watch.

I've already checked out the dock. It's secure, visible from the kitchen window. "Go on. Just don't start swimming unless I say okay."

Shane waves a hand and runs for the door. "Come on, Lauren!"

My little girl glances at me with an uncertain look. Although I tried my best to keep things calm this morning, she was scared. Still is, I guess, and who could blame her?

"How about we all go check out the lake?" Gwen asks, sensing the hesitation.

I hold a hand out for Lauren. "Great idea."

She grabs my hand, and once we're outside, she takes a hold of Gwen's hand with her other hand. We head all the way to the dock like that before she lets go.

Once we're walking on the wooden dock, she's good again. Kicking off her sandals to wade in the shallow water next to it, she hugs her shoulders, shivering a little from the cold.

These lakes are colder than we're used to back home. Brutal seven month winters mean they can take their sweet time to truly warm up for summer.

"Heard about Manny. He'll be fine," I tell Gwen as we both sit down on a log bench built near the shoreline.

Her hand flutters over her chest, relief hissing out her lungs. "Oh, thank God. You heard from J.T. then?"

"Yeah. He's got everything set for us. No more loose ends we should have to worry over."

"Hey, Gwen!" Shane points across the lake. "What's that out there? See that thing in the middle of the water, between here and that island?"

"That's a big ol' pontoon boat," she says with a laugh. "It came with the house...sort of. It floated away from the dock not long before Mother bought the place, and the previous owner just never bothered going after it. I think it's caught, resting on a rock or something."

"We should do that!" Shane jumps up and down for a better look. "Guys, it's just sitting there. We could swim out and get it."

"There's no motor," Gwen tells him. "Bringing it back here might be difficult with just a couple oars."

Shane slaps his thighs. "Aw, shucks."

"How do you know?" I ask.

"Because I swam out to it once," she answers. "It's in okay shape, despite having floated around for a few years. But I don't think we can row that thing back ourselves; we'd probably need another boat to tow it in."

I nod, watching the kids as they forget about the marooned boat for now and chase each other around the dock.

"Does he know anything else?" Gwen pushes her hand into mine. "Does J.T. know if they caught Jackie Wren or if there's even a chance they might?"

"No. He didn't say anything about that. Bet he lost sight of her after this morning."

Jackie doesn't hire morons. Whoever she's got on payroll for cleanup duty, they're very good at concealment, making things disappear. Including themselves.

She stares at the children playing in the shallow water for

a few minutes before asking, "So, what? We just sit here and wait?"

I can feel her frustration intently because I share it. I hate this cat and mouse shit, playing hunter or hunted.

"Not completely. J.T. has all his connections working. They're trying to sniff out a viable way for me to upload the info Keith and I gathered."

I bite back a growl forming in my throat as my mind goes back in time to Jackie's office.

Keith and I were called in for a special briefing with upper management. We should've known then we were screwed, but I didn't know how far they'd go to cover their tracks.

We'd been careful, but someone caught wind of our undercover raids, tapping the company's logistic networks for data.

She didn't waste any time or mince words.

* * *

Weeks Ago

"How much, Miller?" She'd asked the question from behind her glass desk as soon as we entered the office and sat down.

It started out all smiles, as if this were some mishap over Shane throwing a damn baseball through her window.

I'd never even met her before, but I'd seen her icy profile pic in all the company-wide memos.

Some people don't look like their pictures. They're more flawed and more real in subtle ways when you finally see them up close.

If anything, Jackie Wren looks more mannequin perfect

in the flesh. Her jet black hair pulled up in a bob on her head that's just a little too neat. Her lips too blood red. Her smile too contrived.

We had one option: play stupid.

She didn't buy it. But rather than make threats, she offered us jobs.

Different jobs. Inside jobs. Higher paying jobs.

It was a textbook case of keep your friends close and your enemies closer.

Her offer was something we knew we couldn't agree to. Not if we wanted to keep our souls.

How much? She asked the same hellish question three times before the smiles disappeared. And no amount of babbling or shrugging or pretending we had no fucking clue what she meant could help us.

Then the other men came into the room and locked the door behind them.

Then she stood up, giving me a look like she was ready to send her five-thousand-dollar stiletto heels straight through my balls.

Then I knew how utterly screwed we were, watching Keith suffer.

* * *

Present

"There's more that I haven't told you," I say, a heavy sigh on my lips. I watch the kids on the horizon to make sure they're seen but can't hear us.

"Yeah?" she answers dryly, squeezing my hand.

I swallow against the fresh bile burning my esophagus. If

I get out of this without having acid reflux for life, it'll be a damn miracle.

"My signature is on some of those shipping receipts back at Mederva," I say. "Even after I knew those containers had anything but experimental stuff."

Her eyes narrow as she looks at me. "You mean you signed for—" She shakes her head. "Why?"

"There was something we were missing, babe. Something that kept us awake all night, something we couldn't figure out, something damning that might end all this, and digging deep into the muck was the only way."

"What?" she whispers. Her posture tells me she's breathless. "Miller?"

"Jackie's connection. We had to find out who helped mastermind these shipments. Who sourced those poor kids."

"And did you?" her hand tightens on mine.

I nod. "Being on the inside gave us pictures, videos, audio recordings of a late night meeting with Jackie and an off-record visitor who helps orchestrate this bullshit. Publicly, they're a major investor in the research firms profiting off death."

"The mastermind?" she asks. "Who is it?"

I shake my head. "Can't tell you. You'd flip."

"Why?"

"Because this person announced their run for U.S. Senate the day after we found out."

I won't tell her it's the new fuck from Oregon. He's a shoe-in to replace Senator Paul Harris, who announced his retirement last year after coming clean about helping bring down a major weapons smuggling trade thanks to Enguard Security, one of the premier west coast security firms.

We almost reached out to Enguard chief Landon Strauss over this, but there wasn't time.

When Keith and I realized how deep the sewer we'd

uncovered ran, and how our only hope was exposing the entire dungheap at once, we knew we had to keep this tight and act alone.

Otherwise, the true criminals would never go down.

"You're a brave man, Miller," Gwen whispers. I can hear how hard she swallows. "God, if it were me, I don't think I could handle this. Like I'd be tunneling my way across the Canadian border right now, or something..."

"You're plenty brave, Gingersnap. Give yourself more credit."

I mean it, too. I also hope she's even braver than I think. Because she's in this now, same as me, same as the kids and her ma. She's in this till we can keep Jackie Wren and all her filthy friends locked away forever.

I stare at the lake as my mind drifts back in time again. To Keith, forming plans to get what we knew into the right hands. We'd both liquidated everything we owned, started to think about places we could go, but we didn't think we'd have to pull the pin so fast.

Not till that day in the office.

* * *

Weeks Ago

MY LUNGS SEIZE up as we're surrounded.

Is this shit even happening?

A hostile takeover, a mafia-esque shakedown, right here in the office of one of the most powerful CEOs in the country?

Oh, there's no doubt what the intention is. The sleek-dressed men in ties, all wearing earpieces, are modern secret service knights. Or inquisitors.

There are six of them. Three on Keith, three on me.

"I gave you the opportunity," Jackie says, her crimson lips pulling to the side sourly. "One that could've been incredibly rewarding and ideal for everyone."

Neither Keith or I say anything. One of the goons inhales a breath, like he's gearing up for something.

"Did you think I wouldn't find out about you cashing in your company shares?" she asks.

I bite my tongue. That was the one thing we'd both questioned; too much, too soon. Would it flag us?

We'd needed the money to make our escapes, though. Fuck.

Heather, Keith's wife, is supposed to leave for Phoenix tomorrow where they'll catch another plane to Ecuador. She's supposed to take my kids to Phoenix, too, and I'll meet them there to hop another long flight to New York, and then Ireland.

Now it seems like we made a critical mistake we might never get a chance to fix.

Their systems, their investigators, were just better than our plans.

"Miller. One more time," Jackie snaps, drumming her fingernails on the desk. They're the same murder scene red as her mouth. "How much? How fucking much do I have to cough up to make you Boy Scouts behave and forget all this?"

It's not even a question.

Even if I were that morally corrupt, if I could just forget about chopped-up kids being harvested, there's no way she could be trusted to follow through. She'd probably have us shot and buried in the nearest unmarked graves before the checks cleared.

I look at Keith. It's only fair to give him a chance.

He's staring past Jackie, looking through the windows to the city, where the sun cuts through the spotty haze over Elliot Bay and the mountains beyond.

It's beautiful. Normal. Entirely Seattle.

And it might as well be a thousand miles away from the brutal reality hanging over our heads.

"Keith," I grunt his name.

He turns, wearing a deadpan look. First to me, then to bitchface herself.

"Not for sale. Bite me."

Despite the madness, the fear, I grin. That's the man I know, and if need be, I'm proud to die by his side.

"Oh, really?" Her gaze snaps to me again. "How about you, Rush? Going to give me your cliché, tough-talking hero act, too? Such a shame. It isn't even interesting anymore, you know. I've seen men like both of you break and scream like children."

My teeth grit together as those words echo in my brain. Like *children.*

"Go back to hell, you fucking vampire," I spit. "You won't get away with this. Give me time. I'll be the man to bring you down."

She snorts pure derision. "How ambitious. Enough talk. Gentleman, shall we?"

She's not talking to us anymore.

One of the men moves like a gorilla, something heavy materializing in his hand. It's a metal poker from the fireplace across the room, as huge as a tire iron.

He slams it into Keith's leg like he's chopping wood. My anger flares at the sound of a bone snapping.

Shit.

SHIT.

One of the men behind me moves, locking his hand on

my throat. The fiery burn of adrenaline hits me like a drug as the goon takes another swing at Keith's other leg.

They push him to the floor. A second goon lands a kick to his ribs so hard I hear the sickening splinter.

They're going to kill him. Beat my best friend to death right in front of me, and then they'll start on me.

It's too much. This is *not* how I'm dying and leaving my kids.

I think the asshole behind me twitches at the visceral crack of Keith's other leg busting apart.

My turn. I break the hold the goon has on me, bash him in the gut, then plant an elbow in his throat.

As he goes down, I grab his gun.

All hell breaks loose. I know they'll shoot us both, riddle us with bullets, unless I do one thing.

I swing the gun right at Jackie Wren's scowling face. Her bitch mask breaks, and those dark-brown eyes of hers churn with fear.

"One wrong move, and tomorrow the media gets one hell of an obituary. I will shoot her, you assholes. Back away from Keith. And me."

They stare at me icily, all six of them. Jackie's nose twitches and she throws up her hands. "What are you waiting for? Do it!"

The men obey.

The standoff continues for thirty seconds, me swinging the gun by several degrees like a wild man, searching for some way out. I'm able to maneuver around her desk, where I grab her by the hair and push the barrel of the gun against her spine, wrapping one arm around her till it hurts.

"You want to stay alive?" I growl.

She nods frantically. I can't even enjoy hearing her whimper.

"Then listen, only gonna say this once. Your boys are going to pick up Keith, very carefully, and escort us over to your private elevator. I'll wait for them to load him inside, then the three of us will have a nice, friendly ride down to the street. You yell, you scream, you scratch me, you try any shit, and bam!" I yell the last word in her ear, and she jumps. "Let us fucking go, and we'll both settle this another day. Fair?"

She nods again. Her men don't need to be told twice.

Two of them pick up Keith, careful not to mangle him more. He bites his hand to keep from screaming as they carry him to the executive elevator around the corner. I wait till he's in before pulling Jackie with me, then stab the button to the bottom floor.

None of the goons can follow.

"You got your phone?" I growl at her again. She nods. "Call him an ambulance."

Done.

The sirens are already flashing a minute after we're downstairs, pulling up, and I give Jackie Wren another ferocious tug. It gets a few looks from people milling in the hall, low-ranking Mederva employees who probably wonder what I'm doing manhandling a woman worth a billion dollars.

If only they knew.

Keith looks at me as the medics approach, his eyes huge and red. "Miller, goddammit. We have to go. Right now. I don't need my legs to fly and–"

"Just let 'em set your legs. Clean you up. You'll be on the first flight once I talk to Heather. You still got your phone?"

"Yeah. Miller," he whispers, pulling at my pant leg, staring up at me with this lost, hollowed-out expression in his eyes. "What have we got ourselves into?"

"Hell," I whisper. "Now we just have to find our way out."

I don't move till the EMTs have got Keith loaded, taking

him away. Then I march Jackie outside, around the building, to a small park with a sculpture garden that's usually not very crowded this time of day.

There's a statue of a huge angel there. That's where I pull Jackie before whirling her around, slamming her into the stone base so hard she bangs her head.

I don't care if anyone else notices.

I've already got an Uber on the way to pick me up.

"You'll pay for this!" she hisses, her face raw hatred.

"No, you will!" I snatch her phone out of her hand and smash it on the ground, buying a few more precious minutes. "Next time I see you, bitch, it'll be in an orange jumpsuit. I know the instant I let you go, you'll want to storm back into your office and have your men hunt us both down. You'll be on the horn assembling a whole assassin team to vaporize every trace of us. Can't stop that, but it won't be quick for you. You're gonna have a lot on your hands to deal with first, Jackie."

She looks at me, her anger crumbling into confusion. "What are you–"

I point the gun down and fire. Right through her thigh, a part that won't be fatal, even though I wish I could end her right here in broad daylight.

It works. She goes down, too shocked to even scream, clutching at her wound.

I don't hear her howling for help till I'm closing the door to the car, telling the driver to step on it.

* * *

Present

I JUMP at the feel of a hand pulling at mine.

"Are you all right?" Gwen asks. "Miller, where are you?"

"Right here, babe. Sorry."

"Your hand is ice cold," she says, frowning. "I'm afraid to even ask what you were thinking."

"Then don't." I stand. "You don't want to know. I don't want you to know."

She squeezes my hand again. "Okay. It's too bad we don't have some of those remote control bombs you told me about when you and Keith got your cigarettes and socks off that truck."

A shiver zips up my spine. I don't have the heart to tell her J.T. set me up with an arsenal, and several remote detonation charges are just a few of my new toys.

Can't imagine I'll have to use them, but there's no telling how many reinforcements Jackie might call in. She could come here with a goddamn small army, considering I'm the man who shot her.

She stands and nods toward the cabin. "Want to teach me how to grill burgers? The kids are probably starving. Shane, at least. I swear that kid has a hollow leg."

Consider me Ginger-snapped. She's so beautiful, inside and out.

I love how she does that, shifts things, not just the conversation, but the tension inside me. Her voice must be half the magic. It's so bright, so cheerful, sunny and inviting and ferociously tempting.

"That's my boy. Always hungry," I say, touching the tip of her nose. "I'll grill the hamburgers. You can watch."

"Watch and learn?"

I give my head a slow shake. "When you're ready. Don't think the middle of the woods is a good place for you to experiment with grilling over an open fire."

Her eyes sparkle as she nods. "You might be right about that."

"Damn right, I am."

She giggles as we walk up the short trail to the deck, hand in hand. The desire to kiss her flares inside me, but I check myself, reluctantly releasing her hand so she can walk in the house.

I uncover the grill and use a wire brush on the metal rack before going inside to get the bag of briquets. Gwen has the fridge door open, bent over, digging things out. Can't help but give her sweet ass a quick pinch.

"Hey!" She spins about, holding a ketchup bottle. "Keep that up and I'll squirt you with this."

I step forward and reach around, this time to cup her butt with one hand. "Too slow."

Her face arches toward me, fighting another dick-teasing grin. "Oh, just wait."

The temptation is too much. I brush my lips on hers, then jerk back. "That bottle hasn't been opened yet. Guess I'll be waiting a long damn time."

She kisses my chin. "Then maybe I'll work on my bottle opening skills. Or do I need a lesson in that too?"

This girl.

I take the bottle and set it on the counter. While keeping an ear tuned outside, just in case one of the kids comes running up the hill and bursts inside, I grasp her waist and pull her close enough to feel my building hard-on.

The fullness of her tits pressed to my chest scorches my blood, sending raw heat to my cock.

"How 'bout you open something else for me?" I shouldn't ask that, shouldn't do this, but she's the distraction I need right now. Redheaded heaven, right here in blood-red hell.

Smiling, she slides her hands into my back pockets,

grinding against my growing dick. "Like what, teacher? Couldn't begin to guess what you mean."

I bite her earlobe softly, loving how she gasps, before whispering, "Those long, sweet legs for one."

She presses tighter against me. "Oh? And why would I do that?"

Even her voice is mock innocence. Hearing her purr like that wrecks me.

I slide a hand inside the back of her shorts. "The better to slide right into your tight little piece, Red."

"Hmmm..." She fakes a frown, twirling her hair.

I swear to everything holy I almost flip her against the counter and take her right there.

"What a big mouth you have, Miller. And what big eyes. And – oh, *this* right here." She reaches down, running her fingers up my bulge. "Whatever this is, it's very freaking *big.*"

"The better to fuck you with, Gwen. And I mean *now.*"

Enough games. Snarling, I take her hand and lead us straight to the bedroom.

She makes enough room near the bed for her hand to slide around and cup my cock. "There's a window here. If we open it, we can hear the kids."

"Yeah, we can." No argument here.

Look, I know how insane this is, but this need, this storm in my blood...I need her under me, consequences be damned.

She plants a quick kiss on my lips before stepping away. "Go stand by the window."

I reach out to grab her, but she's already too far away. "Where are you going?"

"Go stand by the window, Miller," she says, entering the joining bathroom. "Make sure you can see the kids."

I move to the window. Both Shane and Lauren are still on the shore, happily picking up rocks and throwing them so they'll skip over the water. They're blissfully oblivious, and that's what I'd love to be for the next ten minutes.

It's too soon for anyone to find us here. Not with J.T.'s Eagle watching up the only road, ready to give warning.

Red returns with a foil packet. "Glad you remembered these."

I bite back a grin. I don't tell her that I didn't.

May Courtney strikes again.

She rips the packet open with her teeth and one hand, using the other to unbutton my jeans. I pull down her shorts and panties, half-wondering if we're really doing this, right here, right now. She's adventurous, game for an animal quickie, and I love it.

With my jeans and underwear down around my legs, she rolls on the condom with a satisfying stroke. Then she steps out of her shorts and bends across the bed.

Spreading her legs, she cranes her ass toward me. "Legs open, Mr. Rush. Give it to me."

She's such a delectable little brat sometimes. You'd better believe I'll fuck her like one too.

I grasp her face and kiss her hard. "You're amazing, Gingersnap."

She grasps my butt, pulling me closer. "Only for an amazing man. Funny how that works out, isn't it? I just love how free you make me feel. How safe." She cups my balls. "And how horny. Miller, please. I need you in me now."

Don't need her to ask me twice.

I take her sweet cunt and it's as hot, slick, and eager as I knew it'd be.

My full length slides deep inside her with a single thrust.

"Oh!" She whimpers, opening her legs wider, pushing her ass up toward my abs.

I grasp her hips, holding her in place, slowly pumping in and out of her. No easy task when I want to pound her into tomorrow. "You were so ready for me, babe. Must've been wet the whole way here."

"You do that to me." Her legs brush my ass, teasing. "Get me all hot and bothered."

My hips move faster in response. She moans, and I can't decide if I love it even more than the steady smack of my balls on her clit.

We go hard for a while, and right before she comes, her face twists back for a kiss. I take her tongue the same way I rule her body for the next sixty seconds, loving how her pussy spasms, clenches, and sucks at my length.

Hard to believe I'm still going after that, but I am, pounding up into her at a faster, meaner clip.

With one hand, I fist her hair. The other rolls up her shirt and flips her bra down, so I can fondle her perked nipples while my dick goes to town on her. Nothing's ever felt so good.

The slow burn sustains a primal reaction in my blood, building to a roar. That's when I flip her over, get her under me good and proper, face to face so I can see everything my thrusts do to her.

I dip my head and suck one nipple hard, loving the sound of her muffled moan.

My mouth works harder, then I twirl my tongue around the other pebbled nipple before finally letting it go. "You don't have to be quiet here. Not right now. They won't hear while they're still at the lake, tossing rocks."

"They might," she says, right before laying her head back and moaning loudly.

My forehead dives against hers, pressing our faces together. I lock eyes, burning my gaze into her, wishing even my eyes could fuck her like I'm doing now, slamming my dick to the edge of her womb.

"Miller!" she groans. "Oh, yeah. *Yeah. That's. Good.*"

I know I've done it when a writer can't form sentences anymore. I pull back and drive into her again, several times, pressing harder, deeper, going for the zone.

Her hot little pussy clamps around me as she whimpers again. "Miller, come with me. Come together."

"Killing me, baby. Fuck, you're–"

I can't even finish when it happens.

Her pussy tightens, her flushed lips fly open, and this breathless little whine grinds out as her O hits full force. She always comes harder the second time.

I thought I could go forever, but the tension at the base of my spine explodes the instant I see her coming.

So I bury my lips on hers, smothering her screams, and give in.

White, electric heat sears up my balls and soaks my brain in ecstasy. For the next minute there's just this heat lightning of two tangled bodies, fire-red hair, and the most luscious pair of tits in my life bouncing like they might rocket right off her as I slam into her as hard as I can.

There's just Little Red Riding Cock and the Big Bad Wolf I've become, owning every inch of her.

There's just Gingersnap and me, enraptured in lust, drunk on the best hit of our lives.

I swear I've never come so hard for so long. When I'm finally spent, the afterglow leaves me damn near numb. I flop down next to her like I've lost my spine.

I glance out the window one more time, see the kids still by the docks, then look at Gwen, at her smiling face and sparkling green eyes.

She leans forward, kisses me with full tongue, and then lays her head on my shoulder. "Thank you."

"Not like you're paying me, babe." I laugh, having never been thanked for sex before like I just fixed her dishwasher. Hell, maybe I did fix *something* down there.

"No. I mean, it's almost like a housewarming present, I guess. I wasn't sure about all this, coming up here, these people chasing you...but now I know we'll be fine here. We'll be okay. We might even have a normal life up here, however long it lasts." She reaches over, running her fingers along my jaw, scratching at my beard.

"Well, you're welcome. Come again anytime," I say with a wink.

She giggles. "Seriously, we'd better get dressed now, before the kids decide to come looking for us. It'll be dark soon."

She's right, but even so, I want another round. The world feels whole again after we've fucked.

Planting a few parting kisses on my neck, she whispers, "One more thing: there's no couch here, Miller. We'll have to share a bed. I'll let you decide how you want to break the news."

Shit. I'd noticed that. I'm sure I'll just tell Shane and Lauren whatever I should, but not before I have some fun.

"There's a recliner out there, you know."

"Right," she whispers, her smile never skipping a beat. Then she untangles those long, beautifully Gwen legs from mine and sits up with a backward glance, mischief in her eyes. "We'll have to try that next."

XV: WINNERS AND LOSERS (GWEN)

*S*o call me flipping crazy.

Here we are, in my mother's cabin, hiding from some seriously evil people, and all I can think about is having sex with Miller Rush. Day and night.

We've been here for almost two weeks, and it's utterly unfair how everything he does presses my buttons. Turns me on, even when it should be as boring and mundane as folding socks.

Maybe it's because he's at ease when he's fishing, cooking, or just patrolling the grounds. I only see him tense when he's on his laptop, giving the screen a glare that might burn right through it.

Of course that does something *wicked* to me, too.

Of freaking course. I've become a total fiend for this bearish man.

All his faults.

All his talents.

All his endless, showery affection.

Miller knows it too. He uses it to send me close to the brink whenever he pleases.

Kinda like right now. The way he's staring at my boobs makes me wonder if he can see right through my shirt. My nipples pucker, helplessly lost remembering the warmth of his lips and the jagged, oh-so-sweet scratch of his beard.

It's the facial hair that really drives me wild. I never even knew I had a thing for guys with beards before he showed up and decided to let his scruff grow a little longer, a little more natural, a little more wild to match this frenzied, lumber-sexual life he's taken on.

Lucky me.

It'll be a few hours before anything can happen, though. I push off the dock with both hands and jump to my feet, shaking myself back into the present.

"You two need more worms," I say.

Miller looks over his shoulder and grins. "Two more fish, and we'll have plenty for supper. These are big walleye, could almost give the salmon back home a run."

"Wonderful." I pick up the can. "Lauren, honey, want to help me dig for more?"

She sets her book on the dock and leaps up. "Sure thing!"

I smile, knowing she loves to get her hands in the earth. There's something calming about the cool, dark, rich soil up here.

It's been a cloudy day, with rain off and on, so fishing was about the only outdoor activity for the kids this afternoon. We've all shared the two poles, but Lauren would rather read, and I was satisfied just watching.

Mostly because I often end up missing more fish than I catch, like yesterday, which is half the reason they need more worms.

Lauren and I walk up the short incline to the cabin, and then take the gravel path to the shed to grab a shovel. I'm about to open the door when something catches my attention.

A cigarette butt.

Miller doesn't smoke. Neither do I.

I reach down and hold it up to my face, frowning.

It could've been there before, I guess. An old one I just hadn't noticed. Mother brings plenty of odd writerly characters up here for her retreats, and I'm sure the smokes and coffee and scotch flow like fountains but...

My gut tells me different.

I don't open the shed door. "You know what? We have a few sausages we could eat along with the fish, and it looks like it's going to rain again soon. Maybe we should just say we're done fishing for the day."

Lauren's face lights up. "We could play another game of Scrabble."

"For sure." I lay a hand on her shoulder while scanning the area. "Let's go tell your dad and brother."

We aren't even to the dock again when Shane asks, "You found worms already?"

"Nope." Lauren shakes her head. "Gwen says we're done fishing. It's Scrabble time instead."

"What?" Shane says, giving his pole a shake. "You're crazy!"

A frown covers Miller's face as his gaze meets mine. I give a slight nod, gesturing at the shed.

"Your sister isn't crazy, Shane." Miller reels in his line. "We've got ourselves enough fish to clean."

"And it's going to rain again soon," Lauren says, tilting her head to stare into the overcast sky.

"You don't know that," Shane argues. "It's been cloudy all day."

"And raining off and on," Lauren tells him.

"Good. Fish bite in the rain, don't they, Dad?"

"Reel in, son." Miller pulls the stringer of fish out of the water. "And carry these up to the cabin."

I step onto the dock. "I'll carry your pole, Shane."

He huffs out a breath and hands me his pole, reluctantly taking the stringer full of fish from Miller.

As Shane and Lauren head for the cabin, Miller comes close and asks the inevitable. "What's wrong, babe?"

"There's a cigarette butt on the ground by the shed. I'm sure it wasn't there before."

His eyes darken and he takes the fishing pole from me. "Go to the cabin. Lock the doors."

"I can—"

"Cabin, Gwen. Keep the kids inside."

The idea of him getting hurt scares me. "Be careful. You have the local guy, don't you?"

"Yeah. Gonna talk to him now."

I run up the incline, trying to keep things light by playfully hurrying the kids inside. It's time for an early dinner prep.

So I don't know how to cook fish real well, but I do know how to clean them.

I had to learn last summer while staying up here with Mother, just the two of us. Apparently, her weakness is dealing with gills and guts. She's lucky I don't mind.

Lauren declines to help, taking a page from her, but Shane's more than happy to have something to do again. The window above the sink is open. I keep my ears tuned for any and all sounds while cleaning several big walleye and a couple little sunfish.

Once the fish are done, the filets soaking in a bowl of water in the fridge, Shane asks if he should throw the guts outside.

"Not yet. Let's just wait a little while, okay?" I nod toward the window, searching for an excuse. "It's raining, Shane. We'll wait until it's clear and then throw them down on the shore for the raccoons and turtles to eat."

"Are you two ready to play Scrabble yet?" Lauren asks, trotting over with the game box tucked under her arm.

"No." Shane looks up at me with disdain. "We already played that all week."

Lauren looks wounded. The last thing I need right now is a scrap between the kids.

"You did," I agree, and turn to Lauren. "Sometimes it's fun to change things up. You know, I thought I saw a few more games upstairs. Isn't there a Battleship box?"

"Yeah, Battleship!" Shane belts out, suddenly pumped. "Let's play that."

"But only two can play..." Lauren looks at me, her little eyes searching.

"That's okay, honey. I'm pretty busy, so why don't you two go on and have yourselves some fun? I think I've got some peanut butter cups chilling in the fridge. First one goes to the winner."

I wink at them, totally keeping it a big secret that I'll hand one out to the loser, too. Well, and myself.

I may have a lot to learn when it comes to grilling and setting breakfast meat on fire, but I'm a pretty awesome chocolatier. I learned to make peanut butter cups from scratch on a trip to Spokane once. This adorable little place called Sweeter Things had a free class after touring their shop.

Another research trip for Mother – what else? – but I'm glad I got something for myself out of this one.

"Come on, Lauren." Shane runs to the narrow set of steps leading up to the loft. "Let's go play. Bet I sink your whole fleet without breaking a sweat."

"We'll just see, Admiral Buttface." She sticks her tongue out and races up the stairs after him.

That's one crisis defused.

I quickly scan the house, looking out each and every window for any sign of Miller.

I don't see him. It's raining harder than it has been all day.

My heartbeat sticks in my throat, pulsing at a sick, angry rhythm. My mind conjures up the worst scenarios, the things I haven't really had to think of for days.

But part of me knew we'd gotten too comfortable here.

Knew the sky could fall any freaking second and –

There's a blur. Sudden movement in the woods almost gives me a heart attack.

Until I realize it's Miller and run to unlock the front door for him. He bounds up the steps and through the door I hold open.

"What did you find out there?" I ask.

He brushes his hands through his dripping wet hair. "Nothing."

I grab his arm and walk into the kitchen to grab him something to help dry off. "What about the man J.T. sent to watch the road?"

"Eagle's there. Right on schedule for making the rounds."

"Does he smoke?" I rummage around in the drawer for a towel.

"No, and he says no one has come anywhere close to turning down this driveway since he arrived. He checks for tire tracks several times a day." He kisses my forehead and takes the towel, giving his head a rub. "That cig could've been rotting there since last year. They don't decompose too fast. Though it looks fresher than I'd like."

"I just never noticed it before. Do you think..."

"No, Gingersnap. I don't. Probably our nerves getting the best of us, making a mouse into an elephant. Still..." He wipes the rain off his handsome face for good measure. "It was wise to check it out. No telling when one clue could mean everything."

"Booyah!" Shane yells from the loft, so loud it's barely muffled.

I grin. "Battleship. Pretty serious business up there."

He nods, smiles, and sets the towel on the counter next to the bowl of fish guts. "You cleaned the fish?"

I stand taller, lifting my chin. "Surprise."

He grabs my hips and pulls me closer, and I'm loving how he digs his fingers into my flesh. "Think you'll keep doing that to me forever."

Knowing the kids are too engrossed to come rushing down, I loop my arms around his neck. "Only good surprises, I hope."

"Very fucking good," he growls, running one hand between my legs.

I bend my knees, gliding against his weight, his support, his incredible muscles. There's nothing quite like having a man who's truly your rock, physically and emotionally.

His lips take mine then, eager as ever. And that's how I nearly melt into a mushy-feely puddle near his feet. When the kiss breaks, my shirt is soaked, saturated with the water he'd picked up.

Grinning, his hand skims up my body and cups my right breast, squeezing hard. "Sorry."

"Yeah, you look real sorry."

He gives me another kiss, his tongue leaving no doubt about his true intentions. "I'll go toss these fish guts by the lake while I'm still soaked. By the time I get back, you'd better be wetter. Fully ready for me, babe."

My eyes round, and I try not to smile.

I snap the towel at him as he picks up the bowl instead. He jumps out of the way, laughing as he walks out the back door.

I shiver at the sudden blast of chilly air. That's the thing about the Northwoods. A single heavy storm can change the temperature by thirty degrees almost instantly.

The front of my shorts are wet too, in more ways than one, so I head to the bedroom.

"Gotcha!" Sounds again from above. This time, it's Lauren. "How do ya like that, Captain Poopypants? I *won*."

"Best two out of three!" Shane shouts desperately.

"Fine, you're on! Bet I sink you even faster this time."

I grin as I walk into the bedroom. Those two are so delightful.

I've never enjoyed anyone living honestly, doing their thing, more than these kids. Except for their father.

That thought makes me smile brighter as I shut the bedroom door and yank off my shirt. Even the cups of my bra got a little drenched. With a sigh, I hang the shirt over the rail of the log bed and walk to the closet for a dry shirt and bra.

I'm still digging when I hear the door pop open. Turning, I instantly cover my front with a dry shirt, until I see Miller's grinning face.

"Surprise," he growls, more rain water dripping off him.

Dear Lord. He's got this whole rugged, beardy, furiously sexy movie star look happening, like he just stepped out of the rainy final battle scene in some wild thriller flick. Like he's done kicking butts and ready to lay down the law with his lady.

I point a finger at him. "Stay away, Mister. You already got the whole front of me wet, and I don't want to have to go fishing for more new clothes." I set the dry shirt aside to unhook my bra and step out of my shorts.

He turns, clicking the lock shut on the bedroom door. "Let me help."

"No," I say, even though the thought excites me. "You're wet."

"Stop projecting, Gwen." He walks toward me with mock sad puppy dog eyes. "How 'bout I give you a choice – a clean towel or letting my tongue figure out just *how* wet you are?"

Holy Toledo. I swear, the look he gives me could read my mind.

Shaking my head, I point to the bathroom. "Go towel off and then we'll talk."

"Doesn't sound as fun and it's not part of the deal." He totally ignores me, grabs me, and pulls me forward. "Your choice. Towel or tongue?"

Pure heat courses through me. From the way he growls it in my ear to the fire in my pulse. This defiant, ridiculous, irresistible man just might burn me down.

"Miller. The kids are awake," I remind him. But my argument is verbal only. My pulse won't stop racing, and I already *know* the look he'll give me once his fingers reach between my legs.

He pushes my breasts against him, flush with his chest. "Door's locked, and I know my kids. They'll go all day trying to outdo each other given half a chance. Means we should go too, Gwen. Go fucking *hard.*"

I'm trembling. My arms fall in surrender and I let him take over.

Those big, calloused hands roam my breasts, two at once, leaving me delirious.

It's almost shameful what he does to me. How hard it is to fight, how fast I give it up, how *insane* I come when he's in me. Is it fair to classify a man as a drug?

"Another wet spot," he growls, dipping his head and running his tongue down my throat, then my cleavage. My toes curl up.

"That wasn't a wet spot," I whisper, loving the thrill rippling through me, his hands going places, everywhere they please.

"No?" He nips one nipple, shooting me an icy look. "Was it there then?"

"Wrong. Keep going. Lower, I think."

He lifts a brow. "Little minx. I know it was rain there for sure. But if you're that hard up for me to taste your pussy..."

Oh! My clit aches. Savage anticipation building, braising every bit of me.

Walking backward, he pulls me away from the closet, across the room, straight for the bed.

Before I even know it, he flips me onto the mattress with my legs hanging over the edge. His hands go straight for my thighs and shift them apart.

"Fucking bliss," he growls, slowly inhaling my scent. "Knew you'd be wet for me, Gwen. Knew I'd put you in heat."

Guilty. I can't even try to deny it when he cranes his face forward. His stubble rakes my skin, soft and coarse, a delicious contrast that's only overpowered by his tongue finding my clit.

My pussy throbs. My knees shake. My eyelids flutter like they might just float off my face.

I can't hold back a groan. "You're just making me wetter," I whisper, raking my fingers through his thick, dark hair as his tongue winds tighter.

He growls his promise into my skin.

Then – oh, baby, then – he takes me apart piece by flaming piece.

Miller Rush was born to bring a girl down in fits.

I flop over on my back, feeling him spread my legs wider. His tongue goes deep, hard, starting so soft, so languid, and then burning faster and hotter like a napalm fire.

He sucks. He licks. He teases. He owns.

This man, this beast, already knows my own body better than I do. In no time at all, I'm a shaking mess, stuffing my own wrist against my lips to avoid screaming so loud they'll hear us upstairs, even through their shouting.

Two of his stern fingers plunge into my pussy. He finds the spot that makes the rest of me scream while his tongue dive-bombs my clit.

I bury my hands in the bedspread, knowing I'll need to hold on for this ride. I'm gone in less than twenty seconds.

Coming!

The fireball in my core explodes, incinerating every nerve, reverberating through me like an echo strummed to perfection by a rock star.

It *hurts* how good he riles me, carries me to heaven, and then lets me fall, slamming back into myself with a shaking, furious whimper.

I could go on and on about the unbearable heat, the growly sweetness of his tongue, the static hum of my own skin as muscles twitch and every extremity I own curls.

But there's a point where ecstasy with Miller Rush gets *truly* indescribable, and I'm so *there.*

Pleasure gushes, cascades, and finally lets me float back into my own body after what seems like forever. Then my legs fall slack on the bed; my body goes limp. Thoroughly drained by him.

He gives me a few parting licks before finally lifting his head, smirking like the sun just ate the moon. "There, babe. All dry now."

I laugh, shaking my head. "You're crazy."

"And you fucking love my insanity." He leans over me and kisses each nipple, then skims more up my throat until we press lips.

He's more right than he even knows.

Because I've obviously fallen hard for him, and I don't think I'll be getting up anytime soon.

I don't even want to imagine the state of my heart if this doesn't work.

If I can't spend the rest of my life with him and Shane and Lauren.

If somehow, some way, I can't become his wife for real and a mother to them.

But I'd probably die a few times if I told him these things.

So I just lay there, relishing the afterglow. Then, rejuvenated as always, I sit up.

He's gone. The bathroom door shut.

I glance at the bedroom door, wondering, then jump off the bed and run to the bathroom.

He's barefoot and shirtless, pulling down his pants that hug his hips so devilishly by the time I'm inside.

The hard-on he's sporting makes me proud. "Miller?"

"Gonna shower first," he says.

I shut the door behind me, hands poised on my hips. "You aren't getting off that easy."

"No?" His sly smile comes again, haloed in scruff I could just kiss for days. "Figured you'd join me."

"If you insist..."

I shake my head and reach out, folding my hand around his cock. Every time I touch it, I'm amazed at how soft, yet rock-hard, it is. Like steel wrapped in velvet, equal parts gorgeous and enticing and lethal.

Stroking it gently, but firmly, I sidestep, forcing him to move with me. Once his back is against the door, I kiss him hard. "Not so fast. It's my turn to mess you up."

"Babe, I–fuck!" he snarls, fingers tangling in my hair.

I've dropped to my knees, taking his cock deep in my mouth, all the way to the back of my throat.

Feeling how he shudders just might be the best thing ever. And knowing it's from the pleasure I'm giving him? Priceless.

"Gingersnap." He huffs out a breath. "I—"

I pull my head back, sucking his cock all the way to the head, smacking my lips as I release the tip. "You'll lean back and enjoy this, Miller Rush. Just as much as I did. Fair is fair."

He cranes his head back, another growl bleeding out of him. "Shit, I already am."

I swirl my tongue over the head of his cock, loving how the muscles in his legs flex.

Gripping his base, I pump him up and down, stroking the entire length while taking him deeper. I fondle his balls while sucking.

He tastes so good, manhood incarnate with dark notes of earth and musk.

I love how velvety his skin feels against my tongue, the sides of my mouth, massaging my lips.

I suck him until I'm breathless, then brush my tongue over his balls, replenishing my lungs to take him in my mouth again. He starts pumping into me.

It's so good, so amazing, this terrible urge builds inside me all over again.

I didn't even know giving a blowjob could do that.

With him, it's a given.

He growls, pulling my hair a little harder. I encourage him, reaching behind his thighs to squeeze his strong butt, loving how he thrusts harder, faster.

My pussy won't wait long. We need a finish so we can get to the next part that much sooner.

So I cup my hands over his balls, around the base of his cock, and suck him like mad. My tongue digs into that little spot I know he loves, right under the crown of the cock.

I'm rewarded with a snarl, him hitching my hair so strong it's almost painful. "Gingersnap! Fuck, gonna–"

I know. And I have no earthly intention of stopping now. I glance up and gently needle him with my teeth.

"Gwen," he growls again, his legs twitching, his huge chest rising and falling as his breathing goes wild.

My lips go down, taking him as far as I can go. That's when he throws his head back and shows his teeth.

His seed comes in a hot, indecent, totally chaotic flood. I swallow as best I can, but even I can't keep up.

I'm just sucking harder as his come fills me, spills down my face, splashes my tits like some kind of animal marking.

It's as crude as it is heavenly. So I let my own climax go, taking as much pleasure as I'm giving.

I suck until I feel him groan and relax. Despite the Miller storm in my mouth, I feel weirdly relaxed and satisfied too.

So I draw back, letting his cock slowly ease out of my mouth, cleaning my lips with my tongue. Seeing a droplet still on the head of his dick, I lick it off too, then tongue his cock lovingly one more time.

"Goddamn, that was glorious." He pulls me up by my shoulders.

I kiss his lips, squeeze the dormant hard-on still in my hand. "Now, we're even."

"Bull." He wraps his arms around me, his hands drifting to my ass. "I've got ideas, babe."

"Oh, you really want to go best two out of three?" I can't help thinking of the kids when I say it, hoping they'll stay busy with their game a while longer.

Laughing, he hugs me tighter. "You already won, sucking me off like that. But I'd be an idiot to walk away without a real fuck."

My pussy tingles, full of need. "Maybe you're right."

After another long hug, another kiss, I step back, knowing the kids will get bored with their game sooner than later. "I cleaned the fish, but you'll have to cook them."

"I know." He kisses my forehead, resting his lips against

mine. "But you're nuts if you think I was talking about dinner."

Without another word, he pulls me into the shower. There, underneath the steaming water, he shows me how wonderfully wild his 'ideas' get.

Miller mounts me from behind, pinning my hands to the tiled wall in front of me. He shifts my legs apart, biting my shoulder, marking me for real this time.

He's lucky I'm good at covering it up after he gets rough. And he's doubly lucky that, even though I'll *never* admit it to his face, I kinda like it.

One thing's for sure – I definitely don't hate how hard he takes me under the shower.

Piston hips, roaming hands, fingers palming my breasts and pinching my nipples. The raw, wicked friction of his cock inside me is enough. Especially when we've been at it for so long, there's no need to warm up again.

This is a *real fuck* just like he said.

I don't even like that word, but God, do I love this.

His growl, his rhythm, his incredible weight and strength behind me. How he shatters me once, and again, and brings me apart over and over on his incredible cock. I can't even tell where one climax ends and another begins.

It seems like an eternity before he snarls, before his hands squeeze my breasts, yanking me back into him. We didn't even remember the condom this time, but thankfully, I'm on the pill and I trust he's safe because *oh, hell.*

Miller grinds into me, thrusts up with a growl that could split the world in two, and buries his length to the hilt like he's *trying* to knock me up. Then the same unruly seed I sucked out of him pours into my pussy, my womb, his balls unleashing everything.

It's kind of amazing how hard, how long, how freaking much he comes.

And the wild, manic heat of him erupting inside me brings me off all over again. I barely have time to fumble, cranking up the shower, praying the noise hides the howl ripping out of me.

* * *

LATER, when I can actually stand again without my knees giving out, I kiss him one more time and leave the bathroom, get dressed, and pad out to the kitchen. Shane and Lauren are still upstairs bombing each other's fleets like they're reenacting Midway.

Outside the window, the weather's turned from rain to a full-blown storm, complete with thunder and lightning. Thanks to the generator, we don't need to worry about losing power. Miller filled it this morning for backup, so we should be good again until the day after tomorrow.

Guessing at what he'll need to fix the fish and sausages, I pull things out of the fridge and set them on the counter.

He comes out of the bedroom, fully dressed in Minnesota flannel that looks so good I want to tear it off him all over again. But the kids finally come running down the steep steps.

"I won. I won!" Lauren squeals. "Best two out of three. Can I have my reward, Gwen? You said chocolate."

Miller looks at me and grins. I remember the peanut butter cups and flash them a smile.

"Of course. Let's make it dessert after dinner, okay? Must be a lucky day for us girls."

Because I won best two out of three, too, I think to myself.

Miller laughs and pats Lauren's shoulders. "Good job, baby girl. Keep it up and maybe I'll have a kid who goes to West Point."

Shane kicks glumly at his other heel. Miller sees him and slaps his shoulder, too.

"Be a good sport, son. Sometimes you learn as much losing as you do by winning."

"Even in 'war?'" He makes quote signs with his fingers, knowing full well it's just a game.

"*Especially* in war. All the way back to George Washington and Alexander the Great, probably. Hell, sometimes I think we only came out on top in Afghanistan and didn't get another Vietnam because the officers learned a thing or two."

Shane's expression eases and he nods. "Well, I guess that makes sense."

Across the room, Lauren frowns and plants her little hands on her hips. "Daddy, did you two play Scrabble without me? You and Gwen?"

"Nope," he says.

We know what she's thinking. He's trying so hard not to smile I almost burst out laughing myself.

"No one would play Scrabble without you," Shane says, rolling his eyes. "You're like the only one who really likes that game. Making words. *Sheesh.* That's about as fun as a spelling test." He looks up at Miller. "What game did you guys play?"

I clear my throat, blushing. "Well, um..."

Miller walks over and picks up the bowl of fish filets. "Oh, ours was more of a contest."

"Cleaning fish." Shane nods, taking a good guess. "Gwen's really good at that. Fast, too. I watched her earlier."

"She's good and fast, all right." Miller winks at me. "And since the girls won, the boys have to cook supper. Come on, Shane."

The little boy makes a face and scratches his head. "Aw, okay. I guess that's fair."

"You guess?" Lauren jabs him. "That's more than fair, Admiral."

"Don't worry, the girls will do the dishes," I say, returning Miller's over-the-top, totally not heart-stabby wink. "We want everybody happy here."

Shane grins. "Now that's fair!"

"Why don't you two go work on your stories while Shane helps me cook?" Miller asks.

I love how he does that, encourages some me time with Lauren and my notebook. I've told him it isn't easy to make the words flow sometimes.

In fact, it's hard freaking work. Sometimes I think the main reason Mother does her research trips is just to clear her head.

But Miller gets it. He listens. How many girls would *kill* for a man who does that?

He's read more of my story, too, and even made a few helpful hints on the intrigue whenever I've gotten stumped, or a little too freaked to keep going. On the one hand, being up here in a cozy cabin hoping the bad guys don't come is great inspiration.

But it's also insanely hard to figure out where the line is between fiction and real life.

All in all, I'm further along on this story than I've ever been, and still really like everything about it.

Lauren and I each claim a recliner and delve into writing. We throw happy glances at each other once in a while, whenever a noise or laughter from the kitchen catches our attention.

Like everything he cooks, the fish and sausages turn out perfect. It's a kind of fish stew with plenty of spices served with piping hot rice on the side. Hot, steamy, and delish on a rainy night.

Lauren and I keep our end of the deal, cleaning up the kitchen afterwards, and then I give both kids a few chilled peanut butter cups to munch on.

The storm has passed by the time we're winding down, but it's still drizzling. I pull up the weather app on my phone, which shows another wave of Doppler green blobs heading our way.

"Gotta love a place that reminds me of home," Miller says, staring at the screen over my shoulder. He reaches down and takes my fingers in his, squeezing wonderfully.

We pass the evening playing games, including a round of Scrabble, until Miller announces it's time for bed around nine.

The kids both give us hugs goodnight.

"You know, this *is* kinda like home, but better. I like this place, Dad," Shane says, pausing on the stairs leading up to the loft. "Even though it doesn't have TV, it's fun."

"I like it, too, bud," Miller says. "Great view. Good fishing. Awesome company. What more could a guy ask for?"

Judging by the glint in his eye when I look over, I've got a pretty good idea. My body tingles, and I cough into my hand, hiding my blush until after Shane scampers off.

A short time later, after the light up in the loft goes out, Miller stands, reaching for my hand to lead me to the bedroom. "Up for another contest?"

I grin, setting aside my notebook after reading things over.

Though technically, I'd only been staring at the pages and editing like a snail, waiting for silence from the loft. "Best two out of three again?"

He shrugs. "Or three out of five."

"Or five out of seven," I say, loving the fire crackling in his eyes.

I turn out the lamp next to the chair and leap up into his arms.

XVI: EYE TO EYE (MILLER)

*W*hether it's the fresh woodsy air or the primal satisfaction that fucking Gwen senseless leaves behind, I'm not sure, but I've never slept as well as I have the last few nights.

So when my eyes open, I lie still for a moment, wondering what woke me.

It's still dark. Nowhere near morning when the dawn's first light flits through the mist rolling off Rainy Lake.

This darkness should be peaceful, lend itself to sweet dreams.

Instead, I'm wired.

There's no denying the tension pulling at my body, the way the hair on my arms pricks up.

Something's out of sorts here.

Silence echoes in my ears as I listen for something I'm not sure of till I hear it.

There.

Shit. It's a muffled sound, almost like a scraping, out of place in the quiet, cloudy night.

Slowly, I ease off the bed, cross the room to the one small

window in the bedroom, and carefully peel back the curtain. It's as dark out as a horse's ass.

My eyes focus, pinpointing an area where I may or may not have seen something. A motion.

A faint flash, a movement, a deer, a bear, a damn intruder.

I'm not sure if I'm right. Nothing but my gut to go on, but something's out there. Or *someone.*

"What is it?" Red whispers, turning over.

I walk back to the bed, not meaning to scare her. "Don't know, but go get the kids up, quietly. Take them down to the basement."

Now wide awake, she climbs out of the bed and shimmies into the clothes she'd removed when we came to bed. I grab mine too and throw them on.

Knowing she hates the dark, I grasp her hand and squeeze it real tight. "We can't turn on any lights, babe. Not if–"

"I know," she whispers. "I'll be okay."

I nod.

Wanting to assure her there's nothing to be afraid of, I say, "Just stay quiet. I won't let anything happen to you or the kids."

"I know that, too." She kisses me quickly. "Just don't let anything happen to you, either."

"I won't." I have to bite my lips together then to prevent something else from slipping out.

Words I haven't said to anyone except my kids in years. Not since Willow.

The L-word.

"Love you, Gingersnap," I growl, wishing I had time to appreciate the sparkle in her eyes. Instead, I hold her hand as we cross into the living room. "Don't come out, no matter what you hear."

"Got it. We won't. And Miller...I love you too." She kisses

my cheek again and lets go of my hand in order to climb the stairs.

It's hard as hell, but I have to forget the tear she wiped off her rosy cheek.

If it's more than just a black bear milling around our place, I've got bigger worries than figuring out what love means.

I move to the windows on the front of the A-frame cabin, and once again shift only a small piece of the heavy drapes to take a look.

It's just as dark on this side, almost pitch-black.

There's a string of miniature solar lights hanging off the tiny porch roof. They glow about as strong as fireflies, but they're probably at half power tonight, casting the dullest orange glow.

Just enough light for me to see the boughs of one of the tall pine trees move.

Shit.

Wind wouldn't do that. A small animal could, maybe, or a bigger one like a bear, but my senses wouldn't be this prickly over anything that couldn't talk.

I sense more than hear Gwen and the kids creeping down the stairs, and then through the door under the steps that goes down into the concealed basement. It's more of an old storm shelter than anything, the one part of the house that isn't fully modern.

When the door closes with barely a click, I walk over to a trunk in the corner and tap my thumbprint since it's too dark for the code. There's a mechanical *thunk* as it unlocks. One more goodie J.T.'s buddy Eagle rigged up for me.

It's where I stowed my duffel bags. One side still has the other half of the cash, and the other has my emergency weapons cache.

I insert the magazines and tuck two 9mm handguns into

the waistband of my pants, then pull out a cushioned bag holding several flash grenades. They're tactical specialty, hardly more powerful than most firecrackers, designed to blind the enemy rather than hurt them.

Lastly, I grab the case holding the remote control for the explosives I buried around the perimeter of the cabin. They're an option of last resort, if I need a diversion or a big, strategic boom. Without the remote, they pose no threat to anything.

I put the minis in one pocket and tuck the remote in the other, close the trunk, and walk to the kitchen area to sneak out that door.

I consider texting Eagle, but refrain. He'd have already sent me a text if he'd seen something. I hope he's still alive.

Hell, if I'm lucky, that movement I saw could be Eagle making a deeper probe to check something, so I ease out the door and plant myself against the wall, walking to the edge of the small deck.

Scanning the area slowly, I let my gut tell me where to pin my focus.

It's too damn dark. I ease down, not wanting to wait, and elbow crawl my way to the steps, slide down them, and crouch near the bottom of the deck.

My ears catch a sound I *can* make out. I hold my breath, listening.

A twig just snapped. Stepped on by someone's uneven foot.

Whoever did it stops. For more than a minute, there's not a murmur. I grit my teeth together, readying myself for hell.

They're out there, all right. Just waiting, making sure no one else heard or stirs inside the house before they make their next move.

Fuck.

The air locked in my lungs ignites. I let it out through my

nose, slow and quiet, so it doesn't distract my hearing a single iota.

A thud sounds then. A big one, along with a muffled grunt.

Head down, I run to the shed, the source of the sound.

Weird. Still nothing but silence echoes in my ears. I ease along the wall to the backside, then stop at a brief flash of light.

There's someone down the driveway, scanning around with a flashlight.

It could be Eagle, but my gut says it's not.

I slip back around the corner of the shed and then make a mad dash into the woods, where the big pines have thick, low branches. I grab them as I move so the boughs don't sway, then shimmy up the tree, finding a spot with a good vantage point to see the road.

I don't have to wait long before I can count heads. *Four of them.*

From the way they walk and the height differences, it's three men and one woman.

Ears fully tuned, my gut boils when I hear her. Jackie Wren's voice, her low, whispered, frustrated words.

"Why the hell hasn't Lex signaled?" she hisses. "I can't believe this. Out here in the middle of goddamned nowhere when I should be in DC for a conference."

The man ahead of her swipes an annoyed hand through the air. I almost laugh at his signal.

Jackie Wren never knows when to shut up.

I've sat through enough company meetings to know that woman lives to hear herself talk. She thinks she's the next genius in industrial biotech. Not the soulless, hateful beast she actually is.

"What the hell does it mean?" she hisses again.

Nobody answers.

"He must already be in the cabin," her goon answers, his gravelly voice low.

The hair on the back of my neck stands up.

In the cabin? *Fuck.*

Micro-inch by micro-inch, I twist and glance down at the ground.

Eagle's there, looking up at me, this dark, muscular silhouette among the leaves and pines. He holds up one finger, then points into the woods.

I give him a thumbs-up. The thud I'd heard was him, taking down one of Jackie's goons on the perimeter.

He then points to the trees along the driveway. I give another thumbs-up, knowing he'll be sneaking through the woods, and hopefully ambushing Jackie and her goons before the fucks see it coming.

I don't hear a sound as he walks away, fading into the woods.

"What about Boone?" Jackie asks, her voice shriller. "Why hasn't he signaled?"

My nerves tingle. Lex *and* Boone.

Eagle had only taken out one front runner. That means there's another asshole out here somewhere.

The man walking ahead of the others cuts his hand through the air again.

"Why does he do that? String us along forever?" Jackie again. There's a sound like dirt, rocks kicking up and spattering the ground again. "Ugh! I can't even walk out here. Where *is* he?"

I have to act, before her other man surprises either me or Eagle. Draw out him out from wherever he is.

"Up your ass, Jackie," I growl into the darkness. "That's where he's gone."

They all stop. The front man's gun shimmers as he swings it toward the shed.

"Miller Rush?" Jackie whispers. "Finally. The man I've come a *very* long way to see. You know why I picked you over Keith, right?"

Dammit, I know. The fact that she's tripping over her own feet probably means she's still not fully healed from the hole I left in her leg.

She lets out her nasty, high-pitched laugh. "What's a lady got to do so you'll come out and play like a big boy? You can run, but you can't hide, Miller. Not from me. Not forever."

I say nothing, my fist tightening on my gun. It's too dark for them to pinpoint where I'm at without a lot of effort.

"It's adorable how you thought that little trick would work, sending us after your car down to Texas. It barely got as far as Iowa before we heard there weren't any kids. No little Lauren. No Shane. I wonder if he's just as big a clumsy badass as his daddy? Hey, maybe we'll all find out soon! I bet he's up there in that house, isn't he? It's almost a shame Lex will have to ruin his sweet widdle dreams."

My rage burns hotter, hearing her talk about threatening my children. I want to strangle this bitch.

It's bait.

I know better than to answer except on my own terms. And now, I'm ready.

"I'm not running or hiding anymore, Jackie," I bite off. "Matter of fact, I've been expecting you. Took you forever to drag yourself here. Must be that bum leg."

"Fucking prick," I hear her swear under her breath before she regains her evil poise. "Hasn't kept me from wearing my nicest heels out here just for you, Rush. The tall ones with diamonds in the tips and hundred-year-old ivory heels. The boys, they told me not to do it, said I'd have trouble walking on this turf, but you know what? You really want to know?"

Like hell I do.

I can't even see her face through this darkness, but I

know she's grinning like a Cheshire cat when she says, "I wore them so I could pluck your shitty eyeballs out, one by one. And then I'll make both your babies eat them before we toss your carcass in that big lake. As for the brats, well, I'm sure we can find *something* to do with them."

Goddamn, I'm gonna *kill her.*

She and the men are looking frantically toward the shed. It's doing exactly what I want it to do, bouncing my voice off the sloped roof so they think that's where I'm at.

"But you know, call me crazy, it doesn't have to go down like that. No kids or steely-blue eyes need to be harmed. Do you want to make a deal, Miller?"

"For what?" I growl, knowing it's total bull. She's trying anything she can to flush me out.

"We both know the answer to that. Every man has his price."

I scan the road behind them, trying to see Eagle again, or the other goon.

Too dark.

They're still coming, but not close enough.

The front man who's scouting ahead just needs to take two more steps, and he'll be in range to get the full brunt of a concealed blast.

I can't set it off before then, or they'll scatter like rats.

"I don't have anything you want, Jackie, and vice versa."

She laughs. "Don't lie to me. Not after all the trouble you went through with Keith breaking into encrypted systems." She's talking to the shed, and all three men are busy scanning the roof. "Tell me, Miller, have you heard from him lately? Ran off somewhere deep in the Ecuadorian rain forests, didn't he? Nasty places, I hear. Lots of predators."

I squeeze the remote so tight my knuckles pop. I haven't heard from Keith since I got the new phone and sent him the cryptic text about jellybeans. J.T. told me last week he'd made contact with people he knew down there, and they'd let him know the instant they heard something.

So far, nothing.

I hope he's had better luck than me shaking these Mederva pricks.

"Oh, now, cat got your tongue?" Jackie starts walking again, her ridiculous heels crunching the ground, and so do the others.

"I wouldn't come any closer if I were you," I snarl.

"Why's that? Don't tell me you have company? We've been watching since yesterday, and we know it's just you, your kids, and that twitchy redhead who for some ungodly reason decided to sign her death warrant, following you here. They're still in the cabin, which Lex is dousing with gas right now. And after he's got your kids out safely, we'll all have a nice, big bonfire. Unless, of course, we can come to an agreement to get you to cough up those files you *stole.*"

Shit, maybe she does want the data. Is she that insane, thinking I'll hand it over?

My eyes shift back to the front man. His next step lands him exactly where I want him.

Holding my breath, I tap the red button on my remote. The searing blast knocks him on his ass and sends his gun flying. Then hell opens up.

Jackie crouches down, covering her head, shouting, while the other two men freeze in their boots.

"That's why I wouldn't come any closer, Jackie," I whisper into the night.

"You arrogant idiot!" she yells. "Stop. Just give me the damn footage you stole from my security cameras and we'll leave. We'll–"

"I collected a hell of a lot more than footage off your cams, Jackie." My turn to laugh. I let that sink in for a bitter moment, then add, "But it's not really mine anymore. It's about to make one hell of a headline. Almost as good as the one I almost made, writing your obituary."

"Don't lie to me, *Miller*." She stands up, my name like a curse on her lips. "I'm the only one who wants what you have. The only one willing to *pay* your stupid ass for it."

Disbelief fills me. "Is that what you still think this is all about, Jackie? Money? You think you can buy your way out of this?"

"What else could it be about?!" she barks into the night. "Seven figures, Miller. Think about what that could buy."

She sounds unsure now. Like she's sold off her soul for so long she can't possibly fathom why I care about those kids she's helping fucking murder.

"Four million dollars!" she calls out loudly. "All you have to do is just hand everything over."

"Bitch, you couldn't pay me enough to give you anything. Not what I'm after. What you're doing at Mederva is wrong."

"Hardly! No one's getting hurt! Do you even *know* the diseases those labs are close to curing thanks to this? How much longer it'd take without our leg up? Or are you that dense? Those kids are already dead and on ice every time they show up!"

"Shut the fuck up." Anger rips through my veins like a current.

Perfect timing. There's movement, a shadow that has to be Eagle creeping around the cabin, his rifle coming up. Two more seconds and we'll end this, but we don't get the chance.

A bloodcurdling scream splits the air, turning my blood ice-cold.

I recognize who it belongs to.

Same with the hoarse shout from a man who must be Lex. "I've got the little girl, Ms. Wren!"

Shit!

Lauren, Shane, and Gwen, all flash through my mind, my

heart, my soul at the same time. Eagle ducks back around the corner, just as thrown as I am.

I don't even give the Queen Bitch a second to smile.

Snarling, I jack my thumb into other buttons on the remotes for all the mines near the front of the cabin. Then I leap out of the tree, praying I don't snap a leg.

XVII: SPLASH (GWEN)

y lungs burn, gasping for air, choked on fear and the overwhelming stink of gasoline.

I can barely see through the tears stinging my eyes, but my ears are still working just fine. Lauren's scream has me spinning around.

"I've got the little girl, Ms. Wren!" a man roars.

Think again, jackass!

I grab Shane's arm, pulling him out of the lean-to shed that houses the generator. "Now, Shane! Run! Just like I told you. We'll be right behind you, big guy, I promise."

He gives me a harsh look, biting his lip, but he knows how serious this is.

There's so much determination in him as he bolts right out of my arms. I know where he gets it.

While Shane makes his escape, I barrel toward the faint outline of a man in the darkness. He's running to the edge of the cabin – another group of people? – with Lauren in his arms.

No sign of Miller.

I *have* to get her back.

I hate that I lost her to begin with, but as soon as I smelled the thick, vicious gasoline scent hanging in the air – a ton of it – I knew we had to move. Get the hell *away* from the cabin before the man rummaging around inside lit the whole place up.

We didn't have a choice but to flee into the night. But the bastard was waiting, and he tore her away from me, taking off around the corner before I could catch up.

I don't know if there's more of them.

If there are, splitting up like this at least gives us a fighting chance.

My eyes focus on Lauren's captor. He's shorter than I am, but that's all I know.

He may be armed. He may be brutal. He may be a flipping coward.

Whatever he is, I'm about to find out, and suffer the consequences a thousand times over if it means she goes free.

I plow right into him as hard as I can. For once, my tall, nearly Amazonian bones help me out. He's pure muscle, like hitting a wall, but I think I've caught him by surprise.

He topples over, just long enough for me to snag a fistful of his hair. A split second later, the entire world goes *boom*.

Several explosions erupt in a messy circle around the whole property, sending bright orange up like flares and dirt raining down.

Oh, Jesus.

It's like the Fourth of July, only louder, and a thousand times scarier. The flashing lights show me exactly what I need to see as I wrench harder on the man's hair, forcing him to turn. He's still doubled over in shock. I seize the chance to land a hard knee to his face.

"Let go of her!" I'm screaming, frantic, pulling at her arm so hard I'm worried I'll break her.

The man roars, swearing at me, his foot caught on something. His eyes glow pure menace as the fading explosions illuminate his face.

No time to stare, to hate, to fear. I need Lauren back, and I need to put distance between us and those explosions, now, before they risk reaching the gasoline-soaked cabin.

My instinct does the thinking for me. Pulling back my other hand, I plant a fist directly in his throat and then kick him in the groin.

It works.

As he doubles over, I grab Lauren's arm one more time, breaking her free, and swing her over my shoulder as I run, run, *run* for the lake.

"We have to swim now, honey," I tell her. "Just like I said in the basement, remember? All the way out to the pontoon boat."

"I know, Gwen," she says, sniffling in this heartbreaking way. "I think...I think I can."

"You'll be fine, baby. I've got you the whole time, you and Shane both." Yes, I'm crying, and I don't have the time.

We need to move.

I'm scared for her, for everyone, but this was the only plan I could throw together. More noises ring out behind us.

Gunshots this time, bullets zinging through the air, and another deafening blast goes off as my shoes finally crunch the rocky gravel around the lake before scampering up the dock. It's still painfully dark, but I can hear Shane, splashing just off the end, waiting for us.

"Ready, Lauren?" I whisper, pulling off her shoes and then abandoning mine before I kick my legs into the water. "It's now or never."

She gives me a nod, folding herself into my arms. I try to cover up the splashing sound as we submerge. I point Shane at the boat, barely a shadowy outline in the ink smear of dawn.

I told the kids to stay down for as long as they could. To only come up for air or stay in sight of me, and to not kick their feet above the water, hoping that'll prevent anyone from seeing us.

I surface, watching the water until I see each one of them come up and then go under again.

Even scared witless out here, I'm proud of them. *So very proud.*

I keep surfacing every few strokes, making sure they're never more than a couple feet away, and then swim a few feet behind them, urging them on until the pontoon isn't just a distant landmark anymore.

Shane touches its metallic side first and then swims around to the backside, where I'd mentioned there's a ladder. He's quick on his feet, strong, and he's there to help Lauren up after him.

Once I'm on board, I do a quick scan. It's been a while, but I don't see any weird leaks or abnormalities that would make our little refuge unsafe. Thank God for small favors.

"Get down, guys," I whisper, knowing how the water carries sound, even through the commotion and flashes I still see coming from land. "Stay on the floor, heads low, until I tell you different. Got it?"

"Sure!" they both whisper, eager to listen, even if I can sense the terror in their voices.

The worst part is, I'm not even sure it's for us. There's no telling what happened to Miller, and my heart beats with a sicker, heavier thud every spare second I stop to think about it.

I barely made it here with the kids, and we're not even safe. Not yet.

I can't lose him, too. I can't–

There's louder shouting coming from the shore, but it's too dark to see anything.

For the first time in my life, I'm not bothered by the dark, knowing there are worse things in it. I'm also pissed because it seems like the sun will never rise. I'm sure we've lost five or ten minutes waiting through this chaos, and it's no lighter than when we jumped into Rainy Lake.

I hate this with a vengeance.

The man I love is out there somewhere. Vanished. Fighting. Possibly hurt. And I can't see a freaking thing!

"Gwen, look!" Shane says, tugging at my hand. "That's Dad! He's...he's yelling for us."

I squeeze his hand so he'll pipe down and perk my ears up. It's suddenly eerily silent across the murmuring waters. My heart skips a beat, waiting for his voice.

"Gwen! Shane! Lauren!"

It couldn't be anyone else. Hearing him, knowing he's alive, stings my eyes. And I know he wouldn't be calling unless we were in the clear.

I leap up to my feet, waving. "Miller! *Mill-errrr!* Over here!"

"Dad!" Shane joins me, and I hug him tight.

Then Lauren pops up too, cupping her hands over her mouth. "Daddy!"

"Where are you?" he roars.

"The boat! On the pontoon boat!" I scream, right before fresh sobs cut me off, gathering Lauren and Shane to my sides. "We're all here!"

I kneel down and hug them closer. You know that awkward moment when your heart just ruptures at the seams and touchy-feely stuffing bursts out?

Yeah, I'm living it. I can't believe we made it.

The thought of someone hurting them almost made me snap. Literally.

Ginger-snap. Just like he calls me.

The woman who loves their father and loves them.

The woman who'd give all four limbs to keep them safe.

Right now, the freaked out girl who just wants this to be over so we can have a second chance. A real life that's just like our good times here, without the constant danger and armed stalkers looming over us.

"Hang on, I'm coming!" he roars across the shore.

At the sound of Miller's voice, I release the kids and jump onto one of the seats to see into the water. It's finally getting lighter, just enough so the lake looks more like dull liquid mercury than a seething dark mass.

Our eyes are glued to him as he sails through the water, so swiftly and fluidly I wonder if even I could learn a thing or two from his swimming.

"Dad, there's a ladder back here!" Shane shouts, running to the end of the boat.

Miller climbs aboard a moment later, his hair dripping, rugged and sexy and perfect.

I hang back a second, giving him a moment with the kids. But when he steps up next to me, I nearly melt as those huge, inked, overprotective arms I feared I'd never feel again totally envelop me.

"Thank fuck you're safe," he growls, kissing my hair, my forehead, my lips.

Lauren and Shane go quiet, nudging each other and smiling. Honestly, I can't stop myself from smiling either. Because if there's nothing left to hide, if this strange, beautiful thing we've made has a fighting chance, then even this hell was *worth it.*

I cling to him, not wanting to let go.

Never. Ever.

"Hey, Dad, what happened to the bad guys?" Shane asks, rubbing his eyes.

Miller keeps his arm around me as he rubs Shane's head. "They're at the cabin, all tied up. A couple fled, jumped into their SUV and skedaddled, but Eagle's keeping watch on the others."

Shane pumps a fist into the air. "Wow, so cool."

"You were so brave, Daddy," Lauren whispers, throwing her arms around his leg with a sunny smile.

No argument here.

What he did out there, with barely any help, was nothing short of saving our lives.

Miller kneels down and kisses Lauren's forehead. "Don't count yourself short, baby girl. You swam all the way out here in a crunch. I'm proud of you."

Lauren blushes, looking up at me. "I had a lot of help. Gwen said I could do it, and I did. And Shane...he was all right."

"All right? I yanked you up the ladder!" Shane folds his arms in such a melodramatic pout we all burst out laughing.

"You did good, son. Everybody here did their part," Miller says, leaning down to kiss Lauren's head before looking up at me. "Especially Gwen. In the *dark,* no less."

So, I think he's trying to make everyone here blush. My turn.

"Wish I could say I faced down my fears but...I found bigger ones. Some guy was pouring gas all over the cabin, we could smell it from the basement. It was almost suffocating. We had to take our chances." I shake my head. "I'm sorry we couldn't stay put like you asked."

Fury crosses his face. Pure rage, hatred for the monsters who would've lit us on fire, if they'd had half a chance.

"Don't apologize. You did good, babe. Real damn good."

My nose itches and I search the shoreline again for obvious flames. "Miller, is the cabin...?"

"Still in one piece last I checked. We got lucky. If I'd shifted those charges a foot or two closer, odds are your ma would need a new place to play Thoreau."

"Thor-who? Dad, Gwen also beat up that guy who tried to take Lauren! I watched the whole time from the dock. You should've seen her." Shane throws a few air punches. "*Pow, pow!* Down he went."

Miller grins at me and nods.

"Like I said, we got lucky, Shane." He turns to the benches lining the sides of the rails. "Let's see if we've got any paddles in this boat so we don't have to swim back to shore."

There are paddles, long oars, but because of how high the railing is, Miller and I have to sit on the front of the pontoons in order for them to reach far enough into the water. They're truly a last resort option.

As we start paddling, an odd, mournful howling splits the air.

I freeze, a shiver coursing up my spine. "What's *that?*"

"That," Miller says dryly, "is Jackie Wren. Soon to be former CEO of Mederva Therapeutics."

Nervous urgency makes me start paddling again. "Where is she?"

"Tied up on the front porch, along with her goons. Eagle's got them on lockdown till I get back. Soon as J.T. lets me know the data's in good hands, she'll be out of our sight in handcuffs."

Relief fills me. I knew from the beginning he'd find a way out of this without getting hurt, and without his children suffering.

He's that kind of a man. One you can count on day and night, through thick and thin, hell or high water.

A bona fide hero who'd be forever book boyfriend worthy in Mother's eyes – and okay, in *mine* – but there's nothing freaking fictional about him.

This is too real.

Too beautiful.

Too obviously, I hope, the start of a well-deserved Happily Ever After.

* * *

IT TAKES FOREVER to get across the small stretch of lake, but we do it. By then it's finally morning, the sun sweeping over the misty lake, the islands farther out coming and going like hazy mountains.

Finally, he helps me down the ladder and ties up the boat next to the dock.

Before lifting the kids out, Miller glances at his phone. "Operation Loose Lips underway, according to J.T. Two major press offices just confirmed receiving what he sent."

"Lucky you, Dad. Loose lips and no sinking ships," Shane yells from the top of the ladder, smiling like he's too clever for his own good.

I just want to know it's almost over. *For real this time.*

"Miller?" I whisper, glancing at him as I help Shane down first, and then Lauren.

"The cops should be here any minute. Let's keep the kids inside, assuming there's still somewhere in there that doesn't reek like a fuel tank."

"Of course," I say. "They need showers and clean clothes, anyway. I'm sure one of the bathrooms will be fine."

He kisses my temple. "Thanks, Gingersnap. Couldn't have done it without you."

Liar. He totally could've, and would have, but I'm glad he appreciates me giving everything I could to the cause. To us.

I usher the kids through the back door, trying to avoid the worst places drenched in gasoline. It's not as bad the further we get into the house. Seems like the creep who did this started near the staircase and didn't get far before we fled.

Miller disappears to the front. Though I'm itching to find out what happens next, Shane and Lauren are my top priority. I also can't say I mind escaping a run-in with that horrible woman who engineered all this. Maybe Miller and J.T.'s friend can stay calm, keep their emotions in check, but I'm not sure I could do the same.

I'd want to slap her across the face and then keep going.

The kids are both wet and shivering from the lake. Now that there's less excitement, it's easy to remember how cold it was swimming.

I grab a small throw blanket off the back of one of the recliners. "Lauren, why don't you jump in the shower first?" Tucking the blanket around Shane's shoulders, I add, "You be ready after her, boy-o. I'll go scrounge up some dry clothes in the meantime."

"Gwen, what'll happen now? Now that Dad's taking the buttheads to jail, I mean?" Shane looks at me, his eyes big and bright. "Are we gonna have to leave?"

"For a while, at least, just to fix up the damage and give somebody a chance to come by and soak up the gas," I tell him. I know full well that's not what he's asking but...

It's hard. So incredibly difficult dealing with questions I'm afraid to even ask right now.

Truth is, I have no idea what will happen. But as long as it involves Miller and these kids, as long as we're together, I don't care if we wind up being the first family with a one-way ticket to Mars.

I give him a quick bear hug. "Don't fret, Shane. Your dad will let us know real soon. I'm sure there's nothing to worry about."

"But I like it here. And Lauren loves this place too, all of it. I want to stay in Minnesota," he says, flopping back against the wall like his poor little legs are just done supporting him. "We're happier here, way more than we were in Seattle."

"You'll be happy every day after this, too," I say, patting his shoulder. "Your dad–"

"But that's just it, Gwen. Dad gets to be *Dad* ever since this stuff started. He doesn't have to work so many hours. We get to see him, and even when he's stressed, he's just...happier than a clam, really. Some days back home, he wouldn't want to do much except take us out to eat and stare at the ocean. I blame it on all the rain."

My heart wells in my chest and something I don't want to acknowledge stings my eyes again.

God, I really do love these two little people. "Right now, let's not worry about where you'll live. Nothing much matters except keeping you two dry."

I shouldn't be allowed to hand out sage advice.

Easier said than done, not worrying what'll happen next.

Like where Miller and the kids will go now. Back to Seattle?

That was their home, Mederva or no Mederva. They put down roots there, made connections, and the kids probably have a school and friends out there...would he really give it all away to settle down here?

Again, various heartbreak city scenarios play out in my head while I gather clothes for Lauren and Shane, and then make sure they're showered and upstairs.

It's barely early morning. Their late-night excursion has worn them out. They crash, falling asleep almost the instant their heads hit the pillows.

Just as fast, I go downstairs and straight out the front door.

I'd snuck several peeks out the windows while seeing to Shane and Lauren, and I need to get out there to find out what's happening. It's been a couple hours.

There are several men tied to the big deck posts, under

guard, and the woman I've seen before. She's the same one I'd seen with Manny.

There were two other men with Miller earlier. I'm assuming one is Eagle, the man who'd been guarding the driveway, and the other looks like J.T. He must've burned rubber the whole distance here the second he heard about the commotion. He'd been with family up north, a little closer, maybe two hours from here.

Unsure who the new big white suburban I'd seen flashing a few minutes ago belongs to, I ease the door open cautiously.

Okay. So, by now, I shouldn't be shocked in the slightest by who I see talking to Miller near the porch steps, but *come on.*

"Mother?" I hiss, blinking several times to make sure she's really there.

"Gwendolyn! Oh, darling." She rushes up the steps and throws her arms around me. "I knew you'd be fine, but just had to see for myself." She glares at J.T. "Thank God I hired a P.I. to follow the first P.I. I'd hired. And had my very own pilot waiting to fly me up to the little airstrip here."

"You...what?" J.T. asks, his eyes bugging out.

"Oh, I knew you wouldn't tell me when I'm needed," Mother says with a sigh. "Nobody ever wants me to join in the fun until after the fireworks."

"Because we had it on lockdown, ma'am!" J.T. slaps his thigh, his mustache twitching. "And you could've done better for your money with the other guy. I shook him halfway up here hours ago. Not much of a night driver, apparently."

Mother shakes her head. "Good help is tremendously hard to find. But I knew where you were headed."

J.T. takes a step toward her. "May, listen up, you can't go gallivanting onto an active crime scene like—"

"Crime scene? Last time I checked, this was still *my* cabin.

Even if she's a little worse for wear and needs a change of perfume." She wrinkles her nose, waving her hand in front of her face for effect. "Lord, I hope that gas hasn't soaked through the floorboards..."

"Let me handle that too, please." J.T. says sternly. "The carpet's also evidence the sheriff will want on file once he gets here with his boys to take the trash away."

"You know perfectly well I'm not helpless. My very own interior designer has worked miracles in–"

"Stop!" I yell, stepping between them. I've had enough. "None of this matters right now, Mother. Everybody's safe. They've got them tied up. The renovations can wait."

They both blink. I glance at the people tied up and walk down the steps to stand next to Miller.

"Sheriff's on his way," Miller says. "Just taking damn near forever. He has to come from the other end of the county."

"It's one of the biggest in the state," I tell him, slipping my hand into his as footsteps echo behind me.

"Ah, the man of the hour. Miller, come here, you have to see this," Mother says, holding up her phone. "Over five hundred thousand views and counting. And it's only been live for an hour."

"What views?" I ask.

"People are kicking it around like a hot potato on every social media site," she says. "Hundreds of shares already."

"Of *what?*" I demand again, this time looking at Miller.

He shakes his head. "No clue what she's talking about, babe."

"Some very *interesting* data was sent anonymously to a full-service marketing agency with a soft spot for a little vigilante justice. They knew the best way to get it out there with no chance of any cover-ups." Mother grins. "It's all about hashtags now. They're calling it #MedervaSickos, but I

319

personally adore the new one I saw trending a few minutes ago – #JackietheRipper."

"The *what?*" Jackie Wren snarls, lifting her head, visibly unnerved.

"Calm down, dear, you've secured your fifteen minutes of unholy fame right alongside Enron and Ted Bundy," Mother says, turning her nose up in the air. "Along with a very prominent Oregon politician, who was arrested on the tarmac just now before he could take off for Hong Kong."

"No!" Jackie's cruel mouth turns into a ring of horror. She struggles against the restraints binding her hands together and thumps her tied feet against the porch floor. "You can't do that to him. You can't!" She glares up at Miller. "You *really* should've taken the money and run, you ungrateful fool. Do you have any idea where this little crusade of yours ends? You're making enemies who'll put a price on your head for double anything I stupidly offered."

He shakes his head, not a hint of fear in his eyes. Even though my blood hums with nerves, I love this defiant, unshakable man more than ever. "This was never about money, Jackie. You're a slow goddamn learner."

She kicks her feet against the porch floor harder. "Everything's about money!"

"Not this time." Miller glances at the big police SUV coming up the driveway, flanked by a couple smaller cars. "You'd better save some breath. Looks like the sheriff's here. You can explain it to him while you enjoy your first day rotting behind bars."

"I didn't do anything illegal!" Jackie roars, turning her face to the sky, the veins on her neck bulging. "Anyone can donate their bodies to science."

Miller's face turns to cold stone. "Those bodies weren't donated, you Dracula bitch. You were buying them off murderers and selling them piece by piece to line your own pockets."

Disgust roils my stomach. There's a patch of stinging nettles on the ground.

I can't fathom how he's remaining so calm, so peaceful, when all I can imagine is snatching those weeds up and jabbing the thorns in Jackie's remorseless face.

She strains mightily in her chains one more time, flashing us both a hateful look, and then goes limp with her face pointed at the ground. "You idiot. You asshole. You don't even know what you've ruined."

"Wrong. I know more than I ever wanted, and so does the entire world now. It's all there in the data that's being released," Miller growls, storming over. He looks so huge standing over her, his shadow long and dark across her sour face in the early morning light. "And while we're talking about ruining things, here's one more lesson."

He bends near her feet and swipes off – *her shoes? Huh?*

"Wait, no. Oh, no, no, no, no, no – no!" Her face goes pale, tortured, as she watches Miller carry her expensive looking heels all the way to the dock.

I learn one more thing today. Sometimes the dull sound of a *splash* – two of them – can be enough to rip out someone's soul.

The sheriff's vehicles finally stop, and several men are making their way to the porch by the time Miller comes back, grinning with his eyes. An ambulance follows, parking behind them.

A couple of Jackie's men could use medical attention. The one I'd punched and kicked has been staring at me, craning his throat.

I've never purposefully hit someone before. In theory, I should feel bad, but for this monster? I just can't. Thinking about how he snatched Lauren and started running makes me want to punch and kick him again.

"J.T. Riggs?" the sheriff asks. "Is that you or are my old eyes lyin'?"

"The one and only!" J.T. holds his hand out to the sheriff, his greying mustache bobbing. "Been too long."

"What in the hell are you doing way up here in my neck of the woods?" the sheriff asks while shaking hands. "And what's with these snakes you've got wriggling on stakes? You playing vigilante again, J.T.?"

"Got a real doozy on our end. Get ready for reporters, Sheriff, you're gonna need to tell the hotels and lodges in town to expect major company soon." J.T. takes hold of Miller's elbow. "This here's Miller Rush, and I just helped him take down a dragon..."

He introduces Miller to the sheriff as the three of them walk off toward the cars, out of hearing range.

It's the first time it really feels like this might be coming to an end.

God.

Sure, it's hardly the end of the beginning. I know a case like this will bring weeks of work over the next few months, maybe even years. But if it's Miller leading the charge with sworn statements and high-powered prosecution cases, and not Miller playing action hero...

I can't help but smile.

The sheriff waves at his deputies, directing them to help cover the EMTs while they assess injuries, without untying anyone just yet. I step out of the way and follow Mother back to the porch.

Mother wraps an arm around my waist and encourages me to move inside, back into the kitchen.

"I can't believe it," I whisper. "We're *safe*. For realsies, I mean."

Mother gives me a look like she's offended I'd even second guess her handiwork. "Leave everything to me. If you're still worried about that woman and her threats, give it a day. She'll be singing a very different tune."

"Hope you're right. I guess J.T. really knows his stuff getting this out there. Just in the nick of time."

"J.T.? Oh, no, he facilitated communications, but he wasn't my main contact with this lovely PR push." She pauses for dramatic effect, more than a little mischief in her eyes. "That was your old friend Manny Stork."

My heart jumps up in my throat. "Manny? *Get. Out.*"

Mother winks. "From the hospital bed, no less, where they're still helping him with complications from his broken ribs. Anonymously. Said he couldn't pass up a chance to settle the score with a woman who'd put him in the hospital with no one to sue."

A flash of something I can't even define flares inside me. "Mother, Manny's dumb ideas are the *reason* we're in the middle of this."

She grins. "I know, bless his greedy little heart. Don't hold a grudge, dear. He's handed you a nice tall drink of *hubba-hubba* complete with munchkins, Gwendolyn. And now he's learning to clean up his own mess for once. We got very lucky."

I open my mouth to protest, then close it.

She's not wrong.

Sometimes, it doesn't even matter when truth turns out stranger than fiction.

Sometimes, it just drives you freaking crazy.

XVIII: JUST REWARDS (MILLER)

The sun is up by the time J.T. and I drag ourselves out of the sheriff's office.

Now we have almost an hour's drive back to the cabin. Gingersnap wasn't kidding when she said these northern Minnesota counties were huge.

Part of me actually looks forward to the drive back, winding through rough, narrow roads tucked in shadowy pines and birch trees with just the odd yellow Moose Crossing sign breaking up the scenery.

It's almost fucking over. We survived.

Manny's data dump worked better than I dreamed. His marketing people knew what bits and pieces to throw together into online videos for maximum effect. Now it's gone so viral it's hitting the cable news circuit, and arrests on the West Coast have already been made.

Later today, life will get very interesting for some leeches in Congress.

Keith called a short while ago. It was damn good to hear his voice, even as he raved about how his eel of a lawyer must've been a miracle worker. The bloodhounds who'd been pushing them deeper and deeper into the Ecuadorian forests for weeks disappeared almost overnight.

I'll call him later, tell him the truth.

Right now, the sheriff thinks the only thing Gwen and May had to do with this escapade is renting me the cabin. J.T. Riggs is smooth as silk and silver-tongued.

Hard to believe we started out thinking all we'd need were a few dark flights overseas and a fake wife.

We were in over our heads but running too scared to realize it.

We got our intel, though. That part we'd always been good at. Jackie and her goons won't be in Minnesota long. She'll be extradited back to Washington within hours.

The sheriff already confirmed the FBI raid on Mederva Therapeutics' headquarters. The Feds won't leave a single coaster unturned before they even consider letting anyone back through the doors. And now that it's hitting the media with a vengeance, there's no putting Humpty Dumpty back together again to sweep it all into a black hole.

"I'll drive," J.T. says as we cross the parking lot.

"No. You've done more than your fair share. Let me. I'm too spooled up to think about nodding off."

He nods, tossing me the keys to his Jeep. "Should have plenty of gas."

"Should?" I ask.

He laughs because it's the one detail he's overlooked. Every man has his weakness.

Luckily, the gas station is just across the street. We wouldn't have made it much farther.

Despite the coffee he drank at the sheriff's office, and the large cup he'd purchased at the gas station, J.T. is snoring within ten minutes of us being on the highway.

I grin, only hoping I'll have that kind of stamina when I'm his age. It's not easy, but I have to admit, things would've turned out differently without his help. That goes double for May and Gwen.

My heart thuds at the thought of her.

So maybe that fake wife part worked out just fine.

I've never liked asking for help. The only person I'd ever accepted help from was Keith. Gwen knew it early on, and in her own way, told me so.

She said sometimes it takes more courage to accept help than to refuse it.

Turns out, she's right.

It hadn't been easy partnering up with May and then J.T. To believe he knew what he was doing, to trust turning over our data, and then to sit back and wait while he damn near saved our lives up here.

Truth is, I hadn't had an option.

Now, I wouldn't change a thing about how it all played out.

In the end, Gingersnap did the impossible. She changed my mind.

All while she brought the warmth and light and love back into the abyss of my Miller-verse. Her grace, her beauty, her sex are pieces of me now.

And God forbid I *ever* forget those bright, shiny tears in her eyes last night, when her heart cracked open and she said the unspeakable.

Love, dammit. This redheaded phoenix of a woman loves me the same way I do her, and you *know* it's serious when I said it first.

I've never regretted it for a nanosecond, and I never will. Not after coming horrendously close to losing her, to losing my kids, and knowing on an even deeper level everything I'll always need is right *here.*

I reach up and thump my chest, grateful J.T.'s still sawing

logs in his sleep. The old man doesn't need to see me carrying on with myself.

Now, I've just got to figure out how to make my claim on her permanent.

* * *

J.T. LETS out a sleepy groan and yawns like a cat, then stretches his arms out in front of him and scratches his head. "Little bit of shut-eye felt good. Want me to take over, Miller?"

"Nah, ten more miles and we're there."

He nods. "Sorry. Didn't mean to leave you all on your lonesome for so long."

"No problem." Figuring this is as good a time as any, I say, "Listen, thank you, J.T. For everything you did last night and over the last few weeks. Things wouldn't have turned out this well without you."

He scratches the side of his whiskery face. "You know, Miller, I make three hundred dollars an hour, plus expenses."

What the hell? Most guys just say you're welcome.

The sudden business talk surprises me, but if May hasn't covered all his fees for sticking his neck out...fair's fair.

I look at him, wondering what he means. "I'll make sure you're paid in full out of my own pocket. No worries."

He waves a hand and chuckles. "May's already covered everything. How do I put this?" He glances out the side window, thinking. "I'm just saying, me personally...my fees are three hundred dollars an hour, plus expenses." He turns toward me. "I make a damn good living doing what I do. Putting skills I got from Uncle Sam to good use."

Slowly, I nod.

"P.I. work made a good life for me and the missus, and

our little brood. Got us five kids and a whole crop of grand-kids now."

"Congrats."

He covers a yawn with one palm. "Thing is, I'm getting mighty old. Didn't realize *how* old until this job gave me a real challenge. I'm used to midnight runs. Most of the times it's a custody dispute. One parent taking a kid from the other. I get a call, find the kid, and bring 'em home overnight. Quick. Easy. Done."

"That happen a lot?"

"More than folks know." He rolls his window down an inch or so for some fresh air. "But cases like this, with real meat and potatoes, they're the reason I started this business. Just can't keep up with 'em anymore. And now I'm thinking I should teach a young lad with the skills and the wits all the secrets I've learned over the years."

"One of your sons?" I ask, unsure I want to follow where he's going.

He laughs. "I have five daughters. Not a one of 'em would let their husbands work for me." He taps the dash. "Here's our turn."

I slow down, turning into the driveway up to the cabin as an odd thrill zips up my spine.

I shouldn't. Not on a whim like this, inserting myself into what could be the start of a life-altering decision. Not without talking to Shane and Lauren first.

But here, right now, it's like someone just handed me a ticket to stay in the Land of Ten Thousand Lakes.

"You got anyone in mind for retirement, or what?"

"Matter of fact..." His eyes almost sparkle as he looks at me. "You're in need of a job, ain't you?" He rolls up his window. "Once you finish testifying that is."

Shit. He should know that could take forever.

A wave of disappointment washes over me. "Don't know

how long that's gonna take, J.T. Could be months, probably years tying up loose ends with a machine this big."

"Logistics never scared me. We'll talk about it later." He nods out the windshield. "Right now, I think you've got more important stuff to decide."

My grin eats my own face when we pull up and the cabin's door flies open.

Gwen, Shane, and Lauren rush down the steps, with May close on their heels.

I park the Jeep and open the door as Shane, running faster than the rest, arrives beside the vehicle and almost leaps inside.

"Can we, Dad? Please. We'll be super good. Like super, duper, uber good!"

"Please, Daddy? I'll make sure Shane behaves," Lauren says, arriving next, bouncing up and down on her heels.

"Hold up, guys," Gingersnap says, laying a hand on their shoulders. "Your father doesn't even know what you're talking about yet."

Her smile fades slightly as she looks at me. "You haven't had a wink of sleep, have you? We can do this later..."

Sleep? I'm not sure I even know the definition when I see her – really, truly *see* her – soaking in her fresh, wholesome beauty.

She hooks her arm through mine the second I'm out of the vehicle. "Bet you haven't eaten, either."

"Sure haven't!" J.T. says from the other side of the Jeep. His stomach growls like a bear.

"Get in here and eat with us." She grins up at me. "Don't worry. Mother cooked this time."

I have to chuckle at how her green eyes shine like turquoise. "I wasn't worried, babe. You're a quick learner."

"Liar." She just laughs as we start walking, leaning to whisper in my ear. "That's okay. I love you anyway."

A jealous growl roughs up my throat and I stop, pull her face to mine, and lay my lips on hers real thick. I can't wait another second, even if it's just a taste.

This woman. This kiss. This life.

Shane and Lauren run to the house ahead of us, chattering to each other like their lives depend on it. "What are they all keyed up about, anyway?"

Gwen sighs. "Mother. She wants to take them home with her and get started tearing out the carpet right away. Turns out, she's got a big photo shoot tomorrow to promote her next movie and just loves the thought of showing off her 'grandkids.' Her words, not mine." Her cheeks go rosy pink.

I almost snort. And here I thought *I'd* win the award for inappropriate, over-possessive freak.

"Surprising they're so excited, honestly. I have to damn near dress the kids myself for their yearbook pics."

"Well, her latest book was set at a ranch, something 'based on a true story' that happened over in some little town in North Dakota. Guess this girl who inherited an oil company from her gramps made a lot of headlines recently. His will set her up to be married to this guy and a lot happened but...now they're married for real. Happily Ever After, horses and all."

"You mean this stuff happens in real life? Crazy." I say, sarcasm dripping, winding my hand down her back. "Still not seeing the appeal for Shane and Lauren. *Especially* Shane."

That boy's almost at the age where romance might be the only dirty word he's afraid to use with his friends. Can't wait for him to get hit full force by some little girl knocking him on his knees when he's old enough.

"Well, they're taking photos at this local farm place, and she told the kids they can go horseback riding." She shakes her head. "I said we had to wait until we heard from you. I wasn't sure when, or even if, you'd be back in time."

My heart clenches at the unshed tears welling in her eyes.

Leaving last night was chaotic. It's hard to believe we're able to have some normalcy and privacy again. Just the two of us might be a damn dream.

I fold an arm around her shoulders. "Of course I was coming back. ASAP."

"I know, but...I wasn't sure how soon you'd have to leave for Seattle. You must have stuff to do there, unfinished business."

"Yeah, but nothing too major. I'll go back in a couple weeks. It'll take some time for everything to get lined up before they'll need me to testify."

"Hurry up, Dad!" Shane shouts from where he's standing with the door wide open. "We're starving."

I look at her and grin. "First time I'm not sure I believe his catchphrase. Don't think he's as worried about me eating as he is to get going with your ma."

She blinks. "Oh. So you're ready to send them off? I wasn't sure after, well, *everything.*"

"Babe." I let my eyes shut while a new sense of freedom washes over me, knowing I *can* let the kids be kids again. "If May doesn't mind, and if you don't mind...I sure as hell wouldn't mind some alone time later. Just the two of us. Leaving each other sore for days." I lean in, growling that last part in her ear.

Fuck, do I love the way her cheeks redden a notch. More like cherry than soft pink this time.

Later, I'll make her redder, riding my face. Or maybe I'll just find out how flexible those long legs of hers get doing some moves for the next edition of the *Kama Sutra.*

"Trust me, Mother doesn't mind. She never would've asked if she didn't want them to go with her." Frowning, she adds, "Why would *I* mind?"

"Because you'll be alone. With me and a bed and no clothes."

She giggles as that brush fire on her cheeks turns into an inferno, trying to break away from me, rushing up the steps.

I bound up after her, and in no time, tuck into the nice meal May threw together. It's some kind of stuffed chicken with rice and vegetables. Simple, fulfilling, able to get my mind off how hard I'll take my woman for five minutes.

No small miracle.

Then I talk to J.T. a little more while Gwen helps the kids pack and sees them off, all in record time.

Eagle checked in briefly, too, said he'd swept the area, and then left while we were eating. He also heard the cops in the next county apprehended the stragglers who'd gotten away from Jackie's crew, and they're being held for questioning now.

The instant it's over, with everyone gone, I feel like I just took a shot of pure espresso straight to the arm.

Sleep? Fuck sleep.

Knowing Gingersnap and I might be the only two people for miles has me wide-awake and hard as granite.

"They'll be fine, Miller," she says as we walk back inside the cabin.

It takes me a second to realize she's more worried about Shane and Lauren than I am.

So maybe I did hug them extra tight before I turned them over to May. "Yes, they will be. I never would've let them go if I didn't know that for certain."

"I know you wouldn't have." She shrugs. "I just already miss them."

I grab a blanket off the back of one of the chairs and take her hand. "Think I know a way to get your mind off that..."

Her shy smirk is adorable, heart-shaped lips pursed as terrible things enter her brain, even as she shakes her head. "Oh?"

I read her mind. Grinning, I pull her out the back door. "Boat ride, first. Before dark."

She frowns, looking down the short hill at the dock. "Have you forgotten that pontoon doesn't have a motor?"

"We've got paddles and an anchor. I'm game to work for my next meal."

No confusion here. The fiery gaze I aim her way says what's on the menu.

* * *

I LOVE how she's game for anything and races me to the dock ten minutes later.

We jump aboard, untie the landing rope, and use the paddles to push the boat away from the dock. Dropping mine, I grasp her waist and pull her against me. "We'll just let it float where it wants to. Sound good?"

She nods, looping her arms around my neck. "And just what're we going to do as it floats where it wants to?"

I slide my hands under her t-shirt, staring into her eyes.

Never ceases to amaze me what she does to me. My entire body tingles, sweet anticipation winding everything tighter than a drum. "Whatever we want."

Her coy smile bristles as she licks her lips. "Anything?"

My dick stiffens. So fucking ready for her mouth.

"Especially anything."

She releases my neck and steps back, kicking off her sandals. The next thing to come off is her t-shirt.

I sit down to kick off my boots and socks, watching her, how the bright sunlight makes her skin glow as she slides down her shorts. My mouth almost waters as I stand, tearing off my belt.

She's much faster than me, and it only makes me harder, knowing she might want it even more than I do. Her tall, lush body bares itself to me in all her glory by the time I'm kicking my jeans away on the floor.

"Want to know what I want to do?"

"Hell yeah," I snarl, yanking my shirt over my head. I see she's moved in the split second my shirt blocked my vision.

She's standing on one of the cushions. Her entire body glistens under the sun, peaches and cream I want to savor forever. With a grin that makes her eyes match the glow of her skin, she opens those plush lips and says two words.

"Skinny dipping!"

In one graceful move, she dives off the edge of the boat like a mermaid.

I rush to the side and see where she's swimming beneath the water before following her. "I'm game, woman."

More than game. I might just want to run the board.

I find her in the water, grasping her bare waist to mine.

We surface together, treading water as our slick, aching bodies press against each other. "Love how you think."

She laughs and leaps sideways, back under the water with a parting kiss. *Little minx.*

Her long, lithe body glides through the water like a fish, teasing me like the hungry fisherman.

We play a game of water tag. Touching enough to entice, knowing it'll make what comes next even more fun. More adventurous. More intense.

Soon, it leaves us both wanting more, and after a long hellfire kiss that steals our breath, we head back to the boat.

She arrives first and puts her hands on the ladder to hoist herself up. I grab the handles below her hands and pull myself up behind her. My dick grinds against her ass.

I swear I could take her right here. Right now. Right the fuck like this.

Laughing, she spreads her legs and presses back against me.

Her aim is perfect. My cock glides into her pussy, wet heat replacing the cool water. I feel the sudden contrast in temperature right down to my balls.

She's so ready for me and I love it. Same for how she tightens her muscles, pulling me in deeper, whimpering against my hand.

I slam into her, driving all the way in till my balls hug her skin.

Perfect, perfect, so fucking perfect, I want to throw my head back and howl like a Neanderthal.

She lets out a long, lustful whine as her hips start pumping, edging to meet my rhythm. "Right here, Miller. Give it to me hard and fast. Right now, baby."

My dick works faster, eager to take her raw, hoping I never lay eyes on another condom again with this woman.

My hips go berserk, racing to ecstasy, my lips searing her shoulders, her neck, every time she leans into me and tilts her face back.

Fuck.

Gwen doesn't hold back, freely moaning, groaning, and tensing at my thrusts, and I know she's about to come like dynamite.

Her body stiffens. Her breathing shallows. Every inch of me screams to spill my release into hers, so I sandwich her against the ship, fucking so frantically it's like we're boiling the lake.

"God, Miller, coming!" she grunts through bared teeth.

I fist her hair and tilt her head back for me, sealing her lips in a frantic kiss as my dick swells.

We come together.

We come so hard, so beautiful, so wild I think we're one with the current.

* * *

A FEW BREATHLESS MINUTES LATER, we're both laughing as she lets go of the ladder, slipping back into the water, still leaking me. I let go, too, and we both have another swim, sinking below the gentle waves together several times.

It takes us a little while to recover from *that.*

Looking at me with a half-serious frown, she says, "You stay off this ladder until I'm in the boat."

I feign ignorance, flashing her a puzzled scowl.

Laughing, she grabs the other handle and leaps up the ladder, all the way to the top, before turning and wrapping herself into a crouched ball. "You know why, Miller Rush."

Damn right I do.

Lucky for her, taking her again on the deck of that boat is just as good as having her in the lake.

I scale the ladder and plop down next to her. "Think you just tried to drown me, babe."

"Did not!"

She lays her head on my shoulder and adds, "I mean, that'd kinda ruin all the fun."

I wrap an arm around her, bring her close, loving the soft, subtle pressure of her skin on mine. "That the only reason?"

"No." She lifts her head to look at me. "I don't want to paddle this thing back to shore all by myself."

"So sex and muscle, that's all you want from me?"

She snuggles a bit closer, kissing my shoulder. "Your cooking isn't half bad, either."

I chuckle. Happy, relaxed, and temporarily sated, I lean my head back and close my eyes, just enjoying the moment in the cool evening breeze. Naked and alone in nature with the woman I love.

"Careful. You fall asleep out here like this and you'll still get sunburned." She runs her hand over my abs, biting back a hungry look. "Some things would really suck to get burned."

She's right, but I'm so tired I don't want to lift my head.

"Come on." She sits up and pulls on my arm. "Let's head back to the cabin and take a nap."

I lift my head and open my eyes to see how far away we are. While I'm contemplating if we should paddle or just swim the distance, my body tenses.

A second later, I see why. Two people rushing down around the side of the cabin. One of them looks like J.T., his gold chain flashing in the evening light.

Gwen reaches for my hand, her fingers going tight. "What's he doing back so soon? And who's that lady?"

I shrug. I don't know. But my gut tells me what I thought was over isn't.

XIX: PEARL DIVING (GWEN)

I'm trembling from head to toe, but this time, it's not fear.

It's exhaustion.

I'm so effing sick of bad guys, right now, I swear I could rid the earth of every last one of the creeps myself.

Following Miller's equally tired, silent lead, I get dressed, keeping low to the floor. Whatever J.T. wants, he's milling around down by the dock, not so patiently gabbing with his mysterious lady. She's tall like me, but platinum blonde, and dressed in so much black she looks like she's ready for Halloween in May.

Once we're decent again, we quickly get the ship back to shore, and I work on tying it up while Miller walks over.

I hear them talking urgently by the porch and only catch pieces.

A politician's wife. Cheating bastard. Affair. Designer shoes. Jackie the Ripper.

That last phrase leaves me chilled and confused.

Another thing I'm done with – more surprises.

So by the time the pontoon boat's secure, I rush over,

waving, watching the trio turn toward me. "Who have we got here?" I ask.

"Adelaide Palm. Soon to be ex-wife of Congressman and Senate candidate Logan Palm from Oregon."

I do a huge double take. The woman just stares and sniffs at me like I'm not even there.

"Holy...you mean the same representative Palm who's always in the news for his theatrics?" I don't like politics that much, but even I recognize the name. "Didn't he get arrested or something last year for pitching an illegal tent in a tree over healthcare?"

"That childish *stunt*," Adelaide snaps. "He always was quite the actor, though. Had you fooled and half the country. I even believed he was up there the whole time, too, until I found out he'd hired a lookalike to spend three days up there fasting and then surrender himself to the Portland police. Logan was long gone before the yellow tape and the camera crews arrived, busy screwing his mistress at a swanky hotel across town."

I'm gobsmacked. Also dying to know just what this has to do with us.

"I don't understand." I shake my head, my glance dancing from Miller to J.T and back to Adelaide. "If you're Logan's wife, what are you doing all the way out here while he's been arrested? He *has* been arrested, right?"

J.T. clears his throat, giving Miller a look.

But Adelaide jumps in first. "He'll have bail posted tomorrow unless there's definitive evidence linking him to that Ripper Whore. Now, when I first got in touch with Mr. Riggs here and heard about all this going down, I could've just called. But I wanted closure. So I chartered myself a flight to International Falls and here I am."

Her eyes flash anger, but her smile is almost eerily calm. My stomach churns. I'm so freaking lost.

"Babe, you know I hate to ask after everything we've been through, but we need your help." Miller lays a hand on my shoulder and gives me a look so serious, my blood drains.

"Help? What do you–"

"Shoes," he growls.

"Huh?"

"Shoes, babe," he tells me again.

"Shoes, Gwen," J.T. echoes. "A one of a kind pair of wonder-feet cooked up by a crazy designer who used diamonds on the heels and scorpion blood in the dye for the liner. Adelaide here's got the receipt, found it a while back and planned to turn it over to her lawyer planning a divorce...but he's guilty of a lot more than a mistress and to really bring him down, we need some real bones." His ash-grey mustache twitches, and he sighs, looking across the lake.

That's when it finally dawns on me.

"Crud. You mean?"

"Yeah. Same damn pair I hurled in Rainy Lake before they hauled her off in handcuffs. No wonder she looked like I snapped her golden goose's neck. Turns out, I was doing her a favor, tossing away evidence."

"Oh."

Adelaide's eyes brighten. "Your husband here says you're an amazing swimmer."

Husband?! My eyes search Miller's. He just grins and doesn't correct her. Technically, I guess he's half right, considering how this all started.

"You know I hate to ask, but I think you're part dolphin. Gwen, would you please–"

That's all I need before I'm running for the dock.

Hearing Miller Rush say *please* instead of barking orders in his adorable, oh-so-grumpy way is worth a favor or two.

* * *

EVERYTHING HURTS by the time I finally track down those flipping shoes.

Against the mess of dark rocks and sand at the bottom of Rainy Lake, the five-figure designer heels blend into the darkness. I probably wouldn't have ever found them if not for the shiny metal flash.

They're tangled around something, and it pulls loose with me when I grab the small chain and *pull.* It dislodges those shoes. Just in time, too, because I don't know if my lungs could handle yet another ninety-second run without oxygen.

Miller's there on the dock when I come up gasping, extending a strong hand to pull me up. His huge, proud, perfect smile is reward enough.

Part of me also adores how Adelaide snarls, snatching the heels from my hand. "I *knew* it. And to think he never bought me a pair of slippers..."

J.T. takes the shoes for safe keeping and tries to console her. I collapse in Miller's heavenly arms as he showers praise in beast-man speak. "You did good, Gingersnap. Got them in record time."

It's nice to be even for a change, instead of him saving my bacon. Literally.

My heart flutters anyway. His endless grin, hallowed by that irresistible scruff, says more than words ever could.

"But wait, there's more. Special delivery," I whisper, giving him a kiss as I push my little discovery into his hand.

"What's this, a locket? A book?" His blue eyes lid, and he flicks the small silver box open with his thumb. "Looks empty."

"Thank Mother for that. She always said I'd fill it up once I found my words and kept on saying it every time she saw me wearing the stupid thing. It was a present for my sixteenth birthday. Barely big enough to hold a good luck charm or something. I never bothered. Last year, I got so frustrated waiting around for my muse, I threw it away, right in the lake."

His eyes light up. For a second, he looks like he could kiss me like a hurricane. Then, he actually does.

His tongue says it a hundred times on mine before he pulls away and speaks. "Good thing you did, woman. You just helped a mess of people find a whole lot of words to help put away Wren and Logan Fuckface."

"He'll sing like a canary in a couple weeks," J.T. says, walking over, Jackie's incriminating heels now neatly bagged. "Just wait. His kind don't last long in prison."

The rest is just a blur. I vaguely remember J.T., Adelaide, and Miller talking a while longer before we walk them to his Jeep. I don't even know where my silvery book locket disappears to and wonder if I imagined the whole thing.

J.T. looks at Miller and me then. "Sorry, kids, but this old man needs to get these shoes in the sheriff's custody, Adelaide to the airport, and then some serious shut-eye."

"No need to apologize," I say, stifling a yawn. "We need some sleep, too."

I had gone back to bed for a few hours after he'd left with the sheriff, but hadn't slept well alone, and any reserve energy I'd had left, I'd spent dredging up those stupid shoes.

The second we wave J.T. goodbye, Miller and I go straight to the bedroom. Too tired to care about my clothes and hair still being damp with lake water, I undress and throw myself into bed.

Miller does the same. I snuggle in close, and as his huge arms wrap around me so tight, so loving, so grateful, I let my eyes drift shut.

* * *

WE SLEEP like the dead until dawn.

It's early. Five o'clock, according to the old clock next to the bed.

Miller's gone. His side of the bed still feels warm, but I hear the shower turning off, and then his heavy footsteps padding closer.

He's buck naked, corded muscle and animal ink moving in fluid, sexy strides.

If I wasn't wide awake before, I am now – especially when he catches me mid-stare.

"Didn't mean to wake you. Go back to bed if you want, Gingersnap."

"Nope. I slept like ten hours and I'm feeling...better."

Let's be real, it's hardly the right word for waking up to Miller Rush in the buff after the last twenty-four utterly insane hours.

I reach up to brush the hair out of my eyes and am appalled at how my hair feels like a matted mass of straw. That's what I get for going to sleep with wet hair. "You know, I need a shower too."

His eyes glow. Miller grabs the tie of my robe and pulls me up, then closer. "You're in luck. I need my second shower of the day to be a functioning human being. I hear if we take one together, it'll use less hot water."

My heart instantly thuds, even as I feel inclined to say, "The hot water heater is that little box on the bathroom wall. It's called heat on demand. It warms the water up as needed."

He kisses the side of my neck, running several rough fingers against my thigh. "Too early to talk so dirty, babe. Not unless you want that little heat box inspected."

Laughing, I lean my head back, giving more room for his growly kisses which won't be stopping anytime this century. "I mean, if you insist..."

He starts walking, forcing me to move backward while he's still kissing my throat, my cleavage. "Come on, my mermaid-girl. Let's go see how much heat we can conjure up wet."

Nothing could wipe the smile off my face. Being called his is only part of it.

In about sixty seconds, I'm going to be receiving the best wake-up call of my life.

He unties my robe while still coaxing me backward, his hands going behind me for a squeeze that curls my toes. "Looking mighty hot already. Fiery phoenix red. You ready for me?"

I know what he means, but it makes me think of something else. All the unknowns, the unanswered questions, the terrible idea we could be living on borrowed time before he decides a fake wife he's lived with for a couple glorious months is more trouble than it's worth.

"Gingersnap?"

I stop walking and pinch my lips together at how even that simple, silly nickname warms my heart. Our eyes lock. His are blue moons, passion overflowing, but there's hesitation, too. Curiosity.

Does he know what I'm thinking?

His slow, fierce kiss tells me he might. Then he says, "Less thinkin', more fuckin'. Can't give any more than that right now, Gwen. Not till the timing's different."

"I don't need more than that right now, Miller." That's not a total lie. Because honestly?

I don't know what I need. What I expect. What I'll do if him and the kids jet back to Washington next week, or decide they want to live in my townhouse forever.

"Talk to me," he growls, pushing his forehead to mine. His fingers must be burning up when he touches me, running them up my jaw, tilting my face to look at him. "What do you need, beautiful? It's your morning for saving the last act yesterday."

"Just a shower," I whisper, smiling into another kiss. "And *this.*"

I reach for his seething cock, so hard and thick it's no easy task to curl my entire fist around it. As usual, I can't tell who wants it worse today, and I kinda like it.

Grinning, he pushes the robe off my shoulders. "That I can give, Gwen, and then some."

I drop my arms so the robe falls to the floor and lean against him. I feel his hard-on pressing against my stomach, and know he's fully aware of my breasts flattening against his chest.

We're too far gone for more words.

Our lips tangle, our hands roam, our voices drop to guttural moans and heavy breaths, and somehow, we fumble our way through the bedroom and into the bathroom without breaking tongues.

I step into the shower, my awed gaze scaling his body, every last inch of bare muscle and ink. Forever amazed – what else?

He has to be the best-looking man on this earth, with or without clothes.

Those eyes are so lightning blue. They were the first thing I'd noticed and still do every time I look at him. I love how they shine, sparkle, and shimmer, especially when he's looking dead at me.

The rest of him – his chiseled jaw, his wide, muscular neck, broad shoulders, brawny chest, rippled stomach, tree trunk legs, even his bare feet, are the essence of perfection.

God didn't break the mold when he made Miller Rush and hurled him into my life.

I think he went through a few hundred before he found the perfect mix of bear, of soldier, of father, of lover, of *man.*

And there's no mistaking that part when he takes his sweet time kissing my neck, helping shampoo and rinse my hair. Then his hands take me places I'd never find anywhere else while I'm this shamefully wet.

Endless teasing licks give way to deep, hard conquest. His tongue takes mine and his thumb finds my clit before he drops to his knees. He brings me off once on his hands, riding his tongue, his beard, his growl.

I scream myself hoarse, two feral fingers and a mouth like Zeus' working deep in my pussy, prepping me for what's next.

I can't take any more.

My back braces against the shower wall. I throw one leg around his waist as he pins me against the wall, gently by the throat, and pushes his glorious cock into me.

His long fingers hold my face open for his lips, his tongue, his teeth as he goes hard. He holds nothing back, a cascade of sweet fuckery. Hard, languid thrusts become quaking, fast, clit-searing swipes inside my body, every inch of him buried to the hilt.

"Miller!" I gasp his name so hard I see stars.

His name barely gushes out as he brings me to the peak, pushing me over.

Coming!

Just like that, he messes me up *so good* when my shrill whine melds with his thunder, when I'm shaking on his tattooed wall of muscle, when my pussy creams every inch of him and his seed goes so deep it burns.

I'm scared the pill won't even be enough. He's going to trash my freaking birth control and leave my ovaries smoking if he keeps taking me like this.

But not so scared I stop, sinking my teeth into his lip, urging on our sweet delirium.

It's truly indescribable.

Truly as close to heaven on earth as anything can be.

Miller stands, holding his cock in me while the water steams around us, and keeps me from collapsing.

Knowing he'll never, ever let me fall is paradise.

With him, I've found my inspiration, even if I might've misplaced that stupid book charm necklace again.

And my muse doesn't sail down from the sky to whisper sweet nothings in my ear.

My real muse just growls, stomps, and leaves me so dizzy I'm still trying to figure out what hit me.

XX: NO PLACE BETTER (MILLER)

Two Months Later

"ARE we gonna finish the gazebo today, Dad?" Shane asks while we're loading the pickup with boards at the lumber yard.

"Sure are," I tell him. "A few more trim boards are all we've got left."

"Then we get to paint it, right?" Lauren asks. "That pretty white shade May picked?"

"Yep, made to order."

She smiles, rocking happily up and down on her heels. Can't blame her. The extra beat in my step today feels as bright as the sunshine outside.

Can't believe how fast things have moved.

Well, shit, maybe I can, considering everybody involved. There were plenty of people who wanted the case against Mederva to go down rapidly, rather than a slow drip feeding the national media frenzy.

They've survived as a shell with fierce government oversight, back to distributing legitimate equipment. I know a few in the new leadership. They're good, clean people who'll make sure no stone's left unturned, and in time, they'll rebrand and restore their reputation.

The new crew in charge even gave both Keith and I large severance packages, which I almost refused. But with FBI auditors involved and entire armies of lawyers, they assured me the blood money was confiscated to pay out damages, and anything I was entitled to came from doing legitimate security work. I didn't believe it till I saw it myself in Seattle on a brief trip a few weeks ago.

"It'll be done by the time Gwen gets here, right?" Lauren asks.

"That's the plan," I say, loading the last of the wood in my truck.

The big black vehicle was the first thing I got after selling off the Equinox.

New wheels, new life.

Not just on our end, either.

Even perma-idiot Manny Stork appreciates breathing again. Seeing what came down with Mederva, he realizes just how valuable Gingersnap is to his firm, and she's enjoying working a few real cases on a very part-time basis whenever she's not writing.

To everyone's delight, Gwen finished her first novel a month ago. It's in the hands of an agent right now.

It's good, too. I've read the entire thing more than once.

Parts of it are so close to real life, hardly anyone will ever guess it isn't fiction through and through. Only a few of us know the truth.

It's hard not to feel a lick of pride when *based on a true story* means ours.

I close up the tailgate, smacking dust off my hands. "Let's

get moving. Should be finished by the time Gwen gets here this evening."

"Will the paint be dry by then?" Lauren asks.

"Yeah." I nod to the back seat. "Climb in."

As usual, we're off to May's for Friday night supper. Gwen has no idea we've been building the gazebo in her mother's backyard all week. Mainly because I asked the kids to keep it under wraps. We're lucky this place is so huge nobody really notices unless they have reason to.

"So why the big secret, Dad? Why do we gotta be all hush-hush?" Shane asks as we drive away from the lumberyard.

I inhale sharply, holding the breath in my lungs.

Here's my chance. Now or never.

I've needed to talk to them about my plan for weeks, ever since Seattle. It affects the whole family, their lives just as much as mine.

"Well, tonight, after supper, I need to ask Gwen something. But I want to know what you think about it first." I flex my fingers on the steering wheel, surprised at how my palms break out in a sweat.

Shit.

It's the right thing to do, I tell myself. I know it is.

Now that the biggest rush of evidence and interviews is over for the team prosecuting Jackie Wren and her henchmen, I've got my life back.

I'll start working for Landmark Defense in a few weeks. It's a massive defense company based out of St. Paul that J.T. referred me to. I'll still help him with P.I. work on the side. Landmark's been more than generous with time off for other obligations.

Guess the owner, Hunter Forsythe, once a single dad himself, is fully committed to family coming first. He took a personal interest in my case and the rest was history.

All in all, everything's fallen into place faster than I imagined. The rest is up to me, to reinvent myself, my family, my life in a better image.

"Think about what, Dad?" Shane asks.

"What do you want to ask Gwen, Daddy?" Lauren echoes right behind him.

"Well, I'd like to ask Gwen..." I take a deep breath and swallow. "To marry me."

"Awesome!" Shane fist-pumps the air with a grin, his blue eyes flashing my shade.

"Daddy, that's wonderful!" Lauren shouts, one octave below screaming. "The best thing ever! Oh my gosh."

"It's a big step for me, for all of us," I say, trying to calm their enthusiasm so they understand the consequences. "You've never had a mother before. It's always been the three of us. If Gwen says yes, it won't just be three anymore. We'll be a family of four."

"And maybe *five* if Gwen has a baby," Lauren says.

Shit. My daughter's two steps ahead of me.

My jaw goes tight because I know how right she is. Knocking up Gingersnap isn't even a question if we tie the knot.

It will happen. Many times.

"That's another thing, guys. Another kid's a real possibility someday. How would you feel about that?"

"Having a bro would rock!" Shane says without even a second to think it over.

"Or a baby sister! That would be ideal to help look after Shane," Lauren says, flashing her brother a dirty look. "Please ask Gwen, Daddy. I know she'll say yes. Just know it."

"So you're okay with this?" I ask one more time. "Both of you?"

"Yeah!" They both belt it out together.

I try not to grin. "And you'll keep it a secret? Won't tell

anyone about me asking Gwen tonight, including May?"
Especially May.

"Scout's honor," Shane says, crossing his chest.

"It's a promise." Lauren nods firmly.

My veins are humming. "Great. Let's get this gazebo done. After we eat, I can take Gwen out there and ask her to marry me." I glance over my shoulder at their smiling faces.

"Oh, Daddy, I can't wait," Lauren whispers.

Neither can I.

* * *

I FUMBLE MORE things finishing off the structure than I ever have in my entire life. Nothing major, but little odds and ends I have to double check and smooth over several times.

By evening, the gazebo's done and freshly painted. It almost glows wedding white under the late afternoon sun. *Fitting.*

"You've outdone yourself, Miller. This turned out even better than I expected," May gushes, hugging my arm. "Simply gorgeous, sir. It adds a lovely finish to the entire yard."

When she says yard, she means acres of rolling green landscape and trees. She's not wrong, though.

Pride wells in me. It does look pretty great. With its gabled top and waist-high railed sides, it's almost picturesque. Sitting where it belongs in her manicured lawn makes it stand out.

"As soon as the paint dries, I have some strings of twinkle lights I'd like hung around the bottom of the top," May says. "Oh, and speakers for the corners. We need a little music to please the ears as well as the eyes."

"In this heat, the paint should be dry in an hour or so."

"Lovely." May spins around, looking back at me over her shoulder. "That gives us just enough time before dinner."

"And a swim?" Shane asks hopefully.

"Of course," May says. "After all the work you and Lauren did, you can splash around all afternoon."

May and I have an understanding when it comes to the kids. While they're at her house, she can spoil them to her heart's content, but whenever push comes to shove, I'm still their father with final say.

Just like she's Gwen's mother. And it's only right I ask for a final blessing before popping the question.

I wait till we're done with the afternoon snacks her people serve, and after I've got the twinkling lights and speakers up, before accepting another beer and sitting down on a chair next to the pool where Lauren and Shane are swimming. It's a safe distance where we can talk privately.

"My, just *look* at her now. It's hard to believe little Lauren wouldn't leave the shallow end a few months ago," May says.

Anyone watching can see the love she has for my kids. When she looks at them, her eyes shine as bright as Gwen's do. I'm thankful for that, finding someone who loves them as much as me and their future mother.

And someone who, I think, approves of me, too.

"A lot's sure changed in no time, May." I take a swig off my beer. "A whole heaping lot."

Fuck, I'm babbling. I've never had to do this before. Ask permission to *marry* someone's daughter.

It's more unnerving than I'd anticipated for a grown-ass man.

"Something on your mind, Miller?" May smiles, her instincts sharp as claws. "Go ahead. We're practically family."

"Ironically, May, that's what this is about. Family." I smile back at her. "No easy way to say this, so...I'd like to ask Gwen to marry me tonight."

She lifts a knowing brow all the while biting back a smile, her face turning mock serious. "Like to ask, or *will* ask?"

"Will ask, if it's okay with you."

Honestly, even if it isn't, it's coming anyway. But it'd sure be nice having her ma's endorsement.

"Oh, Miller, of course it's all right with me." She leans over and squeezes my hand. "And I hope she says yes."

I huff out a sigh. "I do, too."

She pats my hand. "Let me tell you something I told Gwen a few weeks ago." Her gaze deepens, turning fully serious. "Love is more than great sex. Don't get me wrong. Wild bedroom acrobatics are certainly important, too, but love goes deeper. Far deeper. It's there all the time. Making you grin for no reason. Making you thankful. Making you whole."

I nod. She's just described everything I feel for Gingersnap.

"Good advice," I say.

"It should be. Lord knows I've written enough books to know and lived one broken heart that told me what to avoid..." May leans back in her chair. "Okay. You've got my blessing to ask Gwendolyn to be your wife, but on two conditions."

"Conditions?"

She holds up two stiff fingers for effect. "One: if you ever hurt her, I'll have you killed. And two, if you ever think about moving away from Minnesota, about taking those sweet children and my daughter away, know that I'll be hot on your heels. I have the money for ten more homes just like this one."

Shit.

I'm not sure which one of those is scarier. Probably the second because the first one's out of the question.

"Understood," I say. "One hundred percent."

"Good." She leans forward again, her elegant smile reappearing like she'd never just threatened murder. "Now, how will you ask my lucky little lady?"

"I thought I'd wait till after supper, while showing her the gazebo. At some point, you'll go off with the kids, leaving us together."

"Perfect! I have some planters we can move out there for a little color, and I'll..." She stops and looks at me. "You don't mind if I set the mood a bit, do you?"

"No, May, I don't mind." I lean closer. "Long as you don't mind watching Shane and Lauren overnight."

She holds up a fist. This might be the strangest thing of the day, fist-bumping a middle aged lady with more money than some city treasuries, but it works.

"Deal," I tell her.

Real sincerity fills me. I lean over and give her a hug. "Thank you, May. Thanks for everything you've done."

She hugs me in return. "Thank you, Miller, for loving my daughter in a way I always knew she'd be loved. It was simply a matter of her finding the right man and bringing him home."

A FEW HOURS LATER, I'm the most nervous I've ever been without armed men involved.

I'm sure Gwen has fallen in love with me, but is she ready for forever?

She's a smart girl. Cautious. Leery of many things.

She claims it's because she's a chicken, scared of her own shadow, but that's not true.

She has more guts and gumption than many guys I know. I'll never forget how she handled things during that night of hell at the cabin. Her quick thinking saved my kids.

But she is careful. Even when it comes to her writing, she avoids launching deep into subjects she hasn't experienced. Something she got from May, I think, who has to try everything before she can put it into words.

Her ma pressed Gwen into the same mold and that's what keeps her on her toes.

Marriage isn't something May ever forced her to try, though.

I don't want her to think that's what I'm forcing, either.

"You've barely touched your steak," Gingersnap says quietly. "Is something wrong with it?"

"Nope. Immaculate as ever." I shake my head. "I'm just not as hungry tonight. The kids and I had snacks here today, and you know how big your mother's snack breaks get."

She grins. "Lauren said she swam all afternoon. How'd they talk you into that? Or should I say, how'd *Mother* talk you into it?"

I wink at her, taking a bite of steak, chewing like it's the only thing keeping my jaw intact.

It's gonna be goddamn rough if I haven't wifed this woman by the end of the night.

"Gwen, darling, did you read that email I forwarded about the next writer's conference? It's the end of September, in Minneapolis, so you won't have to book a motel room if you don't want to. I've already booked mine. I hate city driving, but I could cancel it to ride with you, or could add you to my room..." May takes a drink off her wine and continues on about the conference.

Gwen nods along, and when May finally stops talking long enough to take another sip of wine, she says, "It's too soon for me to go to a conference, Mother. I haven't even gotten feedback on the manuscript I sent to the agency yet."

"Oh, that hardly matters," May says. "I've told you before,

lots of unpublished writers attend. It's how they learn what to do, and not to do, in order to make their work shine."

"How old do you have to be to go, May?" Lauren asks.

Of course she's totally serious.

So's May when she says, "I'm not sure, sweetheart, but I'll find out. I'd love to have you attend with me."

"Really?"

"Yes, really." May sets down her napkin. "As a matter of fact, let's go call right now and find out. Shane, you can come, too."

He freezes and horror fills his eyes. "A writer's conference? Uh..."

"I meant you can come with us to make the call." May stands. "In my office. We'll have our dessert there. It's chocolate cake."

"With white frosting?" Shane asks, suddenly a hundred times happier.

"Yes, sir." May holds out a hand to Lauren.

Both kids look at me.

I nod, and they leave the room with May.

Now, it's zero hour.

Gwen looks at me and shakes her head. "What am I missing?"

"Missing, babe?"

Like the fact that I'm about to shove a ring on your finger? I think to myself, stomach churning.

Her green eyes flash as she looks at me slowly. "I mean...didn't the kids seem unusually quiet, and Mother more chatty? I swear she's talked my ear off ever since I got here, without really saying anything important."

"That's unusual?" I ask with a snort.

She bursts out laughing, and I join in with a chuckle.

"No. Okay, maybe." She sets down her napkin. "Or maybe

it's just me. Seems like I've waited forever for this week to end."

"What? Don't tell me Manny's jerking you around again?"

She grins. "Nah, he's been a good boy. I just really want to sleep in tomorrow."

"You, sleep in? Instead of bounding up at six a.m. to tear up some words?"

She shrugs.

I set down my napkin and take her hand. "Babe, I'm game. You want your beauty rest, just say the word, and we'll keep the kids here tonight. I'm sure they won't mind."

She leans over and kisses me softly. "Whatever works, Miller."

It's now or never.

Standing up and pushing my chair back, I hold out a hand to her. "Join me for a walk? There's something I want to show you."

"Sure." Taking my hand, she follows me down the hall.

Before we get to the door that leads to the pool and beyond, I pull a scarf out of my back pocket and hold it up.

Her frown is adorable. "Um, what? Is that one of Mother's scarves?"

"Yeah. The better to blindfold you with, my dear."

Her face scrunches. "You're joking, right?"

"Do I joke with surprises?"

"Okay, okay." Laughing, she turns around. "Blindfold me then. Maybe we can do it again later."

My dick stirs at what she's implying. But for once, I really want the image of Gwen naked, blindfolded, and prone out of my head so I can do what I came here for.

Claim her like that for the rest of my life.

Knowing she trusts me enough to cover up her eyes here or in the bedroom gives me the extra shot of courage I need.

So I slip the scarf over her eyes and tie it on the back of her head.

"See anything?" I whisper in her ear, loving how she shudders against me.

"No."

"Hold my hand, babe. It's right this way."

"Just don't let me trip over anything."

I chuckle. "Like there's anything out of place. You do know we're at your ma's house?"

"True." She tightens her hold on my fingers and then folds her other hand around my arm. "I'm ready."

I lead her to the door and open it. A rush of chirping crickets and other night sounds instantly serenade us.

"We're going outside? It's probably dark enough now that I wouldn't need to be blindfolded."

"You do with the lights. We're gonna walk around the edge of the pool, then into the grass," I tell her.

"Okay. What's next?"

"I'll take off your blindfold and present your unicorn, duchess."

"Oh my God. Don't tell me...Mother bought Shane and Lauren a pony, didn't she? Now I get why they all ran off together. I know Lauren wants one, but seriously, leasing it would be so much easier than driving over here at five in the morning to feed a horse."

"You'd do it, though, wouldn't you? Get up early every morning and drive them over here to feed it?" I know the answer, but ask anyway.

I'll never get sick of hearing how much this angel loves my kids.

"It won't be easy," she sighs. "But...if that's what they wanted..."

I grin, pressing my lips to her shoulder. Her hand comes

up slowly, caressing my face, feeling the rough shadow around my jaw I know she adores.

There's no fucking way I'll screw this up.

I'll convince Gwen to be mine forever, or I'll go down the biggest loser in history.

It takes forever to get to the edge of the lawn. The lights May had me hang up are twinkling like little stars all the way around the gazebo. I let go of her hand and step behind her to untie the scarf. "Close your eyes. Don't open them till I say."

"You're crazy, Miller. You sound so serious." She giggles, oblivious to the fact that I am.

"Eyes closed?"

"Yessir."

I untie the scarf and wrap my arms around her waist from behind. "All right, on the count of three, open your eyes. One. Two...*three.*"

"Holy Toledo!" She sucks in a deep breath and lets it out slowly. "You...you built Mother her gazebo?"

"Sure did."

"It's gorgeous. Totally picture perfect. I bet she loves it." She turns, pressing her hands against my shoulder, giving me a celebratory kiss.

"And you?" I growl, kissing her back, trying to *focus* before I'm drunk on her lips.

"It's too perfect. Everything she talked about for years, and it looks so lovely with those lights. Guess we'll be doing dinners here sometimes."

Shit, okay.

Deep breath.

Slowly, I step around her and take her hand. "There's a reason I finished it today."

She frowns as we walk toward it, my heart drumming something fierce. "Oh, you mean she was that impatient?"

I say no more, remembering how May said it'd be the perfect place for a wedding.

We climb the steps and enter the brightly lit octagon space, stepping onto freshly laid tile. Several green plants line the interior in their huge Grecian urns, and soft music plays through the white speakers hanging in the corners. "Looks like the perfect place, doesn't it?"

Still frowning, she forms a half grin, studying me. "Perfect place for *what?*"

"Gingersnap, you already know," I whisper, coming closer, leaving no space between us.

Then I reach into my pocket, pull out that little silver book locket I've turned into a ring box, and kneel.

XXI: THAT'S MY HUBBY (GWEN)

A shockwave rolls over me so fierce it turns my knees
to rubber.

I almost hit the floor as Miller goes down on one knee in
front of me, holding a familiar necklace that's been missing
ever since that day at the lake.

Holy crap.

This can't be happening. It can't. I never saw it coming.

Maybe in my wildest dreams, I always thought it could
happen someday. *But right here? Right now?*

I've heard Mother mention weddings for her shiny new
gazebo but...

Oh, he's talking. And I can barely breathe.

"Gwendolyn, I thought I only had love for two special
people a few months ago. Never imagined anybody creeping
into my life and burying themselves as deep as Lauren and
Shane. Then there was you. I found you in the darkness, this
beacon of light I never knew I needed." He looks away for a
moment, and I try to wipe the first of many messy tears with
one finger. "Babe, every day we've had together counts as the
happiest of my life. Despite being on the lam, chased down

by some pretty evil pricks, I always had you, and that was plenty. That's all that mattered. Call me crazy, but hell...I want to keep you, Gwen. Forever. And I know that only happens if I make it real, make it official, make it last."

Oh God.

Oh. My. God.

My ears strain against the dull roar of my own heart, and he's not even finished.

"I'm done with pretend, Gingersnap. Because the first time we kissed, I knew your stupid boss never set me up with a fake wife. He played matchmaker without even knowing it." He flips open my locket, just the right size to hold what's inside. "Marry me, Gwen? Marry me right here in this gazebo, and I'll build us an ever after with the same love and care I used building this place, every last day of our lives. Let me be your muse."

I press a hand to my mouth, desperately trying to blink away the blurriness caused by tears of pure joy. The gold band shimmers in the light and the large diamond glistens like it has a light on inside it.

It's embarrassing how long it takes me to remember how to speak.

But it's hardly every day a man as incredible, infuriating, and screaming hot as Miller Rush asks you to spend the rest of your life with him.

"Miller!" I shout his name and drop down to my knees in front of him, throwing my arms around his neck so hard he rocks back. "Yes! Yes, yes, yes, yes, *yes.*"

I kiss him, over and over again, thoroughly short-circuited by happiness.

He stands, bringing me to my feet alongside him, all the while never taking his mouth off mine.

I'm still in total shock.

"You're sure, Miller?" I whisper, hoping to God he is. "I

mean, what about the kids? Did you ask them? Are they okay with us–"

"Babe. Take a look." He pivots his gaze over his shoulder, nodding at the house.

At first I don't see anything. Then as his hand squeezes mine, I notice Mother's office window is lit up. There's a huge sheet of paper hanging in the window with several lines written in a black marker.

PLEASE SAY YES, GWEN! BE OUR MOM!

In small print, below that, it says, *And let May be our grandma!*

It's amazing I don't just fall right over. By the time I look back at Miller, he's lifting a brow.

"Satisfied?"

I laugh, wiping a few more stray tears from my eyes. "Well, that answers how the kids feel. But what about you? I know how you feel about help...and marriage is having someone there to help you, all the time."

So I'm not trying to talk him out of it, I just want to know he's not making a mistake, doing something he'll regret.

Blame my inner chicken. But I have to be *sure.*

He nods. "Never been more sure of anything, Gwen. I welcome your help. Now and forever."

My fingers flutter as he grabs my hand, holding it up. I try really hard not to drop dead on the spot.

The way he looks at me while sliding the ring on my finger makes my heart double in size.

It's love. Pure, beautiful, glorious love. The same love I mirror every time we kiss and wish it would never end. Then he slides the locket back around my neck, a new chain attached that fits perfectly.

I think it's the first time in my life I don't feel awkward wearing this thing.

Turns out, I just needed the right muse, the right man, and I'm so lucky they're one and the same.

"Nothing to be afraid of," he whispers. "What I'm feeling is so strong, so real, it'll see us through anything, babe. Day and night. Good and the bad. Light and dark."

Ah, here come the tears again, rolling down my cheeks in hot trails. I couldn't stop them if I tried. "Miller, I'm never afraid anymore. Not when you're here."

"Love you, Gingersnap. Today and tomorrow and till I draw my last breath."

"I love you!" It comes out like a squeal and I pinch my lips together, nodding toward the house. "And I love them, too. You and Shane and Lauren...I swear I'll always be there, too. Day and night. Good and bad. Light, dark, grey, whatever!"

Smiling, he pushes his forehead to mine, brushing the hair away from my face. Then, cupping my cheeks, he pulls me into a blue-eyed kiss that incinerates any doubt I ever had.

* * *

WE'RE STILL LOCKED in that kiss, making out in each other's arms, when a voice floats through the air.

"Did she say yes, Dad? Did she?" Shane asks.

"Yeah, tell us, Daddy, please!" Lauren seems even more impatient than her brother.

And then, "Darling, please answer them!"

Mother. Ugh.

Laughing, we both throw our heads back and yell, "Yes!"

"Yes." We repeat it again, turning to face each other, smiling at my new fiancé like my grin might just fly off my face.

Another question bounces off the gazebo, slightly different versions asked by the two kids and Mother. *When?*

Miller lifts a brow, looking me over.

I shrug. "Whenever you want. Right now. Tomorrow. The next day. Next month. I don't care, however long it takes to throw something simple together." I kiss his chin. "You being my husband, Miller, that's all I care about."

"Sweet coincidence. That's all I care about, too, Gwen."

Laughing, I glance at the house, and then at the foot of the gazebo stairs, where Mother and the kids are waiting.

"Maybe we should let them decide when?" Glancing at the gazebo, I add, "We already know where."

"You sure about that?" He turns, side-eyeing our little gaggle of family spectators. "Letting them decide?"

"Totally." I press tightly against him. "Frankly, I'm worn out deciding. I have other things I'd rather do right now."

Growling, his hands wind down my back, catching my drift. He gives my butt a delicious squeeze with both hands. "Fine. It's settled. The kids are spending tonight with your ma, just like we talked about. Let 'em figure it out then."

I nuzzle his neck. "I love how you thought of everything."

He subtly grinds his hips against me. "Ready to tell them?"

I'll never get tired of this.

How easily he makes me crave him.

How he sets my body on fire.

How wonderfully natural every kiss, every caress, every night with him feels.

It's been like that since we first met, and I know it'll stay that way for the rest of our lives. I draw in a deep breath, just to steady myself for the journey home. "Ready."

"Good. Then we'll get the hell out of here," he nearly growls every word again.

Laughing, we leave the gazebo and meet Shane, Lauren, and my mother near the lawn.

The whole trio are as giddy as I am. And after I tell them

they can plan the wedding, I'm not sure whether it's Mother or the kids who do more bouncing up and down.

Actually, Shane isn't quite as excited at the idea as Mother and Lauren, until I tell him he's in charge of the cake. Including the taste testing. Then his little face lights up like Christmas and the promises he makes us never stop.

We say our goodbyes and leave then, hand in hand.

The drive back from Mother's house seems to take hours rather than minutes. His hand rests on mine the whole way, pressed to my knee, fingers laced and warning what's to come.

You know you've found Mr. Hell Yeah when he can make you this wet with nothing more than his palm.

We're out of the truck with the garage door still lowering when we lock arms, stumbling to the door. Neither of us wants to let go.

The door opens, and the coolness of the air-conditioned house enhances how the air between us sizzles.

We make it as far as the living room before stripping, letting our clothes fall where they may.

Miller runs a hand down my arm, around my waist, and I tremble with need, with want, with pleading.

"Fuck, babe. Didn't know I could be this happy," he says, bringing his lips to my throat.

"Same. Oh, but I am. Now and forever."

Snarling, he tosses me on the couch in one swift movement. The passion between us is too hot, too intense, too reckless to wait another second.

I spread my legs, more than ready for him. "Welcome home, honey," I whisper.

He laughs, driving to my depths in one stroke, guttural pleasure ripping up his throat.

Folding my ankles around him, I hold him there, relishing this moment, this connection, this perfect heat. It's amazing how a few words and a life changing promise make sex even better.

The bond between us just grew stronger, and tonight, it makes things hotter than ever.

I pull his face down, raking my nails down his back, desperate for his tongue. It comes as his hips pump harder, shoving my butt into the seat, all delicious tension as he takes me over.

"Goddamn, I love it. Love how tight you are. Love how good you taste. Love how you can keep up," he says, pushing himself faster, harder.

The way he's moving, driving into me, is everything.

Despite the urgency, he takes it a little slower then, drawing out the pleasure, simmering our intensity to unbelievable heights.

I can barely breathe, barely think, all because of him.

But I guess that's what it's like with Miller Rush.

When I swear I can't take anymore, when my knees and toes and hands can't stop shaking, he moves faster, takes me further into sheer bliss. I cry out, arms and legs locked around him, screaming like a crazy woman.

Coming!

My climax hits with a force that's all consuming. He's right there with me, holding me tight, his cock pressed deep, hurling hot liquid jets into me. Even the aftershock leaves us gasping, drunk on the realization that *yes, we're doing this. Yes, it only gets better.*

Our eyes meet. His, like mine, are passion and love overflowing.

We both laugh, knowing this is only the beginning.

* * *

Months Later

"You look like a real life princess," Lauren says, walking around me in awe.

Her and Mother picked out my dress, an amazingly simple gown of white silk that I absolutely love. I've never felt truly beautiful before, but I do right now, and I can't wait for Miller to see.

Kneeling down, I plant a kiss on her forehead. "I feel like a princess, thanks to you."

"I always knew Daddy had a little Prince Charming in him," she says with a wink.

I look out the window, into the backyard, where white chairs are set up in a circle around the gazebo, and people are already mingling. "He certainly is."

Mother laughs. "I believe knight in shining armor fits him like a glove."

I flash a smile her way. "I think you're right. I'm just lucky I get to marry my hero."

"And I'm so happy for you, darling." Mother puts an arm around Lauren and gives her a hug. "Happy for myself, too, let's be honest. I get a son and two lovely grandchildren all in the same day. How awesome is that?"

"Pretty awesome," I say. Full of emotion, I blink back a few tears. "Thank you, Mother. For everything."

She shakes her head, then gives me a glance that's oddly authentic. "No. Thank you for letting me be your mother. I know that hasn't been easy at times."

I give her a hug. "I wouldn't have had it any other way."

A knock sounds on the door.

"Come in!" Mother chirps.

"It's almost time, everybody," Heather says.

Her and Keith arrived in Minnesota two months ago, shortly after Miller asked me to marry him. Miller helped get Keith an in with Landmark Defense, a new job and a new life for two best friends. They've been living in one of the townhouses next to us while their new house is being built.

Surprise-surprise, right next to the new one we're building. It's less than a mile from Mother's house, about as close as you can get without intruding on her spacious land.

Heather waves at Lauren. "Maid of honor goes first. Right this way, little lady."

Lauren picks up her bouquet and, keeping her chin up, walks to the door.

Mother gives me one last kiss on the cheek, and then hooks her arm through mine. "Ready as you'll ever be?"

I nod like mad.

As we leave the room together, she leans to my ear and says, "Thank God, Gwendolyn. I've been dreaming of your wedding day ever since you were a little girl."

I know she has. And just when I tell myself I can't possibly be more thankful for Miller, I am.

Because when he agreed to let her and Lauren and Shane plan the wedding, he meant it.

He's never questioned a single idea they presented. Neither have I. They're all a part of this, a part of our lives, merging together into one happy unit.

"I hope it's everything you've ever dreamed of," I say.

"Oh, much more, darling. I couldn't even have written an epilogue this perfect." She laughs. "But you did."

Even though it's reality, I can't stop blushing every time she reminds me.

Two weeks ago, I signed a contract for the book I'd written, as well as two more with a major publisher. The commitment makes me nervous, but I know I can do it. With Miller and the kids, I don't think limits exist anymore.

We stop near the door that's hanging open, leading out to

the lawn full of people, and Miller, standing in the center of the gazebo.

"Here you are, Mrs. Rush," Mother whispers, wiping a tear from her eye.

Warmth fills me from my toes to the top of my head. I give her a quick peck on the cheek. "Thanks, Mother."

She nods her head toward the organist. All the people in their chairs rise as she and I step out the door. Friends and family and extended relatives we haven't seen in ages.

My eyes instantly go to Miller, and my heart thuds at the raw appreciation in his eyes as he scans me from head to toe. I let my appreciation of him show, too.

He's so freaking handsome in his black tux. Then again, he's handsome in everything. And when he's not wearing anything at all.

Keith completes the scene, standing there with a grin that could burn right through everybody with his flaming red hair that's even brighter than mine, a perfect contrast to his navy blue suit. I'm grateful for his friendship, his influence, one more powerful force who helped sweep Miller into my life.

But soon, with so many distractions, I can't focus on anything except my soon-to-be-husband.

He lifts a dark brow, and a giggle tickles my throat, knowing he's undressing me in his mind.

It's only fair, considering I'm doing the same to him. We both know how important a healthy sex life is to a marriage. Good thing we've got that part down pat, plus a lifetime of delirious practice ahead.

We have so much more than just great bedroom acrobatics, too.

Today, Miller becomes my best friend. My husband. My everything.

He keeps the adventures coming every single day, and I

suspect they'll only be coming faster and more furious after we've said our vows. That should be scary for someone who's been one with a hen her entire life, but it's not anymore.

Because I'm no longer afraid of anything. What could I possibly have to fear, hitched to a hero?

Our union, the ceremony, is a short, heartfelt service.

Traditional vows. Promises. Totally us.

He's a man of few words, and I'm so freaking nervous and giddy I'm scared I wouldn't be able to remember a single line with everybody staring at us. He holds my hand the entire time, fingers laced through mine, squeezing with a grip that promises me *fifty, a hundred, a thousand years.*

It promises forever.

And it binds us together as we share our first kiss as husband and wife.

He kisses me with such fierce, proud passion I'm beet red by the time it's over. But I'm actually happy when I come up for air and see his grin, hearing the raucous cheers around us, with two screaming kids louder than anyone.

Before we exit the gazebo, we let our announcer do his thing. He tells everyone that besides marrying their father, I've officially adopted Shane and Lauren, making me their legal mother.

The guests go ballistic as Miller shakes Keith's hand one more time. Then, along with Shane, a groomsman, and Lauren, the maid of honor, we strut back down the aisle. One family.

My perfect family.

There's a huge spread of delicious food, prepared by Mother's chef. Drinks running over, dancing everywhere, and a gorgeous cake that looks so divine, part of me doesn't want to cut it. It's been personally baked for us by Wendy Forsythe, Miller's new boss' wife, and her adorable family shop in St. Paul called Midnight Morning. If there's anyone who knows a thing or two about perfect weddings, it's her.

It seems like there's a hundred hands to shake and even more things to taste. I should be absolutely exhausted, but as the night draws on, I wonder if marrying this incredible man gave me a second wind for life.

While the party's still in full swing, Miller and I wind up a short distance away from the pool, talking with J.T. and his adorable wife, Margaret, when a group of children runs past us. A little boy, no more than three, trying to keep up, trips.

"Joey!" Margaret screams as the child tumbles into the pool.

Without a hint of hesitation, Miller does what he does best.

Spinning, leaping, and still in his tux, he swan dives into the pool and goes after the kid, surfacing with him a second or two later.

J.T. takes the boy from Miller's hands, muttering endless apologies. I kneel down next to the pool as Miller grabs the ladder railing to climb out.

God. Just when I thought my heart couldn't be fuller, or my admiration any stronger, there it is.

I'm so flipping proud of this man.

Proud to be his wife. So proud that every time he growls *mine,* I can give it right back.

Planting a grateful kiss on his lips, I reach for his dripping tie, pulling him closer. "You just *had* to do it again, didn't you?"

Shaking the water from his hair, we both laugh as I get splattered.

"Do what, Gingersnap?" he whispers, coming in closer for the next part. "Get you all wet?"

"No, but yes. I mean...make me love you even more."

Yes, it's sappy as all hell, but who cares?

I kiss him again with the full force of my own pulse, lost in rapture. I don't even care that he's getting my dress all wet, or that everybody's staring and smiling at us, or that the kids can't stop bouncing up and down and chattering at how awesome it was.

Nothing else matters besides the man lovingly attached to my lips, tangling his arms around me.

It's amazing to remember how one messed up call put us here. But it's his kiss that'll keep messing me up for a long, long time to come, in all the best ways.

That's my freaking hubby.

My hero. My rebel. My best mistake.

EPILOGUE: IT'S THE LITTLE THINGS (GWEN)

Five Years Later

"*Moooooom!*"

I glance into the kitchen from where I'm sitting at the dining room table, catching up on emails I've put off for a week. Shane has his head stuffed in the fridge, as usual.

"I'm right here," I say, which also means *you don't have to shout.*

"Oh." He shuts the fridge door. "Sorry. I didn't see you. Have you seen my chemistry book?"

I look at the closed fridge door, and then his empty hands. That's weird.

I frown. "It's Saturday, why would you need your chemistry book?"

"Because I have some homework."

I stare harder at him.

"Who are you and what have you done with my son? First you're not plucking the last crumbs out of the fridge, and now you're talking homework?" I gasp, running my hands down my cheeks.

He laughs, his voice cracking a bit. "Very funny. We gotta go to the store. Even I can't wolf down mustard on blueberry yogurt, about all we've got left."

It's hard to believe how much he's grown in five years. Our mischievous, sweet boy is turning into a tall, kind-hearted, and not-so-shockingly handsome young man. He's almost as tall as me, and getting more muscular every year.

I grin at him. "Homework on a weekend, though? What's really up?"

"A bunch of us are meeting over at Max's house tonight. Keith said we could use his shop for the project we're working on. Dad said it was okay."

I nod. "Dad told me you were going over there, but I must've missed the chemistry project part." My spine quivers. "Does Heather know you're turning her place into a makeshift lab?"

He rolls his eyes. "Yeah, Mom, she knows."

I have to smile. He looks so much like Miller that I almost feel sorry for the girls in his school.

As his mother, it's my right to know no girl will ever be good enough for him.

Not until she proves herself.

Thankfully, I remember that's still years away.

"If I was you, I'd look in your backpack for your textbook first. That's where we found your U.S. history book a couple weeks back, remember?"

"Oh, right. I was trying to forget that one, though." He smiles, holding up a finger. "I'll take a look and see what I can find. Thanks, Mom. See ya later!" He opens the fridge again, grabs the last apple, and then kisses my cheek on his way out through the dining room.

"Love you, too, big boy." A second later, I run a few

steps through the house and call after him, "Hey, don't forget to be careful, Mister. If you blow up Keith's shop or something, you'll help us cover the hike in insurance premiums."

"Nah, I won't!" he yells back at me.

"Have you *seen* this guy? Don't trust him, Mother." Lauren says dryly, pushing her way past him and into the dining room. "Oh, and have you seen this?"

I glance at the piece of paper she's holding up. The blank backside is turned toward me. "Hmm, what is it?"

"A note from Abby's preschool teacher." Lauren lays it on the table. "It says she needs to bring treats for the last day of school next week. I know you've been busy with the series, so...FYI."

Oh, little Abby.

The sweet joy she brings into our lives every day still amazes me. Born ten months after Miller and I got married, she's truly made our lives complete. She's a little bit of Miller, a little bit of me, and a whole lot of rambunctious, happy little girl.

We're lucky she has a big brother and sister to look up to.

Lauren's grown up too, turning into a beautiful young woman who absolutely adores her baby sister. I'm so happy the terrible teens haven't gotten *too* wild yet or soured her sweetness with even a smidge of bitter.

"Yes, I saw that," I tell her. "Thanks. We'll let Abby pick out whatever she wants to take for a treat when we go grocery shopping tomorrow."

"Pick out?" Lauren looks appalled. "Don't you think we should make something, Mom? With your skills and mine and especially Dad's, we can–"

"We can't, honey. The school doesn't allow homemade treats. They have to be store bought and individually wrapped." I don't mention the no peanuts rule.

"Store bought? Awww, don't they know how full of preservatives that factory stuff is?" She picks up the paper.

I try not to grin. While Shane's getting into heavy metal and messing with test tubes, Lauren's turning into just a little bit of a health freak. And that's okay. All things considered, there are worse things for a teenage girl to be.

"We need to look for a different preschool next year, Mom. I haven't been impressed with this one. Anything homemade is healthier than store bought. Everyone knows it." My princess puts her hands on her hips, satisfied she's read her decree.

"Hey, Abby likes her school," I say. "So do your father and I."

Lauren shakes her head, defiant as ever. "Because they let her finger paint! What kid doesn't love finger painting?"

"None, I suspect. But tell you what, when you have a beautiful bouncing baby all to yourself, I won't stand in your way if you want to send them off to the nearest Amish school."

It takes a second for it to sink in. Then Lauren's little brow knits and she sticks out her tongue. "That's hardly what I meant, and you know it."

"Okay, bossypants. How's your latest fantasy story coming? Your grandma said good things last I heard, and if she likes it–"

"Grandma's amazing, but she doesn't know fantasy. I've got some world building to do to get it right. The guy at the last seminar we went to talked a lot about that, and he should know since he's had a hit series about dragons. Turns out, people really care where their magic creatures come from, whether that's fire-breathing lizards or house cats striped like tigers."

I smile, loving how her work-in-progress has its nucleus

all the way back to the first story we ever did together. Things could've gone down so differently then.

I don't miss *that* kind of excitement – not even a little – but I'm thankful every day I helped my knight slay himself a real beast called Jackie Wren. She's spending her fifth year rotting away in a Federal supermax on a life sentence.

Lauren walks into the kitchen and peeks out the window above the sink. "Hey, Mom, is Abby still outside with Dad?"

"Yep, should be out by the swing set," I tell her.

"I'm going to go get her. It's time for us to get ready."

"Get ready?"

She gives me a look like I've forgotten her birthday.

Oh, jeez. I haven't, have I?

I'd been so deep in the last book of my latest mystery series that I've barely even let myself breathe.

"We're going shopping with Grandma today. I told you, remember?"

I shake my head, hoping that might help the fog that's been lingering thick for a few days now. "You did. Sorry." I do recall her mentioning it now. "What're you shopping for?"

She grins. "It's the end of April, Mother, which means changing up our wardrobes." She waves her hands. "Time to trade in the sweaters, scarves, and boots for shorts, swimsuits, and sandals. And nobody has better taste than–"

"Don't say it. I know," I say with a sigh.

I think it's cyclical, these little attitude flourishes. There are times when she reminds me so much of my mother that I wonder if somehow, some of her blood got into Lauren's veins.

"Sorry I'm so scatterbrained, honey. Just don't let Mother get too insane with little Abby, okay?"

It's a serious request. If I thought Mother was being ridiculous spoiling Shane and Lauren, ever since her new infant granddaughter showed up...oh my God.

If we didn't make rules, I think Abby would have her own throne room and a couple elephants by now.

"Gotcha. No worries, Mom," Lauren says, walking back into the dining room to give me a quick peck on my cheek. "There's no need to be sorry, either. You were under a tight deadline last week. I'm starting to realize how crazy that gets."

There's the girl I love. She might be older and sassier and very busy figuring out what kind of lady she wants to be, but I know the end result will be a woman who kicks butt.

At her core, Lauren's loving, kind, and understanding, and I don't think that'll ever change.

"No fooling, I was. I'm just glad that book is done and sent off."

I'm also very thankful how well my writing career is going.

I'm not at the level of my mother, but I'm getting there. Maybe a few more books and one of them will strike gold with some major movie deal. Then *I* can be the one to make the kids' faces turn red when I spoil the stuffing out of my future grandkids.

"I'm proud of you, Mom. Not just for making all the best-sellers' lists. You just do so much around here for everyone, and yet...you're always still smiling. Never stressed. Always happy. I hope I can be just like you someday."

I wrap an arm around her waist, reeling her in closer. "Thanks, sweet girl. It's pretty easy when my family makes me the happiest woman alive."

She hugs me and then steps away. "I have to go grab Abby and get ready. Grandma will be here soon."

"All right. Love you."

"Love you, too, Mom."

Moments later, Miller walks into the dining room.

Naturally, I stop and stare.

It seems like this man gets a little hotter, a little bolder, a little growlier with each passing year. And now that he's fully acclimated himself to Minnesota wear, and he's walking around half the time in flannel?

Dear Lord.

It's a miracle I get any writing done at all when we still spend most of our free time in bed, whenever the kids are busy elsewhere. It hasn't gotten easier finding time for each other with a growing family but dammit, we do. And I wouldn't trade a single fiery night with this man for anything.

"How's it going with the emails?"

I lean my head back so he can give me a kiss. "Hard to believe how fast they pile up." I run a hand through my hair. "I just...I don't know, hubby. Feeling so foggy headed lately I'm having a hard time remembering anything. Guess the last book took more out of me than I thought."

He grins, an even happier gleam shining in his sky-blue eyes. "Foggy-headed? Forgetful? Tolerating that mud Lauren pushes?"

He reaches over my shoulder, tapping the rim of my glass. I stare down into the turmeric-lemon tea. It's something Lauren came home raving about for its anti-inflammatory properties after her last big yoga class ended.

Normally, I can't stand the stuff, but today? It's not half bad.

Wowza. Maybe I'm more tired than I thought.

"Babe," he growls, nipping at my earlobe.

I bat him away, laughing. "Hey, come on, working. What're you grinning so big about, anyway?" Guilt pools in my stomach. "Oh, no. What did I forget now?"

He shrugs nonchalantly, padding into the kitchen. "Nothing I know of, except maybe...*nahhh.*"

"Maybe *what?*" I shoot him a dirty glare.

"Well, Gingersnap, do you remember the last time you were foggy and forgetful and suddenly got a hankering for the weirdest shit a human being could put in their mouth?" He winks at me.

No?

Oh. Wait.

Ohhhh.

My heart dives into my belly and then swings back up again.

"Holy hell!" I shout, throwing a hand over my mouth.

It can't be...can it?

Clicking on the calendar icon on my laptop, where I record and track everything, I scroll back a month. Then two. A bubble of freaky, stunned joy starts in my stomach as I twist to look at Miller.

"Last time I was like this, I was..."

"When you were pregnant with Abby," he finishes for me, smiling like a cat who just ate the bird.

I bite my lip before admitting the possibility, "I haven't had a period in two months."

He nods. "I know."

I stand up. "You know?"

Nodding, he walks over and grasps my waist with both hands. "Gwen, it's me. Of course I do."

I loop my arms around his neck, breaking into a grin. "Yeah, you would."

"Happy?" he asks. "Just like when we found out about Abby?"

There's only one way to answer.

I kick my legs up, hugging my hands around his strong neck. Right on cue, he sweeps me up into his arms, reenacting the scene when we found out the first time. "How about you, Miller? Ready to be a daddy for the fourth time?"

"Damn right," he growls, pulling me closer, swinging me around in a circle.

Then, when my feet finally touch the floor again, he kisses me with enough passion to turn my knees into butter.

He's kind of good at that, you know.

Breathlessly, because his kisses *always* do that to me, I lean my head on his shoulder.

"Another baby," I whisper. "I can't think of anything more perfect. Right on schedule to keep our lives fun if the kids head off for college in a couple years, so little Abby isn't alone."

"What's my reward?" He kisses the top of my head. "For timing everything just right?"

Oh my God, is he serious?

Judging by the look on his face, it's a given.

"In case you forget, it takes two to make a baby, buster." Laughing, I quirk an eyebrow, running my fingernails gently up his chest. "But maybe you'll find out tonight. I have a few ideas."

Miller opens his mouth to answer, but the front door opens first, and a familiar voice calls, "Yoo-hooooo!"

Speaking of timing...

I pull my head up, press a finger to Miller's lips, and whisper, "I'll make a doctor's appointment so we're totally sure before it gets back to anyone too obnoxious."

"Good plan," he tells me before craning his face up and shouting, "In the dining room, May!"

The next half hour is a whirlwind. Something Mother always causes whether she means to or not, getting the girls out the door for their shopping trip.

Miller stands next to me as we wave bye to them from the front door. Once they're out of the driveway, he closes the door and slides his hands under my shirt, a truly wicked glint in his eye.

"We're alone. How 'bout we talk rewards early?"

My entire body tingles. I dip my hands under his shirt, sliding my fingers up his hard, inked body. "Just talk?" I bite down on my smile, loving how he scowls.

"Fuck no. I should show you how you got pregnant."

I laugh. "You know how that happened, do you?"

He shoves my shirt up high enough to expose my bra. "Matter of fact, I'm an expert."

I lean back, giving him full access to my breasts, sighing as he moves in for the kill.

"I guess I'll believe you, if you've got the proof," I whisper, teasing him into a frenzy.

He growls like thunder as his beard rubs my cleavage. "Nothing I'd rather do, Gingersnap. Now or any day."

There's nothing I'd rather do, either, and just like him, I'm eager to prove it.

ABOUT NICOLE SNOW

Nicole Snow is a *Wall Street Journal* and *USA Today* bestselling author. She found her love of writing by hashing out love scenes on lunch breaks and plotting her great escape from boardrooms. Her work roared onto the indie romance scene in 2014 with her Grizzlies MC series.

Since then Snow aims for the very best in growly, heart-of-gold alpha heroes, unbelievable suspense, and swoon storms aplenty.

Already hooked on her stuff? Visit nicolesnowbooks.com to sign up for her newsletter and connect on social media.

Got a question or comment on her work? Reach her anytime at nicole@nicolesnowbooks.com

Thanks for reading. And please remember to leave an honest review! Nothing helps an author more.

Still Not Yours

Still Not Love

Baby Fever Books

Baby Fever Bride

Baby Fever Promise

Baby Fever Secrets

Only Pretend Books

Fiance on Paper

One Night Bride

Grizzlies MC Books

Outlaw's Kiss

Outlaw's Obsession

Outlaw's Bride

Outlaw's Vow

Deadly Pistols MC Books

Never Love an Outlaw

Never Kiss an Outlaw

Never Have an Outlaw's Baby

Never Wed an Outlaw

Prairie Devils MC Books

Outlaw Kind of Love

Nomad Kind of Love

Savage Kind of Love

Wicked Kind of Love

Bitter Kind of Love

Made in the USA
Columbia, SC
28 February 2020